I0646714

imPERFECT
FAE

C.N. ROWAN

VINCI
BOOKS

By C.N. Rowan

The imPerfect Cathar

Vinci Books

vinci-books.com

Published by Vinci Books Ltd in 2026

1

Copyright © C. N. Rowan 2023

The author has asserted their moral right to be identified as the author of this work in accordance with the Copyright, Designs and Patents Act 1988. This work is a work of fiction. Names, characters, places and incidents are the product of the author's imagination or are used fictitiously. Any resemblance to actual persons, living or dead, places and incidents is entirely coincidental.

All rights reserved. No part of this publication may be copied, reproduced, distributed, stored in any retrieval system, or transmitted in any form or by any means, including photocopying, recording, or other electronic or mechanical methods, nor used as a source for any form of machine learning including AI datasets, without the prior written permission of the publisher.

The publisher and the author have made every effort to obtain permissions for any third party material used in this book and to comply with copyright law. Any queries in this respect should be brought to the attention of the publisher and any omissions will be corrected in future editions.

A CIP catalogue record for this book is available from the British Library.

Paperback ISBN: 9781036710767

The EU GPSR authorised representative is Logos Europe, 9 rue Nicolas Poussion, 17000 La Rochelle, France contact@logoseurope.eu

Foreword

Welcome to imPerfect Fae, book three of the imPerfect Cathar series. You could read this book on its own. But only in much the same way as you could eat Marmite straight from the jar. Or smear it on your eyeballs. When of course you should only spread it liberally on human flesh before devouring it.

But I digress. The point is this is the third book in the series, and I really do recommend you read imPerfect Magic, book one, first if you haven't yet. If you have, good! I hardly need to warn you about all of the terrible bad language and gore that lie ahead. Also – even more horrific – UK SPELLINGS! Anticipate more u's than you can throw a stick at – humour! honour! labour! which frankly sounds like a bad dictator poster slogan – and none of your z's, thank you very much, not today.

Right. On with the show. Let us see how Paul is handling himself since last we left him. Any bets?

Chapter One

I drink, therefore I am. Descartes said that to me after I took him on a four-day bender. Inspired all his later work.

The best thing about having your magic eaten? Getting shit-face drunk after.

Magic and alcohol don't mix, really. Not in the "I drink this, then sniff that, and next thing I know, I've got five new tattoos and I'm trying to chew a police officer's leg off" kind of way but in the "magic is too damn powerful, so booze can't mess with your synapses seriously unless you start mainlining methylated spirits" sense. I am really, really enjoying finally getting smashed off a few simple pints though. It allows me to forget just how much of a shitshow the rest of my life has devolved into.

Whenever the booze haze I've been wrapping myself up in for the last four or five days (a sense of time is the first thing I let go of, swiftly followed by decorum) starts wearing thin, I quickly find myself drowning in all the misery I seem to have encountered recently, mainly brought upon by myself. How did it all go so badly wrong? Let me count the ways…

First, my dead wife, best friend, and son all turned out to be surprisingly ambulatory and sadly not in a *Walking Dead* sense. Shows how crappy everything is going for me when zombified loved ones would be the better option. Instead, my best friend, who I thought had died saving my life, reappeared hundreds of years after that event, having spent all of that time planning my downfall as a side event to destroying the world. Then my murdered wife showed up, now no longer even human, in service to a powerful coven of witches who ordered her to watch over me because the river monster I dumbly made a deal with in my grief while mourning said wife (because you know, she was supposed to be dead) decided to eat the magic of one of their daughters. I thought we were sorting some stuff out — me and my dead wife, not me and the river monster, I hasten to add— finally getting some of that closure but nope. She double-crossed me at the worst possible time, revealing she had even more secrets when surprise, she turned out to be in cahoots with our son — whom I believed had been ripped from her belly to be used in some messed up ritual as she lay dying. And what exactly was that "worst possible time?", you ask.

After I killed a fucking demi-goddess. But not before she'd eaten my magic. Not my best day ever. Not even in the bloody top ten.

Then I had to go kill the scum-sucking, murderous river monster I shared my territory, the city of Toulouse, with. Except I couldn't kill Franc because it would have also murdered all the homeless he kept tethered to him with his *talent* as insurance against such an act.

2

Ah, but no worries!

I bring my tumbler of whisky to my lips and basically inhale its contents, remembering the rest of my sorry tale.

No worries because Aicha Kandicha, my *ex*-BFF and a ninth-century Moroccan princess turned cold-blooded killer, wasn't okay with us striking a deal that would see Franc leaving my area only to start eating kids somewhere else. So she cut off his head, damning who knows how many poor souls to death. Those in Toulouse were safe thanks to Isaac, my mentor and good friend, protecting them with angel-fuelled magic, but I watched dozens outside of Isaac's protection die just like Franc did. And we'll never know how many more he had outside the city boundaries.

'Damn you, Aicha,' I mutter as I turn the empty glass upside down, wondering where the hell all my alcohol went. 'I begged you not to do it, but you did it anyway. You did it anyway…'

And so our friendship is done.

Pulling the glass to my chest, I hold it close. 'Whisky,' I murmur, 'you're my only friend…'

I'm slumped across a bar. I think. I don't even know which bar. Honestly? I don't know if it even is a bar. I might well be sat at a table in the park. Or on a bench. Or the pavement. I've spent a fair bit of time perfecting my slumping action on each of those recently. I am approaching mastery. Just a little more alcohol, and I'll have it down pat. I search for the drink I'm sure I have some-where at hand.

Sadly, it seems to have decided to take a stroll when my attention was elsewhere. Tricky little buggers, drinks. Moment you turn your back, they've either gone for a walk, or they're in need of topping up all over again. Sneaky fuckers.

Something cuts through the alcohol haze wrapped around my head. A noise — a blocked, muffled sort of noise that I've heard before. That means something. Something I need to be aware of. Need to do something about.

Blearily, I push myself up into a sitting position. Apparently, I'm not at a bar, after all, but on the damp wooden deck of a canal barge. Oops. Simple mistake to make.

The noise comes again, which is unreasonable of it because I'm still trying to get the world to calm down and stop whirlygigging like a Wurlitzer after the regrettable decision to move. Squinting my ears as hard as I can, I try to focus on it, on why it seems so familiar.

Ah. Realisation comes and burns just the tiniest touch of the alcohol away. Not a lot — not enough to bring me even close to sober. But enough to get me on my feet and moving, half-vaulting, half-tumbling over the barge's gate and down onto the towpath. Without falling into the canal, which is a real and present danger. But right now, I'm more interested in being dangerous.

Because what I heard was the noise of fear. Of a woman's fear. Muffled by a heavy hand.

It says something of how shit the world we live in is that it's a sound I've heard often enough over the centuries to recognise immediately even through the heaviest of booze clouds. Half-sobs masked by weighted grasping fingers as men look to take, as always, what isn't theirs. By force and a malicious greed that soils us all as a species.

Not while I've got anything to say about it.

There. In the shadows of a closed-up squat factory, the concrete façade with splintered boarding and shattered glass. I can pick out shapes. The way they're moving makes me fairly sure they're people. Mind you, everything else is dancing around constantly; the pavement keeps trying to move away from my foot each time I put it down, and I'm having to concentrate really hard not to go arse over tit every single step.

As I stagger towards them, I start to distinguish features enough to be able to perform a rudimentary headcount. Three. Or four. One of them might be a bollard. Or he might be kneeling. I can't tell at this distance —and this level of drunkenness— if any of them are male. But I'm prepared to lay money on it for all of them. All except their intended victim.

As the sound told me, they're restraining her. One of the fucking shameful excuses for a human being has his pork-sausage fingers half-shoved into her mouth, keeping her quiet enough while his friends root through her belongings. I've got no idea if they're going to be satisfied with stealing her valuables or if this is just the warm-up, the amuse-bouche before the main course.

Either way, I'm not standing for it. I mean, I literally *am* standing for it in the sense that it was the only thing capable of dragging me back to my feet, unsteady and swaying though I may be.

But this is my city. And shit like this? Gets dealt a smackdown.

'Oi! You sorry sad sack bunch of wankers!' is what I try to yell at them. Unfortunately, I chose far too many words starting with S, so most of what comes out basically sounds like a snake having a stroke. The 'wankers!' is clear at least. And enough to get their attention.

Good. Let's fucking rumble. I step forward, bringing my fists up to a classic pugilistic guard...

Which is enough to completely off-balance my body as it was previously relying on my hands to keep its wobbling under control, like a tight-rope walker's pole. Now that they're not splayed to the sides but are pulled up tight in front of my face, my foot skids off sideways and I go splashing face-first into a small pool of foul-smelling water.

Nope. Not water. The Good God damn it.

By the wheezing chuckles emanating from the group, I've not struck them paralysed with fear by my menacing entrance.

Right. Never mind. Take two.

I drag myself back up, only buckling once, kneeling back in the puddle because, obviously, having my top half soaked in stale piss isn't enough.

Normally I don't use magic on the unTalented. But these guys are fucking scum. And I'm properly annoyed now.

'Right. You fucking asked for it,' I slur and launch myself into what might just pass for a run. Albeit more where I lean in the direction I want to go and rely on my legs to work fast enough to stop me from faceplanting back onto the concrete.

And as I gather up speed, I pull on my *talent*, drawing it to me, ready to set the fuckers on fire, ready to make them burn like a fucking Bastille Day fireworks display. As I near, I stretch my hands forward and push my power out...

'Oh, do you think he's one of those street magicians? You know, like Dynamo?' The rough timbre carries vague curiosity tinged with boredom. Not the vocal reaction I generally look for.

'Yeah, I saw that too! Little poof of flames. Whaddya reckon? Bit of black powder up his sleeve?' A second voice sounds even less impressed than the first one.

Oh. Right. I'm not packing the big guns magically now. Not even a Super Soaker. Fuck. Forgot about that.

Never mind. I've got hundreds of years of street fighting

and martial arts experience at my fingertips. I don't need magic for a bunch of shitheels like these.

I'm leading the charge now with my right shoulder, and Bored Goon Number One's voice definitely came from my right. My vision's blurring like the world's shittiest shakicam home movie, but I don't need to see. I've got training. *Instinct.* I place my foot, and miraculously it plants solid. Using that, I pivot, twisting from the waist, bringing a spinning back fist crashing round...

And missing the bastard by a country mile, smashing straight into the brick wall behind him.

I hear the pop, but the pain's too diffuse and blinding for me to work out exactly how many knuckles I broke.

I'm quickly distracted from that anyhow. By the fist crushing my cheekbone.

My neck doesn't snap —I can tell that because I'm not dead or severely paralysed— but my pain receptors aren't convinced because they're screaming blue murder. Or, at the very least, aquamarine murder. The left side of my face is on fire, but the right side doesn't get left out for long because I hit the floor hard, grazing most of the top layer of skin off as I go.

Not my most graceful entry into a fight ever, it would be fair to say.

I might not be sure how much damage I took to my neck, but there's no question at all to the amount I take to my ribs when a heavy shoe crunches down on my chest; it breaks at least one rib. Instinctively, I curl in on myself.

And now I'm a prone target.

The kicks rain down, shot after shot to my sides, then my back as I roll around like a shell-beached turtle.

Getting my arse handed to me by a bunch of unTalented thugs. Fuck my life.

Of course, I may be drunk. Scratch that. I am drunk, and those first few blows basically put me out of action. But I'm not completely done. And even without my magic, even pissed out of my skull, if I didn't manage to break my own hand on that wall, I'd stand a decent chance against these goons.

So instinct does what it needs to. A foot flashes past my peripheral vision, and my hands lash out of their own accord. I've got a grip. By wrapping both my arms around his leg.

Ah, fuck it.

I open my mouth and bite down hard, squeezing my jaw together. Then I twist and tear my head backwards.

Considering the mouthful I spit out, I reckon someone's going to have difficulty standing up for a while. Intact calf muscles are useful for that sort of thing, and I've just gouged a steak-sized chunk out with my teeth.

Screams and swearing erupt, and there's a momentary lull in arriving beatings as everyone tries to work out what the fuck just happened. I use it to get back to one knee. Ah ha, you fucktoboggans. Now we'll see what's really up.

Except I feel a swift punch to my side, a jab that seems to keep going, not bothering with practicalities like stopping on contact with solid flesh. And a familiar pain, as sharp as whatever caused it, comes screaming up through my insides as I topple forward.

I've just been stabbed.

Oh, they got me good. I can't tell what they've punctured and perforated yet, but more than one organ I reckon. My lungs are struggling, but that might be the shock. Or one might be ruptured by the blade. Both are possible.

It's funny. I'm already soaking — in booze, in the stale piss I slipped in. But I can still feel the difference, can still feel how much blood pumps out of the hole. The warmth spreads along my side, then my back as I perform a rolling slump over, and there's a lot of it.

I'm a dead man. Just a matter of time.

Through the greying blurs that make up my vision now, there's only one bit of good news. The shithead who stabbed me is standing over me, his blade wavering. Probably the first time he's ever taken a life. Wait till my body disintegrates. That's really going to shit him up for a minute before the magic kicks in, and he forgets all about it. His mate, who's now half a calf muscle down, is sat on the floor, bawling and snivelling, which warms my soul, and the third of their trio is trying to wrap what looks like an Armani jacket around the gushing hole I made in his leg to stem the bleeding enough for them to get out of here.

And there's no sign of the woman. She managed to hightail it out of here while they were distracted with murdering me.

Good. That makes it all worth it.

That's as much as I'm allowed to see. The smeghead who stabbed me's regained a little of his shaken confidence, at least so I gather by his sudden snapped off kick to my jaw. His heart's not fully in it —it can't be; I don't lose any teeth — but it's enough for me to end up kissing the concrete again, my eyes closed.

Lying in my own blood. Stinking of piss. Killed by some mortal hoodlums. I think I might have reached a new low.

Ah well. Won't be alive for much longer now. The Good God knows I'm going to need a drink again after this particular humiliation. I wonder if they'll do a runner, leave me to bleed out. Or whether they might gather some collective strength, goad each other on, and stab me again to finish the job.

In the end, the answer is neither. Because although my eyes are closed and absolutely determined not to open, I hear a familiar voice. One I've been avoiding since I got back to the city a week ago and went on a bender instead of letting him know about the shit-heap of a situation I'd just got back from.

'You stupid sods. This is what you were taught is right, is it? To terrorise women? To kill brave but *bloody stupid* —' Okay, that part is definitely addressed at me. ' —drunks who try to do the right thing? Fine. You'll all remember this. Every single night, you'll have this scene come back in a dream. And that woman? She'll wear the face of any woman who's ever mattered to you. See your mother, your sister, your one true love who got away. See them cower and scream in terror from your actions and feel that shame because you gave them that feeling. You planted that trauma in their heart and marred them with it. Carry that forever and may you never get a night's peace ever again. Now get out of my bloody sight before I forget I'm a pacifist.'

I manage to crack my eyes open a tad, and the area is bathed in a silvery light, like the moon decided to pop down to have a guided tour around the streets of Toulouse. Except it's not from a celestial body.

It's from a celestial being. An angel. It's the light of Nithael radiating out of my mentor —who's also the nearest thing I've had to a father in the past eight hundred years— Isaac.

Boy, am I in trouble now.

'Well, this is a right bloody mess you've made here, lad.' Yep. That's a distinctly pissed-off tone right there in his voice.

'I might have got a bit pissed, 'Zac.' That's a valid excuse, right?

'I think that might count as the bloody understatement of the year, lad. Getting jumped by a trio of unTalented hoodlums? What the bloody hell is going on?'

Two bloodys in one sentence. Isaac is definitely pissed. Mind you, there's a clear answer to his question. 'Well, right now, 'Zac, what's going on is I'm dying.'

'Ah, damn it.' I feel him crouch down to check on me. His arm comes behind my shoulder, lifting me up, cradling me to him as my life leaks out all over his crumpled shirt. My vision clears enough to allow me to focus on his face. More lined than mine, he looks to be in his early forties, but his tight brown curls and sparkling eyes combined with his kindly demeanour garner attention wherever he goes in that "sexy college professor" sort of way. Not that he cares. Or even notices.

'I'm a mess, 'Zac. Best just to let me die. Come back afresh.'

'Except I've spent a week trying to track you down, lad.' There's the recrimination again. 'I'm not eager to go hunting again.'

I shake my head, which turns out to be a bad idea considering the swelling forming around my neck. I wince. 'I'll ring you straight away, promise. Sorry.'

Gently, he levers me up into a sitting position, holding me on either shoulder so he can look me in the eye. He purses his lips, then nods. 'All right, lad. You better bloody do.'

Then he lifts a hand away and clips me hard round the back of the head.

'Ow! Fucksake, 'Zac, what was that for? I'm fucking dying here! Literally!'

'Well, one, for making me so bloody worried for a whole bloody week. And two, because you're going to get out of having a bloody hangover that you full well bloody deserve, so you can have a ringing head right now instead! And maybe it'll remind you to bloody ring me as soon as you come to, you bloody idiot.'

As my vision fades to black and my life fades away, I can only think one thing.

Six bloodys. In one go.

Isaac is seriously pissed off.

Chapter Two

Back in a new body, feeling like a new man. Which sucks. I want to feel like a drunk old man, thanks very much.

Sobriety is an unpleasant, unwelcome shock. Far more so than dying and coming to in another body in Purpan Hospital's morgue. I'm used to that. Happens all the time. Being sober is something I've purposefully avoided for...

I'm not sure exactly how long. Vague memories of my last conversation with Isaac drift back to me. I'm pretty sure he said a week. A week-long bender.

Nowhere near long enough.

I made Isaac a promise, though, so I reach into my etheric storage, pull out a burner phone and give him a call, letting him know where I am. He's got to be at least fifteen minutes away, maybe even more if he has to walk back to his car.

I promised I'd let him know where I was. Didn't say I'd be sober when he got here.

I grab the last of my emergency stash from my storage —a bottle of Dalwhinnie whisky, which is better than I deserve or got served in the last few days— and settle down outside the hospital for him to arrive.

By the time he gets there, I've necked near on the whole bottle, and I'm feeling in a much better mood.

'Are you bloody well drunk again, lad?' Hmm. He doesn't sound pleased. I'd have thought he'd be impressed. A whole bottle of whisky in less than half an hour. I'm impressed. And thirsty. I think back and correct my earlier thought. *Nearly* a whole bottle of whisky in less than half an hour. So where's the bit left?

'Did... did you move my drink, 'Zac?' I slur, peering blearily up at the face, feeling incredibly proud of myself for having identified my *talent* mentor and only remaining friend. Especially as he is weaving around even more than my head is. And in the opposite direction apparently. I frown. That is very inconsiderate of Isaac. At least move in the same sense as my drunken rhythm.

'I'm guessing from the glass around your feet you dropped it.' Isaac pulls me back up. He lifts my chin so I have to look him directly in the eye. That isn't something I want to do right now.

"S not right, 'Zac, taking a man's drink like tha'.' I address his brother, who's residing inside the same body as him, along with two angels. 'Jak, tell him. Bet you needed a few after so many... so many...'

I blink. There is a word missing. *So many time?*

No...

'So many *years* in that skull,' I say triumphantly. "S not right. Can't drink in a skull."

I pause again.

"Could make a cup from a skull though. 'S very goth,

that. If we made a cup of Almeric's skull when you were trapped in it, would it have made you drunk? D'y'thin' we coulda poured it through the eye-holes?'

I consider this.

'No, 's a bit tinny... tinery... teeny-weeny. Might spill some. 'S no good, that. Too risky. Sorry, Jak.'

Another thought strikes me.

"What about you, Nan? Can you get drunk being an angel? 'Zat why you came to this plane, eh? Bet the higher planes are *shit* if you can't get any booze. Rather go to the toasty place. Better musicians 'n all that too, innit?'

The thought occurs to me I am carrying an awful lot of this conversation. All of it, in fact. I force my eyes to focus despite them insisting that it is far more effort than it is worth just to know what is going on. Isakob isn't listening to me! No. Not Isakob. Isaac and Jakob. They might be sharing the same body, but they're still different people. Isakob is just a portmanteau. No, an *aicha*nteau. No room for that now though. I squint my ears to make myself hear clearly.

'...I don't think he's in a fit state to do that, the poor boy.' I can distinguish Jakob's vocal style from Isaac's. That tells me two important things. First, that they are having a conversation between themselves instead of listening to the wisdom dripping from my lips. *Rude*. Second, I definitely am not drunk enough.

'On that, I think we can agree,' Isaac says, 'but time's wasting, and he's going to feel even worse later when he gets his head on wobble. Nith, I know it'll hurt him for a moment and you don't like to do that, but it'll save him a huge amount of grief afterwards. The only other option is I kill him now and pick him up in a sober body. So would you do the honours, please?'

Isaac grips my arm again, and a moment of other-worldly peace floods through me. A cleansing sort of peace. I suddenly realise what it is they're doing, which means it is already too late to stop because it is done. Nith, one of the angels residing in his body, burnt the alcohol out of my body. Multiple days of accumulated hangover, which was beaten back into the corner by never being sober, rears up to come and start slicing off parts of my brain with an angle grinder. Physically, I know it's not the case but my mind is convinced I'm due it. To be fair, I definitely am.

'Ugh. Owwwww.' Those don't feel like witty famous last words, and considering I feel like I am about to die any second, I need a better epitaph. I try again. 'What the hell, man? That was a bitch move.' Still not one for the head-stone but a better expression of what led to my untimely death, at least.

There is sympathy in his regard. Just not as much as usual. 'I think there's only one of us who's been behaving in that manner, my lad.'

Harsh. 'It's been bloody hard, Isaac. I've lost them all. What's the point?'

'Has it, lad? As hard as being trapped in a skull by a maniac who tricked you with love for hundreds of years like Jakob was? Or as hard as Aicha's five years of being tortured to the limits of her instant regeneration by Nazi scientists? I'll tell you what it isn't as hard as, my boy.'

I wince. Aicha's suffering is almost as monumental as her stoicism. Almost. Isaac leans forward conspiratorially.

'It isn't as hard as having to raise a lad new to the Talented world, accompany him through his adventures, trials and tribulations, and then find out, at the end of it all, he's become a proper whiny little bitch wanker.'

I am agog. Gobsmacked. Isaac never swears, and he is

certainly never mean. I don't know if I am more shocked by the verbal backhand he's just dealt me or by all the recent spates of resurrected dead loved-ones-turned-enemies.

'That was a trifle harsh, 'Zac,' Jakob says. 'He's been through a lot, the poor chap.'

'We've all been through a lot. There's a lot more to come too, if I'm any judge.' Watching the two brothers taking turns driving the body seems like justifiable schizophrenia. It's not a disorder if you have two actual personalities sharing though. Or four, if you count their angelic companions, but they never speak through Isakob's mouth or "take turns driving it". 'I never thought I'd see Paul Bonhomme, the last bloody Perfect, call it a day because things got tough.'

There's only one possible reaction to that. To sulk. So I do so with aplomb.

It's a quiet car ride back to my house but not a comfortable one. Isaac is glowering, fuming so hard if he were wearing a kipper tie, he'd have smoked it. I'm staring out of the window, studiously avoiding looking at him, and wishing we could get there quicker so I can get out of this confined space I'm being forced to share with a furious, disappointed father-figure. When we pull up at mine, I can't get out of the car fast enough. The fact there's alcohol inside my house is also a motivating factor.

I astound myself with my hand-eye coordination by threading the key into the lock the first time —something I have been far too inebriated to manage for the past few days — and in we go.

I head straight for the kitchen and swipe a bottle of cheap shitty whisky that I use for making hot toddies in the winter months. I'm not in the mood to be picky. I take a massive swig —

And then promptly spit it out across my clean, albeit dusty and neglected work surface.

'That's fucking water!' I feel flummoxed, flabbergasted. And pissed off too.

Isaac waves jazz hands at me. 'Ta-da! Reverse Jesus.'

I look around frantically, my heart thudding in my chest. 'How much? How much of it did you change, you bugger?'

He sighs dejectedly. 'How much would you expect, lad? We need to talk, and I need you sober. I'd also like you to be less abjectly pathetic and raring to sort out the fucking mess you're in as well, but I'll settle for the one out of the three I can do something about.'

I slump. Dejection is considerably less fun when not drunk. Most things are. I think about that for a moment. That isn't true. I wasn't having fun for the last few days. I was seeking oblivion, the absence of anything. That included fun.

The disappointed crossness dissipates a little from Isaac's expression. A touch of his usual sympathetic nature comes through. 'I get it, lad. Of course I do. Eternity can get too much for any of us, and this has been a catastrophic couple of weeks. Were we on the other side of it all, I'd have allowed you to wallow in misery again, same as last time you lost her. This time, though, she's not lost. *We can find her.*'

I straighten up at that. 'Have you? Found my wife, I mean?' I'm not ready to ask about my son.

He shakes his head, and I deflate back into the chair. 'Not yet, but I have an idea where we —and I do mean *we* this time, lad— might start. That means you need to be sober and get your head back in the game.'

I look at him. There is a gleam in his eye. He didn't waste the last few days getting tanked up like I did. He found a lead. 'Come on then, old man. Spit it out. You're like the cat who got the cream. What have you found?'

Isaac grins triumphantly. 'I know where to find Gwendolyne.'

Bloody hell. I'm glad I'm sober. The news would have bowled me over otherwise. I could kiss him if it wouldn't be a form of torture banned under the Geneva Convention considering how badly I stink right now. Gwendolyne — Susane's mum, my mother-in-law. She is a serious lead.

Chapter Three

Drunken sot or intrepid adventurer? Time to decide if I am Gwendol-in or out.

After getting somewhere close to presentable, or at least less like Pepé Le Pew in terms of personal stench, I head back downstairs to find that, while Isaac has not, in fact, cooked up a concentrated caffeine shot for me to mainline straight into my veins, he has filled my largest mug. Fuck all those people who say they don't want sugar because they're sweet enough. I just want my coffee to be as dark and as bitter as my soul.

Pulling up a chair at the kitchen table, I manage to sit with considerably more aplomb than the last time I sat down. I'm feeling more human after my shower, which is ironic because I'd love to have more of my god-like magic back and feel considerably less. 'Gwendolyne. Where?' I ask, not beating around the bush. No, I am slashing my way through the bush with a machete, sprinkling bush killer as I go.

'Hello, Paul. How are you, my lad? Feeling better? Been a bit down, have we? Perhaps burning some bridges we might not have wanted to? Maybe, just maybe, forgot to come and have a chat with us before getting blotto for—' Isaac consults his non-existent wrist watch sarcastically. 'Almost a week? Well, never mind, I'm sure we aren't working against the clock or anything.'

I am worried about the amount of squinting I am doing. If the wind changes, I'll end up looking like a villainous gunslinger at a showdown for the rest of my life. Still, I can't help but squint at Isaac. 'Is that actually you, Isaac? You didn't pick up another lodger, did you, 'cos I know Jakob wouldn't be this sarcastic.'

He huffs, leaning forward, fixing me with his gaze. 'It's me all right, you bloody idiot. I've been worried sick about you for the entire week. Aicha's gone off radar. I can't reach her. Franc's dead, which is no bad thing, but I had to get a courtesy call off the bloody Mother of the Sistren of Bordeaux to tell me to look after you because, apparently, you've lost damn near all your magic. You didn't think I might want to know that? Or that I might be a tiny bit bloody concerned? You're a daft bugger sometimes, Paul Bonhomme.'

'Takes one to know one.' Oh, Good God. Apparently Melusine didn't just eat my magic. She ate my maturity too.

'Slow hand clap for the comeback of the century, ladies and gentlemen. Come on now, 'Zac. I know you've been worried, but he's here and sober now… And near as damn it powerless, Jak. And apparently unable to stop himself from sulking. Now, where is Aicha?'

Bloody hell. I didn't tell him anything. After the whole double-cross by my dead/alive wife and getting my *talent* eaten by Melusine, I took the easy option of taking a cyanide pill instead of going home to see Isaac. I woke up in a new body in a poorly lit basement. By the smell of the place, whomever's corpse I just hijacked hadn't been doing so well for a while. It wasn't the most positive start to a new body and had only added to my depressed state, so I hit the bottle. Or bottles. Without ever once thinking of contacting Isaac.

I look at the man who's been here for me for the last eight hundred years. It is difficult, almost impossible, to meet his eyes, and tears form in the corners of my own as I try to do so. Good God damn it, I am ashamed. Letting him down hurts so much more than letting myself down.

'I fucked up, 'Zac. Like, I really fucked up. I know it's not the first time, but this is on a previously unprecedented level. This is on some "burning down your parents' house by smoking a spliff while they're out" level. Only worse. I really cooked the goose on this one.'

'Okay, lad.' He smiles at me, his enormous heart as clear as ever. 'Why don't we start from the beginning?'

So I do. I tell him about Franc's death, about my argument with Aicha for beheading him, about the shitty state I'm in now due to Susane's double-cross, my apparent offspring being all grown up and a powerful asshole fae, and getting my *talent* eaten by Melusine. He sits there, listening quietly and nodding sympathetically until I mention the part about giving Melusine's heart to the daughter of the Mother so she could get back the magic Franc had stolen from her.

Holding up his hand, Isaac stops me. 'You gave her the heart, and it gave her back her eaten *talent*?'

I nod. 'Apparently Franc and Melusine were related. He was her nephew.'

'You did that even though it could have given you *your talent* back? And you're feeling *ashamed*? Bloody hell, my lad, it's a hard road of self-flagellation being a hero, isn't it? Makes me very glad to be a scholar rather than a crusader.'

I shudder at his choice of words. 'Never a crusader. Fuck those Crusading assholes.'

Isaac gives a slight laugh, a note of embarrassment on his part in there. 'Aye, poor choice of words. Look, what about the situation with Aicha?'

I sigh, feeling the powerful urge to down a pint of absinthe. Through my eyeballs. 'We are done. If you can find her, good luck to you, but Kandicha and I are done. Finished.'

'You really think she deserves that?'

I shake my head. 'It's not about what she deserves. Hell, I know I'm the one in the wrong. But she's gone, and it's for the best. I'll not have her carrying me like some fucking bedridden family member to and from the nearest toilet. If I can't shit on my own...' I'm struggling with the metaphor I started. Isaac rides to my rescue, pulling me out of the hole I was digging, then drops me into a gaping pit instead.

'So you'll just defecate in the bed instead? All that means is you end up in a shitty state, and someone has to come and clean up the bloody mess afterwards. Not exactly a brilliant solution, that, is it?'

He has a point, of course. It's just a point I am going to determinedly ignore. 'What was this about having tracked down Gwendolyne, anyhow?'

He picks up the deliberate change of subject —Good God love him— and rolls with it. 'With us and the whole

Sistren looking for your ex…' He frowns as he waits for me to clarify what she is now that she's not dead, but I'm not in the mind to get into that right now. Besides, I have no idea what the legality is for a dead wife coming back to life… Especially since I've also died and been reborn numerous times since then — albeit in a different way to her. 'Ah…' He clears his throat. 'With us all looking for Susane, I am pretty sure she and your son have gone to ground somewhere.'

I frown at the mention of my son. He presented himself like a fop, a louche in the style of the landed rich of the early twentieth century, but he didn't fool me at all. There's a coldness in him and a hardness lingering just below the surface. Susane, one of the strongest women I've ever met, seemed terrified of him. That doesn't speak of a healthy mother-son relationship.

And that, right there. That is a reason to sort my act out. Because I have some serious questions to ask Suse —I don't take getting sucker punched lightly— but I also need to understand. The fear in her body language when he appeared. How he put that there. And how to take it away again. Because no woman should have that reaction to their own son. And I need to understand him too — if that reaction he's instilled in her is a result of his trauma. If it's possible to help him. And if not, then work out how to get her away from our long-lost son, to save her from all she's ever wanted and missed since her very first death.

Isaac paces up and down the room. 'Anyhow, I got to thinking. With Susane most likely gone to the fae world, our best bet of finding her is through Gwendolyne. Now, she's never forgiven me for introducing you to her daughter, and I doubt she ever will, so I've not quite found her, but I've picked up word that the Cagot have settled in Castet, up in the mountains. I suggest we head up there. If she's still alive, that's where she'll be. If she isn't, maybe someone will give us some hints.'

I look at him doubtfully. 'If she's that upset with you, maybe it's better I go on my own?'

Isaac stops dead and swivels slowly to look at me. 'What are you talking about, lad?'

I smile weakly. He doesn't look fooled. 'I just meant maybe she'll talk more easily to me on my own?'

'You really think she's more cross at me for introducing you than at you for stealing her daughter and letting her get murdered?'

My smile gets so weak and watery, it is the "coffee from a motorway services" of smiles. 'Yes?'

Isaac huffs, then pulls up a chair, swivelling the back to face me. He sits astride it and leans his chin on the top of the backrest. 'Right, what is going on, boy? Why don't you want me coming with you all of a sudden?'

I sigh, scrubbing at the nape of my neck, searching for the right words. It requires me being honest with myself first. Then being honest with him. I have no idea which is harder. 'I don't want to lose you too, Isaac.'

He chuckles, not getting it at all. 'Lad, I've the two most powerful beings that we know of on this plane riding in this one body alongside Jakob and me. I think I'll be all right.'

'But you nearly weren't, man!' I am so frustrated that he doesn't get it. 'You so nearly weren't. And two of your Dream Team spent hundreds of years locked away in a fucking skull! When we fought those werewolves at L'Astronef, if Nith hadn't stepped in and saved your life, you'd have had your throat ripped out. By a mangy little werewolf, 'Zac! You're a fucking whizz on the research front, and when you've got the time to search out secret names and work those into your castings, you're a next level Talent.

Problem is, on the fly, you're entirely reliant on the Elohim, and they don't play the game the way I do.'

I gesture victoriously. 'If I mess up, then it's a case of pop the metaphorical coin in the slot, pick up a new body, and then "Ready, Player One". If you get it wrong, if Nith makes the wrong call...'

My eyes prickle. It is an unbearable thought. 'I can't lose you, 'Zac. I... I couldn't carry on. It'd break me. I can't risk it.'

The man who is my father in every sense except biologically smiles the saddest, most loving smile I've ever seen. He puts his hand on the nape of my neck, where I've been trying to rub a hole in it, and bumps his forehead gently against mine. 'I love you too, you bloody idiot.'

He lets go and leans back. 'Thing is, you know as well as I do, there's no such thing as real immortality, just being really, really good at not dying. One of these days, I'll be gone or you will. Considering your tendency to hurl yourself headfirst into danger, most probably you. I'm not such a fool as to be unaware of the risks. Still, I support you every time you ask me to, like when you go off to do something ridiculous like, I don't know, volunteering to fight a dragon-shifter fae for someone's daughter you never met and getting your magic eaten in the process.'

'Yeah, I know, but still...' I can hear the whiny tone in my voice. It doesn't make me feel full of pride. Full of hot air, maybe.

He shakes his head gently, watching me the whole time. 'It's not your call to make, boy, any more than it was mine the millions of times I wanted to tell you not to be such a bloody fool, not to risk yourself in some idiotic way or other for someone else. I never mollycoddled you, my lad. Don't start doing it to me now. I'm not senile yet.'

He has me bang to rights. I nod my assent. 'All right, you win. So how do we get to Castet?'

His smile widens, all brilliantly white teeth. 'I've got the Model S fully charged. Looks like I'll be driving for once.'

I cover my eyes and try to stop my groan from being audible. I am so used to it being Aicha or I who drives. This is going to be a nightmare.

Chapter Four

"T'es la" in French means, "Are you there?" The Tesla salesman obviously wasn't all there, letting Isaac drive off in this overpowered deathtrap.

If I ever doubted that Isaac is magic, the drive lays that to rest when I witness his astounding chronomancy in action. It is incredible how he can defy the time-space continuum. After two hours into a two-and-a-half-hour trip, we are still less than halfway there. His mastery of wibbly-wobbly, timey-wimey stuff is incredible.

'Jesus, man, that wasn't even a stop line.' The only thing stopping me from punching the ceiling repeatedly in frustration is that Nithael will probably put me in some sort of protective bubble for my sake and that of the driver. Then they won't be able to hear me complaining. That would be outrageous.

'I'm terribly sorry, dear boy, but I'm still getting to grips with it. It's harder than it looks. You're doing a grand job,

Jak. Thank you, 'Zac. I'm afraid I'm not sure Paul agrees, poor chap. He'll get used to it. Why are you gripping the handrail like that, lad?'

Watching them switch control of the body while driving down narrow, twisting mountainous roads —Isaac having insisted that the scenic route was "just as quick" despite the evidence of a route planner and reality itself— is utterly terrifying. How does the handover work? Do they have to let go for a millisecond? You'd think, considering my ability to come back from the dead and Isaac's angelic protectors, I'd feel reassured. Nope. Not at all. Scared out of my wits. Fear is irrational...unless it comes to Isaac's driving. Or him teaching his brother how to drive using a single shared body. With me as a passenger. Screaming internally for hours on end. Then it seems entirely rational.

'Can I please, please drive for a bit?' My voice is as thin as my blood feels. Considering how hard my heart is pumping, you'd think it would be the opposite. Super-compressed. Maybe that energy is all being transferred over to my nerves. They certainly feel charged up to the max. God, I need a drink.

'Nonsense, lad. You sit back and relax. Yes, it's been a most stressful few days for you. Exactly. It'll do you good to put your feet up for a bit...'

'Jesus Christ, that's a corner. Steer, steer for the love of fuck. And stop switching control constantly. Argh.'

The journey quiets down after that. I avoid looking at him as I am sure they're simply carrying on the conversation internally, and if I see the miniature twitches representing them exchanging control, my eye muscles will start spasming in rhythm.

At least looking out of the window is easy on the eye. The villages we drive through are gorgeous — the houses a mixture of utilitarian farm buildings that have been reclaimed, nineteenth-century labourer dwellings with cracks and holes that are quaint to see — but doubtless draughty as hell when the mountain storms blow up — and the crosspatch wood of half-timbered buildings dating back to the Middle Ages. Blossoming flowers adorn walls and windowsills, adding to the sense of a people more comfortable in their proximity to awe-inspiring nature.

In-between, the mountains get closer. The landscape becomes less pastoral, the gentleness giving way to a more tectonic shaping, hills lumping one against the other like kids squabbling for a prime position in a class photo. The temperature is dropping too. We are approaching the evening, and the difference between day and night is as plain as, well, as day and night.

By the time we approach Castet, winding up and down the lower mountains on ever narrowing roads, the only thing that has stopped me from biting all of my nails to the quick is that they no longer look like *my* nails. Isaac has been far too polite to mention it, but I am starting to not look like myself. Literally.

The illusion I've always cast subconsciously over my new bodies, since the first time I reincarnated, has been my longest woven spell, and I never even had to consider it. Now my fingers have plumped out, and I've swollen all over, most noticeably around my belly. I've never had a beer gut before. It feels a bit of a two-fingered salute from the universe for my self-indulgent behaviour of the last few days.

I avoid looking in the sun visor's mirror. I've already suffered some negative psychological effects from what I've been through over the past couple of weeks. I don't want to see that my nose is a bit longer than normal or my cheeks are a bit more fleshed out. I do still look like me but not entirely. It's like a double exposure and it puts my own face into the Uncanny Valley.

I don't mind the idea of going to see a shrink, but it'd be hard if they couldn't understand that when I say, 'I don't recognise myself when I look in the mirror,' I am being literal. Still, I am in a pretty crappy place and one could help. Perhaps when this all calms down, I'll put the word out on the grapevine. See if there are any Talented psychologists out there.

I snort. The idea that I'd expose my psychological weaknesses to someone else Talented, especially someone I don't know…it is almost as ridiculous as the idea that things will ever calm down.

Isaac looks over at me, causing me to nearly keel over from the minor heart attack I get from him taking his attention off the road. Again. I'm not entirely sure the shrieked garble of syllables I produce count as actual words, but they obviously work because he looks back in time to avoid driving off the side of the road and straight into the ravine beside us. While I might want nothing more than to spend the rest of the trip hyperventilating into a paper bag, I make a conscious effort to keep my panic attack silent until we arrive in Castet.

The old village is as pretty as it is narrow. We have to stop and back up to let a campervan go past at one point, there not being enough room for us both. After they pass, we come to a stunning lake, the mountains reflecting in a surface so clear, Narcissus would insist on taking a couple of lifetimes to appreciate it properly. A river feeds the water as it burbles over rocks, deceptively calm and peaceful. You don't get a lake like this formed by small waters. There'll be wild rapids further up, happy to pull in the unwary and weary.

Apparently, I am incapable of even contemplating a moment of tranquil natural beauty without getting my goth-thoughts on.

'So what now then? I don't suppose your contacts provided you with something as useful as an address? A set of GPS coordinates? A collection of riddles, leading to the address? A puzzle box that either *might* open a portal to hell or *might* lead us to the Cagot community?' The deal enforced on the Cagots by the fae king is shitty in the extreme, albeit typical of a fae's idea of a just and reasonable reaction. Their ancestors killed his chosen people, the ones he had wanted to gift with a second life as fae kin after their death. So Oberon cursed the Cagots to take their place and to live miserable, ostracised existences on society's periphery. Them and all their descendants forever and ever. Arsehole.

Isaac looks indignant as he parks on the side of the narrow road. If anything wider than an anorexic moose comes down the lane, he's going to lose his wing mirror. 'Bloody hell, lad. I've narrowed it down to one small village in the Pyrenees. You want the moon on a stick.'

I bounce up and down in my seat. 'Ooh, yes. Can I get it on a particularly big stick? Then once I've eaten the moon, I can use it to *hit you every time you take your eyes off the road.*'

There is a loud *harrumph* from the driver's seat. Then the car goes quiet.

'So you've really not got any idea at all?'

He jumps out of the car and heads to the boot. I dread to think about what he might be carrying back there; it rattled around as we veered our way here. He comes back with a small suitcase, which he pops open. Inside is a neat black suit and tie.

'Can't beat a bit of legwork, can you, lad?'

'I really hate you sometimes, Isaac.'

The next few hours involve us trawling up and down the street, knocking on doors, posing as everything from religious missionaries to door-to-door salesmen. It's about as exciting as it sounds. By the time I've run the gamut from Jehovah's Witnesses to Pastafarians and invented McDonaldism (free salvation with every Happy Meal) — I'm about ready to burn the place to the ground to get some fucking answers other than getting the door slammed in my face or told where I should go and what I should do with my long-dead mother when I get there. Until we finally hit paydirt with a passing farmer who apparently skipped middle-age and went straight for the middle ages in terms of his attitudes. A veritable rumour factory, his tale of lesbian Wicca devil worshippers who've bought a small holding by the Port de Castet, full of random strangers coming and going, along with the accompanying description of the heathen harlot in charge, matches both with Gwendolyne and the Cagot lifestyle.

We jump back into the Tesla, only pausing to take off the ridiculous disguises, and head farther up the mountain towards the Port de Castet.

Chapter Five

It is more than a pleasure to see the white stone walls of Isaac's house. The limestone seems to reflect the moonlight, to absorb the waxing globe's powerful silvering. After more than six decades away, it is as close to a homecoming as is possible for a man who has outlived all his family by centuries. My time studying under Ahmad Al-Buni down in Andalucia was as instructive as it was mind expanding — literally, at times, with the substances the sorcerer brewed from strange herbs obtained from far-flung locales,. Now I return, the proud pupil eager to show his old master all the new knowledge I have gained, to show him the chance he took on a lost and fallen broken man was an investment well made. I'll not stay too long, I think. After seeing other places, other wonders... there's a hunger there now, a longing to seek out other teachers, to find new marvels hidden from the unTalented. To revel in this world of wonders I've gained access to. But I know full well there will only ever be one Isaac.

And if I am honest, there is also a driving need. To

prove myself…worthy. Of a certain woman I met under the shadow of Montsegur's fall and who has loomed large in my dreams and desires ever since. A promise I made to her and to myself, that once I gained my power, once I was a Talent in my own right, then I would seek her out.

And now, nearly three hundred years later, my apprenticeship with Isaac complete, my knowledge grown and my reputation following suit, I am not far off being able to claim that title. And my desire has never dimmed or diminished. Not for a single second.

But first I'll take a moment with a man I love as a father, enjoy some calm. Compose myself and my heart before making a decision as to where I head next. Whether on for some further learning. Or in search of my heart's desire. Whether I feel worthy of her yet.

So it is with a strange mixture of lightness at the return and longing to be gone again that I arrive back at the house I called home for more than two hundred years. Stranger still to feel like I'm going to enter it as something approaching an equal with the rabbi inside. Not magically —he's still more than a match for me in that regard, even discounting his angelic companion— but as a man. I've grown, travelled, learned. I'm like a man back from a war he left for when but a boy, finding his village shrunk along with his parents, who are now doubled over a walking stick. Expanded horizons change every perspective. Though Isaac will not have shrunk at all. Somehow, that man's heart just keeps getting bigger, more open.

It is as I am about to close the distance that I feel it. Al-Buni taught me many advantageous abilities. Not least is to keep myself open to the presence of Talent nearby while maintaining my own bundled down deep inside. Now I feel a sensation, a shivering ghostlike touch on my senses.

Talent. And not Isaac. His magic I know almost as well as my own. Same for Jakob. Even the others of the Hachmei Province, the Jewish elders and magi who protect the Montpellier Hebraic community, I'd recognise.

No. These are strangers.

And if I am not mistaken, strangers lurking in observation of Isaac's abode.

Anger flashes through me, sensing the Talented leaning against the wall in the comfort of its night-time shadows. My gentle master is not without enemies. Other Talented have sought him out, seeking to replicate his magic and rituals that called down Nithael, the Bene Elohim who now shares his physical being. All are politely refused. Few are pleased about it.

My mind is awhirl with the images. My presence was a valid excuse for the rejections for him while I was there; how could he take on another while he already had an apprentice as pig-headed and difficult to train as I was? It never bothered me to play the fool to underline the impossibility of his situation.

My absence will have created whole new questions. If I had left, why would he not take on another now? It would have made refusing without bruising feelings and egos all the harder. And many with magic are not used to accepting an honest "no" to their whims and desires.

There. Another, across from the first. A second spark of *talent* half-muffled down a darkened alley. Far enough back to be hidden in shadow from human eyes. Close enough to keep watch on the home of my mentor.

Good intentioned men do not observe from dark alleys. Looks like I have arrived at just the right moment. Passive magic, such as detecting other Talented is not all I've learned under Al-Buni's instructions.

The first thing is to take enough distance that my magic will not alert the bastards as theirs has me. I flow silently back down the road until it is only by straining my magical senses that I can detect the villains. Then I slip my hand into my parting gift from Al-Buni.

On my leaving, the sorcerer taught me how to find a pathway between the worlds. Not far. Not enough to risk being lost into other realms — a risk he warned me of if I ever tried to tear a doorway large enough, although it would be almost impossible to achieve. No, this is more like the magical equivalent of a treasure chest. And I can keep all the things I value the most there.

There is little I value more than a razor-sharp blade right at this particular moment.

My sword pulls free of my 'etheric storage', as Al-Buni called it with a snickering whisper. It seemingly cuts through the invisible air and rends it in two. A good start. But not yet enough.

The night is well lit, the moon full and carrying all of Artemis's force, to light the owl's hunt and guide its talons home. Now I will be the night-time hunter. And that means I must not be seen. Nor sensed.

The physical senses first then. Nearby, the trees stand proud and firm, unmoving and as ancient as the land itself it seems. Their boughs are hung with darkness, like throws draped to dry by the riverbank on laundry day. And as then, a person so minded might borrow them. If they knew how.

I reach out with my *talent*, constantly aware of those threats, ensuring I am not drawing in their attention as well as what I need. Confident they do not sense me, I pick the shadows from the branches like pinching up fine silk from a mercer's roll. Then I wrap it round me like a cloak, garbing myself in the night.

When I am sure I have drawn it tight enough so as to ensure I remain unseen, the next task is to hide my power. Already drawn in tight, now I bind it, wrapping it up within my heart, containing it within one of the focal points of power aligned across the body that Al-Buni displayed to me. A form of magic from well beyond Algeria, I believe. A sign of how well travelled he himself has been in his search for illumination.

Until I release the binding, I'll not be capable of much magic. But that is why I drew my tempered steel first. Holding that and the night-hiding pulled around me should be more than enough to deal with these miscreants, whoe'er they be. If not, I can undo the binding after the element of surprise is no longer needed.

Now the brightness of the night is of no concern. I set to creeping towards the bastards who seek to threaten my master. No need to bother his peaceful thoughts, his pacifistic tendencies with these whoreson vagabonds.

My new life was born, baptised in blood and fire. I'll not shrink from either anymore.

They remain split up. Good. Easier to deal with them one at a time. The one pressed against the wall is close enough as to be half-visible now, though the shadows, both those they hug and those I've draped around myself, obscure any clear sight. Still, I'm close enough to be confident their gaze is fixed on Isaac's front door.

Allowing me to creep up behind them, my blade raised, and bring it down like a battle-field arrow.

I've no idea what alerts them. The tiniest taste of my guarded magic. The whispering dance of the downwards blade. A well honed instinct or second sense. Whatever it is, they move in time. Just. My blade clinks against the rough hewn stone behind, pebble-sized chips flecking off.

It seems they have either incredible presence of mind or else the darndest luck. As they spun from the blade, they entered my guard, and though unable to see me, it's no difficulty from the ringing sound of metal on stone to guess where my sword might be. And from there, for a man trained in the art of war, to know where I must be. They turn their twirl into a lunge, driving forward with their shoulder and forcing the air from my lungs hard enough that the sword follows from my hand.

It clatters to the ground like banged pans in a busy kitchen. Not the most auspicious start to my silent assassination.

It doesn't go all my opponent's way though. The collision pushes me sideways, so that they carry on through me, their shoulder sliding off and away, and my dark-shade spell helps me once more. They turn back, trying to seize me, but grasping fingers miss fractionally, closing on naught but night-time air.

I've got enough of my wind back now to hammer them with a fist to their ribs, to repay the theft they made of my own breath, and steal it from their chest.

A wheezing gasp tells me I've done it. Between the building's gathered darkness and that which I wear, everything is difficult to see, but they're bent double and that will do. I follow through with a knee, my hands in concert with the motion to crack their bonce on it.

But they twist again, turning back, and I stagger forward, off balance, my hands flailing.

Instinct serves me well though. Outstretched fingers graze their jerkin and close without thinking, pulling them close. Now I use that weight, the same one pulling me downwards due to my lack of grace, and transfer it onto them, dragging them to the ground, twisting us so I land on top.

Well, that is the idea at least. While we do both head floorwards, it is in a tumbling tangle of limbs that results in us rolling over and over, spraying up dust and muck as we travel across the filth-strewn street.

But when we come to rest, I straddle the villain and pull my fist back to make a pretty mess of their face...

Until it strikes me they themselves are pretty. Too pretty to be a prettyman — a cunning individual. In fact, they are not a man at all.

They are a woman. A beautiful woman. A beautiful woman who has been in my dreams for two hundred years.

The beautiful woman of my dreams that I just punched in the ribs and then rolled through mire made of god knows what across the cobbled floor.

Not the impression I was aiming for the next time I met Susane.

The shock causes my dark-shade to drop, and she is greeted by the sight of my horror-struck visage as I try to utter a thousand apologies that will not come, only leaving me shaping unintelligible syllables, mouthing inanities I cannot get to cleave from my tongue as anything but gibberish.

She looks up at me, blowing a loose strand of hair encrusted in what I hope is mud but fear is not from in front of her face. 'I have heard,' she starts slowly, rolling every syllable around her mouth, a stark contrast to my gibbering, 'some of the younger Cagots talking about doing the deed of darkness, but I'd never realised it involves taking a slide in the shit. Plus, I believe it's customary to ask a lady's permission first. And not with a gut punch neither.'

I look at her agog, struck dumb by shame until she quirks one eyebrow, and we both dissolve into sniggers.

A second later, the sky apparently falls on my head, and a second after that, I am sprawled out among the aforementioned muck, staring up at a blurred face haloed by the over powerful moon. I can't help wondering if she's amused by this evening's farcical goings on. At this precise moment, I'm struggling to see the funny side. Mainly because I am struggling to see.

'And do all such former Good Men turned bad assault innocent women?' *Aah, Gwendolyne, Susane's mother.* Her features slowly quit swimming and shimmering, and I manage to force them into focus. She looks as unchanged as her daughter apart from the scowl she now wears openly. And the billy club she wielded with a threatening proficiency in her hand, based on her stance and my aching head.

'I thought you villains, Talented knaves planning to assault Isaac! Hanging in shadows and hiding down alleys.' My reasoning sounds as weak as my voice does. It's hard to find dignity when down among the mire.

'And so it comes to this, when a lady after travelling cannot even complete her ablutions afore calling on old friends' —my heart rises at her naming us as friends— 'and their errant vagabond of an apprentice.' It sinks back down. Isaac and Jacob are the friends, not I.

'Mother, leave him be!' Susane regains her feet and dusts at herself ineffectually. It'll take more than waved hands to remove the grime now encrusted on her clothes I'd wager. 'He acted as he is wont.'

'Like a fool?' The mother's sour tone makes it clear what she thinks of me, without couching it in a parable for once.

'With good intent. Albeit, as if also often his way, without perhaps the intentions he desired.'

By the Good God, you can say that again. Still, despite the damage I have done her, the street brawl and stinging blows, she keeps her eyes on me, and that grin when she talked of 'doing the deed of darkness' is still there.

There is no harm to be had by trying to make amends. I sweep into as low a bow as I can manage, surreptitiously scraping a lump of foul-smelling muck I'm glad I cannot fully identify from my cheek in the process. 'My sincerest apologies, my ladies, Susane and Gwendolyne. I have long been gone from Isaac's side, and my urge to protect my loved ones is ever strong. I beg your understanding and forgiveness.'

'Granted, my Good Man,' Susane replies, and is it my imagination or was there a subtle emphasis on the '*my*'? Of such things are a million sleepless nights made, tearing apart each syllable and playing it back again and again in one's mind.

If Susane has been charmed by my manners, Gwendolyne most definitely has not. 'My girl, did I never tell you the tale of the world's greatest troubadour who decided to become a bandit king?'

The way Susane is angled means her mother cannot see her face. From her voice, when she replies, 'Never, mother,' you'd believe it entirely genuine. Only I get to see her roll her eyes. I bite down on a giggle. That is unlikely to aid me in my cause to impress Gwendolyne.

'He was entirely too successful. All he had to do was open his mouth and let the sweet sounds come out.' She narrows her eyes at me. 'And nobody would even realise they were being robbed.'

I think it's pretty clear who I am in that particular story.

A change of subject seems the safest bet. 'And though it is ever a great pleasure' —*to see your daughter,* I think to myself — 'what brings you both to our door?'

Some of the sourness leaves her expression but not the wariness. 'That is not a discussion for out here nor for when you are in the states that you are. Plus, they are words for both your ears and your master's.'

She sweeps past me imperiously. The regal impression is somewhat undone when Susane performs the same manoeuvre with a wink so large and a grin so fresh as to make the whole performance border on bawdy.

It puts a smile back on my face even over my aching pate as I push myself back up. And I cannot deny I am intrigued.

Gwendolyne said it was for both my ears and Isaac's. Which means whatever she has to say, whatever it is she needs...

She needs from both of us. Not just my master.

Chapter Six

Apparently paths for walking up mountains are hard. This is something it would have been useful to know before starting.

The road up towards the Port De Castet is steep and very windy. I'm sure your instinctive reaction is, 'Why is there a port up in the mountain?' The answer is, of course, very simple. Sky pirates.

I'm joking, of course.

Sky pirates don't bother with ports or docks.

The Ports in the Pyrenees are large staging areas for shepherds herding considerable flocks, spots where they can rest and feed the bleating masses. Accessing it by road is not easy. Especially when your driver is both hesitant and has multiple personalities wanting to take control of the wheel. Eventually, I persuade Isaac to pull over onto a strip of grass and walk the last part for the sake of my heart. It takes about thirty seconds of walking the steep incline before both my heart and the rest of my cardiovascular system make it categorically clear what a terrible idea this was. While personally, I might enjoy trekking in the mountains and have spent hundreds of years rocking around this country (and many others) on my shanks' ponies, the body I am currently living in doesn't share the same interest in outdoor pursuits.

After approximately three minutes, you can wring my T-shirt out and have enough water to boil a kilo of rice. If you don't mind the rice being very salty. And tasting horrible. And if you were some sort of weird, unhygienic freak who boiled their rice in sweat.

Strangely enough, for a road on a mountain, we keep going up. The slope doesn't give. My knees feel like they might. My lungs? Almost certain to collapse. My heart? Ready to explode and/or seize up entirely any time now. Apparently, along with their appearance, I was also masking the poor physical condition of a lot of the bodies I picked up with my *talent*. My mind keeps saying it is easy. My body keeps saying my mind is full of shit. I find myself in agreement with both, which is a bit odd, to say the least.

Isaac isn't even out of breath. Damn it, I'm supposed to be the all-action hero here, leaping into danger and punching evildoers acrobatically. Instead, I am wheezing like a punctured bagpipe, only slightly less musically.

He takes pity on me. 'I could really do with a quick pause, lad. Hard work, this.' He doesn't have a hair out of place and looks ready to go on a quick marathon while carrying a rock-laden backpack. I am, however, too done in to object to the charity.

We plonk ourselves down on a couple of rocks poking

out of the browned grass like petrified dinosaur eggs. I'm not even pretending to be in good shape. It is a "head between the knees and try to remember how to breathe without feeling like you're about to vomit" scenario. Booze or exercise, both can end the same way if you aren't ready for them or if you aren't charged up with enough *talent* that neither can touch you.

By the time we get up and going again, I probably look less like a crack addict mid-cold turkey. Only slightly though. We carry on up, under the overhanging branches that are a small mercy from the brilliant yellow sky bastard who seems determined to make me pull a Wicked Witch of the West and melt on the spot. Dappled light dances shadows across the path. They carry enough shade to keep me moving. Just.

After approximately the five thousandth bend in the path looping up the mountain (by the way, if the loops are supposed to make it easier to walk, why do I still feel like we are heading almost vertically up?), we hit a rare blessing — a level piece of ground. And the top is in touching distance, the trees breaking to allow views of vertiginous fields full of sheep that, I feel convinced, must have one leg longer than the other. If not, there'd be rolling boulders of wool cascading down every time they tried to walk. I can spot where, in what some call "simpler times" and I call "only simpler to die early and horribly times", shepherds would have taken respite on the plateauing summit and let their herds graze. They'd have earned it.

Before the trees thin, a narrow dirt track bends away and down, and a roof top nestles under the cover of branches. It is a small, simple house as far as I can judge. Solid, well made. Unlikely to draw attention. Almost hidden.

I raise an eyebrow at Isaac. Skilled non-verbal communication seems like a win at this precise moment. He nods, eyeing the property thoughtfully.

'Exactly what I thought, lad. The place practically screams Gwendolyne.'

I've recovered enough to gulp some air down. My scratchy, burning lungs decide to allow me to wheeze out a reply. The generous sods. 'If she realised that, she'd burn it to the ground and fuck off immediately.'

'So let's pay her a visit before she does that, shall we?'

We trot down the track, skirting tree roots that seem suspiciously convenient in their placement, almost as though they want to trip us up. Branches make grabbing motions without moving, and the scree underfoot seems continuously treacherous, shifting as we put our feet down. It is very annoying, and I can see it is getting to Isaac even more than me, especially when a vine-like bough whips his glasses off.

'Right!' He harrumphs and glares. I wouldn't have believed it was possible to subdue a forest by sheer weight of regard, but this is Isaac in frustrated professor mode. Nothing can withstand his force of disappointment. If someone ever learns to harness it, it would solve the energy crisis in one fell swoop. 'My friend and I are here to visit Gwendolyne, who once told me I was ever welcome at her hearth. Apparently, you rambunctious lot would seek to make a liar of her!'

There is a silence. A silence that, although he is addressing a bunch of inanimate objects, feels pregnant with the expectation of a response. A response that better be a heartfelt apology at that, thank you very much. He slowly turns, taking in the whole wooded area surrounding us, daring it to continue to behave so impertinently.

The branch holding his glasses gives the tiniest shiver as

though caught by a momentary breeze, and Isaac's glasses drop into his outstretched hand. He pops them on, taking a moment to arrange them correctly, then nods firmly.

'Right, then. No more of that nonsense, please. We'll say no more about it.' He turns his attention back to the path, which, miraculously, is suddenly as solid and as stable as if a steamroller nipped along it while our backs were turned and a crack team of ninja road builders re-laid the bitumen.

I shake my head in wonder as we carry on towards the house.

The forest pulls itself to a halt at the approach, allowing beautifully laid-out beds of wildflowers to grow around the surrounding edges. Pinned back neat blue shutters of the white-washed cottage allow streaming sunbeams in, no doubt corralled to illuminate the house *just so*, keeping it beautifully light and airy. Nature doesn't want to disappoint Isaac. With Gwendolyne? I reckon it just doesn't dare piss her off.

We tap at the doorway, a fresh azure colour that matches the shutters, and wait. I look over my shoulder at the calm verdant scene behind me, appreciating the momentary peace. The click of the door unlatches, and I turn back just in time to feel the cold metal of a shotgun barrel pressed up against my most private of parts. The pressure isn't hard enough to put me on my knees, but it is certainly firm enough to make me aware of exactly where it is.

My mother-in-law cocks back the hammer. 'Did you ever hear the story of the Perfect who kept turning up where he wasn't welcome?' she asks, a predatory gleam in her eyes. I shake my head. It's surprisingly hard to speak when you can feel one of your testicles slotting into the end of a gun barrel.

She smiles. It is the sort of smile reserved for a wronged woman who has the perceived perpetrator at her mercy. 'He learned how to sing soprano very quickly indeed.'

Gulp.

Chapter Seven

Quite happy to perform a rendition of 'Woke Up This
Morning', but sadly, I don't think that's the sort of "singing
Sopranos" she's after.

Isaac tries to gently push the shotgun away. Then he tries a
bit more firmly. The barrels don't budge.

'This is no way to welcome old friends now, is it?' His
tone carries hints of the same reproach he used to quell an
entire forest, albeit softened. I don't think it would have
mattered if it were sharp enough to slice through concrete.
It isn't going to cut through her steely resolve.

'You're always welcome, Isaac the Blind.' Her tone
doesn't sound very welcoming. 'Your yapping mongrel
isn't.'

'Gwendolyne. Gwendolyne!' The bite of Isaac's tone, so
unusual and different from his usual placid attitude, causes
her to pull her attention away from her desire to prune
away my manhood. She looks across at him, and there's

frustration written on both their faces. 'Gwen, you need to hear what we have to say.'

I nod. Very, very gently. I don't want to give her an excuse for "accidentally" pulling the trigger. Although I might come back in a different body afterwards, I don't want to live through being made into a eunuch. Again. Or having to walk up that damnable fucking mountain in a body, knowing my luck, that's infinitely worse than this one. 'Susane came to visit us. We know about the Cagots. Apparently, our son is alive.'

Her attention snaps back to me, and she stares at me. I can almost see her weighing up what I said and how much she wants to know the details against how much she just really, really wants to shoot me in the bollocks. I sigh with relief when she clicks the safety on and pulls the barrel back. The relief transforms to gasping wretches when she shoves it forward hard. This time, it definitely drives me to my knees. I suddenly decide rolling about on the floor and crying is a useful contribution to the conversation.

She nods appeased. 'That'll satisfy for now then. Long enough for me to hear your story at least, Cathar. If I get bored at any point, I'll let you know somehow, I'm sure.' She leans down, grinning entirely without humour. It is a terrifying effect on her wrinkled face. 'Storytellers get bored easily. Make it interesting, Good Man.'

When I regain the ability to breathe and stand some few minutes later, I follow the two of them in. They didn't wait for me to regain my posture. I shoot a baleful look at Isaac as I come in. *Thanks, buddy*. He shrugs, obviously feeling a tad guilty, but no apology is forthcoming. Clearly, he felt there was more to gain by him coming in and playing along. I am rocking too bruised of a ball sack to get on board with his game plan right now. I lower myself down into the wicker seat of the kitchen chair evidently left for me and look at Gwendolyne.

Have you ever seen someone after a tragic life event, and they've just *aged*? It's not that they've suddenly gained an excessive number of extra wrinkles or half their hair has fallen out. It's as if the grief has sucked away some element of their vitality that fought off the hands of time. A spring is gone from the step, an elasticity from the skin. The wrinkles have deepened, and the eyes have dulled. Physically, there's no real measurable difference between them since you last saw them, but the weight of loss drags them downward as surely as gravity does.

Gwendolyne doesn't really look any older than the day I first met her, but she now sits stooped, bent by the gravitas of loss. Only her eyes hold on to their fire. I can't help wondering how much my reappearance has stirred that up.

She breaks the silence. 'What do you mean, you saw my daughter and you know about the Cagots, Perfect?' She looks me over more closely. 'And why do you look like the boy who decided to go sailing at the top of the waterfall in a leaky apple barrel?'

That's not the worst way someone has told me I look like shit, and I've rarely deserved it more than now. Still, no one enjoys having their faults pointed out to them by their mother-in-law.

'Well, there's a whole host of reasons for that. Long story short, I got my *talent* eaten by the Lady of Lourdes, who turned out to be Melusine herself. I was there trying to get the Mother of the Sistren of Bordeaux's actual daughter's *talent* back —fuck me, that's a mouthful— after that scumbag Franc had eaten hers. Turned out, Susane had struck a deal with the Mother and got sent along to keep an eye on us for her, which is how we found out all about the "two-lives-for-the-price-of-one" *Cagot X-Factor.* Except she screwed us over at the last minute and stole Melusine's wish-granting sceptre for some fae bastard who claims to be our son. She seems pretty convinced of it anyhow. Now I'd like to get hold of them both and have a quiet word in their ear-holes about it. Then a very loud word. A bellowed, screeching word possibly. Then I'd like the sceptre back.'

Gwendolyne listens to all this intently, testing each word for veracity. She never stops staring at me, and if I wasn't recently subjected to the Mother's gaze, which would have made Alexander the Great whimper and hide behind the nearest elephant, I might be intimidated. As it is, I am far too tired both physically and mentally to feel anything at all. I'm not entirely sure after what I've been through recently that I'll ever be able to feel again. I am even less sure that I want to.

'That's quite a tale, Good Man.' She stirs, uncoiling off her chair with a heaved sigh, and stands. She stomps across to the hobs, which are as rustic as Isaac's in style, and heaves a copper-bottomed kettle into place. When she puts out three cups, I know she is taking this seriously. If she makes me a cuppa, then, while she might not yet have forgiven me for the death of her daughter the first time, she is unlikely to groin-punch me again. In the immediate future anyhow.

Gwendolyne's tea blends have always been wondrous, and I inhale the steamy vapour with pleasure before I take a sip. A thought flashes through my mind as I do, that she might be in cahoots with Susane, and this could be poison or at least something to take us out of the game. I wait, looking at her as she drinks hers. I'm confident she poured hers from the same kettle, and unless she is pulling a "spending years building up an immunity to iocane powder" style jig on us, we are drinking the same tea. Once

I am sure she isn't about to die, I carry on with mine. It is too good to waste. Plus, I am sure Nithael would've alerted Isaac if she pulled anything like that on him, and he is clearly enjoying his beverage.

She sits back down, still studying me. I wonder if I should offer her a magnifying glass so she can inspect me even more minutely. Then I realise she'd most likely use it to set me on fire.

Then I remember she can set me on fire even without a piece of glass and the sun's rays.

'She never came to me.' She stirs her tea perfectly; there's ne'er a clink of spoon on cup. I wonder what she is stirring. She didn't offer me sugar, and only a barbarian or an English person, which is basically the same thing, takes milk in their tea.

I shrug. I'm not surprised by her saying that. Even if Susane did visit her, Gwendolyne is hardly likely to confess it straight up, and I don't have the magical oomph to throw my weight around. I need to be far more cunning than that to make sure she's telling the truth.

'Are you *sure* about that?' Yeah, that was super sneaky. Without a doubt, she'll crack under the pressure of such expert cross-examination.

She narrows her eyes. 'Entirely sure.' Well, colour me convinced.

Isaac steps in. 'You'll forgive the doubt, Gwendolyne, but it would be fair to say we've had a time of it of late. Few we've met have turned out to be trustworthy. Some of us have had a few centuries of it, 'Zac.' He rolls his eyes at his brother's input. 'Yes, you had it rough all right, lad. Gwen.' He turns to the chief of the Cagot and flourishes a hand down his body. 'Allow me to present my brother, Jakob, recently returned to us after a sizeable period of imprisonment and now residing in my body; all thanks due to Paul. Look —' He gestures at me with his spoon. *Hold on, why does he get a spoon?* I am feeling quite spoon-less, which is annoying. 'I know you still hold him responsible, Gwen, but it takes two to tango.'

I interrupt, 'I saw a video recently of someone tangoing on their own, so actually, it only takes one to tango.' I falter under two intense glares, possibly five depending on how Isaac's other body buddies feel about it. 'Which isn't relevant and doesn't take away from the fact that, yeah, Isaac is right. And I should shut up. Now. I should shut up now. Shutting up right now.'

I don't really deserve the gracious incline of the head Isaac gives me. His manners really are impeccable. 'Appreciate that, lad. Right, look. We all know he's a bit of an arse sometimes."

I start to open my mouth.

"You were shutting up, remember, Paul? Good on you. Right. He is, but he means well, and he does his best. What happened to Susane was never his fault, and it was ever her choice to go off with him. You know that, Gwen, and you paid him ill with the cheap shot at the door. He suffered. Same as you did. More than you did for he didn't know she'd come back. So lay off him, and let's get to some answers, if you would be so kind. Did you know Susane had crossed back over?'

I see the tightness around her eyes, around her mouth, the skin pinching in as if her mind is pulling it to itself. It is that gravitational grief in action again, and I know for sure she's not seen her.

'I had no idea,' she says. 'I've seen her but a couple of times when she shepherded a newly turned fae across to the Summer Court. She was... aloof would be the best word. I got the impression she was settling well in the Court.'

Despite the sucker punch earlier, I don't take any pleasure in disillusioning her. I don't want to see any mother suffer vicariously through their child. Sadly, it is a prerequisite of the parental condition if you give a damn. 'She wasn't well settled. For the entire time she was there, she was a servant. She took the lowest of the low position as part of a negotiation before indenture to the Sistren after. They negotiated the whole deal on her behalf to allow her back over. I got the impression that initially, she'd done it to get back to see me. Apparently, my ego is precisely that big. It was all part of some plan concocted with this fae claiming to be our kid.'

'I don't even understand how that could be possible. How on earth was he kept alive? And why?'

'Valid questions, and ones I'd love answers to. Sadly, the son of a bitch didn't hang around to give us any of them.'

A silence ensues, so pregnant that even the most lackadaisical father-to-be would leave his pint and head for the hospital. I remain clueless as to why Gwendolyne's letting it drag out. I glance at Isaac, who shakes his head as she starts to speak.

'Are you calling,' Gwendolyne says slowly, enunciating every syllable, every letter, 'my missing daughter a bitch?'

This puts me in quite a pickle. 'Honestly? I just meant it as a turn of phrase, but she's hardly top of my people's Pop Picks right now considering the stunt she pulled.' Honesty is the best policy, right?

'Do you know the story of the idiot magician who got his magic eaten and then turned up, running his mouth to a powerful witch who hated his guts?'

I give it a moment's consideration. 'I mean, oddly specific as it is, I don't think I do.'

'He vomited frogs for a month every time he opened his ill-mannered and poorly controlled gob.'

I decide developing ranidaphobia is a psychological trauma too far. Discretion is clearly the better part of valour here. Isaac steps into the fray.

'Gwen, leave him be, please. It's been a harder time than you'd imagine, and he's done us all much good in the meantime. It's no exaggeration that the poor lad probably saved the world, and everything since has been him paying for it.'

In all honesty, it wasn't me who saved the world; it was Aicha, but I'm not going to undermine any good intentions the claim might have garnered me from Gwendolyne.

She thinks for a moment, then nods. 'Fine, I'll set aside my feelings for now. But however angry you are, boy, and however justified you might feel, keep a civil tongue. It's never too late to learn manners.'

I take a deep breath, then blow it out. 'You're right. I apologise. It'd be fair to say I'm not in peak form. Physically. Magically. Mentally. I'm wrung out, and I'm probably unusually abrasive.' She snorts at that but holds her peace. Looks like she is serious about setting aside our differences. Or, at least, about being polite. 'Look, you once promised me a favour if I took that trip to Rome on your behalf. I know you might count my wooing your daughter as that one, but help us here, and we'll call it officially quits. You'll owe me nothing.'

'What will you do to her when you get hold of her?' There is a quietness to her now. I always got the impression — hell, she was always vocally clear that she considered me brash, immature, almost a clown. Now I hear something else. Even with my magic practically gone, she isn't asking *if.* She is asking *when.* I guess she knows just how dangerous I am after all.

'I promise if she offers me no harm, I'll bring none to her, though I'll defend me and mine. Gwen —' I lean forward, stretching my hand out for a moment.

When she pulls hers back, I almost flinch, but I control it. I can understand, even if it hurts. 'I still love her. I've loved no one else, not before, not since. I spent a lifetime in grief, more than one. Every life has just been a mouthful of ashes and a constantly wagging tongue to hide the taste of an immolated soul. Losing our son hurt just as hard at the start, but I never knew him. That pain went with time, although not the empty hole, knowing I'll never be a father after all. But her loss? That's been a constant companion every second since I found her dead in our bridal chamber. Regardless of her stitching me up, I still don't wish her ill. I'd like to know why she did it, sure. An apology would be appreciated, and I'm not suggesting I can forgive her. But hurt her? Not if there is anything, *anything* I could do in the world to avoid it.'

She sags, the tension leaving her like a shed feather whipped away by the rising breeze. 'Please, Paul. I don't know who this man is, if he's really your son, but Susane would never have done this for anyone other than him or you, so I'm sure she believes it. Save her if you can. From this path she's set herself down.'

'I'll do all I can. My word upon it.'

She closes her eyes and leans back into the curved beech sticks that form her chair back. For a moment, I think she is contemplating my words, weighing up whether she can trust me. Then her eyes snap open, and even I, magic levels depleted as they are, can see the red *talent* fire burning in them before it fades away, and she sighs.

'She's not here. Not on Earth.'

I straighten up. Apparently, Gwendolyne can tell where a member of the Cagot is. Or maybe just her daughter? Either way... 'That's a useful tool. And even with that, you didn't know she was here?'

The implication is clear; I can't help but make it. She sits back up, indignant. 'Am I a liar now, Cathar?'

Isaac raises his hands, pleading for peace. 'Come now, enough. It's an understandable question. If you've such a connection to her, how did you not know she was here?'

Gwendolyne laughs bitterly. 'Do you think it a gift kindly given by Oberon to *make my life easier*? Since when has life ever been easy or the fae ever been kind?'

I nod. 'Nope, they're officially a bunch of bastards. Hey, that's a brilliant collective noun for them. A bastard of fae.'

The two of them look at me askance, and I have no doubt it has left Isaac's cohabiters similarly bemused. It is at times like this I really miss Aicha. Times like this and when someone needs killing with maximum prejudice. So...most days of my average week.

The Cagot queen ignores me and carries on. 'There was once an *escape*. Well, twice, but once where Oberon decided it was my job to track them down. He gave me this "gift" to allow me to find any Cagot, human or fae, that I was required to.

'The escapee was a part of my clan, my extended family on this side of the portal. Life on the other side hadn't gone well for them at all. Worse even than it does most of the time. We tend to either accept a lowly station in exchange for maintaining aspects of our humanity or else burn it all away and embrace the fae, though it hardly means climbing to the heights of courtly life normally. This girl wasn't prepared to do either. She wanted to come back, and she didn't think to bargain for it, just fled when an opportunity arose and the portal opened.'

Her expression is bleak, an incorrigible marking of guilt engraved in a memory where choices were limited and none of them good. 'I had to hunt down someone I'd shared meals and moments with and deliver them back to what is little less than slavery. It's not a skill I want. I don't exactly consult it on a day-to-day basis.'

Okay. She's convinced me she didn't lie to us, and we are getting away from the point. That is my job in a conversation, nobody else's. I pull us back. 'So if she isn't here…'

Gwendolyne nods again, confirming my fears. 'She's in the fae realm. Either Summer or Winter Court.'

Fuck fuckery, fuck fuckery. Fuck fuckeroo.

Chapter Eight

You know why Arthur Conan Doyle couldn't sell people on the veracity of his photos of faeries? Because they fae'ded.

I really, really don't want to have to go into the fae realm. It is full of fae, for starters. Call me prejudiced, but that is more than reason enough.

'Right, so we're going to have to go through the portal and hunt them down in a land full of homicidal magical creatures who see humans as pets, sport, or meat. Possibly all of the above. Outside of that, are there any major problems?'

Both raise their hands. My heart sinks in the same ratio. 'This is not the reaction I was looking for.'

'Why are you waving your hand at Isaac like that?'

'Why am I wavi…seriously? Have you never seen *Star Wars — A New Hope*?'

Blank looks all round. I press on. 'Right, Isaac. You go first.'

'Okay, well, basically, lad, I'll not be able to go with you.'

I grind my thumbs into my eyelids. Perhaps if I smoosh them a bit, I'll see some good news coming. 'Of course you can't. Any reason why not? Fae make you break out in hives? You owe Oberon for two weeks' rent when you two were flat sharing as students, perhaps?'

'No need for the sarcasm, lad.'

'Always need for the sarcasm if you want sane Paul,' 'Zac.'

'Right, well, anyhow, the long and the short of it is that angels and fae…um…really don't get on.'

I look over at Gwendolyne, who shrugs. 'Don't ask me. I'm stuck over here. Oberon only tells me what I need to know. Although speaking of that…'

I wave her silent. 'One thing at a time. We'll come to your problem after. So, what, if we go through and they see you, we're going to have an all-out war? Every fae and their aunt Peasblossom coming gunning for us 'cos they hate the Elohim so much?'

He shakes his head helplessly. 'Worse than that. I can't go through. It's actually impossible. According to Nith — and Nan is backing him up— the angels really despise the fae. Considering Elohims are the embodiment of order…'

'And the fae are absolute agents of amoral chaos,' I finish grimly for him. He nods this time.

'Exactly. Well, anyhow, at some point, they took proper objection to something some faeries had done and came down to their dimension to sort them out. I'm talking flaming swords, world-ending battles of biblical statute.'

'Hold on, hold on.' I hold my hand up. 'Are you saying it was like something out of the *Book of ReFaelation*? No? Anybody?' I put my hand back down, but the silence still hangs about like that last guest at a house party who doesn't understand it's time to leave even though you're stood there in your nightgown brushing your teeth.

Isaac resettles his glasses. I am pretty sure he dislodged them in his attempt to internalise his side-splitting laughter. 'Ignoring that, lad. Right, anyhow, it was long and bloody and only really ended when Summer and Winter Court got together and reinforced their wardings across their whole realm. I'm talking about *all the fae working together, lad*, which should give you an idea about how seriously they took it. Result of that is nothing angelic can get into any of the faerie realms. Best case is we'll bounce back out again.'

'Worst case?' I have to ask.

'We won't.' His expression says it all.

'Okay, brilliant, so I'm going in without backup. Right, your turn, Gwen. What flaw in my flawless strategy have you decided to jimmy a crowbar into?'

'You can't get into the fae realm either, Cathar. Neither of you could even if you didn't carry an angel with you, 'Zac.' She sits unmoving, unmoved by the bad news she just delivered. Mind you, she already knew it. Guess it would have less impact on her.

'Jesus, really? You could have mentioned that earlier!'

'I did try, Cathar. You were too busy cracking jokes and discussing irrelevant ancient history. Doesn't leave much space for anyone else to talk.'

'Well, you should have tried *harder* then. Good God damn it. Right. Why can't I go?'

'Because the portal only allows the fae through. Even I can't get onto the other side. Not while I'm still on my first life.'

I groan out loud. 'Of course not. Any particular reason for that?'

She looks at me unbelievingly. 'Did you never hear the story about the lord who made serfs of his people but left his palace doors unlocked?'

I think it through. 'I'm guessing he got serfed?'

She doesn't even blink. Wasted. 'Something like that.'

I look over at Isaac. 'Is there another way into the fae realms other than via the Cagot portal?'

Isaac rubs his chin thoughtfully. He stares straight through me, and I know he is probably communing both with Jakob and crew and his own extensive memory. It suddenly occurs to me I have no idea, after all this time, how Isaac manages his own memory palace equivalent. I wonder what it looks like, whether they are all gathered in a cosy farmhouse kitchen having an illusory cuppa. Or is it something grander? Perhaps a cavernous ballroom? Although a crumbling castle straight out of Transylvania would seem more Isaac's style. Considering his recent vehicular purchase, maybe his mind palace is some super slick, ultra-modern condo, all glass walls and minimalism taken to the max. There are strange depths hidden under that collegial surface and even stranger tastes. I guess it's true that we can never really know a person, however many centuries we spend in their company.

I can tell the moment he comes back to us. His expression doesn't fill me with hope. 'Possibly? There's nothing certain. I can take us to sites that certainly used to be ways through. There's plenty of rumours and stories we could investigate as well, of faerie circles or standing stones and ways they might trigger and open up. The problem is, it's not just about them being able to be opened on this side.'

'It's that they've all been slammed shut on the other.' Gwendolyne's expression inspires even less hope than Isaac's does. 'The fae — or the courts, at least, are withdrawing more and more. Earth's lands are iron now. The waters are run through with rust, the land is ploughed with shards, and steel is laid from north to south. Plus, they know they'll stand no chance in an all-out open war these days. It'd be a bloody mess for both sides, but since when has that ever stopped humanity sticking their metaphorical penis in an ant-hole just to see what happens? We all know it's only a matter of time in the modern world before everything comes out. Oberon wants no part of that and has closed everywhere off. Even us Cagot, cursed but still his children when we live a second time, he cares little for...'

She sighs, and I can see the centuries weighing down so very heavily on the strong woman who expected to hand off the mantle of leader long ago. I wonder if it is a choice that she's never had another daughter. Whether maybe she can't bear the risk of another child living and growing and dying before slipping away to a magical land where they'd be nothing but a second-class citizen, the same as they'd been here. 'I feared he'd be furious when I told him I couldn't find many of the new Cagots with his gift. My people have spread wider, and we no longer live in a time when marriages can be arranged and children controlled. More and more of our offspring have taken true mortals as their companions. I feared that maybe he'd punish me for my failings in keeping them under control. We all know what happens to the sheepdog that can't keep the sheep safe.'

I scratch my head. 'The shepherd gets a second sheepdog to help out as it's obviously too big a job?'

Gwendolyne laughs, a tinkling melody at odds with the bitterness in her expression. 'He eats the dog when he gets hungry enough instead. I thought I might end up on the menu. What I found was Oberon...didn't care. He was entirely unbothered. More than that, he was completely unsurprised. I suspect he made it happen or else always knew it would happen eventually. In my opinion? It's simply a sign he's preparing to pull back from this world entirely. I sincerely doubt there's another Summer Court portal open other than mine.'

'What about the Winter Court then?' The frustration in my voice is clear and only matched by the woman's dismissive hand-wave.

'Are you mad, boy? There's no safety in the Winter Court, no passage whose price you'd be willing to pay. And only Maeve herself decides who can pass through her portal from either side.'

Jakob pipes up. 'What about the White Lady? Isn't she the guardian of portals?'

It's a possibility. 'That's not bad, Jak. Perhaps we could find her, use the Nain's finger like Aicha.'

'I've got a problem with that as a plan.' Isaac sounds grim. 'Do you know how many have come back from the portals the White Lady has sent them through?'

'Not many?' It sounds feeble even to me.

'Very few indeed. And those who have always say they went where she wanted them to go, not where they'd expected to. We know she's the guardian of the portals. But portals to where? I'd not have you launched off into another dimension even weirder and more bloody dangerous than Fae, if it's all the same to you.'

Hmm. She's not a malevolent force, by all accounts — and according to Aicha — but her wants and whims are beyond the ken of mortals. 'Okay, let's hold on to that as Plan B, shall we? There's no guarantee the Nain could find her again anyhow, and we could lose months trying to track her down. Let's see what else we can think of before we commit to that particular plan of action.'

We sit in silence for a while, sipping lukewarm tea. It feels hotter than my thought process does. Although, at least my brain feels fresh. Fresh out of ideas.

It is Jakob who cracks it. 'Paul, my dear boy, have you ever worn a non-human body?'

I open my mouth to answer, then stop, thinking back over the past eight hundred plus years. I start again, scratching my chin. 'No…no, can't say that I have.'

'Have you ever been in the position where the only available body was non-human though?'

'Again, no. Jak, I like your thinking. You might well be on to something here.'

I turn to see Gwendolyne shaking her head. 'It's a good idea, but they keyed the portal to only let Cagot through without Oberon's express permission. The fae were all called back long ago. Those who've stayed do so against the Horned Lord's wishes. He'll not let them come and go as they please. With my portal, only new fae can pass through. Indeed, the portal pulls at them, causing them greater and greater agonies if they resist its demands.'

Damn it. That seems like a non-starter. I try nonetheless. 'I don't suppose there's a really, really naughty Cagot? Like one who doesn't pay his Cagot tax? Let his elf insurance lapse or whatever?'

It is a total shot in the dark, where the dark is a starless night and the target is a matchstick head half a mile away. Still, if you give an infinite number of monkeys assault rifles, it'll get caught in the resultant automatic spray eventually.

Gwendolyne's eyes light up. 'There is one. Though he's no longer one of mine nor even one of Oberon's.'

I am totally confused. 'I thought all the Cagot belonged to Oberon?'

'He did once. Didn't suit him to listen to me nor to bow to his fae lord. His tastes are…colder than most.'

I look blankly. She sighs, wriggling to get herself more comfortable. Either that, or my stupidity is giving her pins and needles in her arse. 'Did you ever hear the story of the rose who hated the feel of the sun?'

I shake my head. 'Another new one for me.'

'She sold her soul to Winter to wear berries ready to kill and leaves to make a child bleed. Rose to holly by a change of allegiance.'

I clock it finally. 'This Cagot swore fealty to Maeve instead?'

'Aye,' the Cagot queen says grimly. 'And what a price he paid for it too.'

Chapter Nine

I'd better pay attention to this story. Missing information here could be fae-tal. Okay, enough with the fae puns, promise.

I look over at Isaac. 'Are you all sitting comfortably? It sounds like there's a story in there.' I think about it for a moment. 'Are you all even sitting? Do you provide seating in your mind space? Or is there standing room only?'

'Luckily, my brain is expansive, you cheeky bugger. Room for the angelic hosts, my genius brother, and more knowledge than you could ever hope to know.'

'Want. Want and hope are two very different things, 'Zac. Like, I *want* to know about this Cagot she might allow me to kill. I *hope* the story doesn't take too long. Two very different things.'

'I want you to stop being such a rude sod. I hope you'll keep your mouth shut and *let Gwendolyne get on with it.*'

Bloody hell, someone is feeling touchy. Mind you, the

fury behind the self-controlled gaze of Gwendolyne tells me I am liable to start spitting frogs if I don't keep my mouth shut. I wave magnanimously for her to continue. She doesn't fill my mouth with toads. Truly, we are a gracious pair.

'Jack was always different. This wasn't long after Susane's death and rebirth. You know as well as I do it was a different time, and children became grown as soon as they could be, but he was born grown. Born wrong too. He trained to kill as soon as he could and put it into practise the moment it was possible. His mother was the only thing he ever loved, and she was gone from him by the time he was seven, taken by a cold winter and a cruel famine. His father never cared for either of them and set him to work with little to drink and less to eat, not bothered if he followed her to the fae realm sooner rather than later.

'Jack's pleasure in killing served him well for he could hunt the rats through the fields he toiled in, stripping the flesh from the bone while he cut corn. The child was born wild and raised feral, and he hated us all. He hated the Cagot for he saw us all as his father's kin. He hated the fae for they took his mother from him. There was nothing he wanted from any of us.

'I was far away when this happened, and this was before Oberon gave me his "gift". His interest starts with their rebirth, not a moment before. They were near Bilbao, and the hardships of those particular years kept me tied too close to the Pyrenees to do my duty of care properly. By the time I made it that far again, he had turned ten. He celebrated his birthday in style by gutting his drunken sot of a dad and spiking his bones with iron studs on his rebirth. Then he took anything that wasn't nailed down and disappeared off north. I might even have passed him on the trail without knowing.

'I started investigating hard, both into what had happened and Jack's whereabouts. When I found out more details about how his father had behaved and how the local community had done nothing to help or shelter him, I stopped searching for him temporarily and concentrated on reprimanding the Cagots who had failed him. It seemed the more pressing issue.

'By the time I looked for him again, the trail had gone cold. I headed northwards, asking questions of our people. I assumed he would look for shelter there, but of course, he avoided all the Cagot like the plague. By the time I got back, Charlotte, a newly-turned fae, had made her daring escape back through the portal, and Oberon insisted I concentrate my time on bringing her back, finally giving me the "gift".'

The sadness hangs around her so heavily, I am amazed it doesn't obscure her face in a mist of weighted tribulations and tears. It makes her eyes shine brighter, if anything. Gwendolyne isn't one to let the pain dull her down. She lives with her mistakes, both those she's made and those forced upon her. I guess I am one of the latter.

'So by the time you resolved that unpleasant situation, he, what, went over to the dark side?'

'In effect, yes. He built a name for himself as a mercenary. His fearlessness, presumably due to having a second life in his back pocket, combined with a brutal, sadistic streak meant he was famed for getting the job done however dirty or dangerous.

'In the midst of all this, he reached out to Maeve. Don't ask me how. Her involvement in this world has long been less than Oberon's, with her only straying over to take her twisted pleasures when the urge drives her. Having said that, she's also more… understanding, shall we say, of those who can pass between here and there if they bring her tribute.'

She gets up, a hand on the small of her back as she stretches herself out. I can feel aches and pains myself. It tells me two things. One, just what an excellent storyteller Gwendolyne is that I've lost track of how long we've been sat here. Two, how my magic is now officially weak as piss. It can't even deal with this body's built-in obsolescence at work.

She shuffles wearily over to the stove and puts the kettle back on. I'm not going to say no to a refill.

'I told you how a part of us is tied to the portal,' she calls out over her shoulder as she fusses over the hobs. 'It sings to our souls, some harmony that Oberon set ringing in our very being. Sometimes I wonder if Maeve didn't interfere somehow with Jack before he was born, for he was of the cold and dark from the warmth of the womb. The Winter Court called to him, and he answered. He swore fealty while still a human, and she marked him. Marred him.'

I study my fingers as she talks, with half my brain listening. My face is still my own, more or less, but my body doesn't match my expectations. It's weird that they don't look like my own digits and are giving me something like the opposite of phantom limb syndrome. They keep surprising me each time they move even though it is me doing it. There's a reason we say "I know it like the back of my hand", and it's a bizarre sensation to not know the vein lines and skin folds that roll and rise with a simple drumming movement. As she says the last part, though, my head shoots up. 'What do you mean, marred him? Marred him how? Marred all of him?'

My brain pulls up on that, then reverses backwards through the recent tale and pulls out the name she casually dropped in. I really hope I am putting two and two together to get five, but maths only ever fucks me over when it won't be in my favour.

'Only half-marred him, Good Man. Only half.'

Good God damn it. Half-Marred Jack. The Jack of Plate.

Chapter Ten

Of course the only body that I can nick would belong to a legendary psychopath. Of course.

Isaac raises an eyebrow at my reaction. 'I take it that means something to you then, lad?'

Considering my said reaction was to swear like a trooper, get up, kick the nearest doorframe hard with my left foot, then remember that I no longer have most of my magical immunity, resulting in me hopping around the kitchen clutching said foot while turning the air the same colour as Picasso's paintings during his Blue Period, Isaac's assumption isn't exactly Holmesian level detective work.

I limp back and collapse into my chair, my fury spent, my foot throbbing. 'You can't tell me you've never heard of the Jack of Plate, man?'

Isaac looks baffled. 'I mean, I know of the armour style. Jerkins stuffed with iron plates and all that. Uniform of the Jacquerie Rebellion during the fourteenth century. Very popular with the Scots later on, if I remember right. Still, isn't Gwendolyne talking about events in the seventeenth century? It was outmoded by then.'

Gwendolyne tuts. 'The eighteenth century, actually. And he wears — or at least wore then — that outmoding like a vicious badge of honour.'

Judging by his furrowed brow, Isaac's still not following. 'Like a uniform?'

'Like a sign of how incredibly dangerous he is.' Based on Gwen's expression, she knows precisely how much. Same as I do. 'Do you remember what turned the tide of Napoleon's plan to take over as much of the world as he could march his troops into?'

'Of course.' Isaac nods gravely. He's never been interested in war, but its impacts, the effect it weaves on history is another story. 'The same thing that's foiled most others who've had the same idea since. He tried to invade Russia.'

'Right. Except that mystery has never been fully solved by the historians. Sure, Russia, the country itself, can be a murderous bastard to those who don't know how it is. But Napoleon marched in there with half a million soldiers — half a million!— and fled back out six months later, having been decimated. He only had fifty thousand men left, a tenth of those he'd entered with. The Russian army did its job. The Russian winter even more in the campaign's later days. But Jack took his fair share. It's not known who took out his contract precisely —Russia's Commander in Chief Kutuzov perhaps or one of Napoleon's political enemies back here in France, eager to see him finally bite off more than he could chew— but whoever it was, Jack did what he'd been paid for. Men disappeared, died by the hundreds. Entire battalions advanced across apparently empty hostile terrain, never to be seen again. The numbers couldn't be explained by desertion; the number of survivors meant it couldn't be starvation...'

'Because he left one alive to report back.' Isaac's lips thin. These aren't the aspects of humanity's darker nature he likes to be reminded of.

Gwendolyne nods. 'Precisely. And when the terrified lad, sheet-white and shaking like a leaf in a Pyrenean storm, told tale of a man dressed like some actor portraying times long past, wearing armour that offered little protection against a blade or bayonet, sporting a falchion and dressed in antique fabrics who danced around bullets and revelled in the slaughter and drowned a field of wildflowers in their salt-soaked blood, what do you think that did for Jack's reputation? To have ended a campaign and a conqueror's dream? Not with the poor survivor's immediate superiors, of course, or the straight-laced unTalented generals, those who had him sent to head doctors and locked in an asylum where he cried every night and screamed about the man with the melted face. No. But with those who *knew*. Who had either the *talent* or the connect with the seedier side of death-dealing...'

Isaac has it now. 'Then his reputation would grow.'

'Precisely. Between the wreckage made of his face, his antiquated garb, and mannerisms, no one could mistake who had woven that doom. And people then knew who to hire to bring murderous mayhem. Who to fear in the alley's dark, in the battlefield tent's isolation. Inside prison or surrounded by a legion of armed guards. Whenever Jack gets a Talented, well...'

I finish it off. 'They get got.'

'Precisely. Not a terrible reputation to cultivate.' She picks up the kettle off the stove and refreshes our brews before sitting back down.

Isaac looks at me. 'What did you hear of him to get so upset?'

My expression sours further. I have to hope the wind doesn't change; otherwise, I'll be stuck looking like Mr Burns with a hangover. 'I didn't hear anything. That was the problem.'

He looks suitably confused. 'What?'

'I didn't hear a single thing. Not when he found us, when some mercs and I were tracking him. And not a thing afterwards.'

'Why?'

'Because he shoved his blade straight through my ear and out the other. Made it hard for me to hear anything after that.'

'Why were you tracking him, lad?'

I find myself back there for a moment. *We are pushing through the forest, a tight-wound woodland on the Massif Central, hoping to find someone alive, hoping to find a trail to follow.* I was disappointed on both accounts.

I can read the question in Isaac's frown. I'm not one to go hunting people as a rule of thumb. 'Do you remember Jean Du Burnuy?'

He came from one of the wealthiest Toulousain merchant families and was the first of his line to show any *talent*. I kept them under careful observation after one of his ancestors proved to be a keen proponent of torturing and executing women who refused his advances. He had me killed. I returned the favour, burning his factory to the ground in the process.

Du Burnuy, to his credit, didn't hold my summary execution of his ancestor against me. He used the family finances to further his studies. Although he never was a world-shaking Talent, he was a friend to scholars all over, happy to provide financial backing where needed to move the knowledge needle a little more from ignorance towards enlightenment. We never required the money; when you've been around as long as we have, you tend to manage enough smart market guesses or ride enough inflationary tides to be set for however many lifespans you live. Scholars will scholar though, and Isaac got on with him like a house on fire. I wince. Considering what happened to him, that's perhaps not the best turn of phrase.

'Did Jack have anything to do with his death?' The first bubbles of anger flare behind Isaac's eyes. He is slow to rile, keeping his zen-like peace as long as possible. But Jean was a friend, a fellow lover of learning, and I can see how much the idea we might have left his death unavenged is causing him serious concern.

I hesitate, unsure how to answer it. 'I…don't think so. Well, perhaps. I didn't realise the Jack of Plate had a connection to the Winter Court. Look, let me fill you in on what happened.

'De Burnuy contacted me a few years before he died, scared as hell. Said he'd been warned someone had taken a contract out on him. It seemed ridiculous —who would want to kill Jean, right?— but he was convinced and genuinely terrified. He heard the Jack of Plate had taken the contract, and he begged for my help.

'Jean assembled a team of mercenaries to help hunt this man down. I didn't understand where I fit into the picture, but he said it scared him that Jack might be Talented. He just wanted someone along to even the score if it were true. De Burnuy was all about theory rather than practical magic. He knew I wasn't scared of getting down and dirty when necessary.'

I stop. For a moment, I am once more in those close-pressing trees, picking my way back to where I died. *I am on high alert after getting caught out the first time. Fool me once…*

'We had word he'd set up in the forests of the Massif Central somewhere near Dienne. The mercs Jean had hired were standard fare — Germans and Spanish mainly, fresh from war and full of over-confidence bordering on arrogance. I don't suppose either of you have seen *Predator*?'

Blank faces. Damn it, they would have understood instantly if they had. 'Shame because watching that film damn near gave me flashbacks. Except it wasn't some invisible ET with a laser we were up against. It was one man with a falchion. Got me before I even knew he was there. Then took his time with the rest of them.'

I can't even remember their names. I remember how they died though. Badly. Intestinal ropes hung garlanded from the branches like tinsel on a Christmas tree. That led me to the first body, a grim version of Ariadne's string-ball for Theseus, the last of his guts still attached to his insides just about. The next body was some few hundred metres through the oppressive greenery. Hamstrung. He and the rest had been left there for quite a while while Jack had gone off hunting. They were probably the unluckiest. He wasn't pressed in the slightest when he came back for them. He had the luxury of taking his time. Not that any of the others had really died any better.

'I always wondered if he was Talented. There was no evidence of magic use, but the fact he got the drop on me and, of course, that he took me out of the equation first made me wonder.'

'What about Jean then?' Isaac's anger turns to disgust. I think between co-inhabiting his body with an angel and staying for much of the proceeding few centuries in his little academic bubble, he sometimes forgets just how innately cruel and despicable the human condition can be.

I shrug. 'I headed back to his house in Montauban both to deliver the news and regroup. When I got there, he told me he'd reached out to whoever had put the contract on his head and had got it rescinded, that he no longer needed my services. I reminded him I wasn't one of his mercenaries, that this had been a personal favour, and he begged my forgiveness but asked I let the matter rest. Frankly? I did just that.'

'Why on earth would you?'

'He killed a bunch of unTalented mercenaries who were hell-bent on hunting him down. Yes, he was an assassin and evidently a cruel one at that and probably Talented too. Still, he didn't attack me or mine, nor was he making a play for power in the region. Hell, Jean resolved the matter with diplomacy. Would you have us hunt down every person who is sick and twisted? Perhaps we can go looking for serial killers first, eh? Find those who glory in the murder of innocents. But in that case, maybe we should look at some of the front-line soldiers for various armies around the world? Not all of them, but there's always some who'll get a taste for killing in the wrong way. Though they've all been put there by the generals, so perhaps we should have a sharp word with them? Or the politicians who made the call to go to war often to line their own pockets?'

My own ire rose as I went on, and I take a calming breath to get myself under control. 'It's a slippery slope, dude. Before you know it, you'll be the one ruling with an iron fist, and we all know where that ends up. Either the Talented are running the world, or they're minding their business. There's not much middle ground. Going with the former either ends up with a world in chains or us hunted to extinction. Not where I want to end up.'

I can see he wants to argue, but deep down, he knows he doesn't have a leg to stand on. Hell, he taught me this himself when I was on my way to act like a hero, aiming to save the Perfects at Montsegur. 'So does all this link in with Jean's death?'

I bite my lip. 'I didn't think so then, but now? It was so many years after, and his factory burnt down more than once over its illustrious history.' I nod to Gwendolyne, who doesn't know what happened. 'His body was discovered inside it after it went up in smoke one September evening. There was no evidence of arson or of *talent*. The general opinion was an insurance job gone wrong, with De Burnuy setting the fire but getting trapped inside while doing so. I never believed that though. No, I always wondered what Jean was doing there that night. He rarely got involved in the day to day running of the place. That's what his employees were for. Plus with it being inside my territory, he normally let me know before coming to Toulouse itself, even with it being his factory, but he didn't. It never made sense. So maybe Jack went back later on to finish the job on his own time.'

Isaac is silent. I can see him trying to pick holes in what I've said, in what I did. Fair enough. The Good God knows I've got it wrong more than a few times over the years and torn each situation to shreds afterwards, trying to see what I could have done differently.

While he digests that bombshell, I decide to concentrate on the situation at hand. 'So million-dollar-question time,' I say, turning to Gwendolyne. 'If we kill him and I can wear his body, can I get through the portal?'

I see Isaac, previously lost in thought, stiffen. But when

he opens his mouth, it's his brother at the helm. 'We can't just hunt this man down and kill him, my boy! That's...' The silence looms as wide as his shocked eyes as he hunts for the word. *Call it what it is, Jak.* 'That's murder!' *Right you are. And what does it say about me that I'm not in the slightest bit bothered?*

For once, Gwendolyne ignores him instead of me. Yay me. 'If the body were in fae form, you could pass through. It'll recognise you as of Cagot stock.'

Now she turns her attention to Jakob, and there is a rigid fury burning in her eyes. 'You want a reason to hunt down Jack? What do you think he did to earn Maeve's blessing? He agreed to be her hands here on Earth. Killing when needed, taking what's wanted. What do the fae always want?'

Ah, poor Jakob. He rinses out the colour from his brother's borrowed skin, turning chalk-cliff white, his mouth agape. After all he's lived, the horror he saw in service to Ben, he still forgets just how evil we can be as a species.

Because there's only one thing Jack could offer that would've made Maeve take his pledge of allegiance and leave him to run free in our world for centuries afterwards.

The fae, especially Maeve, always want children, and the bastard is stealing them for her.

I don't need another reason to hunt him down. Finding Susane, getting to the truth of what happened, of who the other Cagot fae is is motivation enough.

But if I did...that would be a good enough reason without a doubt.

Chapter Eleven

MONTPELLIER, 10 MAY 1514

Once I clean myself up with a wash and a change of clothes, I hurry down to the hall. The Good God knows I tried to be both rapid and efficient, but somehow Susane has beaten me and looks completely unruffled by our recent wrestling match. Her garb is plain but clean pressed, and she has not a hair out of place. Not that I can tear my eyes away from her face, her beauty only accentuated by the amusement writ large across her expression.

'Well met, Good Man,' she says with a half-bow, her eyes sparkling at my evident clumsiness. I banged my head on a low timber in my hurry to get in and present myself again, now I am actually presentable. 'Your ability to make an impression remains as great as ever. Should I ride you down on horseback and make a dusty ghost of you all over again?'

'My lady,' I reply, finding my tongue, 'you'd ne'er find a happier sprite or spirit in any land to.'

She widens her eyes deliberately, the humour clear in the twist of her lips. 'Why, Rabbi Isaac, what magic is this, that you have taken a rough-cut simple Perfect and shaped from his imperfection a man of manners and standing?'

Isaac, sat to the side, chuckles, tickled by her teasing of me. 'I think he had excellent motivation to apply himself to his studies, milady.'

I tip my head in acknowledgement, but Gwendolyne seems less than amused by our discussion. 'While I hate to impose upon you all to return to the matter at hand, I'll remind you of the clockmaker who carved all his intricate pieces but never affixed the hands, saving them all to do at a later date.'

Isaac plays along, though I notice a small eye roll from Susane. 'Do tell, my lady. What was the result, though I hazard I might speculate?'

'He ne'er sold one, so his money was all gone, and he could no longer afford to buy the hands. The clocks never turned. By waiting too long, they ran out of time.'

It isn't the subtlest image I've ever heard from the Cagot queen. I wonder if it is the urgency of the situation or her own urging to turn the conversation away from my back-and-forth with her daughter.

Isaac, of course, ruminates gravely for a moment on what she said, inclining his head to show the wisdom of her words. I'd be keen to know what she and Isaac spoke about while her daughter and I cleaned ourselves up, Jakob having headed to the East, towards Prague, as mentioned in Isaac's last letter to me while I was traveling. He's still seeking to help those in need, still searching for the good in humanity, still somehow avoiding the disillusionment that strikes most of us in that regard. 'You are, as ever, entirely correct, my good lady. Come now, tell us why you sought us out.'

Gwendolyne sighs and settles herself into the hard-wood frame of a chair turned and rested against the matching table laid with what simple repast Isaac had to hand. I'm hungry after my travelling but in no hurry to embarrass myself once more by digging into the spread. No doubt I'll end up stumbling and sending cheese and grapes raining down on Susane's mother. 'Seven hundred years, Rabbi, and some more as well, us Cagots have been hated.'

A quirk of amusement flashes across Isaac's lips. 'I think, milady, my people might have yours beat for that.'

She half-smirks, giving him an acknowledging head tilt of her own. 'A fair point, my friend. Still, intolerance of other religions seems to ever be the way of man. They hate us simply for being Cagot. But…I have a plan.'

Her eyes flick to me. Apparently, I feature in this plan, and considering the terrifying intellect of the woman who has come up with it, it will be a fiendish part indeed. Isaac waits politely for her to continue.

'Nobody knows the origins of the Cagot *nor will they, young man,*' she adds as I draw breath. I bite down on my tongue and my disappointment. 'But there are rumours. One reached my ears recently, suggesting that we are the last remnants of a certain heretical group once prominent throughout this region. A group known as the Cathars.'

'But that's ridiculous! You predate our heresy by hundreds of years!' I scoff dismissively.

Gwendolyne replies slowly and clearly, enunciating to help even simpletons such as I to understand. 'You know that. I know that. The rest of the world? They don't know that.' She pauses. 'Nor do they need to.'

Apparently, Gwendolyne is happy to let that rumour promulgate. I just cannot imagine a reason for it. 'Why would you wish to claim to be Cathars? We were hardly beloved by the Church, and even in these enlightened times, the Church holds sway with all the noblesse of every Christian country.'

She shakes her head wearily. Apparently, my stupidity is tiring her out. 'I do not claim us to be Cathars, boy, but the *descendants* of Cathars. Descendants now many generations removed.'

'*Limpieza de sangre!*' Isaac cries out as he catches on to whatever she is saying.

'Cleanliness of the blood?' I translate, still confused.

Isaac sighs and holds up a hand to calm the impatient Cagot. 'It's my fault. He's never been the biggest fan of the Church, for understandable reasons. I made him learn Latin and the parts he needed to know to help him with his magic, but he hasn't studied the doctrine too deeply and certainly not all the legalities of how they handle things.'

He turns to me. '*Limpieza de sangre* means how heresy taints the blood. In effect, children of heretics are also heretics, as are their children and their children after.'

'Condemned for the sins of the fathers,' I mutter sardonically. 'Talk about "suffer the little children".'

'Quite,' Isaac says. 'Still, there is a clear legal limit under Church law. Four generations and then the taint is considered cleansed from the blood — hence the term.'

I finally see the shape of Gwendolyne's plan. 'So if you were outcast from society and the Church because you come from the Cathars...' I say slowly.

'Then the taint will now be gone, if the Church authorities do recognise us as such,' Gwendolyne finishes for me. 'Were our petition accepted, we could be absorbed back into society and able to join this wondrous new age. Or at least, not suffer so readily at the hands of intolerant local idiots.'

Isaac nods, clearly approving of the plan, and I have to

say I think it well made too. There is only one thing I don't understand. 'But where do we fit into this, lady?' I ask.

Gwendolyne looks at me disapprovingly, her lips drawn thin. 'Because we need your help. Particularly yours, Cathar.'

The Cagot queen asking me for help. I have to pinch myself to make sure I am not dreaming.

Chapter Twelve

There's a special place in Hell reserved just for child snatchers. I might not believe in it, but I'll still take great pleasure in trying to send them there as fast as humanly possible.

Isaac is back in control, white-cold with rage, and it is now fury draining the colour from his face. 'He's been taking children for her? For how long?'

I have to fight hard to resist the urge to scoot my chair backwards, pushing myself out of the way of a now very angry Isaac. The subtext is clear. How long has Gwen-dolyne known?

She sighs, slumping dejectedly, the weight of the years and her responsibilities clear. 'Although I can't track him accurately with Oberon's gift, I can use it to get a rough location. I've always tried to monitor him...'

She trails off. Sighs again, and once more, I'm struck by how much age is carried in the language of the body as much as the shaping of the flesh itself. I never saw Gwendolyne hunch before, but now she wraps herself inward, curling around the small space in front of her like her hands around her tea cup.

'That's not true.' It's an admission that's hard on her, that much is clear. 'All of this played out against the backdrop of Susane's first death. Since then I've been so alone. I won't bear more children. Not to see the men die. Not to see a daughter who will be forced to take my place if I ever crumble in the face of my duty or accident or a knife-blade from the like of Jack. The only Cagot still living to carry magic in their first life, I threw myself into the care of my immediate people, but the world outside the community? I stopped paying much attention. Sometimes, stories of the Jack of Plate would reach my ears, and I'd remember my duty might extend to those who fled my care as well. I reached out, searched for him, and sometimes, I found where he was, sometimes not.' She looks up, and there's a glint of the formidable woman I lived in terror of while trying to woo her daughter. 'Did you ever hear about the goat herder who forgot the honour of duty under the drabness of the day-to-day?

I've heard enough of Gwendolyne's stories to be able to have a good guess. 'I imagine they died, and he starved?'

She snorts at my impudence. 'Something like that, Cathar. Or else produced a poor and savage herd worth little to anyone. Least of all herself.'

She stares into the swirling steam rising up to dance in front of her eyes for a moment. 'I have never forgotten where he went. Part of my duties is to hold those figures — names, locations, dates— of all the Cagot in my mind. Oberon might not care what happens to us anymore, but he's always wanted his due. And expected me to perform my duty.'

'How did he react to the loss of Jack?' I guess that Gwendolyne has her own equivalent of a mind palace, a place to store all the information the King of Summer demands she remembers as part of her people's penance. I can't help wondering how he reacted to Maeve stealing what was already his.

'He listened and said nothing. All I saw was a gleam in his eye, though whether from anger or amusement?' She shrugs. 'Who can say? He seeks me to fulfil commands, not to fill in as counsel. Ours not to reason why, Good Man.'

'*How long, Gwendolyne?*' Isaac's voice cuts through, weighed with cold fury. He's in no mood to tolerate any deviation from the subject at hand.

Gwendolyne looks up at his voice's sharpness but ducks her head back down, unable to meet his eye. 'I realised when he settled down twenty-five years back. A long way from me and mine, up towards Lille. A news report about a spate of disappearing children around the area he was in caught my attention, became a suspicion I couldn't leave alone. So I went over all the times when I knew he had been stationary for a few weeks. Realised he was stopping every twenty to thirty years or so. Then I went to the papers. Found stories of children disappearing from their beds in the dead of night, with no answer as to how in each location. Every goddamned time.'

She stops, and it knocks me back to see tears in her eyes. I've never seen her express emotions like that, even at the death of her beloved daughter. 'I should have realised, 'Zac. I should have realised what he was up to, should have tried harder and stopped him.'

'Yes, you should have.' I am just as astounded to see the

hard, unforgiving lines on Isaac's face. We seem to have slipped into some reversed-up Bizarro World where everyone is the opposite of their normal selves. Stolen children will do that though. Isaac studiously ignores the tears as long as he can, but eventually, they work through his defences. 'Fine, Gwen, we've all made mistakes and missed things we shouldn't have, but he was your responsibility. If you picked this up earlier, if you brought it to us directly…'

'I wasn't allowed. The one thing Oberon did was command me to leave Jack alone. He specifically forbade me to seek help. It's only because you've come to me about him rather than the other way around that I can tell you any of this.'

Living under a geas, a binding of oaths, is no simple matter. Being leader of a people whose entire existence is effectively a form of geas that has spanned centuries must be almost unbearable at times. I never envied her the mantle she bears, but right now, I pity her more than ever.

I lay my hand on Isaac's shoulder, pulling him back and calming him down. 'What's done is done. Do you know where he is now? Out wandering the world?'

She nods, dislodging the tears, sending tiny sparkling refractions tumbling to the floor. 'He just settled down again. It's been twenty years since the last time he did.'

The bottom drops out of my stomach. He is about to start up again.

'Where?' I manage through gritted teeth.

She looks at me, culpability imprinted in the concentric rings of her eyes. It is funny. I can't remember a time when she looked at me with any emotion other than distaste or hate. All it took was for her to have spectacularly fucked up too. Funny old world, and by funny, I mean absolutely fucking tragic to the degree that I wonder for a moment if

Ben didn't have the right idea to destroy it entirely. I shake myself mentally. Those are dangerously bleak directions for a wizard to head in. It leads to natty black outfits and plans for world domination. Possibly even monologuing and cackling. Never a good look.

'Lyon.' Her voice, normally so strong, so confident, trembles a little, the volume not much above a whisper. 'He's settled down in Lyon.'

Fuck sake. I groan. That's the fucking Tarrasque's territory.

Chapter Thirteen

Jack has made his own bed. Now he needs to Lyon it. While I nail big fucking iron spikes through his head, then steal his body. I look forward to it immensely.

We don't hang around long after that. Gwendolyne already exceeded all expectable rules of hospitality by providing me with not one but two cups of tea and refraining from putting cyanide in either of them. I'm not going to tempt her by asking for a third, and besides, I want to get on the road.

I'm eager to strike out directly for Lyon, but whichever way we go —either up and across by Clermont-Ferrand or across, then up via Montpellier— we'll be passing through Toulouse first, and Isaac wants to stock up on various supplies.

'Fine. But one of you's driving. One. Only one. If you want to change over, we stop and take a break. And you're getting us out of the mountains, 'Zac. This ain't the place to

93

be teaching the niceties of road safety. They're hardly roads, and they certainly aren't safe.'

They grumble. Both of them. Simultaneously, which makes both my ears and my brain hurt. However, they give in, especially when I tell them about the detour I want to make before we leave the Pyrenees.

We don't have to go far out of our way. Winding down towards lower ground, we pass through Oloron-Sainte-Marie, beautiful and dying, the medieval buildings that cling to the riverbanks having fallen emptier and emptier as the years went on. There is no work here, and as children grow and leave for different lives, the ancient town ages, each parting youngster a lost spark of vitality. Still, it isn't far before the signs of wealth and good living appear, evidence of prosperity, of a plausible future written into the country-side in genteel housing and close-knit new builds. We wind our way past medieval architecture once more, but this time it's lived in and loved by locals and tourists alike.

As we walk through the secret entrance under the gorgeous old church that dominates the town square, Isaac is practically vibrating with excitement. It surprises me when we manage to pass through the narrower earthen passageways without causing some sort of landslide because of his seismic activity. The cave shrinks, forcing us to duck, and I can picture him accidentally drilling his way up and getting his head stuck in the roof.

When it widens out, we find ourselves standing over a vast cavern, one I am becoming entirely too familiar with. The most remarkable thing about it would normally be the amazing dripped-stone stalactites on a surface too round to be natural, yet too ancient for humans to have carved. Would be, were it not for all the furry tentacles slapped over the surfaces, stuck on by their sucker pads.

I knock on the rough granite wall next to one of the said feelers. I can grab it and shout into it. That's what I did the first time I was here as they are all, in effect, ears with listening holes in the suckers' centres. I can't say I'm not tempted as the owner of them said doing so gives him a headache and talking to him does the same to me.

But he is doing me a favour now. We are building a working relationship, so a minimal amount of consideration seems only right. Look at me, learning and growing with time.

The tentacle peels itself away from the wall with a noise akin to a Velcro strap being slowly pulled free. It hovers around us, and if I didn't know it was a listening apparatus rather than a nasal extension, I'd say it sniffs us. Anything is possible down here though. But Lou Carcoilh is no Snuffle-upagus. I suppose the *Sesame Street* character might resemble him a bit...if he got hosed down with nuclear waste or if Jeff Goldblum put him through a teleporter with a garden snail.

The earth of the corridor rumbles, and we catch our balance so as not to tumble down the sloping passageway. It is a long fall if we do, probably fifty metres at least. I'm not confident in my ability to bounce back from that.

From the gargantuan stone archway opposite us at ground level, Lou appears, dragging his gigantic carapace behind him.

The philosopher, David Hume, said it was impossible to imagine anything outside of our own experience and that anything fantastical we think of is just a concoction of different aspects of things we've encountered. So for him, a dragon was just the combination of a lizard with the concept of wings and the idea of fire being expelled. For me, dragons are a bit more than a philosophical idea, being spectacular pains in the proverbial rear.

I don't know Lou's origins, whether he is some type of faerie or the offspring of some mind-boggling creatures or deities. Another possibility is he was some ancient warlock's pet project, literally. I can imagine said magic user picking the characteristics he wanted — the invincible, magic-proof shell and waggling eyestalks of a snail, the shaggy brown hair of a mammoth, the pliable neck and razor-filled mouth of a spinosaurus, and the tentacles and suckers of an octopus. Then he must have eaten an entire bag of special mushrooms and drank six gallons of sweet mead before assembling the creature.

Which is why the tentacles are ears as well (because who doesn't want to hear through their tentacles?) and why they're stuck by the hundreds to the creature's lips. Wanting his pet to be constantly slick and dripping, he gave it the ability to secrete mucus like a snail before further beating it with the ugly stick for a day or two. And to top it all off, he made it as large as a small mountain. The lesson to take away? Don't create magical beings while you're tripping balls.

The gigantic snail-dragon-hallucinogenic nightmare looks up, his eyes swivelling in my direction. They pull back and blink, then the mouth, which is capable of biting a camper van in half without even noticing, spreads into a fang-revealing smile.

'Mither Thnack!' The tone of delight is completely unforced. He is really pleased to see me, so much so, his lisp is even more pronounced on my "name". I feel like some monstrous dog-kicking bastard for not being equally delighted. The tentacle hanging in front of us swivels, its sucker pad facing us. 'High five, buddy!'

I groan. This is why I'm not equally delighted. We'll be stuck here forever if I don't give him some skin. I awkwardly hop up and slap the pad, which is as big as my torso. My feet don't touch the ground again afterwards.

'Lou,' I say through gritted teeth, my legs pedalling furiously.

'Oh, sorry, Thnack, jutht a minute.'

He waves the tentacle I am stuck to slowly at first, then faster, more and more furiously until my teeth are chattering and my eyes are rattling in my skull. In the end, he scrapes me off like dog poo, rubbing the appendage and my face against the jagged rock wall of the passage until I plop off, grazed in multiple places and covered in Carcoilh goo. Not the best start to a conversation with a monster I've ever had. Although, I still have all my limbs, and the surrounding countryside in a five-mile radius isn't on fire, so it's also not the worst.

I pick myself up and attempt to dust myself down. All that happens is I send gloopy lumps that look like giant loogies everywhere sliding down the walls as if an ogre with bronchitis just coughed them up.

I feel a faint glow surround me that I'd label as white, as it is beyond what eyes from our plane are capable of identifying, no matter how *talented* the person is. It is best not to study angelic magic too hard. You'll end up weeping bloody tears and garbling in tongues. I speak from experience.

My grazes heal, and the slimy substance disappears. Turning, I nod my thanks to Isaac, who gives me a supportive wink. Yeah, who needs Aicha? She'd have just taken the piss out of me and left me dripping in slime.

My thought process is interrupted by Lou's attempt at a discreet cough, which makes several of the stalactites vibrate dangerously, like they can tumble down at any moment. 'Are you okay, Mithter Thnack? You looked terribly sad for a moment there.' The stalks twist around, peering past me. 'Where'th the other thnack? You know, the clever one?' The giant snail wags his tentacle at me. 'I don't think it'th a very good idea, you being out on your own. You need her to keep you safe.'

Ouch. Apparently, even Lou Carcoilh thinks I am incapable without Aicha. The Good God knows what he will think when he realises I managed to get my magic eaten. I wave a hand at Isaac.

'Don't worry, Lou. I've brought along the smartest person I've ever met. He'll make sure I only use plastic cutlery and wear a protective helmet at all times. Say hello to Isaac.'

Isaac was waiting for the introduction, and he steps forward smartly. He peers at the giant cephalopod in wonder. An academic with a new subject to study is like a young child with a new toy. And only slightly less likely to pull the limbs off it accidentally.

'Hello there, Mr Carcoilh, and a pleasure to finally meet you.' There is a breathlessness to his voice. He really is in seventh heaven, getting to see the creature first hand. 'You are truly magnificent. Magnificent, sir!'

Lou preens, smoothing the hair on the back of his eye orb with a tentacle like a fifties rocker, using his natural goo like hair gel. 'Well, thank *you*, sir. Finally, someone who truly bloody appreciateth me for the natural wonder I am. It'th about bloody time, but still, thankth ever so much!'

I interrupt the love-in. We don't have time for this. I mean, I never have time for this but even less so today. 'Right, that's lovely. I'm glad you two are now best buds. Sorry, Jak, we don't have time —'

'Who ith Jak?' Lou asks.

'Ah, yes. Lou, this is Jakob too. Well, Isaac and Jakob. Well, Isaac and Jakob and Nithael and Nanael actually.'

Lou scratches the top of his serpentine-like head with an appendage. 'Is that what they mean when they say someone is called something elthe at the weekend?'

Lou Carcoilh loves modern media. Problem is, he physically can't get out of the cave, having grown too large over the centuries. Plus, he made some mysterious deal back in medieval times with some mage, possibly Merlin himself, where he agreed to stay put. He isn't exactly surreptitious either; he might get away with being outside for a little while, but sooner or later, he'd have the army coming, looking to cook him up and serve him with parsley.

What he can do, though, is send his tentacles out into the town above. At night, they are naturally camouflaged, practically impossible to spot. Everything he knows is from listening to radio and television in the evenings via a sucker stuck to someone's windows. I shudder at the thought of the mess he leaves behind. The local window cleaner must make a killing. I wonder what story the locals have come up with to justify the slimy deposits found regularly on their glass panes. Atmospheric phenomenon or something, probably.

Point is, as he only gets to hear and not see, he concocts some pretty strange ideas about what things can mean. For instance, he is mortally afraid of bazookas, although I'm not sure he really knows what a bazooka is.

Not for the first time, I promise myself that when things calm down, I'll bring him some sort of audio-visual hook-up like a projector and a generator down here so he can watch films and TV properly. I'll even lend him my Netflix password. Unless Netflix is reading this, in which case, I definitely will not ever lend him or anyone my Netflix password.

I shake my head, wondering how I am going to explain drag to what, I hope desperately, is an asexual creature. 'No, look, that's a turn of phrase that is used when someone identifies, perhaps, as the opposite sex but only feels capable of dressing in such a manner on the weekend.'

Lou considers this. 'You mean to say you dreth differently? I hate to sound like an ignorant bloody specieth, but you all look the same to me. If you're all human, why would anyone care about how someone elthe dresseth? Are they worried they'll fall madly in love with them or something? Soundth pretty bloody insecure to me.'

I realise my mouth is hanging open, and I shut it by force of will. Apparently, even a giant snail-dragon the size of Notre-Dame, trapped under a mountain, can understand that instinctively. Yet, a whole swath of humanity struggles with it. Perhaps we'd be better dying out as a species and letting the insects take over. I, for one, will welcome our cockroach overlords, as an undying immortal.

'I mean, you're right,' I start, then stop, flustered. I've completely lost what I was going to say. 'Bloody hell, Lou, you don't have half a way of derailing a conversation!'

Lou cranes his neck up towards Isaac, putting his pad between us, and whispers at a volume that a seismograph could pick up. 'He'th a bit bloody snappy today, ithn't he? Ith it hith time of the month? That would certainly explain thingth.'

I cover my eyes in despair. Maybe he doesn't get it, after all. 'That one's a biological process, Lou. I don't get a time of the month. Only women do.'

He waggles his eye stalks back and forth at me like Wall-E trying to focus, and when he speaks again, his voice drips with horrified sympathy. 'You mean you're like thith *all the bloody time*? I'm so, so sorry for you, Mithter Thnack.'

I wipe my hand down my face, pulling hard in frustration at the bags under my eyes. It's amazing I don't pull them so far down, I end up with handbags instead. Sadly, it doesn't wipe away the pain caused from making conversation with Lou Carcoilh.

Isaac, for once, comes to save the day without making matters worse. 'Listen, old chap, I'd love to get into some details about how much of a misery guts Paul is and even more into how your feeding off magic goes. Only, we're on a bit of a mission, and time is of the essence.'

Lou blinks rapidly, excitement clear on his face. 'Ooh, a mithion! Ith it *top secret*?' he hisses. If a tower-block-sized gastropod could bounce up and down, I'm sure he would be. Thankfully, I think even he recognises that would end up with it raining stalactites, and he'd end up as snail shish kebab.

I nod quickly, grateful for something that means we can talk less. 'Absolutely. Totally top secret. Can't talk about it at all in any way. In fact, we need to stop talking now, honestly, and just go. We stopped by to ask if we could grab back one of the skulls, please?'

Lou nods, a furtive air to him, and taps the side of his grotesque nose/snout/beak mashup conspiratorially. 'Of courthe, Mithtah Thnack, say no more!'

Two of his tentacles whip back into his shell before rapidly reappearing, each bearing a gleamingly polished human skull. I don't need to have my full *talent* back to feel the power radiating off each of them. These are the magical equivalent of plutonium rods.

'Which one of them do you want to take then?' He rocks them back and forth in the air, and for a moment, all I can think about is Lou breaking into a juggling routine. I shake my head, trying to dislodge the thought, and point at the skull of Arnaud Almeric. Even without the skin on, I can recognise him. He still looks like an utter bastard.

Lou drifts the skull over to me gently, which only makes my futile tugging to free it from the sucker pad look even more ridiculous. Thanks, good snail buddy. Eventually, I work it off and pass it over to Isaac, who looks at it, then me doubtfully.

'You haven't even told me what you want it for, my lad. And are you sure you want me to carry it after last time?'

I worry at my lip with my teeth, weighing how much to say. Especially with the literally sticky ears of a hundred tentacles listening in. 'I'm hoping we won't need it, but let's just call it an insurance policy. As for you carrying it, better you than me, dude. You'll be able to shield its presence. I'll pop up on every Talented's radar like a Whack-A-Mole ready to get smacked down.'

Isaac nods. He's picked up on my careful choice of words, and while he might not understand why, he's prepared to follow my lead. So he tucks the skull carefully away into a battered brown satchel.

I turn my attention back to the giant snail-dragon, who's been surreptitiously trying to creep a couple of his tentacle-ears closer to us to listen in better. They scamper back, and his eyes swivel innocuously to inspect the ceiling. I nearly panic, thinking he is choking when he starts spitting globules with a wheezing 'th' sound all over the ground in front of him until I clock he is trying to whistle. Never the easiest thing to do when a plethora of tentacles are attached to your mouth. Plethacles. The new word is wasted without Aicha to run it past.

'Right, Lou, appreciate it. We'll drop this back to you ASAP. Look after the other one for us, will you?'

'No problem, Mithtah Thnack,' he responds brightly. 'Drop it back anytime, and if you do one day remember that Lou isn't my name, it juttht meanth "the", that would be bloody amazing. Bit much to athk though from such a tiny thing, I know. Brainth have to be proportionally smaller.'

He starts sliding backwards, but before he disappears, I think I hear him start to rap, 'I like big brainth, and I cannot lie...' This conjures up mental images of him trying to twerk, so I push it from my mind quickly. My therapy bill is already likely to be high enough.

———————

By the time we get back to the car, it is getting dark. It strengthens Isaac's argument for stopping off at Toulouse, but the Good God damn it, I've wasted enough time. I know it is me who did the wasting by getting wasted but still. Now we have a lead, a target. I want to get on. Plus, this shitbag is delivering children to the fae. There isn't a much better motivator than that for pulling on my size twelve ass-kicking boots. Now I just have to hope that I can still tie the laces up without my magic.

I am so preoccupied, I don't really pay attention to the drive back. Pootling up and down the A64 is getting boring now. Although I didn't recently get tortured to death nor am I currently rapidly bleeding out, so that adds a touch of originality to it, at least. I look out of the window, seeing nothing, and brood with a nineties-James-Marsters level of broodery. I max out my Brood Stats. I become the BroodMaster.

By the time we get back to Isaac's, my state of mind flip-flops between utterly exhausted and massively pissed off, mainly because I am aware how unpleasant it has to be just being in my presence. I might be in a dark place, but I still love Isaac, and he doesn't deserve to be catching my miserableness in the neck. I decide to try harder as I go to get out of the car, but he puts his hand gently on my shoulder and stops me.

'Wait here, lad.' I'd prefer if he shouted at me, told me what an ignorant arsehole I was, and insisted I get my head back in the game. The sympathetic understanding writ large on his expression only makes me feel like even more of a wanker.

'What are you talking about, 'Zac? Let's go get some sleep so we can get going as early as possible in the morning.' I pull away from him, ready to get out, to get to bed and pretend to sleep until the morning. I have neither the energy nor the inclination for a heart-to-heart now. We'll have plenty of time for him to berate me on the way to Lyon tomorrow.

He doesn't move and so neither do I. I don't have a lot of choice in the matter. Apparently, angelic body-sharing gives you insane upper body strength. Either that or he's been doing a hellish number of push-ups in between studying obscure gnostic texts. 'You're never going to sleep, my boy. I know when you're hopped up on righteous outrage. I appreciate you humouring me, but I'm older and wiser than you still. You've only got me beat on the ugliness stakes.'

'And wit and charm and — Look, I'm too knackered for this, dude. What did you want to tell me? I get it. I'm burning both ends of the candle to where all I've got left is a tiny, little stubby spark and hands covered in wax. I messed up. Again. I should have been getting on with it instead of boozing, and this is all—'

'Paul! Knock it off.' He cuts off the rapidly accelerating spiel tumbling out of my mouth, then drops the volume back down. 'Listen, man. I know you aren't going to sleep if we go in. You'll be bouncing off the walls until we head off in the morning.' He taps the side of his head. 'There's two of us in here, and Jak's got the hang of driving now, especially away from the winding mountain paths.'

'Eh.' I tilt my head doubtfully.

'Jak's got this,' he says confidently. 'Wait here. Let me pick up some supplies, bits and bobs we might need for taking on this half-marked Jim or whatever he's called, then we'll get on our way. It's less than a six-hour run. Jak can take over mid-way, and I can grab some rest. You.' He wags his finger at me, half-joking, half-scolding. 'You can catch some much-needed Z's and get your head back in the game. I'm here to do the thinking for you, at least, but you know my limits in terms of direct confrontation. It doesn't sound like this fella is going to be inviting us in for a nice cup of tea and a sit-down chat. Hold on, Jak, what is it? *Y*es, just to reiterate, my dear boy. I really have got this down pat now. You relax and leave the whole thing in our capable hands. There, see?'

I must still look unconvinced because he gives me a light shake, enough to startle me and make me look him in the eyes. 'Have a little faith, my boy. Leave this part, at least, to us.'

I exhale, feeling the shakiness in my hands, my nerves. It is the first physical trait of complete exhaustion, and I have to admit I'm close to collapse. I can feel the adrenaline that pervades every nerve, like I'm a struck tuning fork, vibrating internally at 440 hertz. My magic is gone, so I need to be sharp mentally if we're going to stand a chance. I can't rely on *talent* and instinct to win every battle anymore. For what is to come, I need to be in the best mental shape possible, and I am nowhere near that. We are still moving in the right direction, still progressing, so I need to take this opportunity to relax, to recuperate. Isaac knows me better than I know myself.

I nod, acquiescing. 'You're right. I need the rest, and there's no way I will sleep the night in bed. 'Zac, Jak, appreciate it immensely.'

'Leave it to us, lad. Take a load off. We'll be right back.'

I lean my head against the cool glass of the Tesla's door and let my eyes slide shut. I hear them getting out of the car, but after that…? I think I am asleep before they even carefully and quietly close it behind them.

Chapter Fourteen

Don't worry. Bad dreams are only dreams. Until they aren't,
of course.

I wake disorientated in the dark. The cradling movement of
the car, which kept me slumbering, has stopped, and for a
moment, I don't know where I am or even when I am. I was
dreaming of previous lives, in a time long past, when I felt
young. But I'm not those people anymore; I lost those
moments centuries previous. It takes me a minute to
remember what a car is, let alone that I'm in one. Honestly?
For that single moment as I left a dreamworld so convincing
for a reality filled with doubts, I forgot cars even existed.

That is why I come to with such a start. It definitely isn't
from the startle-factor caused by hearing my own snoring or
feeling the cold patch on my chin from several hours of
drool. Neither of those two happened. Honest.

'Call of nature and a change of driver.' Isaac taps his

head and gets out of the batwing door, stretching for a moment before heading for the concrete toilet block. These are perfunctory services, just a strip of grass, some wooden picnic tables, and public facilities that are as basic as is possible, short of just digging a pit in the ground. Still, there is water to wash our hands after. Simple hygiene options like that still makes me inordinately happy. Take that, bacteria! I put the diss in dysentery.

I am feeling a lot more human for some actual sleep rather than just a temporary alcohol-induced coma now and then. Feeling more than human would be even better, but human is a good start. We finish up our ablutions and head back to the car.

'Whereabouts are we now?' I ask. The drive flew by. I don't even know which way Isaac elected to go.

'Just south of Nîmes. Well, southwest if you want to be precise.'

'I do, 'Zac, I really do. Can you break out the degrees of latitude and longitude for me? I'm betting you've got a sextant kicking about in your baggage somewhere.'

'Paul?'

'Yes?'

'You've been asleep for the whole journey until now, and I'm already fed up with you talking. Go back to sleep, lad. I'm going to hand over to Jak and do the same.'

'Night, 'Zac, sleep well. I'll most likely kill you in the morning.'

He eyes me dubiously. 'Were it anyone else, I'd dismiss that as hyperbole. As it is, I don't doubt you'll be the death of me.'

I gape. 'Man, did you not recognise the quote? Shit, I know film and TV isn't your jam, but we need to remedy that ASAP!'

He mulls it over, then he gives me a roguish wink. 'As you wish, lad. As you wish.'

He totally got me, the sly bugger.

I drift off again for a little while, that half-conscious light dreaming that mixes the world with the imaginary in sporadic flashes. My head keeps sliding sideways, sometimes jerking me back to a more awake state, sometimes settling into the rumbling of the window, setting my teeth into a sympathetic vibration. At some point later —it could be ten minutes or two hours— I straighten up, wincing at the muscle I blocked from right shoulder to the bottom of my neck. I turn it back and forth, trying to find the angle that will make the kinks I worked into it with my terrible sleeping position disappear. No such luck.

Jakob is driving. Looking over, I can tell because he keeps muttering things under his breath. I can't hear very much, but phrases like, '...ten and two...' and, '...indicate, then move...' tell me he is making sure he has all the basics memorised. He probably doesn't want to disturb his brother if he's resting.

I am a little worried about distracting him, but we rarely get any real time together. 'How are you doing, Jak?' I ask quietly and calmly, trying not to startle him when he is concentrating so hard.

It still makes him jump slightly, muscle spasms of coursing adrenaline momentarily triggered in his face and hands, though he does a good job keeping it under control. 'Remarkably well, my dear boy, all things considered.'

He resettles, and I have to say his driving has dramatically improved since the mountains. I suppose it shouldn't surprise me that one of the world's greatest scholars is a quick learner.

'It's not too difficult being stuck inside Isaac's head?'

'It's a great deal better than being stuck inside that skull was. I can tell you that much! Honestly, it's marvellous. Better than I could have imagined these past centuries when I dreamt of escape. I feared a disembodied existence. Floating around, a ghost on the air currents, was as good as Nan and I could have hoped for. Instead, I get to spend time with my dear brother once more, plus Nith. I think it must be quite something for them, too, to be in direct communion after such a long time. And, of course, I get to discover such modern wonders as this.'

He tries to wave a hand at the steering wheel but forgets in the moment that he is already gripping it incredibly tight. The Tesla lurches sideways, but the automatic lane guidance pulls it back. My heart follows suit, then settles for beating like a speed typist hammering away on a Victorian typewriter. Lapsing into silence seems like a sensible way to stop my ticker giving out before we even get to Lyon.

It is Jakob who breaks the silence. 'He worries about you, you know.'

I startle, having been staring out of the window, half-mesmerised by the light-pools of orange sliding past against the blackness. 'Isaac, you mean?'

'Yes. He'll never say it, but he worries. He loves you very much. I think in my absence, you kept him sane. I wonder if he would even be here to greet me had you not been around.'

I try to get my head around this. 'What do you mean? Like, around in France?'

'Around, as in around this plane of existence. Have you never considered that, if Nithael can come down here, he can go back' —he flicks his chin towards the car's ceiling— 'up there if he wants to? I must confess to a burning curiosity myself. To see other dimensions, other planes of existence.'

'To boldly go where no man has gone before?' I waste it on Jakob, but I can't resist.

'Absolutely! Plus, I'd look very dashing in a Federation outfit, don't you think?'

Well, well, well. Top marks, Isaac. I'd have thought the two brothers would've squandered their time discussing arcane magical theory, but it looks like he prioritised the important parts of Jakob's education in the modern world as well.

'He thinks of you as his son, you know, dear boy, so I guess that makes me your uncle. So you need to know how he is handling all this. Losing Aicha, who he cares for very much as well, at a time when your magic is so terribly depleted? He's deeply, deeply concerned. Can you imagine how it must feel?'

There is nothing but bitterness in my laughter. 'Jakob, we're currently driving to the other side of the country to chase down a child-stealing psychopathic blade master in the hope we can go to a land of creatures who see humans as a quick fuck or food, probably both, possibly simultaneously, to track down my treacherous dead wife and a son I didn't even know had ever lived. My empathy for people in uncomfortable or concerning family situations is in overload right now.'

'So you understand what it is to have a child who is completely out of control? And who takes rash, impetuous decisions that will probably get them killed?'

I hold up a corrective finger. 'That *do* get him killed. Regularly. Luckily, I just come back.'

'But what if you don't? What happens when you bite off

more than you can chew and go up against someone or something that can overpower your reincarnating, my boy? Ben came blasted close to managing it. That's what keeps Isaac up at night. Literally.'

I swallow my guilt before it manifests as harsh words. Jakob is right to tell me all this. I don't want to hurt Isaac at all, and there is no doubt that the way I rush at things like a bull in a china shop would have aged him prematurely...if he could age. 'What would you have me do, Jak? Retire from the Talented world? Call it a day now, when the stakes are so damn high? Not just for us either. Would you really have me leave a wish-granting artefact in the hands of some mentally damaged faeling? Leave Susane in his hands? She might have set me up, but there's something unhealthy there in that whole happy-family dynamic, and I'm not buying it for a second. And that's before we get into the whole mess with the skulls and Arnaud Almeric. It isn't that easy to just walk away.'

'Then don't walk away from Isaac either, dear boy. You left him high and dry while you went swimming in drink. He was tearing his hair out the whole time, though he'd never show you that. And it's not exactly the first time you've just gone swanning off into danger without letting him know or thinking of the impact, hmm? Maybe you can't change direction. At least let him know where you're going. Let him know you'll be coming home again.'

Over eight hundred years. I've been alive for over eight hundred years, and Jakob manages effectively to make me feel like a stop-out, party-hard teen coming home to find their parents sat at the kitchen table in their dressing gowns, ready at 3:00 am for a serious talk. Of course, they have a reason. They are teenagers. I'm supposed to have grown out of that phase centuries ago.

'You're right, Jak. I've not been doing an awful lot of thinking recently. Correction — I've not been doing a lot of big-picture thinking. I've been zoomed in, micromanaging one major disaster in the here and now after another and not seeing the damage being wrought around it. I'll make more of an effort, okay? Promise.'

'That's all I can ask, dear boy. I care about you too, but I care about my brother even more. I am eternally grateful to you for keeping him company all these long years. I'd prefer not to lose either of you any time soon.'

The conversation drifts away to small talk topics, mainly Jak plugging me for information about various nuances of modern life. I think they are the little things that Jakob feels he should be able to get instinctively and feels embarrassed asking his brother. Why do people still work so hard when there is all this technology? Why do people seem so *miserable*? There is so little smiling, such surprise when he is in control and he offers someone his seat on the train, or he asks a shopkeeper how they are doing. It doesn't make sense to him. I make a mental note to never, ever take him to Paris. It'd break his big, naïve heart.

Eventually, even this fizzles out. Sweeping light shapes dance across the car roof in a steady rhythm thanks to the metronome of the cruise control. It makes me think of my seemingly endless days sped up, flickering past, an empty projector showing nothing but a blank screen. My life mutes, all the sound and fury signifying nothing strips away, and only the emptiness is left for all to see. At some point, the constant rhythm flashing overhead lulls me into dark dreams, haunted by my actions and inactions both and the pain of hunting for meaning over endless pointless centuries.

It is fair to say I am a bit grumpy when I wake back up

not long after. In fact, I might have come to cursing the world, the Grail, the Good God, and everyone else besides. Jakob glances over sympathetically, though I am glad he doesn't let it draw too much of his attention away from keeping the car going straight.

'Bad dreams?' I sometimes wonder if Jakob isn't secretly English with his impeccably good manners and his stunning ability to state the painfully fucking obvious.

I draw breath and force myself to calm down. My dreams are a manifestation of my subconscious. I am torturing myself. It is my fault, not Jak's.

'Yep, the worst. Do you want to know something? Something I've never admitted to anyone, even myself, really?'

He nods slightly. This isn't about his need to know. It is about my need to tell.

'You know how Isaac and I helped Aicha? With the whole "recovering from years of insane torture" bullshit? She had her own room at mine. I always told her, come over, sleep there whenever you want; any time you've got them bad dreams, any time those memories get on top of you, come back. You've always got a safe place to stay. Funny thing is, I wanted her to stay every single night. It wasn't because I kept her nightmares away. Aicha Kandicha is such a badass, she kept mine away too.'

'You should reach out to her, Paul. She's still your friend.'

The Good God knows I want to. To pull out my phone and try a number I know by heart. To force out an apology for pushing her away when she was only doing what needed to be done, what I couldn't bring myself to do. Except I broke that trust. Shattered that compact we'd built, to lean on each other and lend all necessary strength. Because I know she needed my understanding in that dank ancient Roman storehouse. And all she got was my fury, my anger, lashed with a bitter blame I should have kept for myself, that I'd earned, not her.

Because in the end that's what I do to everyone I love and let get close. Make them pay the price for my bad decisions and man-child bravado.

How can I ever ask her to come back, knowing the costs involved?

'As loyal as she is, she's not one to accept being treated like that. She's gone, let it be Jak.'

'Fine, but I'd like to help if I can. Nan says there is something he might do to aid you, if you'll allow him?'

The idea of proper sleep, not haunted sleep, sounds so good, I would let Leatherface cook me up into a head cheese if he could guarantee me a solid eight hours first. Being touched by an angel? Definitely something I can live with.

'Go for it, Nan. Thanks. Both of you.'

I can't *see* properly, not like before, but I can still feel a wing's pinion unfurl and stroke my forehead. It wipes away the last remnants of the lingering dark. I close my eyes and slip away into a dreamless state, genuine rest I need and missed so much.

I wake up feeling refreshed, relaxed, and completely baffled. Mostly by how I feel as it is so damn unusual but also by where we are. The sun streams in through the window; its approach towards the zenith tells me it is closing on midday. A distant burble of shrieks and laughter says we are near a school, probably a primary one based on the innocent joy the hubbub of voices carries. The underlying rumble of traffic advancing and the occasional screeching of brakes tell me we are in a metropolitan area. I am still sun-blind, blinking my pupils back to a size that allows me to see clearly, but when I bang my knees as I try to sit up, I remember more precisely where I am. Isaac's Tesla.

I smash my head on the ceiling when the batwing door swings up and Isaac or Jakob (never, ever Isakob) gets in, and I leap up, realising where we might be.

'Tell me we aren't in Lyon, man.' I stare wildly around, peering out the window at the relatively nondescript cityscape outside. I can see a big river. It could be the Rhône. We could be in big trouble.

'Don't worry, my boy, we're in Vienne. Isaac is still resting, but he was quite insistent we stop here before he handed over the keys, so to speak. Should I wake him up now?' Jakob's worry comes through clearly in his tone. It must be stressful borrowing his brother's body for such a long period of time. Like getting lent someone's pride and joy classic car. Fun to start with, but there must come a point when worrying about dinging it and ruining their prized possession leads to a sigh of relief when you slip them the keys back.

I remember how to breathe again, which is always a useful thing to remember. 'Thanks, minor heart attack for a minute there. We can't just go rocking up in Lyon like that.'

'Why is that, exactly?' Jakob sounds suitably confused. Damn it; thanks, Isaac.

'Your brother didn't explain at all? He didn't tell you who holds Lyon?' A headshake as an answer. I heave a sigh. 'Well, the Lyonnais call him Mâchecroûte, mainly because they have to be bloody different, and they claim him entirely as their own. He's a river monster that lives under a bridge in the centre of Lyon.'

Jakob is desperately trying to puzzle it out. 'Is he some sort of relation of Franc's or something?'

It is a good guess but not right. 'It's even worse than that.' I groan, thinking of what is to come. 'He's the bloody Tarrasque.'

Chapter Fifteen

Wondering if I can do something more fun than talking to
the fucking Tarrasque. Like driving nine-inch nails into
every articulation point on my body.

Good God damn it. I hate the Tarrasque. Mind you, so
does anyone unfortunate enough to ever meet him. Jakob,
on the other hand, looks entirely lost.

'I must confess, our paths have never crossed. Who is
the Tarrasque, exactly?'

'He's a massive pain in the arse, is who he is. An utter
dickhead who would have been wiped off the face of the
earth long ago if he was slightly easier to kill. I mean, I tried
first time we met. Even Isaac had a go at it, which tells you
just what a wanker he is. In the end, we agreed he could set
up in Lyon as long as he didn't eat anyone, mainly because
it meant he stayed on the opposite side of the country
from us.'

'Okay, I get the message, dear boy, that you aren't fond of him. But who is he? What is he?'

'Well, he's basically a dragon, although I feel really mean to dragons lumping him in with them. He's a unique spin on the concept, like Lou, although a million times more annoying. According to legend, he's originally from Turkey and was the offspring of a bonnacon. You know, the giant bulls who fire acidic shit from their rectum as a weapon? Luckily, they seem to be extinct as a species, although I heard rumours of one showing up in Emerald Valley in the US recently. You can imagine with that sort of genealogy behind him exactly how much fun the Tarrasque is.

'He's basically a cross between a turtle and a lion, with a snake tail just to add to the general hideousness. Half animal, half fish, all arsehole. We're not his favourite people either, and now we need to ask his permission to go hunting in his territory.'

'And if he says no?'

'Then we're probably fucked. I couldn't take him down when I was at full power. Now? I'm as much use as a wet fart. Obviously, you're here to supercharge 'Zac, but I still don't think it'll be enough, and both the angels'll be doing their standard "hands off" shit when we go up against him. If we can't get him on board, bluffing and improvising are the order of the day, but I genuinely do not know what we'll do.'

'Well, we better make sure we get it right then, shouldn't we? When do we start, my boy?'

I shrug. 'It depends. Is Isaac fully rested?' I want him on top form for the upcoming encounter. Jakob nods. 'Then there's no time like the present. Give him a nudge, will you? Let's get to it.'

Jakob closes his eyes, then a few seconds later, Isaac opens them. 'Right, lad, are we ready?'

'Ready might be stretching it. I don't think there is any getting ready for having to deal with that ambulatory shitstain.'

'True and justified. But try not to antagonise him until after we've got his sealed approval to go hunting this Jack of Plate, will you?'

Urgh. Not only do I have to talk to the Tarrasque, I have to talk to him *nicely*. I'm starting to wonder if finding Susane and my son are worth paying such a high price.

'Okay, Dad, don't be a dick to the Ancient Mutant Wanker Turtle. Although if he shouts, "Cowabunga," it's going to get tricky. I have my limits.'

'Radical, lad. Right, up and at 'em.'

We get out of the car. Various parts of me click and crack in peculiar and painful ways. The Tesla might be a comfortable car, but even the most comfortable car makes a shitty bed. We parked under a bridge, the main town itself spreading out above us, embedded into the mounting hillside. The Alps are near, and all the land wants to do is pay homage, climbing and descending, miniature ridges formed by the same tectonic activity on a smaller scale. We stroll down towards the water's edge, crossing the main road. The Rhône swirls and eddies, as wide and as wild as the Garonne back home, the gentler hills on the other side so much calmer than the landscape on this one. It is like the Rhône is so powerful it can hold back the mountains themselves.

Isaac leans over the curving walkway barrier that has swan-neck support posts adding a sense of art to its functional purpose of keeping idiots from trying to dive into water that will swallow them whole and never spit them back out. He dangles a filament of *talent* like an angler trying to catch some particularly esoteric fish, letting it rest on the river's surface. However, rather than being carried southwards, back the way we came, back towards the Mediterranean, instead it heads north, towards Lyon, carried on currents no mortal can see. To be honest? I am struggling *seeing* any of this myself, which sucks.

Eventually, Isaac ties off the magical line to the railing, and we sit down on a nearby bench. Isaac offers me a chicken sandwich and a croissant I didn't even clock he was carrying. I guess that is where Jakob went this morning while we were both asleep. I didn't realise how hungry I am, how much I've emptied this body's tanks. Devouring the food in silence, I can feel it giving me a much-needed energy burst. It won't make the forthcoming negotiations any more pleasant, but it might help me keep my wits about me.

We don't have to wait long. Towards the distant curve of the river, as it wends through the foothills, spray shows something large moving through the water. *Fast.* It is like watching a half-surfaced submarine arriving at full speed, and the fact we don't see cars crashing into each other up the road as they try to look at it while driving shows it is magical in nature, veiled from their eyes. Isaac weaves together a *don't look here* and a *keep away* spell, throwing it up across the pathway and the nearby zebra crossing. Anyone coming close will suddenly change their mind and head in the opposite direction entirely. It will keep them away from the Tarrasque. The lucky buggers.

He launches himself up out of the water like the world's ugliest dolphin, water cascading away in shimmering droplets. It would have been beautiful if it wasn't the *fucking Tarrasque*. Beauty and the Tarrasque don't go together.

Even with his dramatic launch, he still only has about a quarter of his body out of the water. That quarter looms over us, at least twice my height. His front flippers crash down onto the railing, buckling it straight down to the second rail, then to the third, wrecking the beautiful guard rail. I bet he won't fix it when he leaves either. Because he is an arsehole.

The Tarrasque's face looks like a lion if said lion was drawn by a five year old who really hated lions. And drawing. I once read that asymmetry was what made visages attractive to us, but I know that to be a lie because the evidence is right in front of my face. His sagging whiskers seem to be stuck randomly to various points on his droopy snout, like the results of a game of Pin The Tail On The Donkey in the midst of a very bad acid trip. His eyes hang at completely different parts of his head, with one down level with his half-curled lip and the other stuck nearly up at his forehead. I don't want to describe the shaggy, uneven mop of hair around his face as a lion's mane as I'm sure that would make lions evolve instantly just so they can hire lawyers to sue me for slander. Behind his head is his giant carapace, an armoured shell that makes him practically invincible to attack anywhere on his body. We can only see some of it poking out of the water, but seaweed bedraggles it, plus what looks like a pair of very sodden paisley curtains caught in a corner where the two halves join. Self-care isn't the Tarrasque's priority.

Looking at his mouth clearly demonstrates that, which, as it hangs just in front of us, complete with malformed, asinine grin, is hard to avoid. And, Good God, I really want to. His teeth are all askew, criss-crossing each other in a walking advert for early intervention with dental braces. They are the length of longswords, with vast patches of what looks like green fur clinging to them. In the gaps between them are half-rotting body parts of various animals, plus what looks like the tail-end of a dolphin waggling about between two rear molars. I guess he took a trip down the Rhône recently to visit the sea.

The medieval texts that mention the Tarrasque talk about him breathing out poisonous gas, which considering his mother shat acid doesn't sound unreasonable as a weird monstrous power. The truth is, he just has the worst halitosis imaginable. If you could parade the Tarrasque around the primary schools of France, you would traumatise all the children into perfect dental hygiene for the rest of their lives. You'd traumatise everyone. Not least because they'd all have had to meet the fucking Tarrasque.

That is what anyone I know who's met him knows him as. Not the Tarrasque. The *fucking* Tarrasque. Just thinking about him is enough to make you swear. But, of course, I have to talk to him. Woohoo. Lucky me.

He grins down at me. A shit-eating grin, a grin that if you were to see it on the face of anyone who wasn't a thirty-foot-tall invincible dragon, would make you slap them instantly. It'd be an instinctive reaction. I don't care how peaceful and loving you are. Trust me. If you grinned at Gandhi like this, he'd bitch-slap you without hesitating. Urgh. Fucking Tarrasque.

'Oh look! It's the last Catarrh and the Jew-Jew Train!' Jesus Christ. That is really his idea of being funny. It doesn't even make sense; I am a phlegmy cough, and Isaac is a child's idea of a racist locomotive? His voice is a burbling thing that dances up and down some weird scale no musician has ever heard of or would ever want to, and each time he speaks, his breath whistles out of his nose, creating a high-pitched whine like a metal chop saw that sets your teeth on edge. And the smell? There's a special type of fermented herring from Sweden called Surströmming. The smell alone is so vile, people often start vomiting when a tin of it gets opened. There are some hilarious videos on the internet of people trying to eat it and failing miserably. I would happily stuff one of each of those pickled herrings up my nose to plug my nostrils rather than smell his putrid breath.

'Oh look, it's the *fucking Tarrasque*.' Damn it. *Try not to irritate the invulnerable dragon monster you need a favour from, Paul.*

His expression closes. He knows how we talk about him, what we call him. There are no illusions of popularity here. Now there is a pout to his expression, his rubbery lips duck-like as he pushes them out. I have no idea how he avoids impaling them on his teeth as they are poking out left, right, and centre.

'You've got some nerve turning up here.' It is a phrase that could sound ominous from the right creature. From him, it sounds like a petulant whine, like some moody teenager demanding to know why a parent dared enter their black-painted bedroom. And now I can't help but imagine the Tarrasque in goth make-up. Sniggering at him isn't going to help the situation.

'Look,' I start, my hand held up in half-apology to diffuse the situation. 'I'm sorry. I'm not here looking for a fight —'

'Yeah, 'cos you know you'd lose, Poo-fect.'

I close my eyes and count to ten. Scatological humour: Good God, it is like negotiating with a massively oversized toddler. His jokes don't get any better or any less annoying than this. I can get through this. I can. And without shoving my sword through his face — or mine. 'Listen, this isn't a contest between us, okay? We're here to do you a favour, actually.'

The Tarrasque screws his face up, his suspicion clear. 'What sort of favour?'

'There's a man, sort of a man anyway, in your city right now. He's stealing children. We want to stop him.'

The Tarrasque rears backwards, batting his huge misshapen eyes. 'Stealing children in my city?' He settles himself back where he was previously and yawns. 'Don't care.'

Of course he doesn't, the overgrown shit-weasel. The only reason he doesn't eat people is because he gave his oath on his *talent*, albeit under duress. Even he wouldn't dare break it. That doesn't mean it bothers him that people are getting eaten by others, even kids. Appealing to his better nature requires him having one. He is the Vogon Captain of the magical world, only more loathsome. I appeal to his ego instead.

'So you're not bothered there's another Power running around your city without your say-so, doing as they please?'

He waves a flipper at me, accidentally clocking a seagull flying overhead. It drops, stunned, into his mouth where he starts absentmindedly chewing it up. With his mouth open. Gross.

'Hold on, hold on, hold on.' He sprays lumps of gull flesh over us as he talks, the disgusting gobshite. 'You're saying that the solution to me having another Power running around my city is to let two other Powers run around my city? And anyway —' He smirks as he leans forward. I really wish he would lean back instead. Preferably horizontally. 'Who says I didn't say so? Maybe I gave them permission.'

He probably would've, but I don't think Jack is the sort

to negotiate based on what I've seen so far. He doesn't rely on magic, so I suspect he's taken the risk of flying under the radar. Half-Marred Jack is legendary for his sadistic nature, but that doesn't mean he is a masochist too. If he could avoid talking to the Tarrasque, I am sure he would. He isn't criminally insane as far as I know.

'So did you?' I drum my fingers against my spine, trying to marshal my patience.

'Did I what?'

'Did you give him permission?'

'Give who permission?'

It is like pulling teeth. Looking at this nightmarish dentistry, I'd like to pull teeth. Maybe it will concentrate his thought process? No, I just have to get through this. I take a deep, calming breath and try again.

'Did you give Jack of Plate, Half-Marred Jack, permission to come into Lyon and steal children away?'

'Never heard of him. Jack who?'

He keeps that same idiot grin up on his face all the way through it. I want to do that thing in cartoons where they blow into their thumb and inflate their hand, just so I can give him the sort of slap he deserves. I count from ten to one in my head and try to keep my rapidly fraying patience intact.

Isaac steps in. I think he can see how close I am to losing it. 'So can we come in and find this fellow if you've never heard of him?'

The Tarrasque looks thoughtful for a moment, then shakes his stupid, stupid head. 'No, I can't do that. Then I'd have other Powers running around my city. Someone told me that was a bad idea!'

Ohgodohgodohgod. I want to punch him so, so much.

It won't do anything, and I'll just get eaten, but I really want to smack him one.

'What,' I grind out, astounded I've not reduced my teeth to tiny white nubs, 'do you want, Tarrasque?'

'Oh, I'd really like a tuna sandwich round about now. One whole tuna, a huge baguette, perfect!'

If he was stupid, I could forgive him, but he isn't. He genuinely thinks he is hilarious; you can see it on his face. All of this is deliberate.

I try again. 'What do you want in order to let us come into Lyon and find Half-Marred Jack? And take him back away with us as well,' I add on. I don't want him trying to stop us from leaving just because I didn't specify it. He wouldn't do it to help Jack; he'd do it just to annoy us.

'I don't know.' He rubs his mangy chin with a sodden flipper, which probably doesn't help with the mange. The wet fur smell that wafts across would normally be unpleasant, but as it masks the odour of his breath slightly, I am busy trying to work out how to bottle it and give him it as an aftershave. 'What's in it for me?'

Now we are getting to the heart of the matter. I don't doubt the Tarrasque knows exactly what he wants, but if I don't push him, we'll be fannying about for hours, him being deliberately obtuse, us wanting to force feed him his own tail. Through one of his tear ducts. I cut to the chase.

'Don't mess about, Tarrasque. What is it you actually want?'

He looks at me, and the grin disintegrates. I think I see the faintest quiver in his oversized rubbery lips, and his weird googly eyes widen further. 'Don't you want to talk to me, then? It's hard being the only Talented creature in Lyon. All the other magic users don't come around. I don't know why.'

I know why. Because the Tarrasque is here. I keep that one to myself.

'I'm on my own so much of the time. Then you turn up, and you're mean, and you don't even want to discuss it all. You just want to get on your way. It hurts, you know? I look all tough and terrifying, but inside…inside… Well, we all want to be loved, really, don't we?'

I think I see the start of a tear forming in the corner of his eye, and I start feeling like a right piece of shit. Isaac obviously feels the same. He steps forward. 'I guess we do, aye. It's a lot to carry. Have you always felt like this? You might have told us last time.'

He nods, sniffling. 'I might have done, yeah, but I didn't think of it.'

Isaac's bemused expression mirrors how I feel. 'Thought of it? It's how you feel.'

'I didn't think of saying it to make you feel bad, you pair of mugs! I don't feel sad at all. I'm the Tarrasque! I'm the bloody king of the Rhône. You pair of sissies. Nyehh, I want love, nyehhh. I want kissy kisses, mwuh mwuh mwuh.'

He puckers his lips, making kissing noises, then sniggers like a dirty-minded schoolboy. Homophobic language to match the racism, amazing. Good God, I hate the fucking Tarrasque. He turns back to me.

'Anyhow, you're not exactly looking ready to fight Poo-aul. Not much magic left in your tanks, by the looks of you. Would you even come back if I ate you now?'

'Try it and find out.' It is a bluff in a way. I'll definitely come back, but it isn't likely to help me find a method of beating him, however many times I do.

'Tell you what! Hey, yeah, listen, tell you what!' The excitement mounts in his voice. He has an idea. I hope it hurts his pin-sized brain like the worst migraine anyone has ever suffered. 'I don't reckon you're in much shape for catching this Jack of Blades character. How about we make a bet? If you catch him by, ooh, let's say, next Sunday at midnight, then you can walk on out of town with him and he's yours.'

Next Sunday gives us exactly a week. That isn't a massive margin for subduing a lethal assassin favoured by the Winter Court. 'What if we don't have him by then?'

'Then you have to be my servant for a year. Oh, and you have to let me eat you whenever I want. Oh, and you have to climb into my mouth. In here. Aah.'

He opens his maw wider still, gesturing at the back of his throat with his flipper, and the pervading stench nearly makes me retch. The idea of getting any closer to him is appalling. To climb in there? The smell would attach itself to my very soul; I'd be carrying it around for a hundred lifetimes.

The Tarrasque grins his shit-eating grin again. 'Just think about all the fun chats we could have. Every single day and night. Eh, Poo-aul?'

Oh, Good God. The idea, the very idea of having to spend a year in the company of the fucking Tarrasque. It is the very definition of a fate worse than death. I need to negotiate and hard.

'A week's too short!' I start. 'We need to make it two weeks, at least. Otherwise, it's just impossible, and what's more —'

'Done!' he butts in eagerly. 'Now swear on your *talent* that you'll honour our agreement, and I'll let you get on your way.'

Damn, he expected that. He went for the old low starting bid to end up with us agreeing on the terms he wanted. The Tarrasque would make a brilliant HR manager for negotiating with the unions in some mega-corporation, which is unsurprising considering he is a total wanker. I got played. By the —say it with me now— *fucking Tarrasque.*

I consider obfuscating, to walk back on what I said and try to get another extension. I can see it in his face though. He isn't going to budge on two weeks now I've made the offer. All I'll end up doing is arguing with him for ages and getting nowhere. Which means more time speaking to the Tarrasque. Something to be avoided at all costs. Plus, if I only have two weeks, I want to get cracking. A year in his company? Even ignoring the fact the trail would be so cold, scientists would study it, marvelling at it as the closest thing to absolute zero, I think a year spent with the Tarrasque would break me for eternity. Climbing into his mouth once would. And I don't think he'd limit himself to making me do it once.

I look over at Isaac, who wavers, clearly torn. I can see he wants to tell me not to agree; even he dislikes the Tarrasque, and I've never known Isaac to dislike anyone. My mind goes back to the conversation with Jakob in the car — the worry that Isaac has to live with every day while I run off doing stupid things for stupider reasons. Is this one of those times again? I take a moment to think it through.

No, for once this isn't just about my pride or me being impetuous. There is something to that fae who claims to be my son. Something in his coldness, in Susane's fear that has haunted me since they left, almost more than the messed-up state they left me in. Sure, I can't lie. Part of me is hoping that if I get my hands on that sceptre, I can use it to give myself my magic back, same as Melusine's heart did for the daughter of the Mother of the Sistren of Bordeaux. That isn't the only reason or even the main reason though.

Susane might have betrayed me, but that look on her face, the terror in the eyes of a formidable woman causes me sleepless nights.

I give Isaac a slight nod, and he clamps down on whatever he was about to say. Bless him. He might not always agree with my actions, but he always backs my plays. I look over at the foul-smelling, mind-bogglingly annoying dragon I might be about to indenture myself to.

'You've got a deal, Tarrasque. Two weeks.' A sudden thought occurs to me. I wouldn't put it past the Tarrasque to be pulling a scam on us, that Jack might have already done a runner, so we can't catch him there. 'At the end of that Sunday, *if* Jack is inside the boundaries of Lyon right now, then I'll serve you for a year.'

'And climb into my mouth whenever I want. Right in, all the way to the back, Bumhomme.'

Christ, I'd go mad. I would. But I have to get this done not just for me but for the world. One year in the Tarrasque's company, suffering his infantile humour and his halitosis though, and I'd go the way of Ben, ready to destroy everything that lives if it means I can escape this reality.

I steel myself. 'And we can do whatever we need to do to investigate?' He nods eagerly. 'Upon my oath, Tarrasque.' I spit, not to seal the deal but because of the foul taste this whole thing has left in my mouth.

He keeps on grinning. I have a terrible feeling about what I've just signed up for. 'Wonderful! Is that how we seal the deal now? Right you are then!'

He spits a discoloured ostrich-egg-sized loogie the colour of an octogenarian's lungs after they've smoked two packs a day since childhood. It sails over my shoulder, astonishingly aerodynamic for a lump of phlegm. I turn my head in time to see it splash across the front wheel and bonnet of the Tesla, coating them both. The tyre explodes instantly, and the toxic spit rapidly eats through the paintwork at the front. It'll dissolve the bonnet in about two minutes, the speed it is going through.

'Oops, that wasn't yours, was it, guys? Oh, I'm so sorry. Looks like you're walking to Lyon. Oh well, beggars can't be *Jew*sers!'

The oaf guffaws like he just discovered the Philosopher's Stone of comedy and used it to somehow turn his racist lead balloon of a joke into gold. Then he launches himself backwards, turning mid-air to splash down as hard as possible onto the water's surface. He motors away upriver, leaving a ruined handrail and two soaked-to-the-skin, pissed-off magic users behind.

Isaac growls, a deep-throated half-roar that makes me wonder if he was bitten by a lycanthrope when my back was turned. Nope, he is just pissed off. 'I hate the fucking Tarrasque, lad. I told you, Jak. Yes, okay, dear boy, I agree he's not the most pleasant fellow to negotiate with — He's a bloody pain in the arse. I wish I killed him back when I almost had the chance. Maybe if I just tried a little harder… Fucking Tarrasque.'

Isaac is swearing again. Things are definitely not going according to plan. Then again, if anything or anyone could make you swear —

It is the *fucking Tarrasque*.

Chapter Sixteen

The only time I want to speak to the Tarrasque is to Tar-ask
him to fuck off and die.

The Tarrasque thought he was being clever, taking out the
front end of the car and the tyre. Luckily for us, the Tesla's
engine isn't in the front. Unluckily for us, there is also no
spare tyre, so it makes no bloody difference. We are still
down a car.

I can see just how gutted Isaac looks, and I am pretty
sure Jakob is just as downhearted. Isaac's vehicles seem to
be first in line to pay the price on recent missions. He
doesn't choose a car on a whim; he invests himself in it, just
like he did his 2CV that Ben blew up. Just like Jakob chose
this one, having wanted to see the marvels of technology
after hundreds of years in a skull.

I decide to steal something nice to cheer him up. I am
delighted when I stumble across a Jaguar I-Pace two streets
back despite me already huffing and puffing because of the

street being cambered upwards. It is funny, this disconnect between how my mind and my body perceive my physical fitness. My mind thinks I should be able to go fell-running through the Pyrenees as I did in times gone by. But my body thinks a slow walk to the nearest McDonalds sounds like way too much effort, and maybe we should get a take-away delivery instead if we are hungry? I call Isaac over. Well, more I wheeze loudly enough that eventually Isaac notices and comes to make sure I'm not having a heart attack.

'Can you open this for me, please?' I am running on empty *talent*-wise.

An affronted look crosses Isaac's face. 'But that's not ours, lad.'

'It will be once you open it, and we jump-start the fucker.'

'No, it won't be! It'll be *stolen*.'

Good God love me. I had to suffer an entire conversation, extending to more words than, 'Fuck off, will you?' with the Tarrasque, and now Isaac is having a moral conundrum over us long-term borrowing a car. I pinch the bridge of my nose, mainly to stop the frustration shooting like flames out of my nostrils.

'We need to get to Lyon now. Ideally quicker than now. Yesterday would've been good. We'll give whoever owns this their car back later, and if anything happens to it, their insurance company will pick up the tab.'

Isaac looks doubtful. 'Can't we just get our car repaired?'

I gesture wildly. My patience is wearing thin. 'Where? Where do you want to get your incredibly expensive hi-tech ride fixed? Do you see a Tesla dealership nearby? Let's just ring the nearest chop shop, shall we?' I mime a telephone with my thumb and little finger. 'Oh, do you have any spare

Tesla tyres? Plus, a front bonnet to replace the one *dissolved by corrosive dragon spit*? No, but you can order some and get them in a couple of weeks? Perfect, I'll be just about to enter a year of bonded servitude to the *fucking Tarrasque, so* —'

'What are you miming?' Isaac pops in, causing me to blink slowly, my mouth dropping open as he completely yanks on the reigns of my rant, forcing a sudden turn of my horse that I wasn't prepared for.

'What?'

He raises his hand, his fingers spread to the side of his face to mimic mine. 'What is this supposed to be?'

'It's a phone.'

'But that looks nothing like a phone? What's your little finger supposed to be? A headset microphone?'

'This, 'Zac, is the international hand gesture to signify a phone.'

'Since when?'

'Since *will someone just open the goddamn door?*'

'All right, lad,' Isaac says. 'No need to get your knickers in a twist. Still, there must be another way…'

I shake my head. 'Not another way that is quick enough to get us where we need to go. We haven't got time to waste. I'm sorry. If we weren't pressed, I'd find another way for you, and if I had enough magic to pull a bunny out of a hat, I wouldn't ask you to do it. But we don't, and I don't, so please, dude. Steal the car, and let's get out of here.'

'Right, okay, fine.'

We stand there for a moment. Isaac looks in the driver's side window, studying it. He bends over, checks the front tyre arch, then bends further still to look underneath the car itself. He straightens and goes back to peering through the glass, his hand shading his eyes to get a clearer look.

'What are you doing, 'Zac?' This isn't doing my blood pressure any favours.

He shrugs, looking embarrassed. 'I've no idea what to do to get into the car using *talent*, lad. I can't even see the lock to *pull* or anything.'

I cradle my head in my hands and fight hard to resist the urge to sob. 'It's an electric car, man. Electric. Like the car you own. It doesn't have a manual locking system, for crying out loud. Have you never used your *talent* to manipulate technology?'

He flushes again. 'Well, I don't really get on with most technology that well. The Tesla was a present for Jak. I blew all the fuses in the house once, if that helps?' He gives me a hopeful smile.

'Brilliant. So if I want you to turn this car into a completely useless hunk of metal, then you're ready and able. Otherwise, you're as much use as a chocolate teapot. In the summer. On a beach. In Barbados. You know what? Just forget it.'

I start up the street purposefully initially, then change my walk to something of an amble, looking like I'm apparently distracted by the architecture displayed on the hillside looming on our right. So much so that I bang clean into a young man somewhere in his mid-twenties, at a guess, rake-like and as ill at ease with the world as his overly large suit is with his frame. He goes sprawling, and I am there in a moment, my arm crooked under his elbow to help him up, abject apologies pouring out as I get him to his feet and brush him down. With a last exculpation, I pat his back, check him up and down for damage, and send him on his way. As he passes Isaac, I wave the set of keys I lifted from his pocket.

Isaac bustles up, his eyebrows knitting together in

concern. 'That lad didn't look like he could afford for us to be taking his car, man!'

I sigh. 'Agreed, but he can use the ten grand I slipped into his pocket to dry his tears on.' I grabbed it from my etheric storage as soon as I gave up on trying to get Isaac to open the Jaguar. I might be a bit of a bastard, but I'm not entirely heartless. 'We haven't got time to buy a car or rent one. We need to go! Now let's see what we've won.'

I head to where the guy was coming from, clicking as I go. Something beeps behind a mud-flecked white Land Rover. I groan when I pass it and turn to wag a furious finger at Isaac.

'This,' I say. 'This is why we can't have nice things.'

It is a Renault Super 5 from the early nineties, an unreliable workhorse of a tiny three-door hatchback, the pride and joy of no one ever. The bi-colour red and black is a nice touch because it hides a load of the rust and makes an easy guiding line for the cracks in the frame to use for splitting the car in half. It's so small, I half-expect a couple of dozen clowns to spill out of it, and the only suspension it comes with is the suspension of disbelief that a car manufacturer could have ever considered it to be road worthy. I turn back to Isaac again.

'Do you think I can go after him and swap the money and the keys back?'

Isaac claps me on the shoulder, his grin reminiscent of the Tarrasque. I consider telling him so, but there are limits, however annoyed you are. 'I quite like it! Reminds me of my old 2CV. Anyhow, weren't you just telling me we don't have time to mess around, lad? Fire her up, and it's Lyon-Ho!'

He is still chuckling by the time we contort ourselves into the prerequisite shapes required to get into the car. I get the motor to turn over without it coughing so badly it chokes itself to death or falls out the bottom of the engine mount entirely. I'll take that as a win. Time to get ourselves back on the road.

We only have a bit over a half-hour drive to run. Vienne is the last place to the south that really counts as a town in its own right rather than a glorified suburb. Now we blend back into the metropolitan, countryside breaking for warehouses and outgrown villages subsumed by industrial areas, the green breaking against the concrete, a temporarily halted wave just waiting for the humans to go, for the last motor to wind down and the last light to turn off before it creeps on in and swallows the modern world whole.

We are on the bridge at Pierre-Benite, crossing over the Ile de la Table Ronde, a wildlife preserve I always mean to visit, mainly because the name, the Island of the Round Table, makes some naïve part of my heart hope I might find it to be the secret location of Camelot despite it not being in Albion. And it not having existed in Arthurian times. It still seems a plausible bet to me. Isaac speaks up.

'So Jak and I have been talking, what with everything going on — Do ask him. We all need to know. Jak, you're seizing control unintentionally again... No, you said that internally that time, well done... Yes, I will, hold on. One of us at a time, all right? Look, the point is, we want to know what the plan is, lad? How are we going to find this Jack of Plate in such a limited amount of time?'

I smile, tapping the wheel to the Nigerian afro-pop the radio picked up on our return to civilisation. 'Well, that's where I managed to get one up over that overgrown catfish.

He was so eager to agree, he said we could do whatever we needed to in order to track down Jack. The enormous advantage of the Tarrasque holding Lyon is no other Talented are going to be anywhere nearby if they can help it. Sure, there might be the odd natural Talent but not many of them, and they'll not be drawing on their magic. Jack might still be human, but if the Winter Court's given him extended longevity, he'll be exuding fae magic constantly. So the plan is simple. You set up a load of basic alarm wards all over the city. Nothing dramatic, nothing that's going to tip him off. Just a simple warning caused by the presence of magic we can track. We let him trigger a few, narrow down his area of operation. Then we wait till he triggers another and follow him back to his HQ.'

Isaac frowns. 'Why follow him? Does it matter where we take him down?'

I nod grimly. 'It matters immensely. Look, I can't be sure, but if I know how the fae work —which is a stretch 'cos let's be honest, I don't think the fae know how the fae work, really— then he won't be just picking up one or two kids. He'll have a shopping list of traits from Maeve: *talent*, *looks*, *sex*, *race*.' Isaac blanches in the seat next to me. Wooden fencing on our right blocks the Rhône from view while squat tower-blocks from the sixties and seventies hulk down on our left. I take a left turn at the traffic lights and find a place to pull over. This elephant in the room needs addressing.

I twist myself round as much as the cramped seating allows to look at Isaac directly. 'Let's not have any illusions here. This guy? He's a kid-snatcher and a cold-blooded killer. And where those kids will go is even worse than being held captive by him. The Winter Court is no place for any human, let alone an innocent child. It's the main reason I accepted the Tarrasque's shitty terms, it's why I'm making us keep moving forward, it's why we *will not* fuck this up, and why we are going to catch this fucker. We don't know how long he's been hunting here or how big an order Maeve placed. If we're lucky, he'll still be at the observation stage — checking out potential candidates, weighing up who to take to fulfil his side of the bargain. If we're unlucky? He's already got a massive haul of kids stashed somewhere only he knows about. Assuming we manage to capture him and he won't talk, I want to know where they are. He's exactly the type of bastard who'd leave 'em all to starve to death if he knew he was done for.'

I pat Isaac's knee, startling him back out of a dark reverie. 'We're on the good side here, man.' I look him dead in the face, letting him see how entirely genuine I am. 'This is a messed-up situation, but we can't allow it to continue. We've got to protect some other people's children before we can think about our own. I need you watching my back, not worrying about it now.'

I can see the strain and the determination on his face. The latter makes me proud. The former breaks my heart. I wish I could send him back to the calm safety of his serene little house and workshop to tinker with theories rather than having to get down and dirty with me. Problem is, I need him. The kids need him. And it is a mirror of what I said to him. I need to help all those other parents. That means I need to ask more of my own for the time being.

'So what do we do now? As in right now, lad?' I can see he is eager to get on with it. The thought of kids in danger was all the motivation he needed. Doubtless it is the same for Jak but probably not good enough of a motive for Nith and Nan. But hopefully, at least, they won't deliberately resist, knowing about the threatened innocents. I try not to get distracted by how much their shortened names together sound like a sitcom from the seventies, or that 'Zac and Jak sound like an over-caffeinated kid's show from the noughties. I wonder, given I've trained my brain to retain memories for over hundreds of years and to make them accessible when I need them, if one day, I might train it to concentrate.

I turn off the car and hand the keys to Isaac. 'Now? You're going to take this wondrous example of the combustion engine in action and head around, setting up wards. I'm going to take a walk into the centre, try and find an apartment hotel for us to set up in.'

Isaac frowns. 'You don't want me to drop you off, lad?'

I shudder. Half an hour in this rust box was more than enough. It is like a reverse Tardis, even smaller on the inside, and it looks minuscule from the outside. 'Nah, I'll walk. Knock yourself out with the Super 5.'

I hop out as Isaac struggles to pass even his rather compact frame from passenger to driver's seat. Rolling my neck until it cracks, I watch as the Dinky Toys mobile pulls off from the curve. Good, that'll keep Isaac busy for a while. Now to do a little exploration on my own.

Chapter Seventeen

I look astounded at Gwendolyne, Queen of the Cagots. 'Did you just ask *me* for help? I never thought I'd see the day.'

'Yes,' she says through gritted teeth. I think I see Susane nudge her lightly in the back. She adds begrudgingly, 'And if you do so, we will owe you a favour. *I* will owe you a favour.'

I smile my most charming smile. It does nothing to change the sour expression on her face. 'Well, of course, milady, however I can help. What service do you need of me?'

'Most important is that you brief Susane in the doctrine of the Cathars if she is to plead ancestry.'

'Susane?' I frown, not understanding. 'Not you, yourself?'

Gwendolyne shakes her head. 'I have duties to attend to here that press too heavily upon my shoulders to allow me to take a sojourn for months to the Holy See, heart of the Pope's power and domain. That is the second favour I would request. Susane must speak for us, but she has *talent*. We know the Church does not look kindly on the Talented, although they are, as ever, hypocrites, and have their own magicians who work for them, whose magic is apparently a holy blessing instead of the demonic curse it is for the rest of us.'

She hesitates. 'Susane has not had...the range of training you have nor is she much skilled in masking her *talent*. I'd ask that you accompany her, shield her. Keep my daughter safe upon this journey.'

'As a rabbi, I do not think I'll gain much of a welcome into the Vatican itself!' Isaac's laughter is easy, easier than it's been since I returned. He always had a soft spot for Gwendolyne and the Cagots.

'I don't think you need to announce yourself as such, you old fool,' she replies wryly, her lips twisting against her will. 'I have full faith in Susane's power with words, but her Power itself is a danger to her. Will you help her?'

'Aye,' I say hastily. All heads turn in my direction. 'Of course we will, won't we, Isaac?'

He raises an eyebrow at me. 'Apparently so.'

I know the reason he thinks why I am so ready to commit, and he is not entirely wrong. I have been dreaming of time with Susane, literally, and have been hoping we get to know one another more fully. A two-month journey to Rome and back will work perfectly. What he doesn't realise is how much his well-being is also a factor. He has been too long stranded in the machinations required to protect his people and has been too lost to worry about his brother's well-being, Jakob having been more and more distant and more often absent. Isaac's concern for his brother —a laughable scenario considering his angelic companion, in my own carefully kept counsel— came through strongly in his missives to me, and I don't doubt it's weighing heavily on his mind. A voyage together, made only the more pleasant by Lady Susane's company, will do him the world of good. Too long stuck in one corner of the wide world is no way to spend an eternal life.

Of course, he doesn't see that though. He keeps shooting what he believes to be subtle glances between Susane and myself, where in fact, were he to scrawl a giant Enochian rune in the air showing a love heart and arrows firing off towards us, it would be considerably more subtle.

Gwendolyne's eyes narrow. 'I expect you to act as chaperone for my daughter, Rabbi, and keep her safe. Am I clear?'

His eyes snap back to hers, flustered at getting caught out when he believed himself to be so subtle. 'Of course, Gwen. Happy to act as such.'

My adopted father will keep the woman I love safe from my terrible clutches. Wonderful news.

Chapter Eighteen

LYON, 17 APRIL, PRESENT DAY

In the jungle, in the urrrrban jungle, Lyon sleeps toniiiiight. And a butt-ugly lion/turtle/snake monster mash-up, but the less said about him, the better.

I didn't lie to Isaac to get rid of him or to keep him safe or anything daft like that. He cohabits with two angels, making him probably the most indestructible thing on the planet as far as I am aware. No, I worry he won't agree with my course of action. Or even if he did, that he won't be able to control himself. I can't risk it.

I have an idea, which is why I swiped Almeric's skull from Lou in Hastingues. The skull resonates with the same magic as I do, the only type of *talent* that Melusine wasn't able to swallow whole — my reincarnating power. It obviously has something to do with when I broke the Grail, and I really want to investigate that as soon as Life stops tapping me on the shoulder and then headbutting me on the bridge of my nose every time I turn around. The way I see it, it should be sympathetic towards reincarnation, and the Cagots are the very incarnation of reincarnation. Or something like that. They differ from me in that their *talent* springs from fae origins, but I've come up with something that might just solve that problem.

I fish out of my etheric storage the Nain Rouge's finger. He owes me a favour after he tried to trap me in a twisted version of an escape room to get free rein to torment Toulousains. When that failed, he bargained with me to save him from being turned from a red dwarf into an even redder, even shorter red dwarf should Aicha jump up and down on his head until it exploded. He promised us each a favour. Aicha used hers to get him to take her to the White Lady of the Pyrenees in order to negotiate some unspecified deal to pass Melusine's barriers when I was held prisoner. He still owes me my favour, but it'll be no use using it here. We are by the entirely wrong set of mountains to get his attention; I need to be in the Pyrenees to use it. Still, that doesn't make it useless.

I carefully balance the finger inside the mouth of the skull. I don't have the time nor the magical energy to put up a *don't look here* spell, so I get more than a few curious glances. Still, we are back in the big city. Weirdos are ten-a-penny. Goth weirdos? Even more common.

I am not a force to be reckoned with magically anymore, which means I need to think. It is a terrifying prospect, but it isn't my life on the line. It is a bunch of kids going off into potentially eternal servitude to a creature who would take the words: "cold", "cruel", and "inhuman", as a compliment. I can't mess around.

There's a very simple spell, one of the first I ever learned, that turns a needle into the equivalent of a compass for magic. It's not very precise —the minute you're even close to a Talented or a powerful relic, it'll just start spinning wildly— but it is good practise for getting yourself into an aligned state with the *talent* flowing around you. It also helps a young magician with useful tricks like differentiating between forms of magic, and as they get better, they can use it to find a specific Talented individual or a certain artefact if they are well enough attuned to them to know what they feel like. Isaac and I used to engage in long-roaming games of Hide and Seek when I first started out to get me to learn his signature. At the time, I thought it was so I could get used to the differences. Later, I wondered if it was so that, wherever I was, if things went wrong, I'd be able to find him.

I've always been good at attuning. It surprised me to find out not every Talented can see differences between other forms of magic like I can. It's like synaesthesia for different forms of power, and even before my official training began, I was able to tell people's magical signatures apart when they were right in front of me. Now I struggle, with my *talent* so desperately reduced, but I can still do it if I really apply myself. What I am hoping for this time is to channel that ability into the simple magic compass spell.

The spell is in Latin, which makes life easier. I am fluent enough to make some simple alterations to the words. Honestly, when you've been doing magic as long as I have, normally the intent and theoretical understanding is enough, but as I am so limited now, I need to use every possibility I have to increase the chances of it working.

'*Sicut vocat ad similem*
Talentum talentum
Gustus in aliis
Oculos trahit ad locum.'

I wait, the skull held level on the palm of my hand as I

try not to dislodge the Nain Rouge's finger. It is no simple task; I'm sweating, and if I'm not careful, the skull will be slipping and sliding everywhere like someone suffering from vertigo on an ice rink. Or Paul Simon when he gets nearer his destination. I don't have much to give magically anymore. I have no idea if it is enough.

Slowly, painfully slowly, the skull rotates. Considering how lethargically it turns, it is probably a good thing I am sweating so much. Lubrication to aid my weak-ass magic. Still, there is definite movement, and it equally definitely comes to a halt. I asked it to look where I need to go, like the skull of the navigator from the Monkey Island games. It seems my spell worked.

I give the skull an affectionate pat on the top of its cranium. Turns out, in death, at least, Almeric isn't a totally useless bastard. 'Here's looking at you, kid,' I murmur, then set off down the street, following the gaze of a fae-finger-fed dead man's skull.

There are more than a few wrong turns. My spell is weak, and it looks like Half-Marred Jack has been here for a while. Sometimes, the skull will head off down an alley and then just point at a wall for a moment before turning around to send me back in the direction I just came from. I know I am taking a risk by trying to find the highest concentration of fae magic in the city given that would be Jack himself. If he kills me, he'll get his hands on Almeric's skull, which is a terrifyingly powerful magical relic. But I have to risk it for the children. I lived hundreds of years, thinking my son might've been ripped from Susane's belly for some twisted purpose. Then, when she returned, I thought he might have been sold to the fae for her resurrection. And though neither of those things happened, stolen children is still a trigger for me. Mind you, so it should be for anyone with even a crumb of humanity left in their decrepit souls. Apparently, not for Jack though.

I am led to a narrow backstreet on the Croix Rousse, to an old closed-up shop front, the faded blue signage unused for long enough that it no longer even shows the previous name, the corrugated metal shutters slammed down tight over the windows. I set myself up on the opposite pavement, studiously ignoring it. Taking my phone out, I look like I am searching for directions or suchlike, then walk to the building. Surreptitiously, I turn the skull round in every direction. It always turns back, faster by far than it has moved previously, always pointing back to the building. Location confirmed, I hustle off as quickly as possible. The risk I took has paid off. I don't want it to end up costing me instead if Jack catches me outside his hide-out.

Depositing the finger into my etheric storage, I head back towards the Rhône as quickly as I can casually manage, hoping I didn't give myself away by lingering too long. It looks like it was a misplaced hope. I freeze, and my heart stops beating for a second when an arm slams across my chest, stopping me in place.

When I hear the voice, I start breathing again. 'Is this where the hotel is then, my lad?'

Isaac rumbled me. Still, better him than Half-Marred Jack. 'You know what? It was such a lovely day, I thought I'd take a bit of a stroll first, clear my head after the chat with the Tarrasque. And my nostrils.'

'I know you've been for a walk. Do you know how?'

I shake my head.

'Because you triggered several of the alarm wards that *you asked me to set*. Bloody nitwit.'

I groan. 'You didn't alter them so that we don't set them off?'

He harrumphs, the grumpiness a cover for embarrassment. 'I set them so as I won't trigger them. I might have, well, forgotten to do the same for you. But —' He raises a finger in triumphant highlight. 'It's a bloody good thing I did because it means I've caught you out sneaking.'

'Sneaking? *S-s-s-s-sneaking?*' He blinks, nonplussed. Man, I nailed Gollum as well. 'I wasn't sneaking. I had an idea, and it was one I needed to keep to myself. And it paid off. I know where he's based himself.'

The excitement grows on Isaac's face. 'C'mon then, lad. Let's get there now. There might be some young'uns there needing out.'

I shake my head, pushing him so that we start walking in the opposite direction, away from Jack's building, and watch as his excitement changes to confusion. 'Not yet, Isaac.'

The confusion deepens. 'What do you mean, not yet? We can't leave the children in his clutches, man!'

'I know, and we won't. Not for long anyway.' I feel disgusted with myself. It is despicable, leaving them with a psychopath like the Jack of Plate for even a second longer than necessary. But it is necessary. 'If we go there now. If we rescue those children this second, and Jack isn't there, or we don't catch him? He'll be gone, in the wind. Free to start up all over again.' And with him, my chance to get into the fae realm will also be gone. I can't help thinking about the last part even if I don't vocalise it, and it makes me sick to my stomach that I allow it to be a factor in my decision-making.

I clasp his arm, trying to clear the desperate worry from

his expression. 'Listen, 'Zac. If you know where it is, you won't be able to help yourself. I know you. Better I keep the knowledge to myself for now. But once we catch Jack, we'll head straight there and free anyone he's got captive.'

Isaac's jaw is so tight you could play 'Duelling Banjos' on it. 'You better be right about this one, lad. You better be right.'

I smile sadly. 'I know. Honestly, I do. Hold up.'

We come out onto a more standard Lyonnaise street now, the architecture dominated by Napoleonic designs, elegant white-faced multi-storied apartments highlighted by carefully dotted trees that transform it into an impressive boulevard, but that isn't what grabs my attention. It is the flash of patterned canvas that isn't from some middle-aged lothario's half-unbuttoned shirt. This has the distinctive cut of a waistcoat-style jacket. A cut that hasn't been in fashion for even longer than canvas shirts. Several hundred years longer.

'Here,' I hiss and shove the skull into Isaac's startled grasp, then shoot off down the road. I don't think there are many people rocking around Lyon in medieval garb, unless there is an unannounced Renaissance fair going down or fashion took a particularly strange turn when I wasn't paying attention.

As I hurry down the crowded street, weaving through bodies, trying to move quickly but not draw attention to myself, I draw parallel to where I believe the person I am trying to follow is, albeit on the other side of the avenue. My position rewards me with another glimpse of the man wearing the strange attire through a break in the bustling thoroughfare. It doesn't leave me in any doubt that I've found the right individual.

He's obviously wearing some sort of glamour that works

on the general population but not on Talented given the fact people are walking right past him without stopping to point and stare or to be violently sick. The right-hand side of his face isn't a pretty sight.

Queen Maeve has large hands. Large long-fingered hands with cruel curving nails to top them off. Their imprints are clear on his face. One digit is curved up the length of the right side of his nose and passes to the top of his forehead, while the others fan across his cheek and down to his neck, the palm pressed on his chin, lips, and cheek.

We're used to seeing ruined-faced monsters. Freddie Kruger's burns. The pain fetishist's wet dream that is Pinhead. I suppose the closest look to Jack's is the acid-burned Two-Face from the *Batman* stories — one half of it perfect, the other exposed tendons and muscles, breaking his visage and his mind in two. Still, that is nowhere near as horrific as what Maeve actually did to the Jack of Plate.

Where her fingers pressed, they passed straight through, cutting down to the skull itself, remaking the flesh and muscles underneath like clay. She muddled them like a child with multiple pots of playdough, mixing together the different subcutaneous layers, recreating them so that they are thin patchworks of the different tissue types spread over the bone beneath, which almost shines through the opaque material left in place. His right nostril is there, but the nose above it isn't, the breathing hole visible, and the clawed digit-shaped curve pressed into his forehead is like a signature written in nerve-endings. I have no evidence that the pain signals still get carried through the congealed mess left underneath, but I'd lay money they do and are constantly firing. I bet Half-Marred Jack is in continual agony. It seems like the kind of thing Queen Maeve would do just for the shits and giggles.

The gap in the crowd closes again but not before I see him turn off down a smaller side road. I dash across, albeit still trying to do it surreptitiously, so I probably look like I just shat my pants and am hurriedly trying to get home before anyone near me smells it. Not quite what I was aiming for.

As I reach the mouth of the alley, my eyes glimpse beige fabric as it turns onto a side road half-way up. While still trying to look nonchalant, I hustle up there as quickly as possible. I reach the road in question, only to find empty tarmac in front of me. Casually, I saunter along it, checking between the parked cars. It is possible he clocked me and is waiting somewhere to jump out. I am prepared to take the risk. Worst case, I lose this body. Isaac has the skull, at least, so I won't lose that.

I reach the end of the side road, only a hundred metres down. Nothing. No one. It opens onto another backstreet that runs parallel to the first one I turned onto. There is no sign of him. I saunter back to the other road and turn right, heading away from the major boulevard we were on. Maybe I was mistaken, and he didn't go off down the side road. Maybe if I backtrack, I'll find some sign of him...

I get said sign when a knife presses into my throat.

'What are you after then, prettyman? I'm not one who'll be glad of a stalking shade behind me.' The voice is low and gravelly, twisted and distorted in how it forms words, with a whistling timbre behind it.

Ah.

'Just a little chat, Jack.' I spread my hands out in submission as soon as the blade pressed against me, and I keep them there. 'Not looking for any trouble.'

If I can keep him talking long enough for Isaac to catch up, then we'll be golden. Nithael can subdue him, and we'll be out of here, job done with time to spare. Sadly, Jack doesn't want to play ball.

'I'm not much one for chatting. Even less for following. I'll bid you a good day, sir.' There is an all too familiar additional pressure and sweeping movement across my throat, and I keel forward to bleed out.

Chapter Nineteen

Finding liberty in a funeral home? Just call me Morgue-an Freeman.

Another day, another city, another death, another funeral home. I've always preferred coming to in a home as opposed to a morgue. It normally means I'm wearing clothes, if slightly overly formal, and it's easier to walk out the front door and get back on with the rest of my day.

I pull another burner phone out of storage, promising myself to go hit the wholesalers ASAP, and call Isaac.

'You're back, my lad! Whereabouts are you?'

'I'm…hold on.' I turn around, searching for the road name. 'I'm outside the Croix-Rousse funeral home. On the corner of…Rue Philippe De Lassalle and, er…Chemin Du Vallon.'

'Right, I'll be right there. Stay put. No more flaneuring, all right?'

He puts the phone down on me. I must have really pissed him off. Oops.

The Super 5 screeches up in next to no time, and Isaac leans over to pop the passenger door open. I hop in, chagrined.

'Well, who'd have thought it? You got yourself killed the first day we get into Lyon. There's a lesson to learn here. What happens if we plunge off headlong into danger without thinking it through? We end up...'

'Getting ourselves killed and ending up back at square one.' It is the monotone repetition of a naughty schoolboy forced to state the rule he was caught breaking yet again by a desperately disappointed headteacher.

'Not even square one, lad. Now you've alerted Jack to our presence. He'll be gone, surely. In the wind. Off to somewhere else.' Isaac looks glum and rightly so. If that is the case, I've just sold myself to the Tarrasque for a year. I still hold out hope though.

'Not necessarily. He's got himself all set up here. He doesn't know that we know where his hiding place is. Hell, he doesn't even know I'm not on my own. I don't know how it works to get Maeve to open a portal, but I'll lay money that they've got an arranged rendezvous and that the locale isn't far from here. He's still got to move an unknown number of unwilling, terrified kids there somehow. Someone like that is going to have a meticulously laid plan they'll be unwilling to deviate from unless entirely necessary. Not least because I can't imagine Maeve is someone who's understanding about unplanned changes or delays. Plus, I'm pretty sure he left before my body vanished, so he doesn't even know I'm back.'

I really hope I am not deluding myself. I think Isaac can sense how thin the veneer of optimism I've painted over my concerns is. He might be concerned about me, but he knows I am the one who'll end up paying the most if this all falls apart.

'He's a swift bugger, isn't he?' He keeps his scan of the mirrors going. If he was anyone else, I'd say he was worried about being followed, but Isaac is just conscientious in obeying the rules of the road.

I nod. That confused me too. 'I don't get it. Okay, I mean, I get I wasn't exactly 007 in my spy-craft, but I watched my six. I was on alert. I just checked down the main alley and the side one. I don't know how he got the drop on me.'

'Again.'

'Yes, thank you for pointing that out, 'Zac, again.'

'I know.'

There is a silence, a silence heavily laden with smugness radiating off Isaac. I saw the episode of *South Park* where San Francisco got covered by a "layer of smug". I feel like the car is full of it, to where I am practically choking.

'Oh, c'mon, dude. Okay, you're amazing, and I screwed up. We are not worthy to be in your genius presence, and all must weep nightly upon the realisation that they, too, are not Isaac the Blind. The heralds shall carry forth notice to town-criers throughout the lands, and they shall all cheer to know that one who lives is so damn clever. Truly, they shall say — '

'All right, lad, you're layering it on a bit thick now.' He flushes, but I can tell he secretly enjoyed the flattery even if I went over the top on it. He pulls into a loading bay on the side of the street and puts the handbrake on, though he leaves the engine idling. 'Well, I arrived just as he disappeared. He left a small *don't look here* on your corpse, rifled through your pockets, and then was gone. In fact, he was so damn fast about the whole thing, he didn't even see your body dissolve away after, which might just help with not spooking him. It's where he disappeared that made me realise how he got behind you.'

Isaac points at an exquisite Renaissance-era doorway next to us, the solid studded panelling painted a dark green. A brass plaque hangs on it. I squint to read it and then snap my fingers.

'Of course! That explains it!' I feel both simultaneously better for having worked it out and worse for not having thought of it before. 'He's using the traboules to get about.'

Isaac nods, the wide smile on his face well earned. 'Aye, lad. He's using the traboules.'

The traboules of Lyon are one of those hidden wonders that, oddly, aren't more widely discussed. The word is a vulgar bastardisation of the Latin *transambulare*, meaning to cross, and they weren't ever meant to be something mysterious.

Lyon used to be the centre of the French silk industry by royal decree, and the silk workers needed speedy access to the rivers to drop off heavy loads of the precious fabric so widely prized by the noblesse. After 1540, all silk manufacturing in France had to be done in Lyon, and the city grew wealthy because of it. As they built new houses and factories, they specifically followed a little-known architectural quirk dating back to the fifth century, adding in covered passageways that allowed access across the roads (mainly oriented north-south) to the river directly on an east to west heading. They internalised access to buildings with beautifully covered enclosures, even elegant towers. Normal front doors, same as what might allow access to any house's courtyard, meant as time went on, it became impossible to tell which are private properties and which are traboules.

Only locals know the hidden ways, and they keep them a carefully guarded secret. It's served them well more than once. Most recently, they used them during the Second World War to aid the Resistance in their actions undermining the Butcher of Lyon, Klaus Barbie. Before that, the silk workers used them in pitched battles with the authorities during their rebellions of the nineteenth century.

Officially, there are a couple of hundred left, with fifty or so accessible to the public — in fact, by law, the residents have to keep these doors unlocked until eight in the evening. Unofficially? They number at least five hundred, and locals in the know claim a lot more. What is undoubtedly true is that there are a hell of a lot more traboules than those labelled with a sign or plaque.

"So... new plan of action,' I say slowly, verbalising my thought-process. 'While we wait for him to set off one of your alarms, we do some research, map out as many of the traboules as we can. Once we get those, we can anticipate what way he might go...'

'And then cut him off!' Isaac's eyes gleam with excitement. I'm just not sure whether it is at the idea of catching Jack or the prospect of doing some good honest research again.

Of course, nothing runs that smoothly.

The first two days, I manage to keep calm. Just about. Isaac and Jakob pour over old maps they managed to wheedle out of the hands of librarians who'd normally have laughed in the face of anyone asking for such precious rarities. The kindred spirit of natural born researchers and caretakers of ancient tomes won out though, and they have them spread across the table to be studied in great detail, trying to discover any forgotten routes through the city. Whenever they found one, I headed out and walked the paths. Sometimes I deposited imbued items, stones or plant pot fragments carrying more of their magical alarm wards, in each of the traboules. Each time I did so, I was convinced that we finally blocked off all avenues of escape for him, and any second, he'd trip one, allowing us to descend on him like the wrath of God. Or, to be feared even more, like the wrath of Aicha. I miss having her wrath around, especially right now. Her calling me a dickhead repeatedly would be a lot more interesting than watching the two brothers jabber animatedly from a single mouth about town planning designs from the nineteenth century.

By day three, I'm teetering constantly between boredom and despair. I guess you could say I am on the bordair between both.

'Are you sure the alarms are working?' My voice isn't getting any less whiny or petulant each time I repeat the question. Which, as I am asking every ten minutes or so, means my peevishness is on an exponential curve upwards.

'Of course I'm bloody sure, lad!' You can plot Isaac's frustration perfectly on the same graph as my peevishness. Jakob keeps having to audibly tell him to relax, to not get so tense, which I'm pretty sure isn't helping Isaac as it is driving me round the bend.

'And they're set to a high enough sensitivity?' It's all very well them detecting magic, but if Jack has to start pulling fucking Dr Strange impressions to get them into action, all whooshy lightshows and the like, then that's not going to help us at all.

'Anything. The smallest glamour. Lighting a cigarette off his blasted fingertip.'

I don't get it. When I ran into him the first time, he was definitely glamoured. You could tell by the fact passersby weren't vomiting when they looked at him, and small children weren't screaming and running away as he passed. I can understand him going dark for a couple of days — getting tracked by a Talented inside the city, even one he now thinks is dead is going to have him watching his tail, looking out for additional enemies hunting him, but eventually he's got to move. Even excluding his own sordid aim of kidnapping kids for the Winter Queen, he needs to eat, surely? I can buy his lair having backup supplies, but there's a limit. And surely after three days with no follow up, he'd be out sniffing around, trying to get back onto whatever schedule either he or Maeve have set.

'Maybe he isn't using magic, lad?' Isaac sounds suitably doubtful, but we've got nothing else to go on, and I can't work out what else he could possibly be doing. So I set out to walk the streets again. Only this time with more drinking.

This sounds considerably more fun than it is because even if Isaac wasn't going to sniff my breath like a perpetually disapproving mum catching a kid half-way through climbing back in via their bedroom window, I can't risk even getting tipsy. Jack already got the drop on me — twice if you count that time back in De Burnuy's service, and the threat to the kids outweighs even whisky's siren-like temptation. And —even worse, possibly— I have to do everything subtly. Which means more time wasted.

I'm glamoured up — Isaac's magic, thankfully — an eye-wateringly complex Kabbalist symbol drawn with fine delicacy onto my forehead, with careful instructions not to even think about sweating. And now I have to get to know a few people. Because we don't know who Jack knows, who he's slipped a few euros to for a heads up if anyone comes asking about him. So I need to identify some likely locals and make my questions seem unsurprising, part of a free-ranging conversation rather than deliberate digging for information.

So I spend the rest of day three and all of day four frequenting some bars and tabacs — the cigarette shops-cum-bookies-cum-alcoholic hangouts that stand in distinct contrast to the classier offerings, like the black sheep of the family at a wedding when no one could come up with a plausible reason not to have invited them. I order cheap pints and then wince as I add a dash of the serum 'Zac provided me with that nullifies the alcoholic effects. Then I get into some serious daytime drinking sessions, discussing the same mind-numbing subjects revolving around poorly understood politics gleaned from similar conversations and bad mouthing celebrities for the most part.

By day five, I know enough of who's who to be confident in those who'll give up information I want to know and who's quiet enough to be of concern, the ones who might be sitting there as paid eyes for Jack. When I'm confident there's only the former and none of the latter in each drinking hole, I turn the conversation towards something that involves terrible disfigurations. Work accidents, chemical spillages. The Hollywood film adaptation of Philip Pullman's *Northern Lights*. Once the chatter gets firmly invested in the subject matter, I casually drop in having seen a fella who looked like he'd had half his face melted off the other day in Lyon. Did anyone else stumble across him? Helluva sight. Et cetera, et cetera. Always watching faces, looking out for people shutting down, like they've been paid for silence.

Nothing. No obvious dearth of conversation, the equivalent of the moment in the old Westerns when the piano playing screeches to a stop and all you can hear is the sound of hammers getting cocked. But equally no information either. Every time I bring it up, people lose interest when I can't produce a photo, hoping to get in a bit of grisly rubbernecking like the cheap thrill-seekers we so often are as a species. Then they move on to a different subject.

Because no one has seen him. Not one person has come across anyone like that in recent times. Occasionally, people will share stories of less-badly marked individuals they've come across before. But it's never Jack.

Five days spent looking for him, and all we know at the end of it is he's not wandering around wearing a glamour —thanks to the alarms not going off— but he's also not wandering around without one — thanks to my new-found drinking buddies. And considering they spend their days sat at the tables outside watching every passing stranger to make lewd comments or looking for someone to mock in order to feel better about themselves, my confidence levels are high that they'd have noticed him.

Five days gone, and all we've learned is that either Jack can fly, which Isaac insists will still trigger the wards as he set them to cover the tops of the buildings too in case Jack used the rooftops, or he's gone to ground for far longer than I expected he would. Or he's come up with something so fiendishly clever that neither of us can think of it. Not difficult with me, but Isaac and Jakob are actual geniuses. It doesn't seem likely.

Of course, there's one other option I try not to think about. That he's gone. That we spooked him so thoroughly, he packed up shop, did a runner, called it a day on this particular hunt. If he left Lyon, then my deal with the Tarrasque will be basically solidified, and I'll be forced into servitude for a year to the world's biggest arsehole. And of course, if he can outwait my two-week time limit, then the Tarrasque wins, and Jack wins. And I lose. But more importantly than that, the kids lose.

By the end, I'm sat in a tabac under a cloud of self-imposed misery so thick that even my new "friends", who normally would be looking on me as a mark, someone they can try and con for the price of a drink or two, are leaving me well alone. My eyes are fixed on the entrance to Jack's road, the one that leads towards the centre of Lyon from his hideout, the one I'm sure he must be coming and going by.

Except he doesn't come nor go. There is no sign of Half-Marred Jack.

Of course, when Isaac finds signs of his doings, it only makes things a million times worse.

Chapter Twenty

I'd love to Jack this all in. Except there's kids involved. So there's no quitting this time.

The phone call telling me to hurry back to the apartment is garbled and panicky but enough to get the adrenaline coursing through my body, so I cover the distance in about half the time it took me to wander to my seat overlooking Jack's road. It's a miracle that I don't take the door off its hinges as I come crashing through, half expecting to find Isaac with Jack's blade to his throat, having overcome Nith and Nan through some fiendish trickery that shouldn't be possible. The Good God knows impossible acts seem to be his specialty.

Isaac points a trembling finger at the TV screen. He's paused the news mid-report, and I'd make a joke of it, applauding him for working out modern technology if I couldn't see the tears forming in his eyes. This isn't the time, clearly. Instead I watch what he wants me to see. Or needs me to, anyway, as he presses the play button. What he wants is for the news report to be untrue. Sadly I doubt that to be the case.

At first I don't make the link. The scene on the screen jerks around as the reporter tries to get closer to what's happening. A man and a woman are being strong-armed to awaiting police vehicles through a tussling crowd of reporters. The man is struggling, shouting furious abuse at all around him, red-faced and teary-eyed, screaming incandescently that they've failed them, failed Teddy. The woman's face is like that of some youngsters I saw in the summer heat of 1916. Wide empty eyes that don't even hide a more than half broken mind. Trauma imprinted into every skin pore. She follows numbly, heading where she is shoved, vacant, the only colour to her skin the bruise-like bags under both eyes.

Then the live images cut, and the report brings up footage from a week ago, the night before we arrived, where the mother sits flanked by gendarmes, making a televised appeal for information. She trembles, her lips quivering with the pain of what she's living, but there's still something there that is missing now. Hope. Amid all the agony, hope.

'… if you've seen him, any information about him, please. Please, tell the authorities. We just want Teddy back. Please…'

It cuts back to the newsroom where the anchor fills in the story. A missing boy, disappeared from his bedroom while the parents watched television in the room below. Initially believed to be a runaway, now the authorities suspect foul play. Kids don't get snatched from their rooms at night. Busy play parks and shopping centres are the hunting grounds of predators, where children can be separated from distracted guardians easily and then vanish into the faceless hubbub. Homes are hard targets. And leaving no smashed glass or broken locks only raises the difficulty level.

Unless of course, you're a professional with centuries of experience and magic at your fingertips. Unless you're Half-Marred Jack.

'He's already got them, lad.' Isaac's tone matches his hand, wavering up and down as he struggles to marshal himself.

'He's already got one, 'Zac.' I try to sound more confident than I am, but I can feel my heart dropping like a stone. If he's already got enough, he may already be gone. And those poor parents might go to jail for something they never did while their child heads to a hellhole a million times worse than human prison.

'But that's the point.' Isaac is practically frantic as he collapses into a seat, swivelling a laptop I didn't even know he owned around to show me the multitude of tabs he has open. 'Look.'

Each tab is a report for a child that's gone missing in Lyon. Isaac's dug deep — some of these are police documents not available to the general public, but I'm not about to ask him how he got hold of them. Magic, persuasion, a touch of both, no doubt.

'Ten kids, Paul! The bugger's got another ten! Surely he's gone now?' Isaac is absolutely distraught, practically tearing his hair out. And what I'm about to tell him isn't going to make him feel any happier, even if it means it's less likely that Jack's gone.

I think about how best to get it across to him. There's telling him, but I don't think he'll really believe me. Isaac always wants to believe the best of people, a trait he shares with his brother. The best thing is to let him see the truth himself.

'Do me a favour, 'Zac?' I say it as gently and as calmly as I can, keeping my voice level. 'Pull up the same details of disappearances from one year ago, will you? Say in one week in June?'

He goes to work, and I treat myself to a very small tumbler of the single malt I brought with me. Just a taste. Not enough to affect my rationale or decision making. Just enough to fortify myself for breaking Isaac's heart a little.

After a while, he looks up, horror scrawled across his features. 'Seven in that week too! Are you saying Jack's permanently hunting in Lyon?'

The answer is, in many ways, far more horrifying than that. 'No. I'm saying that's normal.'

'That's not bloody normal, lad!' The indignance in Isaac's voice is strident, demanding I take back such a monstrous array of words. Sadly, I can't.

'You're right but neither are we as a species. Lyon's population is, what, half a million, give or take? Statistically speaking, you're talking about one kid, maybe two, going missing every single day of the year with those sorts of numbers.'

The colour drains from Isaac's face. I take no pleasure whatsoever in pulling the scales from his eyes over this. 'You can't be serious, lad.' The words are practically a whisper, forced out against a chest pulled tight in shock and grief.

'It's the truth. Cities are always the worst. Most decent-sized capitals see over twenty thousand kids disappear a year. A city the size of Lyon will lose a thousand.'

'A thousand children? How do you lose a thousand children?' Indignation, denial, fury. All there in every syllable.

'Some run away. Some are "accidents" in abusive

homes, which is why the police have nabbed those parents, seeing their tale of a kid gone from their bed as the sort of flimsy bullshit guardians pull out when they went too far in their "disciplining". Some...' By the Good God, it's hard keeping my tone neutral, pouring all this poison across Isaac's image of the world, of humanity, but he needs to know. He has to know. 'Some get taken. By the ones who are monsters in human skin, without needing *talent* or Faerie. Just terrible passions and tastes that they'll indulge regardless of the innocence it destroys in the process.'

'But thousands? *Thousands?*' Now it's a plea. Isaac's begging me to tell him it's not true, a weird reversal of our normal parental role, like he's the kid asking me to tell him the monster under the bed isn't real. Except I know it is. It always has been.

So I nod my head, and Isaac bows his, and I rest my hand on his shoulder as he cries for all those lost to the darkness of our species.

After a while he stills, and he raises his head resolutely. 'So how do we catch him, lad? Tell me you've got something for that?'

Good. For a moment, I wondered if he'd try to come up with some way to protect the children, perhaps to force Nithael to do something, to head off on his own equivalent journey to that Jak took, trying to save the Jewish diaspora from the hate they'd suffered throughout the centuries. Don't get me wrong, if I get my hands on a child abuser, they're never going to see the sun again, but we can't hunt them all down. The Talented world and that of the unTalented needs to stay separated to save everyone. Even the most innocent. Especially the most innocent.

'Well, there is something that's weird, 'Zac. Something Gwen already mentioned. Something that's implausible about this case and made the police understandably suspicious about the couple's story.'

'Them being taken from their beds!' His eyes widen at the implications.

'Exactly. I know he's got a fucked-up face, making him not the most approachable, but it'd be easy to weave a glamour, to snatch a kid out from under a distracted parent's nose. But instead, he has this peculiar modus operandi. Which means —'

'Any cases involving kids disappearing from their beds are his!' Isaac's excitement grows. He's channelling all that misery over the lost children into solving *this* case, saving *these* kids.

'Right! And also there must be a reason why he feels safer doing it this way, grabbing them like this. If we can work that out, we might get a step closer to catching the fucker.'

Isaac nods sharply, and his head is down, focused on the computer again a moment later. I turn away while he's engrossed, head to the bathroom, and stand, my hands wrapped around the sink, gripping the porcelain hard until the shaking I hid from him stops. The Good God knows I may not have any illusions left about humanity, but it doesn't mean I don't grieve for those who suffer because of our darkest elements. There was no way I was going to let Isaac see that though. No, he has enough to process without seeing my pain.

By the time I compose myself again and come back out, Isaac has news. 'Of the disappearances in the past two months, the one last week was the fifth one to include them vanishing from their own bedroom. All of the other four happened either the same night or the night before.'

I turn that over in my mind. 'So he grabbed five. All at the same time or near as damn it.'

'Aye. The authorities are questioning the lot of them. Apparently, they're investigating whether it's some sort of satanic cult or paedophile ring, considering the similarities of their stories.'

I put that out of my mind. Sorry as I am for the parents, I'm sure they'd rather I concentrate on finding their kids. 'Okay, so question is, do we think five is enough to appease Maeve for another couple of decades?'

Isaac rubs his chin, his head shaking slightly, the negative carrying through unconsciously before he even verbalises it. 'I doubt it. If she's anything like the monster we believe her to be, she'd break five before breakfast.'

I manage to avoid shuddering at that image. Just. 'Quite. So Jack's not done, but he has gone quiet...'

Isaac looks up sharply. 'Since we came to town.'

'Right. Or, well, perhaps. Because he seems to grab them in a group. And that happened before we even turned up. Why?'

'Delivering them.' Isaac's tone is grim. 'The longer he holds them, the higher the risk of them getting discovered, even in Lyon, which most Talented avoid like the plague thanks to the Tarrasque.'

It makes sense. 'So he has certain drop off times? A hand off to a contact, a handler of sorts?'

'Or a moment when Maeve tears open a portal, and he best be standing there with the goods.'

Again, that seems bloody plausible. And I see the moment when Isaac realises that means the five kids he stole before we got here are probably gone. He sinks into a nearby chair as though his legs can't support him anymore, weighed down by that knowledge.

He looks up at me, desperation in his eyes. I know that look well. It's the one I've worn more than a few times myself. When the course of action ran outside of my control and I was desperate to do something — anything that would allow me to regain some modicum of input. 'Lad, we've got to go to his place. Now. Take him down. Stop this.'

Fuck. I was ready for this, but it doesn't mean I want to have this conversation. 'We can't do that, 'Zac.'

'Why on earth not?'

'Two reasons. We know the kids aren't there. We don't know if he is.'

'So let's check!' I can so relate to that tone in Isaac's voice, that need to act.

'Isaac, if we go, and we get this wrong... If we trip one of his wards, or we bust on in there, and he's gone...or if it's just one of his hideouts, and it's booby-trapped...then we'll lose him. He'll go to ground, and that'll be the last we hear about Half-Marred Jack, at least within the time frame.' There's a begging edge to my tone, a pleading for him to understand. 'If we don't get any news soon or if another kid goes missing, then we'll go in straight away. Give me a couple more days. Please?'

He looks at me, searching my face, and then nods, though I don't miss the bite of his lip as his gaze drops back to the table. The Good God love him, he trusts my play even if it hurts his soul to do so.

I do my best to pull his thoughts away from the Hail Mary option and back to the subject at hand — saving the kids still here. 'Okay. So we've spooked him, but we think he's not done. Gwen said he's been here for a month or so, and in that time, only five have gone matching his MO. Do you think he'll already know who he wants to take next time around?'

'Probably.' Isaac winces, as though this conversation is physically hurting him. Good God, I hate having to put him through this. Once again, people suffering for having to help me deal with my bullshit. Others paying the price for me. 'If he's such a consummate professional, I imagine he has them all scoped out first, knows all about them.'

'I agree. Plus, if something happens, like one getting sick or them all going out unexpectedly, he can snatch up a replacement. I can't imagine Maeve'd be happy if she turned up for five and only got four.'

'So he's just staying squirrelled away.' I watch Isaac's lips thin, puckering in distaste. 'He's bunkering down —'

'Until he needs to go and pick them up.' I stop. 'Which means when he does, he'll trigger your alarms…'

'As long as it happens in the next week,' Isaac finishes the sentence, the part I left unsaid.

Chapter Twenty-One

I don't care what happens to me. I'll climb into the
Tarrasque's shithole of a mouth every day for the next
century if needs be. Just please. Let us save the kids. Please.

Two more days of us pacing like caged lions, snarling at
each other constantly. We hear nothing, not a jot. No
reported disappearances. No tripped alarms. No sightings
from the bar-flies I pop out to visit, as much to get out and
save both our sanities as out of any hope of a positive
report. Our apartment-hotel, a respectable double-bedroom
affair replete with an only slightly threadbare
lounge/kitchen ensemble, seems to do an impression of the
garbage mashers on the maintenance level of an Imperial
Cruiser — pressing in on us rapidly, albeit without some
sort of junk-hoarding space dragon alien swimming about
in it. Lucky that, as there is enough to worry about already
with the twat-dragon swimming about in the Rhône.

So when Isaac leaps to his feet and shouts, 'We've got

one!' I don't even make a *Ghostbusters* joke. I am already halfway out the door before he finishes his sentence.

Sadly, it is one on the distant south end of Lyon, far away from both his building and our hotel. At first, neither of us can understand how he managed to cover so much distance without triggering more alarms. It is, of course, Isaac who clocks the solution as we pile into the Super 5, which only makes me feel even more foolish.

'The alarm's gone off by the Stade de Gerland,' he says. 'He's travelling about on the metro.' He shakes his head gently in disbelief. I feel like slapping myself. Of course. I didn't even consider the metro, assuming he wouldn't want to get himself trapped underground. There're no alarms to set off, so if he glamoured himself in there, we'd never know. But wait…

'He can't be transporting kids on the trains, can he?' I rub my chin. That would take some major magical power. *Don't look heres* work well as far as spells go in keeping people looking the other way. Frankly, most people couldn't give a flying fuck if two other people reduced each other to composite atoms if they themselves weren't affected. That normally isn't the case with children though.

As a species, rightly, we're instinctively protective of our kids, and that only augments in most people when they become parents. Trying to mask a crying terrified child in an incredibly packed metal tube would be fabulously difficult. People's instincts would enormously pressure the spell, and the chances it would crumble would be high. Even if he knocked the kids out and then cast a *don't look here* on them and himself, the chances are, with all the unintentional jostling, the spell would get compromised. Unless he is seriously more *talented* than we expected.

'Maybe he bespells the kids, making them look like they're willingly accompanying him?' Isaac says doubtfully.

'You know as well as I do, when a person is being jostled and jerked about, holding them under that level of restraint is significantly difficult. I can believe Jack is confident enough to travel underground, ready to fight his way out if need be. I can't believe he's so over-confident as to risk precious cargo.' Not when he has the traboules he can stroll through with no concerns whatsoever. No, I can believe he might take a van, or he might go on foot, but I don't believe he'll take his kidnapped victims back on the train.

'So, in which case, why has he now headed south? What's he up to down there?'

I shrug, a pointless gesture as Isaac is watching the side window for a gap to pull out into the heaving traffic on the Avenue Tony Garnier. 'No idea. Observing a potential target, maybe?'

'In the daytime?' Isaac spots a gap he can squeeze us into, one that is too tiny for anything but our miniscule Super 5. Maybe it has its advantages after all.

He is right though. It doesn't make sense. 'Perhaps stabbing me prompted him to look to changing up his operation? Maybe he's looking for patterns of behaviour? Like them going to the park or something? Somewhere he might grab 'em in the daytime when no one's the wiser?'

It is a repulsive thought, and I can see that Isaac loathes it just as much as I do. Sadly, that doesn't make it invalid. 'There is a large park next to there. The Parc De Gerland.'

Good God, I hope I am wrong about this one. That or that we stop him before he puts any such plan into operation.

We park by the entrance to the park, grabbing a space too tiny for any normal-sized vehicle because of some shitty parking by both the cars flanking it. Again, the Super 5 is proving a godsend. I am being converted slowly but surely. Crappy little cars for the win, apparently.

Pushing in through the pedestrian entrance, we pass a beautifully preserved carousel, the horses all fresh white, the turquoise on the saddles picked out in fresh paint as well. Only the floorboards underneath show the real wear, the scuffed off paint revealing the grey primer on the wooden boards that has been replaced time after time. We hurry towards the play park. If this is part of some sick plan by Half-Marred Jack, then I feel sure that's where we'll find him.

I am worried, honestly. Leaving Jack's hideout alone has been difficult but doable. Odds are there's no one there except him, and even if there is, Maeve won't want damaged goods. She's undoubtedly looking forward to damaging them herself. But if I have to watch Jack take a child from their parents in a moment of inattention and magical misdirection, I'll be in there like a shot to save the kid, and I don't fancy my chances one-on-one with him.

Unless I can keep him busy for long enough that Isaac can get close enough to contain him, I reckon after a second encounter with me, he'll be gone and gone for good. Then my deal with the Tarrasque will fall due.

Still, I'll take the year of servitude if it means stopping him from snatching a child in front of me. I might not be the Good Man I once was, but I've not fallen that far yet.

As I go to rush past a public toilet block, looking everywhere for him, Isaac checks me by grabbing my arm.

'Hold on, lad, what's that?' He points to the far side of the facilities, which is half-overgrown by the adjacent rampant hedge.

I can't see anything even when I squint. 'I can't see anything, 'Zac.'

He looks at me, and damn, that look hurts because he laces it with the one thing I can't handle. Annoyance? Frustration? Sure. Anger, even. But he looks at me with such pity, it nearly breaks me here and now.

'It's still aglow with some trace of *talent*.' The kindness in his voice is that of a parent talking to their eternally slow-witted offspring, and while that might be accurate, it doesn't make it any less painful.

'Mind you, it's obscured by the angle. Plus, all that greenery interferes with the visibility.' Jakob obviously picked up on my distress. Isaac cottons on quickly.

'Yes, er, well, quite. I mean, everyone knows about my visual acuity. Eagle-eyed Isaac, they call me.' Good God bless him, he does his usual trick of heroically replacing the shovel he was digging with...with Ripley's exoskeleton suit from Aliens. Still, his clumsiness is ever endearing, and his ability to make a twat of himself makes me feel slightly better about my own ability to fuck my existence up spectacularly.

We hurry over and carefully pick our way through the branches of thorns that protrude out to embrace the toilets. We get more than a few peculiar looks as we make our way down the back of the facilities, enough so that I can feel myself glowing bright red. I am aware of how it looks. Isaac, of course, is oblivious.

'Are you okay, lad? You look all flushed. Not feeling well?' He doesn't regulate his volume in the slightest, and more heads turn in our direction.

'Isaac,' I hiss at him, 'they think we're going, you know, cottaging.'

He has no idea what I mean. Of course he doesn't.

'What does that mean? Building cottages? Is it like some sort of squatting in public facilities?'

'He means people think we are going to partake in illicit homosexual acts behind this building, dear boy.'

Goodness me, how is it that Jakob, who was trapped for centuries in a skull, gets it while Isaac doesn't. Of course, then Isaac has to be Isaac, always ready to mend the proverbial wobbly table. By balancing it on a stick of nitroglycerine.

'Don't worry!' he calls out loudly, waving cheerily. 'He's like a son to me! He's just going to give me a quick hand over here.'

Several of the gazes change from curious to horrified, and people start hurrying away. More than one mobile phone is pulled out of a pocket.

'That was amazing, 'Zac. Good going.'

'What did I say, lad?' He looks genuinely befuddled.

'Jak, can you explain to him what a handjob is, please, and sorry to make you educate your brother about that. Oh, and maybe if we can get a *don't look here* thrown up before the police arrive? That'd be swell.'

I turn to stare at the blank wall. Well, blank magically. It is a concrete surface in a public place, so of course it has the prerequisite graffiti tags all over it, ranging from beautiful calligraphic signatures to "Bob woz ere". Someone scribbled, "Mais Michael Jackson Est Mort" on there too. Either they weren't paying attention to recent happenings for some time, or they were referring to the lyric by Lyonnaise rapper Kacem Wapalek. What it doesn't have on it, for me, is any magic.

I sigh. 'What am I not seeing, 'Zac?'

He *ummms* and *ahhhs*, obviously worrying about hurting

my feelings again. I spin my hand, signalling him to spit it out.

'Basically,' he says, 'I can still see the very faintest traces of magic here. Fae magic, by the look of it.'

'What sort of magic? A spell? Some creature hanging around here too much, leaving its magical mark?'

'Well, actually, I'd say it's graffiti.'

I shake my head to dislodge whatever is blocking my eardrums as I surely misheard what he said. 'Sorry, did you say graffiti? 'Cos I can see the graffiti, and that's not helping at all.'

'Not this graffiti, lad. Magical graffiti. It's fading away, but it is definitely there.'

I feel the excitement mount. 'Can you read it? What does it say?'

He shakes his head, and my heart drops. 'It's too much obscured already, but…'

I look up sharply. 'What, man?'

'I can't read it as is, but Nithael might be able to push some power back into it, bring it back to legibility.'

I can't help picturing one of those entirely unrealistic police procedurals on television, where the tech support selects part of a grainy, poor-quality image and enhances it to where you can count the freckles on the suspect's nose. At least "because magic" is a more plausible reason for how Nith can pull that off with the fae graffiti.

Isaac raises his hands, and even being as *talentless* as I currently am comparatively, I can feel the angelic power gush out across the concrete wall. As it does so, the letters finally become visible for me, curving shapes in a cold, pale green, the colour of a frost-trapped blade of grass. They hold for long enough that I can read them.

'Atzerapen gehiago jasanezinak dira. Eskaera astebeteko

epean entregatu behar da, edo Erreginari erantzun.' I turn to Isaac, who carefully wipes a single bead of sweat off his forehead with a hankie. 'Dude, you clearly don't practise with your magic enough if that made you sweat!'

'Oh, I'm sorry, lad. I forgot you have a natural affinity to the cold, cruel magic of the Winter's Court, eh? What's that, you don't? Right, so now think how difficult it must be for the angels, sworn enemies of the fae from aeons past, to recharge their fading magic.'

He has a point. I acknowledge it with my usual good grace. 'Meh, excuses, excuses.' My grin shows I am joking. Hopefully.

He waves me away with his hankie. 'Talking of practise, anyhow. How's your Basque these days?'

'Considerably better than my mastery of the Fae tongue, thankfully. Right, let me see. Um, something about no more delays. Ah. Oh, nice.' I look over at him, and my smile this time is genuine. It is the smile of a man who might yet escape having to spend a year with the fucking Tarrasque. 'He's got one week to get the delivery done, or the Queen's gonna be pissed, right?'

Isaac nods, pleased. 'Pretty much exactly, although with less coarse language, albeit a lot more menacing. So it looks like our friend, Jack, is on a deadline as well. Eight days to be exact. Two more than us.'

'Yep. He's going to be forced to get out and get on with finding the rest of the kids he needs and quick.'

A deep frown creases across Isaac's forehead. 'Unless he already has them all? In which case, it'll just be a case of organising delivery.'

I stop. It is a valid point, worth considering. 'I don't think so,' I say after a pause. 'If he already has the kids, he'd have loaded up and rolled out as quickly as possible after he killed me, meaning there'd be no need for a reprimand by Maeve. Plus, he wants to minimise the amount of time he has the kids in his safehouse. Keeping them all subdued and obscured will mean keeping the whole place under a *don't look here*, plus soundproofing spells, which might draw the attention of the Tarrasque or other Talented like us. And if he snatched all the other kids at the same time last time, surely he'll do the same again this time?'

'Unless, as you said, he changes up his modus operandi.' Isaac's expression is granite-like. 'We've got to stop this bugger, lad. I mean properly stop him.'

I pat his arm. 'We will.'

I don't know how yet, but we will. I promise you that, 'Zac.

Chapter Twenty-Two

LYON, 25 APRIL, PRESENT DAY

Seriously looking forward to making Jack into a Jack-in-the-box. A wooden box.

We hop and scramble out from behind the building, the recharged fae graffiti magic fading away behind us like frost in the rising spring sun. 'Keep that *don't look here* up around us, man,' I say as we walk away.

Isaac frowns. 'Why's that?'

I nod towards two burly police officers who are patrolling the vicinity, suspiciously eyeing the male couples. 'I think they got our description from one of the locals you scandalised. I could do without answering any questions about our sexual predilections from the authorities, if it's all the same to you.'

He pales slightly, murmurs, 'Bloody hell,' and then mumbles something under his breath, doubtless reinforcing the *don't look here* spell.

'Yep, that was brilliantly handled. You completely reassured all the locals that we weren't going to traumatise their kids or whatever.' I turn and address an imaginary audience, like the host of some TV game show. 'Didn't he do well, ladies and gentlemen? Round of applause, please. Give him a big hand!'

I watch him wince with some small satisfaction. I guess Jakob explained a handjob to him, after all. Maybe it is petty, but I've messed up so much recently, it is nice to celebrate someone else's faux pas for once.

There are no other traces of Half-Marred Jack. We do a full turn of the park to be sure, our eyes peeled, but we see nothing. I'm not foolish enough to think he's relying only on magic to hide himself now though. He'll be using all the subterfuge skills he learned over the centuries as well. Still, the jacquerie plate-armour jacket is distinctive enough. If he is here, we'll see him, sneaky though he is. Besides, he came here to pick up instructions rather than to act on them.

We jump back in the Super 5 and head to our apartment. The mood is subdued in the car. It isn't easy to contemplate that he might be out there, gathering up young kids right now. Part of me wonders if I made a mistake, if we should just go in guns blazing right now. I know where he rests his head, and I can't bear the thought he might have young ones in there. Although everything we've gathered so far suggests not, suggests he'll grab them all when he's ready to do one big delivery, I can't get rid of that thought about changing his pattern of behaviour. If

Maeve's started leaving him the equivalent of threatening text messages, he's already behind schedule, no doubt having taken a delay to be sure he's safe after my sudden appearance and then death at his hands. If he feels under threat, anything is possible. He could have kids, terrified and crying, chained up in there right now...

'Isaac...' I consider how to phrase what I want to say. 'Could you — could Nithael, rather, tell how many people are inside a building? Like, perform some angelic form of ultrasound?'

'Just because they have wings doesn't make them bloody bats, lad!' He scoffs, then pauses for a moment. 'Although, apparently, it does because Nith just told me he can do exactly that.'

'You didn't know?'

He shrugs, making my heart leap higher than his shoulders as the car careens left and right. 'We share a body, and there's a harmonious union of sorts, but I'm still just human, lad. If I understood everything about Nith and what he could do —' He pauses, then shrugs again. 'Well, I wouldn't be human anymore myself, would I?'

Whether we are, in fact, still human, is a whole different discussion, but that is one for when we have a lot fewer time pressures and a whole world more booze. 'What about if there are wards or whatever?'

There is a moment of internal communing. 'Depends how high powered they are,' he answers finally. 'It'll work either way, but if they're super-charged up, then the scan might alert the inhabitants.'

I think about it but only briefly. 'I doubt they'll be that strong. He doesn't want to draw the Tarrasque's attention, and he's happy to rely on either knife work or a quick escape to deal with intruders. I imagine all he wants is a warning on ingress.'

Of course, if he gets that warning, he's unlikely to hang about. 'How long will it take?' I ask, thinking about the odds of him making a break for it or, even worse, using the kids as a human shield.

Again, I can see he is having an internal conversation of some sorts. I heroically resist the urge to wrench the steering wheel out of his hand while screaming. He snaps back without having killed us. 'A few minutes. We could do it quicker, but it'll increase the odds of revealing we were there.'

'Yeah, let's try not to let that happen. Okay, here's the plan…'

An hour later, we walk calmly up the street, chatting quietly about the latest superhero TV series iteration, keeping our gazes away from the building where the Jack of Plate is hiding out. When we are practically adjacent, we stop at the large metallic door opposite. The buzzer displays a plethora of names. Whether the building was originally built as apartments or adapted later, I have no idea.

We've been keeping our Talent locked in tight, but now Isaac puts a hand on the door handle while he pretends to jiggle a key with his other, my body and his blocking any viewing from the street.

The door clicks open, and we head inside. The hallway is clean grey-speckled imitation-marble flooring with similarly coloured simplistic walls. There is an elevator approximately large enough to hold half a hobbit, but we don't even bother and head straight up the stairs.

A quick check on the drive over showed the apartment facing Jack's building is still empty. I found it in a fit of frustration during those first few days of him being in the wind. The thought was to put his apartment under observation from this one, but there was no way I could have done it without opening the electric shutters rolled down over every window, and Jack would have spotted the change in a second.

The stairs curl back on themselves, mirroring the decorative whorls of the dark oak banister. At the top, we duck right, heading to apartment 105, a one-bedroom place currently available to rent for the same price as the black-market sale value of one of your organs. Per month. I fumble for my lock pick set in my etheric storage, but Isaac just waves his hand like a fucking Jedi Master, and the door pops open. Man, I really, really miss my *talent*.

Inside, the hallway is bare. Luckily, we're here in the day because the previous occupant stripped the place out entirely when they left — and when French flats say "unfurnished", they mean *"unfurnished"*. Lightbulbs, everything right down to —and sometimes including— the kitchen sink. But I've come prepared with a lamp in my etheric storage.

Passing the gloomy, tiny beige corridor, we plunge into total darkness due to the aforementioned heavy-duty steel shutters on the far side of the room. I let Isaac send up a werelight so I can find somewhere to plug in the lamp. Once that's on, he can conserve his magic, as well as reduce the chances of it drawing further attention to us.

I can now see the room is an unsurprisingly empty living room-kitchen with dark fake-wood laminate throughout. Little more than walls and a floor and a few cupboards. A minimalist's dream, I guess.

I try the light switch a couple of times but quickly realise it is entirely pointless; the bare wires poking out of the walls in place of lightbulbs are a good indicator of that. Over in the kitchen (though as they removed the oven, hobs, and cupboards, leaving only a plain plank of wood work surface and a free-standing sink, I'm not entirely sure if it still counts as a kitchen), I find the circuit breaker box and flip on the power. My plug-in lamp springs to life, giving us enough light to see by, and Isaac gets to work.

He sits down on the floor, concentration writ all over his face, no doubt dotting the i's and crossing the t's of what Nith is about to do. I'm not worried; there are four superstar intellects, two from a higher dimension, crammed into that one annoyingly good-looking head. If anyone can pull this off, they can.

I might not be very *talented* anymore, but for this, I don't need to be. The encircling light glows off them like an overpowered Christmas garden ornament that's being used as a WMD in a neighbourhood status war. I am damn pleased I brought the lamp rather than deciding to open the shutters. Otherwise, anyone in the street or overlooking it would be wondering how I created a miniature sun in a thirty-metre-square apartment. The glow's brightness is due to its concentration; the aura of white light doesn't extend much more than a metre from them. If they allowed it to diffuse across the room, it wouldn't be so radiant, but then, it would also penetrate as far as Jack's building and tip him off instantly.

Isaac stays like that, emitting brilliant light for about ten minutes. Then he slowly fades like the last gasp of a sunset when the clouds break before the earth turns its back on her. He opens his eyes, and for a moment, I can feel the collective presence behind that stare, and it shakes me to my core. It's one thing to know your father figure is half-possessed by an angel. It's another thing to feel the force of two Bene Elohim burning into you from his eyes. Then that too fades, and Isaac is there once more.

The smile that spreads across his face is gentle and caring and thoroughly relieved. 'There's no one else there, lad. Just one person. It's got to be him.'

I feel my blood pressure drop instantly from the vessel-popping stress level it's been running at since we arrived in Lyon. He's on his own in there. No more kids. He's not got the others yet. We're still good on time.

And speaking of time, it's about go time in my book.

'Can Nith or Nan cover the roof?' I'm already reaching into my etheric storage for my sword. I'm thinking about Jack trying to make a break for it through a skylight. No doubt he's planned a host of quick escapes from his hideout. We need to shut them all off. 'Even better, can they lock down the whole building?'

'They could, aye...' Isaac's smile wavers and then disappears. 'Oh, *bugger*.'

That doesn't sound good. 'What?'

'Nith has just pointed out that there's a sort of magic he can't protect against, not on a building-sized scale, and when he said it, I realised exactly how Jack is pulling everything off.'

Oh brilliant. 'Anti-angel magic? Not' —I rear back, waving my hands like eye-stalks as I do my best Lou Carcoilh impression— '*bazookath?*'

'Very funny, lad.' Isaac still looks just as grim. Fuck, this really isn't going to be good.

'Okay, 'Zac, the suspense is killing me here. What can't Nith guard against?' I thought the angels were pretty much infallible when it comes to magic. Apparently, not quite.

Isaac huffs as he pushes himself back up to standing. 'Portals, lad. Nithael won't be able to hold him in the building if Jack uses fae portal magic.'

Oh. Oh fuck. Of course. That explains everything.

It also means our whole plan to charge in and grab him is never going to work.

Chapter Twenty-Three

The cake is a lie.

We lapse into silence for a moment, each of us trying to get our heads around this miserable news. It fits, of course, now I think about it. Jack's a pro. The whole "stealing kids from their bedrooms" thing never made sense. There's so many easier options. Unless he can just portal into their rooms and pluck them from their beds and then fade back into the shadows. The sneaky wankpuffin.

Another thought strikes me. 'The portals will set off the alarms though, right?'

Isaac pauses, no doubt checking with the Bene brothers, then nods. 'Absolutely. Fae magic was the main thing we were looking out for.'

'Okay, so that still doesn't explain how he's been getting around without setting the wards off.' Damn it.

'It explains the note left in the park though.' Isaac's doing that kind of awkward half-shuffle from foot to foot. I understand. We got ourselves all geared up. Now, last minute, we've decided we aren't going for the full-frontal assault but haven't worked out what the hell we're going to do instead. For the moment, we're in limbo, stuck between deciding about trying to get Jack or getting the hell out of Dodge and regrouping.

I'm not following his logic regarding the fae graffiti though. 'In what way?'

'Well, if he's the one opening the portals, then they probably have set times and places for him to check in or get fresh instructions. Although, why not just rip open a portal and check in with Maeve directly?'

I can answer that one. 'Two reasons. First, would you want to report failure to Maeve or even interrupt her if she was in the middle of taking whatever sick kicks pass for her idea of pleasure?'

The thought of the kids who were already sent through to Winter flashes through my brain, and I have to fight to suppress a shudder, then clamp down on the thought itself. It's a fucking nightmare, but I can't help them right now. If I get distracted by that horror, I'm not going to be able to focus on catching Jack and saving any other children from the same terrible fate.

'What's the second?' Isaac pulls me back to the here and now.

'Another arsehole. The fucking Tarrasque. Use that sort of magic regularly —literally ripping holes in reality itself— and you're going to draw his attention.'

'True.' Isaac starts to pace. Usually that's my trick, but it looks like even geniuses need to kickstart their brains into action sometimes. 'So what? They set up certain times and places?'

'Probably.' This makes sense. It's speculation, but it feels right. 'Easier for Maeve to get one of her own world-hopping subjects to pop in outside the Tarrasque's territory and go either meet Jack —'

'Or leave him a message telling him Maeve's losing patience! A low grade bit of working like that magical graffiti will be below the Tarrasque's notice, and the fae, whoever they are, can be in and out before they set off his metaphorical alarm bells too.'

'Right.' It's strange. We're not any closer to a solution, but sometimes just framing the problem, verbalising it and putting labels on it can help. Of course, this is the point in the conversation when normally someone would tell us to stop being a pair of nerdy blathering idiots and to actually just do X to solve the problem. And then probably do it for us as well. The Good God knows I've missed Aicha the whole way through this misadventure but never more than this. Plus, I'd love to see her fuck Jack right up. She'd probably just stroll up and casually disarm him in single combat before marring the rest of his face to bring a bit of symmetry into his life. Shortly before ending it.

Sadly, I'm not Aicha. So the only option is for me to try to think my way out. Normally, I'd say that means we're fucked, but right now there are kids on the line, so I have to step up and sort it out. Even the furious, burning need that's been scratching at my brain until now — to know what the hell is going on with Susane, what on earth (or off it, seeing as they're in Faerie right now) the Cagot claiming to be my son is up to — all that fades into insignificance. Stopping Jack, keeping his ice-cold hands off any other children ever — that's all that counts.

'Okay,' I say, trying to think positively, to find that elusive solution to this blasted problem. 'So now we know what his game is, we have to even the playing field somehow. The portal magic — is there anything we can do to neutralise it?'

A wide grin spreads across Isaac's face, satisfaction written into every little crinkle. 'You know what, lad? Now we're talking. We can't contain him in the building. No, too diffuse an area. But can a pair of beings who came here from another dimension, brought by two brothers who broke open the way for them, do anything about someone opening portals? Have a guess, lad.'

I match his smile with one just as wide. We might have a chance after all. 'Okay, that's good news. So how close will you have to get to pull it off?'

The smile wavers, diminishing somewhat. 'Err…'

Damn it.

Chapter Twenty-Four

LYON, 26 APRIL, PRESENT DAY

Getting Isaac close to Jack without him realising is going to be about as easy as getting a Flat Earther to understand basic geometry. In fact, I'd probably prefer to attempt that.

Already, by the next day, I'm regretting not having gone for the direct frontal assault.

At first, I wanted to stay put in the flat so that we'd know the moment Jack moved. Problem was, if I were Jack, I'd keep a damn good eye on the road, meaning we would've either needed to use *talent* to bring us food and drink or else head out to the shops and stock up. Both were too likely to draw Jack's attention for my liking.

Isaac pointed out that, really, it would make no difference if we knew he was in the apartment or not. Sure, him leaving would tell us the game was afoot, but with his portal magic, he could just disappear in a puff of metaphorical smoke and we'd be back where we'd started.

Our best plan remains the original one. Wait for him to

trigger an alarm. Follow the trail when he does. He's on a deadline, same as us. Sooner or later, he's going to move. We just have to be patient.

Unfortunately, "just being patient" has never been one of my fortes. If I were to somehow end up at a sit-down job interview —one of those ones filled with thoroughly irritating questions like, 'Tell us about a time when you exhibited indomitable will?' or 'How would you use your previous life experience to complete the Twelve Labours of Hercules?'— and they asked me to list my strengths and weaknesses, "Just being patient" would definitely go in the latter column. Although, to be fair, I'd probably have lost patience with the whole thing way before then and demonstrated my strengths by hurling the table through the nearest window. Quickest way of egress and escape.

But what I need to do next definitely requires patience.

For I'm trying to train Isaac in the art of subterfuge.

We have a big advantage, which is that Jack doesn't know what Isaac looks like. To a degree, though, that's neutralised by the four-way combination of Isaac, Jakob, Nith, and Nan being far too *talented* to keep effectively under wraps. If Jack gets even slightly suspicious, looks at them just a touch too much, he's going to see all that power bubbling away below the surface, and 'Zac's cover will be blown.

Which means Isaac needs to be subtle.

I may end up enslaved to the Tarrasque for a year yet.

'Why, 'Zac,' I start, pinching the bridge of my nose so hard I'm surprised I don't snap it off, 'are you walking like that?'

We're practising in the flat. Again. And Isaac is apparently getting ready to audition for a job in the Ministry of Silly Walks. Of the many, many things Isaac is capable of, being nonchalant is apparently not one of them. He's got his back entirely rigid while stretching his legs out in front of him one after the other like a pony prancing for a group of judges in a prize show. It's like he had a terrible stroke and has forgotten how to walk or something.

'Just relax! Be more natural!' I shout. He lets his whole body go loose and now looks like a cross between a half-pissed orangutan and Bez from the Happy Mondays hopped up on pills. He goes bowlegged, and he swings his arms back and forth wildly. And on top of that...

'Are...are you whistling, 'Zac?' I almost can't believe it. Almost. If it wasn't Isaac we're dealing with.

'Well, yes. That's what people do when they're being relaxed, right?' Isaac peers at me worriedly, apparently shocked I'm not blown away by his acting.

'When, 'Zac? When have you ever, *ever* heard someone whistling when they're relaxed? Or stressed? Or any other emotion because I don't know about you, but I've *never actually seen someone walking down the street whistling.*'

'Oh. Oh right. Yeah, I guess it doesn't happen that often.'

'Never. It never ever happens, 'Zac. And if anyone were to do so, then they would immediately be flagged as the world's most suspicious individual by everyone in earshot. Which is why no one would ever do it. Apart from, apparently, you.'

'Okay, how about this?' He tries to combine the leg movements of his first walk with the second one's arm swings, making him look like the front half of a centaur trying to be the Fonz.

'Please. Don't ever move like that again, 'Zac.' This isn't going to work. Isaac's never going to get close to him. I tried dressing him up as a pizza delivery guy, which, apparently, meant he had to turn into Luigi from Mario Bros., and personally, I don't call shrieking, 'It's a nice-a pizza pie,' down the street subtle. And clearly, he won't even be able to walk out in public without someone screaming for medical assistance for him; we need a new plan. One that gets him close to Jack without Isaac having to use even the hint of subterfuge. Or we're doomed.

But I'm feeling better about one thing. I've got a cunning plan for after we do manage to block his nifty little teleportation trick. Only...feeling better lasts just long enough for me to tell the nitty gritty details to Isaac.

'We can't do that, lad!' He looks utterly horrified.

'Why not, 'Zac? They're already dead. Hell, it's what happens every time *I* die.'

'That's...that's...different.' Well, that is a crushing bit of logic. 'You don't have a choice in that. This is *grave robbing*.'

'Strictly speaking, it's morgue robbing. We need some dead bodies. Unless you want us to go and harvest some fresh ones?'

'Obviously bloody not.' I do wonder sometimes if Isaac is capable of telling when I'm being sarcastic. 'Think of the families, Paul! Left without a body to grieve, no closure!'

I'm tempted, so very tempted to make a point about thinking of the families who might lose children, but that's too much of a low blow. I'm sure there's another argument that'll make it all clear to him, to get him on side. Sadly, it's not me who normally comes up with such things. And there's no Druze queen with clinically precise words to cut through the bullshit.

Instead, I have no choice but to sigh and ask him, 'What do you want us to do then?'

The next morning, I find myself marching with him to the local morgue and flashing my psychic paper, inventing police credentials for myself and Isaac. Credentials that, apparently, magically transform him into Hercule fucking Poirot based on the way he is craning his neck, peering at everything like he's perceiving hidden truths and occasionally picking up random objects like paperclips and shouting, 'Ah hah!' for no apparent reason while I try to talk to the bemused morgue attendant. Eventually, despite the amateur dramatics over half an hour, I get turned away with a wringing of regretful hands and a notification that I need an authorising phone call from the Police Judiciare headquarters themselves before he can release the bodies to me.

So we trek across to the nearest Commissariat de Police, where, after two hours and a convoluted tale involving diamond smuggling and threats to various crown princes of Europe that has the police chief mesmerised, I manage to get him to make the required telephone call. We head back to the morgue…

Only to find one of the families waiting for us. Apparently, the morgue attendant didn't just wring his hands. He rang the grieving relatives too. Looks like he found something off about our performance. Can't imagine what it was. Oh yes, fucking Isaac. Of course.

'What are you doing with our dad?' The woman's eyes may be red-raw, but her voice is steady. Middle aged, she carries that stolidity to her frame that speaks of settling into yourself, a comfort in becoming more wholly you. She doesn't jab my chest with her finger, but it's a close thing. It hovers just over my chest like she's about to Bruce Lee me and crush my ribcage with a single digit.

'Top secret, dear lady,' Isaac sweeps in magnanimously. 'Can't discuss too much. Matters of state.'

'Matters of state? Dad was a brickie. What did he have to do with matters of state?' Her voice rises, along with a very suspicious eyebrow. I pity her poor kids. This woman tolerates no bullshit. I very much doubt they ever get away with anything.

Isaac, of course, becomes instantly flustered and starts blustering away. 'Oh, umm, well... All I can say is we have to investigate the possibility of murder.'

'Murder?' Now she just looks baffled. 'He died of a heart attack while sat on the loo. How's that going to be murder?'

I intervene before Isaac can put us in any deeper shit. 'Excuse us for a moment, will you?'

I pull Isaac back down the corridor, far enough away that the woman can't hear me. 'Look, 'Zac, enough of this. We've got the required approval. Stop trying to talk her round. She can't stop us.'

'No, she can't, lad.' His voice is surprisingly gentle, and he lays an arm around my shoulders, softly turning me round. 'But look at her. Really look.'

And I do. I take a moment and see the tremor in her hands that are clenched to keep it under control. The jaw muscles clamped tight to bite back the pain. And those red-raw eyes. She's not even looking at us. She's staring at a spot on the wall, and I don't doubt she's fighting against her own pain, trying to keep control long enough to deal with this nonsense we've brought to her and her family at this most unbearable of moments.

'You're taking away her chance to say goodbye. To finish a chapter of her life she never really believed would come to a close, not really. Our parents are gods until they prove themselves mortal. It doesn't matter if you're eight or eighty. We all become orphans one day. If our parents are lucky.'

I think about the worry I carry for Isaac. My desperate desire to spare him from the misery and murder that seems to cling to me like a bad smell. The suffering that comes part and parcel with being in my life. And when I look back, I know what he means with the last bit, about no parent wanting to outlive their children. Because I can see it in his eyes. The number of times he watched me waltz off into stupendous danger ill-prepared and even less capable. How often he had to watch me die. How hard that must have been, even knowing I'd come back. The terror that, perhaps, next time I won't.

I nod and lay a hand on his shoulder. 'All right, 'Zac. Knock off the Special Agent Mulder routine and go talk to them. Take the time you need.'

He nods and bustles off down the corridor. I give him some space. He doesn't need me eavesdropping on whatever he's saying. Whatever words he says to the lady in his low calm voice do the job. She sags, some of that rigidity leaving her frame, and then eventually gives the tiniest of nods before disappearing inside.

He comes back to me. 'Give her five minutes, lad. Then she'll let us take him.' But I can hardly look him in the eye because I've made him complicit in my acts once again. It isn't just wives who will make monsters of even wise men.

It's sons as well, whether by blood or by choice.

Chapter Twenty-Five

'...wise men know well enough what monsters you make of
them.' — Hamlet

It takes the rest of the day to get the other bodies out of the morgue. Luckily, a simple *don't look here* keeps them from asking the relevant questions, like why we aren't driving a freezer unit van but are bundling them one by one onto the backseats of the world's smallest car. We get them back to the flat, and Isaac sets to work, using Kabbalist sigils to preserve the bodies both from sight and rot.

As we start to position them around the city, bickering like an old married couple about possible routes Jack might take, I'm glad that he's still lying low. It gives us the chance to put everything into place. Once that's done, we pull out a paper map and pore over it in the traboule situated off the Maison De Cible, the famous pink tower hidden inside one of the secret passages, as we have lunch. We debate back and forth about possible routes. I'm convinced I have every one covered, and the eagerness to act, to simply *do* starts to build again. Isaac's less convinced and points out various potential flaws in my plans. Despite my insistence I'll just wing it if any of that happens —which is my answer to every problem ever— he comes up with some far better suggestions. I begrudgingly give him permission to use his incredible intellect to save my ass. Truly I am the very embodiment of generosity.

By the next day, I'm starting to sweat. It's like the wait before Jack triggered the ward at the park but a million times worse. What if he's given up? What if we've freaked him out so much, he's done a runner? Maeve won't be happy, but he can make amends later on, find some extra fucking tribute, the shitgriffin. Also, there's the time limit. He has a couple of days more than me. What if he just waits till the last minute? That'll be the worst of all worlds.

I start running over paranoid scenarios. What if he has us under observation? Maybe he's been watching us the whole time, and he knows our whole plan. Or what if the Tarrasque reached out to him and told him about our deal? That sounds like exactly the sort of thing the melty-faced cocktoboggan would try and pull off.

By the night of the 30th, I am a wreck. Tomorrow is the last day. Either it all comes together, or I am doomed. And worse, so are the kids. I spend the whole time in bed tossing and turning, visions of failure haunting me.

And, of course, it is just as exhaustion finally grabs ahold of me and starts to drag me under, in the early hours of the morning, that Isaac runs up the corridor. 'Move it, Paul! He's out and on the prowl!'

We dash out of the building, half-tripping over our own

feet down the stairs. He's nearby, having triggered our warning by the Church of Saint Bruno of Chartreuse, a magnificent sixteenth-century church, elegiac and baroque. It is gorgeous inside and out and faces the Quai Saint-Vincent of the Saone, the other vast river running through Lyon. Isaac points urgently to the small pedestrian bridge, all red industrial ironwork spanning the waters just ahead.

'There, lad! He's just gone there!'

We push on, picking up our pace, crossing the bridge into Old Lyon. The Basilica of Notre Dame de Fourviere looms ahead, the terrain rapidly rising towards its heavenly positioning. I've had enough of holy buildings dedicated to ladies recently, my run in with the Lady of Lourdes having left me traumatised enough. I hope we can avoid that one.

Isaac points down the side of the river. 'That way!'

I pick up the pace, accelerating away from Isaac. Farther down on the right-hand side, I am sure I glimpse that famous plate jacket darting between two parked cars. I cross as well, pirouetting away from the white van that's arriving fast behind; it honks at me. I am half-running now, desperate not to lose sight of him even though Isaac is being left behind me. I catch sight of him again as I mount the pavement, just as he pushes through a nondescript door painted the grey-blue of a half-rain-laden cloud. There is no plaque to announce it as a traboule. The only small give-away is the grating over the doorway, a metal meshwork off a solid bar, commonly used to allow light into the narrow passageway. I arrive in time to catch the door before it swings itself shut. I slip past and let it close, hoping I am quick enough that Jack doesn't notice the delay.

I pull my sword from my storage and use the little magic I have left to cast a *don't look here* on it. I can't hide myself, but I can stop any residents of the traboule from calling the cops. If the authorities come looking and get hold of Jack rather than me, it could end badly.

The gloomy stone passage stretches about a hundred metres, with only a doorway and a few buzzers to mark a shared property on the right. After that it opens up with hints of green. I edge forward, quiet as I can be, sword at the ready.

I come out to a split-level yard with doors to two houses on the left and an overhanging garden balcony of a third house on the right, with creepers of a potted vine crawling inexorably towards the floor. Diagonally across is another corridor, leading out to the road on the other side. I step out and spin just in time, my sword raised to deflect the knife aimed at my back, catching it in the guard and lifting it upwards, putting me almost face to face with Half-Marred Jack.

His eyes widen. Well, his left eye widens. The one on the right sits in the crevice between the imprinted marks of the Winter Court Queen's index and middle fingers. Her blessing burnt away his eyelid, mangling it with the muscle underneath, so it seems almost impossible that his eyeball stays in the socket. It dangles above the ruined mass unsupported, rotating almost in empty space. I try to fixate on the left-hand side, on the information it can give me and not let the ruin wrought on the right disturb me.

'How now, rogue? I know your face somewhat and your *talent* more.' He leans forward, intrigued. 'You're a small and paltry Power, but I know those whose weasand I've sliced, and yours I've done clean and quick. How is it you're back for another helping of my bollock dagger?'

He looks utterly relaxed despite the disfigured features and despite us being mid-clinch. I, on the other hand, am already sweating from feeling him attempt to turn the blade out of the guard-lock. To counter his movements, I am using muscles that I've not used in any body in a donkey's age and that I am confident this body has never used. He is toying with me. I need to keep him talking.

'Maybe,' I reply, trying to keep myself from panting, 'you didn't do as great a job as you thought you did.'

He laughs at that, a strange slurred sound carried from half a mouth. The other side wheezes and whistles like an overloaded steam engine close to exploding. 'Do you mean to say my blade-work were ought but exacting? That's a tedious mistruth to be sitting on such a tongue. I'll ask of you again. How came you to return here for another throat cutting?'

He is pushing me back and down, and my knees are buckling. It shouldn't be possible for him to get that leverage with the smaller blade, but apparently, no one told Jack that. We turn like a slow-motion version of a courtly ballroom waltz until my back presses up against the wall of the over-looking garden, the earliest spring blossoms of the vines tickling the nape of my neck.

'Maybe...you aren't...as good...as you believe...' Talking is hard. Hell, breathing is hard, but if I don't keep it up, both will become impossible.

'Ah, now, that's just rude, prettyman, ain't it?'

I feel the slight twist of his knife in my guard, enough to make me flick my eyes over to see what he is doing. It is, of course, a feint, and he stabs up into my gut with his left hand, the second knife I didn't see him draw pulling across and down, disembowelling me. I sink backwards, down the running creepers as I clutch my intestines to hold them in my body.

I did my job though. I kept Jack busy and distracted. He whips up and round, his blade out to impale the floating parchment appearing behind him. The knife passes through it, but the papers wrap themselves around his hand, glow brilliantly, and then are gone. Isaac is nowhere in sight. The magic he used is unbelievable, countering the gift of Maeve herself, and while the angels might be almost limitless in their power, Isaac is not. He must've turned around and left as soon as he sent it on its way. He'll need some rest before we try to take on Jack properly after pulling off a feat of *talent* like that.

Jack turns back to me, and now there is fear in his eyes. He can feel the binding, I am sure, and has at least an inkling of what happened.

'Who helped you? Who did this? What buggering magic is this?' He hisses, his knife out, ready to cut some truths from my tongue.

But I pulled out the blade he'd plunged into my guts while he was turned, and now I smile. 'See you soon, Jack,' I say with a wink and then thrust the small knife up under my rib, into my heart, and give it a twist. Blinding pain. Then back into the blackness.

We planned for Isaac to head straight to the car and then for the funeral home where he picked me up last time, so of course I come to in the hospital morgue. I go to contact him, grabbing a spare change of clothes from my storage at the same time as my burner phone. This new body is slimmer than the last couple, so I'm not suffering from pudgy fingers syndrome. It makes me feel a lot more like myself. The man I took over must have been ill for a while before dying though because the muscles feel massively atrophied. Even sitting up seems like hard work. It isn't going to make what comes next any easier. I'm half tempted to kill myself to try to get a better body, but given my luck lately, I'll probably have to do it a dozen times or so before I get a good one, and we might not have the time.

I don't expect we'll have to leap straight into action, but it remains a possibility. Now that we've sprung our trap, Jack is basically a wolf with his leg in the snare. Question is, how will he react? Will he exhaust himself by pulling against it? Will he snap and snarl and look to get his revenge on us? Or will he do something unexpected, the equivalent of gnawing his own leg off and disappearing away into the night, hobbled but free? I've plans in mind for the first two. It is the third one that worries me...

As I wait for Isaac to come pick me up, I can't help briefly wondering how much of the past eight hundred years I've spent dying. Not being dead; we timed that once using a nearby spare corpse, and I come back almost instantly, my new eyes snapping open as soon as my old body shuts down entirely. But I wonder how many times I felt the pain, the white hot pinpricks of each nerve ending. How many times I faded to grey, sense and sensation leaking away as the warmth of life gave way to the cold of the grave.

You know when you pass the tipping point, when you step over the precipice you were teetering on, where some slim chance remained that you might yet regain your precious toehold in life itself. But then you start that inescapable tumble down into the abyss. I can understand why people know and accept their fate when they pass that point. It is inexorable. I totally get why they rail against it to the last moment too. I've done it hundreds of times. Spent weeks? Months? Of equivalent time in that agony, balancing before falling, and still, I will do it a thousand times more rather than head to some peaceful eternal slumber. I still fancy a few more rounds on the wheel of dharma yet if it is all the same to you.

Isaac pulls up a few minutes after I find my way outside. I got lost once, heading upwards, and ended up stumbling into the oncology ward. For all the many ways I've died, I've never had cancer. Small blessings. There are a lot of horrible methods for meeting our end in this life, but there's something so insidious about cancer, about our own body turning against us, our own cells swallowing us whole. Cancer can get fucked.

I pop open the car door and get in.

'Where to now then, lad? Back on the hunt? What's the plan?' Isaac's eyes gleam. I can tell he is enjoying being in on the action for once, however much he claims to be a simple researcher by nature. I think it's been hard for him the past few weeks, seeing me and Aicha head off into danger, taking all the risks. The only time he was up in the mix was unintentional, and he was out cold under Enochian restraints woven by Ben, my former student turned destroyer of worlds, for the whole of that time.

'Not quite yet, 'Zac. There's a plan. First thing is to keep monitoring those alarms. With luck, Jack'll be holding back now, running scared. He'll be back at his apartment.' I try to inject a confidence I don't quite feel into my words. 'Let's go there and scoop him up.'

Except when we drive onto his road and Isaac gets ready to throw up a Nith-powered ward covering the building, he stops and shakes his head. 'He's not there, lad.'

Shit. I counted on him going to ground. On losing his portal magic spooking the shit out of him and him retiring to lick his wounds.

Then Isaac's eyes widen. 'An alarm's just gone off. In town.'

Fuck. Looks like Jack is the type to gnaw his own leg off. He's obviously decided Maeve is a whole lot scarier than we are.

If I've not missed my guess, he's going for the kids. Now.

Chapter Twenty-Six

I got it wrong once. More than once. I can't get it wrong
this time.

We head hell for leather for the other side of the Saone
river, pushing the little car to its absolute limit.

'You know the plan, 'Zac?' I hurl him a little walkie
talkie I fished out of my etheric storage. We'll use phones,
of course —we aren't in the fucking eighties— but I just
want a backup to the backup.

'I do. Are you sure of this, lad?' I can hear the doubt.

'I am.' I'm not, but I'm fucking damn well going to
sound like I am. 'It's got to be the traboules now. He's got
no other way of moving the kids. They'll be his plan B.'
And our own plan B better work.

Isaac swears and changes direction. 'He's crossing on
the Pont Marachel Juin.'

I'm not swearing. That works. In fact, it works perfectly.
Fucking hell, we might pull this off.

We screech to a stop, and I bail out. 'Go! Get in position. Stay on the line.' I pull out my phone and am almost running now. The time for subtlety is over. I want him to know I am coming for him.

Isaac shouts directions down the phone line, saying Jack turned up the Rue Du President Edouard Herriot, heading straight for the town hall. I run past the magnificent municipal centre and cross the expanse of the Place Des Terreaux. The water fountain statue dominates the other side, three stories high, a representation of France holding the four major rivers of the country.

Another yelled instruction sends me dashing up the rue Romarin, then spinning left up the rue Saint-Polycarpe, breathing hard. My hurrying gets rudely interrupted when a hand loops round my throat as I dash past a side turning, stopping me so hard I feel my trachea being crushed, and my feet leave the ground at being checked so suddenly. I also feel the hum of magic that is sure to be a *don't look here* spell kicking into operation. Isaac is nowhere in sight.

''What rough magic have you worked up on me then, prettyman?' The voice hisses in my ear, and the jab of a blade presses against my ribs.

'You've already tried that twice, Jack,' I wheeze through the restrictive grip and the bruises forming on my throat. 'It didn't take then, won't take now.'

'Aye, well, there's the rub. I can't seem to make my blade stay 'cept in its sheath. Yet your distempered workings hold me so as I might ne'er be free in this time here afore I head once more beneath, and I'll have an ill meeting by moonlight to explain it. It'll surely make a mooncalf of me.'

'Sorry, Jack.' He squeezes harder. Each word is a tricky gasp to make now. 'It wasn't my…working… I don't know who…he is…'

'Listen now, you cockered whoreson. I'll have no more of your untruths bandied, and time presses hard upon my heels. Though you've returned too soon, I'll take hope that you'll approach too late if you come again, albeit I'd advise against. Meantime, once more, adieu.'

The blade slides in and out like a needle through thread, and as I fall back into the dark, I see him turn through a traboule door. I glimpse the street name as my vision greys.

Rue des Capucins. Perfect. Then I am gone.

Chapter Twenty-Seven

It's been a delightful three weeks, albeit frustrating at times, to be with two of my favourite people, even if one of them I know not as much as I wish. Sadly, Isaac takes his role as chaperon entirely too seriously and keeps a watchful eye on us, ensuring we have little, if any, time alone. But even still, our time together is bringing us ever closer, only reinforcing that magnetic pull we have to one another.

Isaac works on teaching Susane the same magic I used to keep her and her mum from detecting me, showing her how to sense that seed of power inside herself, how to cover it in your own flesh and soul to mute the light. We know the Church holds Talented. If we can stay hidden from their eyes, it will be a blessing. Working any form of magic is impossible without destroying the illusion, but it should be enough to keep her from being burnt at the stake as soon as she walks into the Pope's domain, assuming there are priests gifted with power in the Vatican.

Other than that, I enjoy the journey. I've never travelled along this part of the Mediterranean nor have I ever gone past the Alps and into Italy. The weather is balmy, warm, and pleasant without ever being oppressive, and the well-tended roads make progress comparatively easy as well. While the star of Venice might be on the wane, La Serenissima is still a mighty nation state, and trade passes often between the north of Italy and the west of France, particularly that of the weavers and silk merchants of Lyon. We are farther south, traversing across Nice and the sovereign principality of Monaco.

Rome is exactly as impressive as I expected. I saw traces of the Roman Empire in my travels, even in the northern reaches of Africa, but here? It is everywhere. It appears that every other building — or, at least, every one that's not a hovel holding a family or ten — dates back to the Empire itself. Grandiose, elegant marble is prominent throughout the town, with classical statues and busts on display as often as vegetables might be in a town back home.

We have time to wait in Rome, time to see no small part of it. Petitions were sent on behalf of the Cagot for permission to make their case to the Pope himself, with no doubt many a sweaty bishop's hand greased as the letters made their way across the Alps and down through the Italian states. The Cagot received approval prior to Susane and Gwendolyne setting out to request our aid, but that does not mean the Church welcomes us straight away.

When finally they summon us and allow us entry into the Vatican itself, we are all as ready as it is possible to be. Isaac already disguised himself in Christian garbs — he'd insisted that if Nithael could see he was still Jewish, then so could his god, and that there was no blasphemy in his deception except to the Christian God-Made-Man he didn't believe in. Susane learned to lock her magic down like she wrapped it in iron chains, and I did the same.

They hurry us through the palace — for never doubt that is what it is. I've been entertained by nobles throughout varied cultures, and this is the domain of an emperor. The opulent mixture of art and architecture that defined Rome for over two thousand years is very much alive in here, and the sign of renovation and new art commissions are everywhere. Pope Leo X's election was not much more than a year ago, and prior to the Church, he was famed as both a patron of the arts and of the artists themselves. Already a shrewd politician prior, having ruled well in the lands of Bologna and Romagna, now thanks to him the Medici family occupies the highest office in the known world. He is known both for his talent as a singer and for his oratory skills. It is also widely known that he uses said skills to seduce many a young man who catches his eye and that the death penalty for homosexuality doesn't exist inside the walls of this building. Feasts and fetes are the defining characteristic of the modern Holy See, the Pope's seat of power, and I don't doubt our wait was to allow the Holy Father to sate his earthly desires before we drew him in to listen to our political pleas.

The Pope, Bishop of Rome and Vicar of Jesus Christ, is a man marked by how he lives more than by what he believes. He is a similar age to the one I appear to be, but he is as much marked by excess as lower classes are marked by suffering and poverty. He has a jocular expression complementing his jowls; they lift up when he smiles, making his face additionally expressive. The lines worn into the plump flesh speak of him smiling often, but the eyes show he is no fool. The cunning and quick nature of his character sparkles in them, dazzlingly so. The layers of lavish ostentatiousness bring an almost theatrical aspect to his appearance, only increased by the drapery and majestic grandeur of the throne room.

Susane speaks. 'Your Excellency, Supreme Pontiff of the Universal Church, Sovereign of the State of the Vatican —'

Leo X interrupts, leaning forward, studying our party as we kneel in front of him. 'Yes, I am aware of all of *my* titles. I would know who, exactly, are you? It is rare that we have a woman walk within our walls and even more rare that one would speak to me. You must have made quite an *impression* upon my pontiffs.'

I do not doubt there was a hefty impression paid to at least one of the chief bishops of Rome to get us this audience. Whether the Pope then received his part is another question.

'My lord, I am here to speak for my people. Whilst I may be just a woman —' I know full well how much making such a scraping devaluation of herself must be costing Susane in pride. '— they requested I lead this expedition as I am the only one of my people who speaks Italian.'

It is a reasonable excuse but not one Leo is going to accept. He switches to French. 'Did you really believe I could not communicate in the Frankish tongue?'

Susane recovers smoothly. 'Whilst we were sure that Your Excellence would have mastery of our language, just as you do of all your heavenly-ordained duties, it is improper not to address you in your own tongue. The Church granted our humble request for an audience far quicker than any might have expected. A tribute to how your reign has improved the flow of bureaucracy as much as it has every aspect of life, and no other could be trained sufficiently swift to have presented our case in the allocated time.'

Good God, she is smart. Quick and decisive and able to

fence verbally with not only the ruler of all spiritual aspects of every life in Europe but a master debater, who gained his skills in the notoriously treacherous debating halls of northern Italy. Clearly she makes an equally strong impression on Leo, for he graces her with a nod. Isaac and myself now draw his attention though.

'And who are these stout fellows in your company? Fellow Cagots to keep you safe upon the road?'

'I am her tutor, Your Excellency, ignorant though I am compared to the knowledge owned and gained in these magnificent halls,' Isaac begins. 'They asked me to keep watch upon her and ensure her education was acceptable afore she met you, so as she would not sully your presence further than our distressing ignorance.'

So Isaac can play the game too, as can I, having not long returned from wandering in far-flung lands, negotiating with viziers and kings. But I shall keep it simple as I don't want to draw attention to myself. 'I am but a humble guardsman, Your Magnificence. My sole aim is to keep them safe during their travels. It is an honour to be in your presence.'

I keep my head bowed during all of this. When I raise it, I am shocked to find the Pope staring at me, his eyes locked on, as though I am a pail pulled fresh from the well on a blisteringly hot day. He looks neither at Isaac nor at Susane. Only at me.

'It is indeed an honour for you, young sellsword,' he murmurs, the tip of his tongue darting out to wet his lips under his intense stare. 'An honour, indeed.'

Despite my best efforts, I drew the attention of the Pope. His whole undivided attention. And I suspect his intentions are more carnal than holy. Shit.

Chapter Twenty-Eight

There's more than one way to skin a cat. And this cat has a whole lot more than nine lives. Or skins.

I come to, my eyes cracking open, and check the street address. Good. It's the body I expected. The one outside the traboule Jack just took. I pull a spare blade from my storage and position myself ready and waiting.

The pale-blue door opposite cracks open, splitting the fat cap graffiti tag scrawled over it in two, and Half-Marred Jack strides out, determination written in his stride. His wide-thrown gaze keeps a look-out for Isaac, expecting my partner-in-crime to accost him. He doesn't expect to see me standing there, my blade pointed at the floor, leaning on a concrete bollard on the opposite side of the road. For the second time, fear flashes through his expression. Still, he throws a blade clean for my throat.

I deflect it before it pierces my flesh. He seems to prefer taking out my voice box. I would understand if he had ever heard me sing, but as it stands, I am offended. He dashes off as soon as the blade leaves his hand, heading away from the Church of Saint-Polycarpe, clinging to the shadows as the façade's up-lighting is only angled to highlight the Corinthian pillars.

A hundred metres ahead of me, he runs fast up the rue Burdeau. *Turn left. Turn left!* I'm willing him to listen, to follow the mental instructions. He has to. He's using the traboules; he's got to head for —

No. Shit, no, he hasn't. Because he keeps running straight on. This isn't part of the plan, damn it.

Or not part of my plan anyhow. 'He went straight, 'Zac; he went straight! Not the stairs! Shoot the Wookie!' I scream into the phone, almost incoherent, because if Isaac doesn't hear me, doesn't react, then we might be done…

A wall of crackling energy springs up mere metres in front of Jack. It passes from building to building, angelic neon towering up as high as the shingles. My clever friend has rejigged his alarms. Now instead of sending warnings back to Isaac, they're broadcasting Nithael's energy out through the nearest one, Isaac having effectively reversed the polarity. I wouldn't want to run into it, and I'm friends with the creator.

Jack doesn't even consider it. Without even a break in his movements, he reverses, a natural fluidity and grace I've only ever seen in one person. No time to think about her, though, to miss her. Instead, I use the time to close the gap, and I start up the left of a set of stairs split in two at the exact same moment that Jack darts up the right-hand side.

He's fitter than me, faster than me too, but I'm pushing myself hard. He beats me to the top, but I'm pumping my arms like pistons, driving this body to its limit, intent on keeping up with the bastard…

Too intent. My head clears the step just in time for my eyes to make out a shape speeding towards me. By the time my vision makes it coalesce into the throwing knife it is, it's already passed out of sight. Mainly because it's not possible to look at your own throat.

I gurgle, tasting the blood running down my gorge, the air whistling around the edges of the blade. Before my vision greys, I watch him turn right down the Rue Des Tables Claudiennes. Now it's the last gamble. There's no more Isaac Hail Marys if this fails. If we have this right, we'll have him. If not, he'll be gone in the wind, and I'll be doomed to the Tarrasque's company. And though we might have saved the kids tonight, it won't help the next ones he targets. *Please*, I think to a god I don't believe in anymore, but who will surely, *surely* protect innocent children if they exist. *Please let this work.*

———

I come to on a set of stairs and rush to the edge, leaning on the metal railing to stare down into the courtyard at the foot of Cours Des Voraces. The stairwell here isn't as famous as the Pink Tower, but I don't think Jack's looking to see the sights. He's looking to escape, to lose his tail. And this is the way out I'm banking everything on Jack taking.

The sense of relief is giddying as I watch Jack dance down the steps leading to the base of the courtyard, still moving effortlessly, gracefully even as he throws glances backwards. I lean back and start down my staircase, keeping out of sight. The staircase of the Cour des Voraces is well lit at night, and I don't want him doubling back.

As he reaches the bottom, I step around the corner. I

won't lie. It gives me great satisfaction to see a monster like Half-Marred Jack start at my appearance.

'Ah, ah, ah, Jack. That was very rude. We weren't done talking yet.' I smile as sinisterly as I can. I practised it earlier on Isaac, who informed me I looked constipated, but Jakob was much more generous, saying it was mildly terrifying. Whichever is the case, it seems to work in freaking out the bastard. Either that or my refusal to stay dead. Whichever it is, Jack dashes left, away from me and down the next set of steps to Rue Biderat.

I follow behind him, hurrying though not running, drawing and dragging a sword-blade down the damp stone walls, the grinding noise ringing out, echoing towards Jack, grabbing his focus. I stop at the railing and watch. He's on the last steps, heading for the open doorway, the amber illumination of the streetlights urging him on, promising safety.

As he reaches the doorway, Isaac steps around the corner, blazing with angelic light that turns the night into mid-summer midday. Jack throws his hand up against the blinding glare, trying to shield his eyes. Isaac spreads his arms up and out wide.

'*You shall not pass!*' he thunders, Nithael's energy pouring out of him and surrounding the Jack of Plate, holding him in place with a power from a dimension way beyond our own. Even if Queen Maeve herself was here, I think she'd find it hard to stand against Nithael in his full glory, and Jack is not fae royalty. He isn't even fae yet. He stands no chance at all. By the time I get down to the bottom, he is entirely cocooned in a ball of angelic power, his eyes rolled up into the back of his skull. Well, one eye. On the marred side, I can still see the very bottom of his iris due to the lack of skull it can roll back into. It is vaguely disquieting.

'Well then, lad, how was that, eh?' Isaac nudges me in the ribs, grinning like a maniac.

I roll my eyes at him. 'Seriously, Gandalf the Grey?'

He looks a tad sheepish. 'I've always loved that line. I couldn't resist.'

I drop the pretence and grin straight back, clapping him on the arm. 'You bloody nailed it! Absolutely perfect. Good job, man.'

He looks deservedly chuffed. 'It was too good an opportunity to miss.'

I trot back up the stairs and recover Almeric's skull from where Isaac stashed it by the last dead body, hidden by angelic magic until the right time. If it wasn't cloaked, I'd have headed there the first time I died. Me screaming 'shoot the wookie' and him setting off the barrier also meant he knew exactly where Jack would be heading next, and to drop the cloaking spell. He was heading straight for the Cours, and the double exit there made it a perfect place for him to try to shake a tail. My stashed body blocked the high road, and Isaac's Middle Earth impression caught him on the low road. So I guess we'll both get to Scotland before him.

I grin. Isaac has every right to feel pleased with himself. Not least because his alarm ward reversal trick worked like an Enochian charm. 'Right, now where? Do we take him back to the hotel?'

The levity dissipates. 'No. We need to check out his safe house. Make sure there's nothing we missed. And time is pressing. How long can Nith hold him?'

Isaac looks strained. 'In theory, without limit. But you know what the real limit is.'

I give him a nod. The angels will only help us on the defence. As soon as we take the offence, especially the torture that may be necessary — and that I might put into play even if it isn't considering the piece of child-stealing shit that we've caught...

'Can you whip up something to keep him subdued?' I ask.

Isaac rubs his chin. 'I can, but it's going to be tight time-wise if we do this all in Lyon. Are you sure you don't want to get him out of Lyon and then come back?'

I shake my head. 'What if some children are there? And Maeve comes looking for them when Jack's deal elapses? We know it was empty before, but we've no idea what he was up to during the days he was supposedly lying low. I'd rather risk the next year than risk that. Either way, Half-Marred Jack is finished. That's a bloody big win in the victory column far as I'm concerned.'

Sometimes you must count your victories. Especially when doing the right thing next might just cost you more than you'd ever want to pay.

Chapter Twenty-Nine

Less Jack of Plate. More Jack of Played. Like a goddamn
flute.

It takes us a bit of time to get into Jack's safe house. Not
physically —he has the key on him— but there are wards to
bypass and traps to flush out. It doesn't take a lot of magic
to connect a trip wire to a block of C4's detonator. Not
enough to alert the Tarrasque but enough to make a bloody
mess of any intruder. Jack is justifiably paranoid. A quick
entry could mean an even quicker exit. I don't have time to
go and pick up another body.

When we finally make it inside, I hate Jack even more
than I already do. We search the place from top to bottom,
but that doesn't take long. It is just an empty room, an old
shop or storehouse, its paint peeling with a toilet that stinks,
its cistern cracked, its flush unserviceable. There is a table
and a chair. A small microwave. A kettle.

And cages.

There are rows of cages stacked against the wall. Each individual. Each without comfort — no chairs, no space to move, really. Certainly, no bed. Anyone inside one of those metre-square spaces could stand — or, more likely, hunch up, their arms wrapped around their knees, longing to be elsewhere, back in the safe world they were stolen away from. Good God, I've done some bad things in my lives, things I regret deeply. But I've never hurt a child, never stolen an innocent from their parents to get what I needed. There are certain lines you never cross.

I also find one other item, draped over the back of the chair. It looks like Leatherface's Sunday best. I pick it up on the end of my sword at first, in case it is the flesh it looks like. When I get closer though, I can see it's rubber.

'Oh, oh! The clever bastard!' I shake my head. 'This is how he got about without using the portals or setting the alarms off.'

Isaac's here in a moment. He wants the answer, can't stand that kind of unresolved mystery any more than I can. 'How, lad?'

I hold it up. 'Rubber face. A good quality one too, professionally made, not just a fancy dress shop prop. Covered up his, shall we say, distinctive features without the need for magic.'

'So he never even needed to use a glamour. Bloody clever.'

'Well, quite. Remembering just how clever he is and how fucking dangerous, let's get him secured now, shall we?'

Isaac sets to marking and mapping out Enochian sigils, drawing up a containment field for the Jack of Plate. We tie his hands and feet, and I hold a sword point to his throat. It feels good to be the one pushing on his trachea for once.

He comes to slowly. Centuries of self-control and

training are clear. He doesn't start or panic. Nor does he try to feign continued unconsciousness. Just opens his eyes and takes everything in, studying, calculating. I don't doubt he'll look for an opportunity, a second's slip in our guard, where he can take advantage and be gone though. We'll make sure he doesn't get one.

'This…' I wave my hand at the minimalist décor, 'doesn't look like much for centuries of being a sellsword and kid snatcher. I always thought being a mercenary paid well. Does Maeve confiscate your pocket money?'

He swallows. 'What now, prettyman? I'm set before you like a trussed fowl. For many, it's victory or else a grave, but it seems you have both and neither.'

I press slightly harder against his throat. 'Perhaps you'll find out for yourself, Jack. Might well be that's a kindness compared to facing Maeve empty-handed, eh?'

He sneers, a revolting expression on his ruined face, then spits to the side — a classic distraction tactic. I keep my eyes fixed on him.

'Put him in, lad,' Isaac says, pushing back up to his feet, the symbol drawing completed.

'With pleasure.' I pull back the sword and swing my foot into his ribs, glorying in the crack that accompanies it. Winded, he doubles up in agony, and it is easy to push him over into the sigil marked area next to him.

The marks flare to life, and now uncertainty spreads across Jack's expression. This obviously isn't what he expected. 'What underhanded contrivance is this then?'

In my long existence, there were times where I had to stand in judgement. When I had to condemn those who failed to act as they should, who abused power and authority to take what was never theirs and charge the price on those who should never have borne that burden. I don't think there was ever a more satisfying time to serve in this role, though, than here against Half-Marred Jack.

'Jack of Plate, Half-Marred Jack, whatever name you want to go under, you evil bastard. You killed many, some who deserved it, some who didn't. I'd not hold you for that alone. But you stole *children*. You took them from their beds, from their families, from the safe innocence they should have enjoyed and delivered them into the twisted hands of a being who will torture and torment them if the thought crosses her mind or kill them out of hand just because. All just for a longer span of life. What do you answer to that?'

He doesn't beg or try to justify it. 'Just kill me, pretty-man. Bested am I and bereft. I've no more words. I'm ready to die.'

'That I'll give you. A last thing though, Jack.' I lean in so he can see the righteous fire in my expression. 'We know the Cagot secret. You'll not be coming back.'

Now the fear truly comes. Terror sparks across his face. Even the ruined half seems to come to life, to move under the pressure of the abject horror. He believed himself safe still, that at worst, we'd kill him and he'd come back as fae. Now he knows the truth. He draws in a breath to plead, to do all the begging he claimed he wouldn't do, but I've no interest in hearing it. I run him through, straight through the heart, and let him drop like the sack of shit he always was.

There is a human urge to grieve, to mark the passing of life. Maybe it's a social construct or a way to keep our place among our peers. We must demonstrate publicly our outrage at the lack of denouement, the way life doesn't provide clean beginnings, middles, and ends with satisfying conclusions. A lack of regret at the ending of another is seen as lost humanity in the person left standing. Fuck that.

I don't feel a jot of sadness. Only satisfaction that another bogeyman is dead. I wear that stain on my soul with pride. Tattoo it into my essence. The death of Half-Marred Jack is nothing but a cause for celebration.

Of course, what comes next isn't. Isaac carries on, positioning the skull of Almeric inside the runic circle directly above Jack's. He looks up at me.

'Are you ready, lad?' I can see the concern written across his face. He doesn't want me to have to do this. I don't either. There just isn't any other choice.

Still, I hesitate. 'Are we sure this will work?'

'As sure as it's possible to be. The wards should have severed any connection to the body. Jack's spirit should have been cut adrift, leaving his body free for you to purloin before it turns fae. If it doesn't work, we should get a second crack at it given Gwendolyne said it can take a couple days before the Cagot magic kicks in. Or you might just come back as fae immediately; we really don't know for sure, but we're going to have to get out of here quickly. Time is pressing.'

I check my watch. Eleven o'clock. Shit, this took longer than I realised. 'If it doesn't work, get him in the car and get the hell out of Dodge. We'll try again elsewhere. I don't want him or me and certainly not the both of us to be inside Lyon's boundaries come midnight.'

He shudders. 'Me neither. Let's get this show on the road.'

Pulling out one of Jack's incomprehensibly sharp throwing knives, I plunge it into my chest. Stabbing myself twice in the heart in two days is about as much fun as it sounds. Sadly, I suspect it is still more enjoyable than what is going to come next.

I come to and immediately wish I didn't. I know scarification has become a hip trend, and branding is a part of that, but I've been tortured with red-hot brands more than once. The moment of contact and pressure, as your nerves fire up under that extreme heat, as they scream their dying agonies, melting away under the pressed-in metal, is horrendous. My face feels like someone is pushing a hand-shaped brand continuously into it. It feels as if Maeve herself is forcing her hand deeper and deeper into my head, like she'll reach through and pluck my brain stem like a wilting rose at any moment. I'd rather spend several hours — hell, several days talking to the fucking Tarrasque, which should give you an idea just how horrendously distressing it is. I'm not making any excuses for Jack —he was a selfish, child-stealing prick— but his life was a constant misery. I would've topped myself long ago…although knowing what he had to look forward to after his death might have kept him from doing so.

I draw several shuddering breaths. Even if I was at full strength *talent*-wise, I doubt my reincarnation magic would have healed me. This is a full-strength fae "blessing". There probably isn't much any magic could do to unpick Maeve's gift.

Luckily, there is someone who can ease it, at least. Isaac's hand presses on my face and cools the fiery agonies of my ruined flesh. That coolness spreads, a numbing sensation. It can't heal me, can't undo the deal struck between this body's previous occupant and the Queen of the Winter Court, but Nithael's magic combined with Nanael's can act as a balm, reducing the blinding agony to a point where I can think again.

I blink, then try to ignore the nausea-inducing sensation that causes, what with my right eye feeling like it will tumble from its half-socket at any second. 'How do I look, 'Zac?'

'Like death warmed up, kid. And only lukewarm at that. Do you feel like a fae? Have you any *talent?*'

I examine myself internally for any power as I rub the rounded tops of my ears, checking for non-existent points. 'About enough to set a fart on fire?'

'Same as before then. Yep, you look human still lad, you can quit the ear massage.' He checks the time again and curses. 'Lad, we need to go. Now!'

I don't have a watch on, and I don't want to mess around grabbing my phone. I can take the hint. We still have to get out of Lyon.

We run outside. I am still adjusting to the strange burning feeling, and I stumble, my feet too big, the world too small, the pain too much. Isaac helps me into the car and then starts it up, pulling away and heading north, heading down the quay on the west side of the Rhône.

I close my eyes, meditating, trying to centre myself inside this half-ruined frame, so I feel rather than see us screech to a halt a few minutes later. Opening them, I realise we are on a bridge, four traffic lanes wide, though the sides are remarkably low. It is one of those non-fancy bridges, where it is little more than a road on concrete pillars that just happens to cross an unfeasibly large span of water. It doesn't need intricate cable supports or arcing geometric walls that soar up towards the sun. It just gets the job done, linking one side of the river to the other with no fuss. Behind us is the town centre of Lyon rising up into the distance. In front should be the greenery of the Park de la Tete d'Or, home of the Lyonnaise Botanic Gardens, a welcoming verdant sight in the city suburbs. Sadly, a considerably more hideous thing currently obscures it. The fucking Tarrasque.

I don't know if he has a natural *don't look here* spell on

him or if people unconsciously, instinctively avoid the Tarrasque, but we are the only people on the bridge with him. He sits there, sprawled across the entire thing, his tail still draping over the far edge. The individual sections of his shell have seaweed and scum caught in the edges like mildew in the grout of a shower. He has his usual self-satisfied grin on his gigantic cat-weasel face that makes you want to smash it in with a brick, if you could only find a brick large enough. I can already smell his breath, mainly because Isaac has leapt from the car and is now advancing on him like a man trying to train a disobedient dog, rolled-up newspaper in hand to bonk it on the nose.

'This was never part of the deal, Tarrasque,' he yells as he strides forward, tapping with furious indignation at his wristwatch. 'We've still got ten minutes yet!'

'Oh, I'm not stopping you, you Jew-sy morsel, you.' God, I fucking hate this arsehole. 'I just decided to do a little sunbathing.'

'It's the bloody middle of the night, man!' Isaac is practically apoplectic. I've never seen him so furious. This whole thing is deeply upsetting his sense of fair play.

'Moonbathing then.'

'Fine, you bloody arse.' Isaac turns around and starts heading back to the car. The Tarrasque chuckles, but the chuckle turns into a hawking cough. I can see what is coming and dive out of the side door just before the lump of acidic phlegm splashes across the front of the Super 5 and eats it down to its component molecules.

'Oops! I really should do something about that cough!' He grins at me, nodding in my direction. 'I believe that is the body of Half-Marred Jack, and he's still in Lyon. Tick-tock. Eight minutes to go!' His smugness is unbearable. We had enough time to make it comfortably out of Lyon, but he's just stitched us up. The fucking Tarrasque is going to win after all.

Isaac's eyes narrow. He looks at the gigantic fish-dragon and then back at me. He puts his arm round my shoulders and draws me towards the bridge railing.

'Do you trust me, lad?' Isaac looks as serious as I've ever seen him.

I am shocked he has to ask. 'Goes without saying, 'Zac!'

He nods. 'Good. West shore, okay?'

I start to say, 'What?' but only get the first syllable out. That transforms into a wailing, 'Whaaaaaaaaaaaa...' when Isaac pushes me over the edge of the bridge, sending me plunging towards the water below.

Luckily, I've fallen, both deliberately and not, from great heights into deep water many, many times. I transform my flailing into something more controlled, feet down and ankles crossed, as are my arms.

I breach, gasping for air and swim as hard as I can towards the west, away from the city, having clocked what Isaac meant. The problem is, the current wants to sweep me back under the bridge, back into Lyon itself. Luckily, this body isn't just some heart-attack victim I picked up from the morgue, their ticker having given out due to not knowing the meaning of cardio. This is the body of Half-Marred Jack, assassin and soldier of fortune. The muscles respond as well as any can. He is naturally fitter than I am, and I hold my own against the tide before scrambling out onto the bank, officially outside the city itself.

I look back and witness the most incredible sight. The Tarrasque is held squarely in the gigantic hand of Nitheal. The fish-dragon clearly hurled himself, enraged, off the edge of the bridge after me, no doubt planning to pull me back into Lyon or, failing that, at least eat me once, which would have undone our entire reason for coming here and set us right back to square one. Instead of plunging down into the water, though, the gigantic creature hangs in mid-air.

This is one of the rare moments where I am lucky Melusine ate my *talent*. I can see Nithael, sort of — a neon outline of a wing here, the crackling blue of fingers round the Tarrasque's neck there, but I'm not about to babble in tongues or start bleeding from my tear ducts. The Tarrasque isn't so lucky.

Green viscous fluid that I assume is his equivalent of blood streams down his face, sticking his misaligned whiskers to the hair of his cheeks. His mouth moves, though I can't hear what he is saying, but the look of sheer terror in his eyes is impressive.

What I can hear, for the first time ever, is Nithael. His voice isn't a booming projection nor is it the heavenly trumpets one might imagine. It is soft and clear and something I cannot even begin to describe. It would be like trying to describe purple to someone colour-blind. There are words; there is speech, but it is from outside of our dimension. Unless you experience it, I can't tell you what it is like, except for awesome in the sense of "making one feel incredibly awed".

'You would further break your word, serpent?' Nithael isn't shouting, but the words carry clearly to me. I suspect he wants me to hear. 'A deal you made, and you have done everything you can to dishonour your vow. Foul creature, know that in the aeons past, we would have struck you down for such an action. As it is, begone from our sight!'

And then something wonderful happens. Nithael tosses the Tarrasque over his shoulder like a crumpled piece of paper trick-shot into a rubbish bin so that he goes flying up, up, up and over the entire span of the bridge and goes sailing further still, over the edge and out of sight. I hear the splash; it sounds like an earthquake split off a section of the city that then slid into the enormous river. It surprises me when it doesn't displace so much water as to drown the neighbourhoods bordering the Rhône. Although thinking about it, Nithael would never let that happen, would never endanger innocent lives.

I get up, soaking wet, freezing cold, and ecstatically happy. We might not have killed the Tarrasque, which surely would have made future generations sing our praises for all eternity, but we made the slimy fucker take flying lessons. I limp my way up the bank and then drip along the pavement back towards the bridge, making sure I stay north of it until we definitely pass midnight.

Isaac meets back up with me. Nithael adds to his rapid ascension on my list of favourite beings by drying me instantaneously and warming me up in the process. My exposed right eyeball means the water went up behind it on my plunge, a wretched, sickeningly strange feeling. I'm greatly relieved to be dry after that.

The drive back to Castet is pretty much the reverse of the way it was to Lyon. I "borrow" a car, with plenty of assurances to Isaac that we'll make sure we handsomely reimburse its owner for it. He agrees as well to call the insurance to get his Tesla collected and repaired, although he has yet to invent a story to explain the damage to it. Before we leave the vicinity, he activates the runes he left by the other bodies we stashed, reducing them to ash and cinders. I can see it troubling him. This isn't like when I take a body and my reincarnation magic kicks in with nobody remembering there was a body to miss. There'll be investigations and distraught families with no remains left to help them reach closure. Still, it is a damn sight less distress than the families who would've lost kids would have felt.

The lost kids weigh on me heavily. Logically, I know the ones Jack delivered before our arrival weren't my fault, but it still torments me. It is only the mixture of constant agonising pain and emotional exhaustion that allows me to sleep on the way back, lost in troubled dreams while the brothers share the body and the driving.

I get them to stop off at my house in Toulouse. There is something I need to pick up for my trip to Faerie. Then we decide to consult with Gwendolyne via a scry, considering the Cagot rebirth is clearly well outside either of our knowledge wheels given the fact that I am not already a fae.

Grabbing the body, stealing it from Jack and booting off his spirit means I'm still human, albeit in inhuman amounts of pain thanks to Maeve's magic. The plan is I kill myself and pop back in a newly fae body. Thank the Good God we check with Gwen first.

'Oh, that would never work,' she exclaims breezily. 'Any Cagot who kills themselves don't come back.'

Isaac and I exchange an askance look. 'That might have been useful information to have beforehand,' I say.

Gwendolyne shrugs, not impressed by my emotional outpour. 'I can't guess everything you might or might not do. And I expected you not to act without speaking to me first. Did you never hear the story of the government that decided they were sick of the advice of experts?'

I am ready to tell her the story of the Cathar who put his foot so far up her ass he could wave with his toes through her mouth, but Isaac checks me with a restraining hand. 'Fine, so he can't kill himself. But if someone else does it, we're okay?'

'Oh yes!' She grins, and it is a smile that women have

shown many times over the span of human history to men, when cocksure chauvinists suddenly realised they needed their feminine counterparts more than they'd imagined. Female readiness to draw blood isn't driven by ego but nor is it limited by fear. Women are always prepared to get done what needs to be done. 'I'm more than happy to do the deed.'

I bet she is. I just bet she is.

Chapter Thirty

If the bastard whose body I'm wearing ran off to marry a mythological horned rabbit, would it become a Jack-elope?

Even after we arrive at Gwendolyne's, setting up what is needed isn't straightforward even for the combined mental and *talented* might of Isaac, Jakob, Nith, and Nan. My reincarnation magic is incredibly strong, and they are going to have to try to keep me in place, attached to a dead body for a period of time ranging from several hours to several days. Apparently, the time to come back as a fae varies significantly.

After getting asked nicely twice by Jakob and growled at repeatedly by Isaac, Gwendolyne and I leave them to it as they work on the floor of the living room, her sofas pushed higgledy-piggledy aside to make space so they can draw mind-melting dimensional magic glyphs onto the parquet. We already assured Gwendolyne we'd pay for any damages. She assured us she already knew damn bloody well that we would, thank you very much. It is better to leave them to do whatever needs to be done without our distracting them. I don't want to somehow end up nullifying my reincarnation or blowing a hole in the space-time continuum. Both would ruin my day somewhat.

Outside, it is that sort of crisp mountain morning where the sky is so radiantly blue, so absolutely clear of cloud or contrail that it seems inconceivable that my manhood is trying to climb back up inside my ribcage because of the cold. I sit down on a grassy bank. The village of Bielle is visible, snuggled up into the crook of two of the hills; snow caps the tops of the peaks like the clouds missing from the sky have cuddled the mountains instead. It is idyllic. That is so contrary to my inner state, it puts me even more out of sorts.

Gwendolyne flaps a hand at me, and I scoot over, leaving enough room on the tuffet for her to sink down next to me. She does so, only a tiny grunt revealing that she finds it harder than she lets on. Getting old is rubbish. Getting old for centuries on end is even worse.

'How are you holding up, boy?' She nudges my knee with hers as we both stare out over the pastures to the peaks beyond.

I run through a million flippant answers but dismiss them all. 'Honestly, Gwen? Terribly. I spent centuries dreaming of Suse coming back, waking up crying because for a moment I was holding her, and when I woke, I had to face it wasn't real. Now she has, and her betraying me has left me broken.' I laugh bitterly. 'More so than I already was. Even brokener. The brokenest. None of it seems to make sense. I'm still going, but that's mainly because I don't know what else to do.'

She sighs and rubs her knees. Whether to add warmth

or to take away the pain, I have no idea. 'Poor Cathar. It's never easy to feel lost.' I look at her sharply, but there is no mockery either in her tone or her face. Only a sympathy that hurts even more. 'You do know the story of Hansel and Gretel, at least, I hope?'

I nod. 'I didn't realise you knew any stories you hadn't made up yourself.'

She draws herself up. 'None of my stories are made up! Just because you've never heard them doesn't mean they've never been heard before.'

I wave my apologies. 'Fine, sorry. Yes, Gwen, I know the story of Hansel and Gretel.'

'Who was the monster in the story?'

'The witch,' I answer without thinking and then see by her wince, I gave the wrong answer.

'Was she? She took in two orphans and fed them up. Sure, she planned to eat them, but she was a monster. That was her nature. She laid her trap, and she reaped the rewards.'

It makes me think of Franc, of my foolish belief that our agreement would keep him in line. She taps my leg with the back of her hand. 'Concentrate! Who was the actual monster?'

I sit and think for a while, running the story through my head. Eventually, it clicks. 'The dad. He was the real monster.'

She nods sagely. 'Of course he was. His sole duty in the entire world was to take care of those children, and he abandoned them to their deaths. So, tell me, what did they do when they made it back home?'

I run it through again. It's been a while since I've studied my Grimm Tales. The last time was when Philip

Pullman brought out his retelling of them, which hewed closer to the originals. 'They forgave him?'

Again, a nod. 'Why?'

I shrug. 'Stockholm Syndrome?'

I get another leg-slap. 'That'd make sense if they forgave the witch instead of burning her up. No, that's not the reason they forgave him. Why did the father do what he did?'

I bite back the next flippant answer and consider the question instead. 'Because he was afraid.'

This gets me a pat on the thigh instead of a slap. I feel like the class dunce who finally got an answer right. 'Exactly. He was afraid. Afraid to fail them, to fail his wife. Afraid that they would starve and die, and he would have to watch. So, instead, he left them to their fate, where he could pretend it wasn't his fault. Where he didn't have to watch them wither away. So why did they forgive him?'

I know the answer now. 'Because they loved him.'

Another pat. 'Right. They loved their parents. They loved their father. They knew he'd acted foolishly, stupidly, that he had betrayed and failed them. And they forgave him.'

She makes a circular gesture with her hand, rotating it round and round. 'Love and fear. They drive so much of what we do by presence or absence. They make us do the right thing or drive us to hurt others to keep it at bay. How does it feel, being the Jack of Plate?'

'Agonising.' I don't need to hesitate for that one. 'Horrendous. Miserable. And that's with the angels mitigating some of the effects.'

'And yet he still clung on, living a miserable half-life, committing the most heinous of acts because he was afraid.

Whether of judgement or nothingness or simply the unknown, we'll never know because he's not here to ask, and good riddance. I'm not justifying his actions, not in the slightest. But he was consumed by fear, controlled by it, and he never knew love. Yes, he was a nasty piece of work from the start, but it was sheer, stark terror that drove him to the depths he went to.'

I consider it. 'I'm still glad he's dead.'

'Me too. But I'm also glad he's out of his misery even if it means you must carry it for a while. He was still one of mine, once, long ago.'

'So what's your point, Gwendolyne? That I should forgive Susane for what she did?'

She shakes her head. 'I'm not asking for that. Just understand where it came from, why she did what she did. Was it love? Fear? Both? And —' She hesitates, gnawing at her lip before continuing, 'If the chance arrives, help her. Save her. Even if you can't forgive her. Save my daughter from herself, Good Man.'

I don't say yes, but neither do I say no. I don't think she expects an answer though. She just leaves the request hanging in the air between us. A mother's last desperate hope, stood in the shadow of the gallows.

Chapter Thirty-One

ROME, 24 MAY 1514

There is a disturbance in the court behind us. Several priests murmur objections in the hall, saying a holy audience is already in session, but something quiets them, then the enormous arched gold-leafed doors behind us are pulled open, and three individuals enter.

The first is a high-ranking priest, though did he not wear the robes and trappings of his office, I would be hard pressed to identify him as such. His is not the pale northern skin of the two who accompany him. His shade is closer to mine, and I might have believed him from the Ottoman Empire itself at first glance. But as there are no official church positions there, I guess from his darker tone, he is from south of the Pyrenees, the states and kingdoms that I passed through on my travels southwards. They became a united Spain by the time of my return, officially at least.

With him is a youth, around fifteen if I were any judge. His bearing speaks of noble upbringing, as does his disdainful sneer. His trappings are extravagant and of the style of the French courts, themselves heavily influenced by

Venetian fashion. Haughtiness is an inheritance he wears with more ease and comfort than his heavyweight ermine cloak dramatically flung back off the one arm.

The third man is what I'm presenting myself to be. A mercenary. His hand rests upon his sword pommel, and his scarred face speaks of action seen, though there is a trace of nobility about him too. He dresses plainly in black, head to toe, with no cloak on him that might entangle his hand when it calls for his sword, and he stands with an easy readiness that suggests he can fight at a moment's notice. His whole bearing screams danger to any who cross his path.

Leo X raises an eyebrow. 'What is the meaning of this, Ximenes Cisneros?'

The priest hurries forward. 'My apologies, your lord, but my needs are dual. First, I came as we previewed to present young Charles Hapsburg, who will look to rule in your name and for your honour in the near future. Second' —he waves his hand at our assembled party— 'to intervene afore these blasphemous swine might further pollute your holy ears with their poisonous lies.'

This Cisneros speaks with the fervour and passion of a zealot, and I dislike him immediately. I've seen too many good men and women put to death by his like. The Pope resists rolling his eyes but only just. 'Advance then, Ximenes, and let's have a more private and less dramatic word on what concerns you.'

The priest scuttles up to the foot of the Pope's throne, and hurried exchanges begin between them. I sidle closer to Isaac. 'Any idea who this bastard is?' I hiss at him out the side of my mouth.

'Cardinal Cisneros of Spain, Torquemada's successor as Grand Inquisitor and tutor to the future Holy Roman Emperor, who is the brat he came in with, if I'm to judge.

Forced all the Muslims in Iberia to convert or leave and is supposedly itching to launch a new crusade against the Islamic world. This is not wonderful news,' he murmurs back to me *sotto voce*. I have a feeling that is an understatement.

I risk a look back at the boy who will one day rule a vast swathe of Europe. He lets his eyes roam disinterestedly around the room, utterly uninvested in the pomp and ceremony surrounding him. I guess he's seen it all his life, and it no longer makes much of an impression. The man who accompanies him though…

When I turned my head, he was already staring at me; I am sure of it, though he breaks off his gaze the moment I turn in his direction. Now he stares fixedly ahead, but I do not doubt he is entirely aware of my presence. I try to dismiss it as a natural reaction as I am the only other man presenting as of military bearing in here, but it makes me uneasy.

My attention gets pulled back to the throne, where the hasty whispered conversation draws to a close, though the Inquisitor stays close to the Pope's side, glaring at us as though his righteous fury might keep us back from whatever unholy ignominious act he thinks we are here to perform.

'It would seem,' Leo X says gently, 'that my Grand Inquisitor has declared you all as heretics.'

Isaac regains his tongue first. 'On what charges, Your Excellency?'

'On the charge of being proponents of the Bogomil tradition, now known more commonly as the Cathars.' The priest practically spits as he speaks, his hatred dripping off every word.

I feel the relief passing through my friends. 'Why, that is

the very reason we present ourselves before his Holiness today,' Susane speaks.

'I do not remember asking for your opinion, harlot.' The Inquisitor looks furious at her nerve, but Leo lays a hand gently on his arm.

'I have allowed their petition; we will hear them speak, Ximenes,' he breathes.

Susane draws herself up, pulling in breath as she does so. This is what she has been preparing herself for. 'Your Excellency, the most honourable Cardinal speaks the truth.' A gasp echoes round the room, and smug satisfaction settles on Cisneros' face. It disappears when she continues, 'But it is out of date, by many generations. My people, the Cagot, come from that most heinous heresy, a mark of shame and ignominy that haunts us still. We have suffered ostracism, outcast for generations, and rightly so,' she adds hastily as again the murmuring swelled, a tone of outrage carried in it. 'But we have paid long and hard for the sins of our fore-fathers. We are all good Christian folk, loyal to Mother Church even though we remain forbade to enter with the normal congregation. None of us deny the sins of our ancestors, but we call for *limpieza de sangre* and forgiveness and a fresh start for my people.'

It is an excellent speech — well put, simple but to the point, with just the right measure of deference added. Leo X nods thoughtfully while, for a moment, I think the Inquisitor might burst. Then I catch movement out of the corner of my eye and realise the soldier just signalled Cisneros. The cardinal hurries over to him for some whispered conversation before returning to the Pope's side. Leo witnessed this exchange with some curiosity and now raises the question that is certainly prominent in my mind.

'Who,' he asks in a carefully loaded tone, 'is the warrior you turn to for counsel, Ximenes?'

'Sir Marco di Vico, a nobleman and warrior assigned bodyguard to young Charles,' the Inquisitor answers. 'He is a man steeped in martial knowledge and from an illustrious history, tracing back to the De Montforts themselves.'

A distant offspring of that murderous bastard Simon De Montfort. No wonder I didn't like him as soon as I clapped eyes on him.

'And what,' Leo asks in vaguely bored tones, 'did the good knight suggest to you then?'

'He reminded me that the cleanliness of the blood is called to question. We have heard rumours of heresy, of witchcraft and demonic dealings among the Cagots. That they are friendly with the Israelites, mixing freely with them, and associate with devils and imps through dark conjurings. And also, I have been told that this man' —he points straight at me— 'is a practising Cathar.'

Well, blow me down with a feather. I did not see that one coming.

Chapter Thirty-Two

Ritual magic is ninety percent boredom mixed with ten percent hoping you don't accidentally summon a gizzard-swallowing demon.

There are thirteen marks on the ceiling. No, wait. Fourteen. I just decide that is the final count when one of them moves slightly, and I conclude it has to be a spider probably just about to get back to some important arachnid work after a mid-afternoon nap. So, thirteen.

I've been lying on my back in the circle, staring up for about an hour now. Isaac assured me they were fully ready for me, but as soon as I lay down, it was too late to get back up, the sigil having flared to life, and of course they found several "teething problems", as Isaac called them. Thus, me counting marks for an hour and trying to resist asking them what the fuck is going on while they meddle with forces beyond the ken of humanity. I am even more impressed that

I resist asking for a glass of whisky. Or a bottle. Or fuck it, an intravenous drip.

Eventually, Isaac looms over me, and my brain scrambles to decode his face with him being upside down. His tone is as calm and as patient as ever and soothes my worries and my need to move.

'We're ready, lad. In a moment, Gwendolyne is going to…'

'Slit his throat open and watch him bleed out like a stuck pig.'

'Yes, thanks, Gwen, that. You'll be gone but also still here. I…have no idea what it's going to be like. It could be very dull.'

'Might be very painful too.'

'Also a possibility but not massively helpful, Gwen.'

'Honesty is the best policy.'

I sigh and interrupt them before they can start bickering like an old married couple. 'Okay, thanks, both of you, I get it. Gwen's going to kill me. You're going to make me hang around. I'll come back as a fae. Honestly, that was always the plan, Isaac. You don't need to justify it or make me feel better. Sooner it's done, sooner I'm back. Gwen, do what needs to be done, will you?'

Leaning over the circle's edge, she slides the knife in like a pro, quick and sharp, slicing through the carotid artery neatly and swiftly. I manage a weak, reassuring wink for Isaac and then even the grey fades away.

I am back on the beach. Back on the endless grey sand, and I realise it is the same grey, the grey my vision goes each time I start to die. The last time I was here, the 'NOT YET' written in the sand from my first death was added to by one saying 'OPEN THE DOOR'. I can't see either of them. Perhaps I've come back in some other part of this infinite greyness. I got lost when turning right at the River Styx or something.

I look around in all directions. It is like I'm standing in the middle of the Sahara. I can see nothing except the same slight dunes rolling away in each direction. So I do the same thing I did when I found myself stuck in the middle of the Sahara in real life. I start walking. What else can I do?

I don't know how long I trudge across this dreary, unchanging, unreal landscape. It is neither easy nor difficult. I don't tire, at least physically. The walk just is. There is no other way to describe it. One foot goes in front of the other, steadying in the sand's slight give and then the other foot repeats the process, although I leave no prints behind me. I stick to a sole direction — or what I hope is a sole direction anyhow. With no sun or stars or defining points either near or far, I can't be sure I'm not just going in circles, although my natural sense of orientation is normally pretty good. Nothing changes. It is entirely possible I'm not moving at all. Maybe the sand is moving with me at the same pace, and I am not actually getting anywhere. It is a depressing thought, a grey idea to match the landscape.

I do not know how I get to a shack. There was no approach, no sight of it on the horizon, no acceleration to hurry me to an actual location. It seemed to spring out of nowhere. One moment I was on my endless trek through an infinite, unchanging landscape. The next I'm standing at a wooden door to a shack. It is more like a shed than a shack, ramshackle and tumbling, planks half-detached, yet somehow still standing. The door hangs at an angle, the hinges cracked, so the door hardly holds. The sections making up the bottom half have slid out, so that it scrapes the sand clear below as I pull it open.

I stagger inside and stop, unsteady on my feet. It feels

like I've walked for a lifetime, and my legs don't understand the idea of not being in motion anymore.

Inside it is…cosy. A small fire crackles in a hearth opposite, only missing a tabby cat curled up in front of it to look like it is straight from a child's picture book drawing. Two large armoire chairs face the fire at rakish angles, high-backed, viridian-green fabric run through with swirls of darker green, reminiscent of the whorls of the Fleur de Lys. It smells of pine and fresh baked bread, and I feel safer than I have been in many long years.

Behind me I hear the door scraping through the sand, and a voice, a warm baritone, says, 'You've made it at last then.'

I turn to see who it is, but it feels like vertigo, like my legs won't turn with me, like the air itself has turned to treacle. I turn but pitch forward and down into a swelling darkness.

I come to, greeted by thirteen dirty marks and a highly motivated spider spinning webs. It matches with the way the room is spinning. My mind still thinks I am upright, and I try to turn around, but my body…

Well, my body knows it is lying down. It is also very different from the body I left behind.

Some things are the same, of course. I still have two arms, two legs. The side of my face still feels like someone is holding an iron on it for shits and giggles. But there are definite differences. My teeth feel longer. So do my ears. And I can feel magic.

Oh, I cannot tell you how it feels to feel *talent* surging through my body again even if it is different, alien *talent* to what I had for the preceding centuries. It's difficult to explain *why* it feels different. I think the closest I can explain is the difference between being a fighter jet pilot and being a bird of prey. The former is incredible. Faster than the speed of sound. Devastatingly destructive and precise as a weapon of war. It's still a tool, however in sync the pilot might be with the plane, however much they feel it is an extension of themselves. It will never be the same as soaring on your own wings, as feeling the breeze ruffling your pinions as you turn and soar on currents no one else can see, that you can taste in the very air itself. I'm not just a magic user anymore. I am a creature made of magic, imbued down to the very core with *talent*. Melusine could never have eaten this frame's power, not without eating the flesh and bones itself. It feels wild and delightful, and I giggle at the sensation.

Suddenly, a hand is on my forehead, and the sensation diminishes, so that I gasp. I don't want it to dim; I want it to blaze and consume me. I buck, but the hand never moves free.

'Well, Cathar, I didn't expect you to be fae-struck.' There is a wry, mocking tone to her voice that pulls me up sharply, bringing me back under control better than anything else would have. No one enjoys getting the piss taken out of them by their mother-in-law.

I give her a two-finger salute, and she eases back her hand. The power returns slowly. I'm sure it would be like rushing rapids and sweep me away if she wasn't here, but she keeps it under control, letting me adjust to the differences there are compared to being human.

It is a strange step to take. I've been a man and a woman, even a child a couple of times, but I was always human in my lives before. Now I have to learn what it means to be other. Over eight hundred years, and there is always something new to learn. It is amazing how life never, ever gets dull.

I slowly regain my feet, feeling the giddiness licking at

my senses, trying to get me to surrender to the sensation. Luckily, I've always been a stubborn bastard. I refuse to cave to the pressure no matter how delighted I am to have magic, to have power truly available again. I force it down, determined to master it.

Isaac's face swims into view, and it is strange. I can see the powers, all of them: his and Jak's, and the brilliance of Nan and Nith as well, all separate, yet all tied and tangled together. I know I can reach in and separate the two entities, though making them four individuals again is beyond me. Still, there is an instinctive voice too, an inhuman one, that screams at me to run from the Bright Ones, that to touch them will be to burn and be gone.

'How are you feeling, lad?' I make myself concentrate on the lines of concern marking Isaac's face rather than the layers of reality behind it. Turning my head is confusing, the world sweeping up and down like a ship's cabin on a restless sea. Motes of otherworldliness dance behind almost everything, the weave of a world revealed. I catch sight of Gwendolyne and gasp.

She is still the old woman I know, still the mother of my wife. Behind her, though, I see her in her other form, in the one she'll take when she can finally lay the burden she's carried for so long down. It is like a shadow but made from the emerald of the grass' dance mid-breeze. If Nithael is a neon electricity carved across the ether, the power of pure thought imprinted on our world, then Gwendolyne's shadow is the earth itself imposing its heft onto reality. There is the power of life, the rebirth of death, the endless cycle all swirled up to cloak her shoulders. I see the greens and the dappling as the world moves behind her too, and it is hard not to fall to my knees. I try to speak, try to explain it, but she lays a finger on my lips.

'Shh now, Good Man,' she murmurs. 'Some things are not to be spoken of.'

Her light dims, and I grab control of my seeing, concentrating on the here and now rather than the then and there. I turn back to Isaac, who still waits for a reply, practically vibrating with worry. I try to put on a reassuring expression, although moving my facial muscles seems to take conscious effort to coordinate. They all seem to want to slope off in different directions — up, down, off behind the bike sheds for a sneaky fag. It is very confusing.

'I'm all right,' I lie reassuringly. That Isaac's brow only creases further means I probably didn't quite master controlling my expression to the degree I intended.

Gwen pats his arm. 'Don't worry, rabbi. He'll be good as gold in a couple of days. Just let him get his sea legs.'

'My fae legs,' I answer and giggle before I bite my tongue.

They both look at me quizzically. She doesn't look worried though, more exasperated. I guess she is used to leading Cagots through this intrinsically confusing rebirth process. Good God knows how odd it must seem to those who never knew what *talent* felt like. I've been wielding it for centuries, and it nearly overwhelmed me. The importance of Gwendolyne's role hits me hard. Without her, the Cagot making the change would go insane. Or more insane than fae already are, which is pretty fucking nuts to start with. Mind you, if they all feel like this *all the time*, I can understand why.

Gwen takes me by the arm gently and leads me to the sofa. She pushes me into a sitting position and swivels my legs up, lifting them onto the sofa. I let her guide me without objecting.

'He just needs to sleep a little, get acclimatised to his

new way of being. Once he does, he'll be right as rain. Or,' she adds, 'at least as right as he was before all this. I'm not sure he was rain-level right. Maybe a light misting drizzle.'

I open my mouth to deliver a suitably snarky riposte, but all that comes out is a gigantic yawn. I feel tired, which is weird because I also feel like I was asleep for half a year. Changing species takes it out of you more than changing bodies normally does, apparently. I chew on the yawn, trying to force it back to allow me to speak, but every time, it just comes out stronger.

Gwendolyne rests her hand on my cheek. 'Leave it now, Cathar. I'm sure you've got much to say, what with it being a day with a Y in it, but right now, you need to recuperate. Let it go. We'll all still be here in the morning. For now, boy, just let it go.'

I want to point out I am older than her while petulantly insisting it isn't even my bedtime and I totally can stay up and chat with the adults, but my brain has other ideas. It seems to give up on keeping my eyelids open, so despite my best efforts, they slide shut. I try to raise my hand to hold them open, but it slides under my head instead, making a knobbly, uncomfortable cushion that, nonetheless, carries me away into a deep and dreamless sleep.

Chapter Thirty-Three

Turn and fae-ce the strange. And what a strange face I have
to turn now.

I come to groggily, blinking at the unfamiliar surroundings.
The floor is a mess of chalk scribbles I find instantly reassuring — either someone let a particularly shit street art
chalk artist loose in here, or Isaac is around. I remember the
magic he worked. Then I remember the magic I have.

I sit bolt upright, checking myself internally to make
sure it is still there, then I hug myself tight to make sure it
doesn't escape. Sure enough, I have *talent* again. I feel
souped up and ready to go to war. Now I just have to get
myself prepped for my arrival at Oberon's court.

I get up and stagger through to the kitchen, where
Gwendolyne greets me with a plate stacked with vittles —
fried mushrooms and potatoes, tomatoes and toast, all sorts
of goodness, and the warmest smile she's given me since
Susane's death. We sit down and eat companionably. Then

she asks me what my plan is. When I tell her, the smile drops off her face. She finishes her meal in stony silence, then stomps off. She doesn't speak to me for the rest of the morning, which is fine because Isaac has precisely a thousand questions about what it's like to be a fae, about the resurrection process, and about my time spent in the grey sands outside life. Until we get into the details about what I'm planning in Faerie. At which point he goes silent for a bit before declaring he's heading off for a walk. Alone. Or, at least, alone as you can be when you have three other beings sharing your brain. I have no idea what it is about my utterly insane plans that keep upsetting people when I reveal them.

Gwendolyne storms up as I am making myself a sandwich at lunchtime, her face like thunder. 'Your plan's utterly insane!' Oh, so it *is* that part they get upset about.

I carry on layering cucumber on top of the hummus. Some combinations are too good to ignore even to explain mastermind plans. 'It may well be, but it's the only one I've got.'

'He'll kill you for sure! And if, by some miracle he doesn't, you'll be top of his shit list. You'll make the *King of the Summer Court* into an enemy.'

I shrug. 'That's a problem for future me. Future me will be a badass or an asshole. Either way, better he deals with it than I have to.'

Gwendolyne throws up her hands in exasperation, but at least she doesn't storm off. I am winning her round. Baby steps and all that.

In the afternoon, she helps me get to grip with my powers, to understand what I can and can't do, my limits and the differences to the power I had previously. It's easy for her to guide me considering how insanely gifted she is.

We run a pretence — I pretend not to notice she is a well-spring of *talent*, the likes of which I've rarely seen, and she pretends I'm not an absolute bloody loony with an utterly ridiculous plan. It works well for the both of us.

By evening, I feel I have it under grips. The main gist is simple. I can't impose my will on the world the way I did. But the world is more likely to listen to me than it did before; I just have to be persuasive and charming, and it'll do what I ask. Luckily, I am such a charming man. Just ask Gwen.

Either way, I can't afford any further delays. It is time to go. Astoundingly, Gwendolyne agrees with me.

'There's not much more I can provide you with in terms of training.' She scrubs a set of potatoes, ready to chip them up for a last meal in the human world before I head over. 'It's not like the sort of magic done here, where it's all study and form to channel the natural *talent*. You're only going to learn your fae abilities by doing, by being in situations where you need it. Like, I don't know, going and challenging Oberon on his home turf.'

'Oberon and on and on and on? Hey, does he come off a walkie talkie by saying Oberon out?' Having soaked some red lentils, I am now making them into patties. I'm sure Gwen would prefer a hefty piece of steak, but she is humouring me.

She rolls her eyes. 'That's what you took away from the point I just made? You're a dead man, Cathar.'

I sober slightly. 'I have been for eight hundred years. It's never seemed to slow me down yet.'

We eat a pleasant meal accompanied with a bottle of Irouléguy, a fruity little local Basque red wine. Conversation is slightly stilted, but then it's never been easy talking with Gwendolyne, and it's never been easy for Isaac to watch me head off on some idiotic adventure on my own. He's rejoined us, seeming to have calmed down as well after his walk. We all force ourselves to talk of other things, to pass our time in something approaching companionship, even if there is an edge of contrivance to the ebb and flow of the conversation. We all know it is only a moment's pause before I relaunch myself off into the madness that is my normal everyday existence.

When we finish, I go and get myself ready. I've no idea if I will be able to access my etheric storage on the other side; I discussed it with the other two, and the consensus was "probably not", so I go to attach a sheath and sword belt. Walking around armed in Faerie won't draw as many stares as it will in Toulouse. The cold steel might though…

Walking back to the others, I ask Gwendolyne about my reaction to iron and its alloys now that I'm in a fae body. 'Hey…so will being close to them make my throat swell up and break out in hives or anything?'

'Carrying your sword sheathed won't make you ill nor will pulling it for short periods of time. What it will do is mess with your magic once it's drawn. You won't be able to use any *talent*, but neither will whoever you face. Basically, if you pull it, you'll be in a straight clash of blades until it's done, though your *talent* will hold to it for a short while. More iron than that? Having it in proximity will leech your strength slowly. You'll find it hard to heal, almost impossible, and your magic will be practically non-existent.'

None of that is majorly disturbing. I don't expect to go over to Faerie and start kicking butts and taking names. Oberon doesn't strike me as stupid enough to give the Cagot the same level of *talent* as normal fae. Even if Maeve super-charged Half-Marred Jack, the fae on the other side have been using their magic for centuries, millennia even.

No, talking is going to be of far more use than *talent*. Other than that, I'll have to try my luck with my swordplay.

Gwen takes me out into her back garden. We pass a neatly tended herb garden, walking under the neck-tickling droops of a willow to a large pasture full of blossoming wildflowers, all pastel blues and violets arrayed above the green sea of stems. It is untended, but there is a pattern to the growth, as if nature wants to arrange itself in a pleasing manner for Gwendolyne. I guess there are advantages to being the Cagot queen.

I don't know what I expected — perhaps a menacing oblong of a monolith surrounded by screeching monkeys or a circle of menhirs dropped off by impressively moustached Gauls. Hell, even a wardrobe perhaps...although that would more likely lead through to the Winter Court. Instead, what I get is a mushroom ring about two metres in diameter, the toadstools almost impossible to pick out among the long grass.

'No wonder the fae can snare mortals who wander into their circles. I can hardly bloody see it!' I peer hard, making sure not to cross the boundary until we are ready.

Gwendolyne harrumphs. 'First, boy, I don't want to broadcast the presence of a faerie circle to all and sundry so subtle suits me very well. Second, I need something that can move easily with me, coaxed to regrow when I need to change my base of operations. A mushroom circle works perfectly well, thank you very much.'

I understand. Sticking around the same place for longer than a human lifespan is tricky, especially out in the countryside. Gwendolyne needs to move every few years to keep from people turning up at her door with pitchforks and blazing torches.

'So how do we do this? I get inside, click my heels

together three times, and say, "There's no place like home?" What gets me to Faerie?'

'Just get yourself in the circle. I'll handle the rest.'

I turn around, but Isaac lays his hand on my shoulder. Looking back, I'm shocked to see tears forming in the corners of his eyes. 'What's wrong, 'Zac?'

'Nothing, lad, just make sure you come back, okay?'

I grin. 'You said that last time, and I did, didn't I?'

He searches my face as though looking for something hidden just below the surface. 'Did you? Did you really, lad? Or are you still lost under the mountains alone?'

Damn. 'That's very profound, but I'm here, man. The only thing I lost was my *talent*. Now I'm back, baby!'

He smiles, the expression not even starting to cover the sadness. 'I'll be glad when you are, lad. As will I, dear boy. I'll do my best to take care of my somewhat sentimental brother. Still, get back safely. What he said. Paul...' He looks me right in the eye. 'You're about to do something monumentally stupid involving one of the ancient powers of the world. If it all goes tits up, turn around and bail.'

Gwendolyne nods in agreement. 'The portal on the other side will allow you back through if needs be. Normally you'd need Oberon to give you permission, but I've marked this body as allowed to travel back and forth. If you lose this one, it'll be a different story.'

'Isn't Oberon going to be pissed off at you? Helping me get across, giving me the option to get back? I don't want to get you in trouble.'

She grins. 'Bit late to be having thoughts like that, isn't it, Cathar? I think he'll be less than happy, but I'm counting on him being even less motivated to come over here, to the mortal lands, to berate me.'

'What about when you end up going over yourself?'

Gwendolyne sighs and shakes her head. 'I don't think I ever will, boy. The days of the Cagots are fading. There won't be many more who turn fae, I think. Once my duties are done here?' She shuffles towards the circle, inspecting the mushrooms, making sure none are trampled or broken. 'I've been alive for a long, long time and carried the aches and pains of this frame for most of it. I don't think I'm ready to start again in a new world, a new way. I'll call it a day, I think. So Oberon can spin on it.' She sticks her middle finger up at me while checking the last of the toadstools.

I can't help but admire Gwendolyne. I've always wished we were closer, that she liked me more. Perhaps because she doesn't. Perhaps because I've always known her value and wished she could see mine.

'Right then, enough dilly dallying,' Gwen says, straightening up and brushing down the creases of her dress. 'Time you were on your way, Good Man.'

I tilt my head in acknowledgement, tip Isaac a wink, and step into the circle. As I pass Gwendolyne, she murmurs, 'Remember, Paul. Love and fear. There's a way to be found from one to the other. There's a way to be found back again as well.' I'm not sure she's talking about me. But I'm also not sure she's not. Then she steps back.

The circle closes around me, my *talent* rising in sympathy to the walls of magic that snap into being around me. The toadstools seem to strain upwards, lifting themselves out of the soil, channelling nature's energy to enclose me. Gwendolyne raises her arms and her vibrant green force adds to the barrier, swirling around it, embedding into it. It adds a sense of movement so that the invisible walls seem to turn with the movement of the magic, slowly at first, then faster and faster until I feel like I am inside of a vortex, trapped in the eye of the storm while a hurricane rages around me. It is dizzying, my attention pulled in all directions at once, and it takes all my willpower to stay standing, terrified of what will happen if I buckle forward. Will I fall out of the circle? Where will I end up if I do? Still, the tornado of power twists and then, suddenly, the world twists with it.

It feels like my head is moving while my eyes stay in the same place. I can't understand how they aren't popping out, especially the one on the right, which is only just tenuously held by the melted wreckage Maeve left. My hands feel too large, my spine feels twisted slightly, like I've a crick in every single vertebra that needs cracking. I feel entirely peculiar. It is distinctly distracting.

So much so that it takes me a moment to realise I am no longer in a field. I am no longer in Castet. Hell, I am no longer on Earth. And I am not alone.

Chapter Thirty-Four

This isn't what most people mean when they say, 'Do you want to use mushrooms to go on a trip?'

I am in what, at first glance, looks like a vast hall. As my eyes adjust though, I realise the place wasn't built but was grown. The foliage is just so dense I mistook it at first for a solid wall forming an impenetrable barrier. But in fact, rows of poplars at least twenty feet in height and pressed tightly together form the walls. They all have an initially delicate camber, bending inwards, that increases exponentially towards the tip, where they meet their opposing number from the other side. Where they touch, they wind together like interlocking fingers of two hands.

An expansive table that would be at home in the mead halls of Valhalla runs down the middle of the room, lined with chairs and bedecked in a dazzling feast. Every form of fruit is there, and each looks like perfection. Salads gleam, tiny pomegranate seeds balancing on green leaves that shine more alluringly than diamonds. It is a riot of colour, every morsel the embodiment of the ideal of sustenance. I am glad I had a big feed before leaving, but even with a full stomach, I am drooling over the spread. I don't know if the rules of not eating faerie food apply when you are actually fae, but I have every intention of making it home again. I best not take the risk.

Sitting around the table are all the faerie creatures I've ever come across and a few more besides. Bright-winged pixies dart around the heads of dark squat bogles, who occasionally flap their hands in annoyance. Fae lords sit draped in floaty, almost transparent gowns; thin white gold coronets pull back cascading hair to reveal pointed ear tips. I think I spot one or two who carry some humanity still in among the impossible faultlessness of the others. I wonder if they are former Cagots or else perhaps mixed-heritage, half-fae and half-human from the time when the worlds were closer together. I even spot a Nain Rouge and wonder if it is the one I had my run-in with. As he can meet my eye without cringing, I have to guess not. Plus, I suddenly realise, given the Nain Rouge I know's propensity to move between our world and Faerie, his loyalty probably lies sworn to Winter. Banshees and brownies, dogkin and drakin — they are all gathered, all absorbed in the feasting and festivities.

At the head, his eyes fixed on me, unmoving and expressionless sits the Lord of the Summer Court. Straight-backed and stony-faced, he perches on a throne woven of thorns and brambles reminiscent of the bare-bones of a sculpture, the wire form before the clay gets added to make it whole. He must be at least eight feet tall, and his antlers look as tall again, thin and elegantly carved and doubtless razor sharp, almost brushing the vaulted ceiling. His face carries fae and animal mixed, hunter and hunted, civilisation and savagery, and his unarguable ancient nature is wrapped around him tighter than the brown felt cloak, with snatches of fur visible underneath. The raucous din around him doesn't make his eyes flicker, doesn't make him move a muscle. Nothing draws him in except my presence.

Slowly, the rest of the assembled menagerie realises something has changed. The hubbub stills, quiets. Eyes swivel, first to regard their lord, then to follow his gaze to me. Little by little, all movement stops, all noise ceases, and I am the subject of the intense inspection of half of the ruling class of Faerie itself, a collective with the *talent* to swat me where I stand and cease my existence before it even begins. I swallow loudly. Maybe this plan is utterly insane after all. Still, in for a penny, in for a pound.

'Don't let me interrupt you. Enjoy yourselves.' I wave magnanimously at the groupings around the long table. 'Word reached me there was a party kicking off. I'm always down to rave it up. When's the DJ arriving?'

The creatures are agog. I doubt they ever had a Cagot delivery who gave them lip before. Plus, I'm not the usual dropped off package.

A voice speaks that rumbles like the far-off thunder of an unsettled summer's day. The pressure in the room increases similarly, as it would in the face of that gathering storm. I don't think I'll get any sudden rain to break the tension either.

'What is this that comes to our court?' The depth of the timbre means the words seem to vibrate inside my skull. I mean, I don't see his lips move, so perhaps they do just that. 'A gift from Gwendolyne?'

Finally he moves, leaning forward, and I think it is only centuries of practising being the most pig-headed human I can be that keeps me from bending backwards as waves of power roll off him, pushing against me, threatening to subsume me below their ineffable force. Still, I will not bend. I will not bow. Not to kings or gods or fae. Not today.

He snuffles, a half-sniff, half-snort, his widespread nostrils flaring as he tastes my scent. 'Then how are you marked by the stench of Winter? You smell of decay and death and Maeve's dark workings. And of something else as well. You are of us and yet are not.' His eyes narrow, piercing in his expression. 'What are you, little fae-not-fae?'

I know a cue when I see one. 'Good day to you, Lord Oberon. You're right; I'm not fae, not really. I, er, "borrowed" this body from an agent of your rival, one she stole from you long ago. I seek permission to cross your lands. I seek another one who was once yours but who left your service, along with a Cagot fae who I believe you never even knew of.'

He muses on what I said. It might seem like I am muddying the waters by how I spoke, but fae love riddles. When you must tell the truth, obscuring it as much as possible becomes the game of choice.

'Well,' he replies after a short period of contemplation. 'I can imagine I know who the first is for I keep track of those who cling to the cold even before the leaves start to fall. The second is clear and well known to us, though absent for some small time prior. The third...' A rumble forms in his throat, like the vibration of a rapidly approaching train felt through the tracks you are tied to. 'I would be most keen to meet.'

Perfect. 'Then allow me permission, lord, to go hunting.

I'll find him, then introduce you. You can ask him all your questions. My pleasure to serve.'

The King of Summer stares at me, then he starts to chuckle. It is a sound like a swarm of wasps deep down in a tunnel, heading straight towards the light where I'm standing, and it is precisely as ominous as that sounds. 'Allow a creature of Winter to walk through my forest? Allow a fae-thief to wander without reproach among my meadows? No, I think there are long talks and torments to come for you before then, brave little burglar.'

I sigh. Damn it, it all seemed to be going so well. Fine. Plan B it is. I hold up my left hand clenched in a fist while I rip open my jacket with my right and let them clearly see what I am wearing underneath.

I feel as much as see his eyes track over me, although I also watch his brow knit together in confusion. Initially. Then he hisses, and it carries the sound of a land cracking before an endless sun that scorches away all moisture and life forevermore. 'Iron. You dare bring iron to our lands? Strapping that to your body will not do you any good. We shall peel it from you at a distance right before we do the same to your skin, insolent whelp.'

I grin, adrenaline pumping hard in the face of threatening the most powerful creature I've ever stood before. It is good to be alive sometimes. Now I just have to stay that way. 'The iron isn't strapped to my body, Lord Oberon. It's strapped to several packets of explosives, all of which are attached to this.' I open my clenched fist enough for them to see the detonator I'm holding in my left hand, its button depressed in my grip. 'This is what we call a dead man's switch.'

The Lord of the Wild Hunt grips the arms of his throne and pushes himself to his feet. I underestimated him at eight feet. He is at least ten, and the ceiling branches part around his antlers, allowing them to pass as he towers above me, an undeniable force of nature.

His voice rumbles again in my brain. 'Not yet, it isn't, but soon enough.'

Eep.

Chapter Thirty-Five

ROME, 24 MAY 1514

Being accused of heresy by the Grand Inquisitor himself in the Pope's palatial halls is not somewhere anyone wishes to find themselves. Yet, somehow, it is exactly where I am.

The charges are entirely unjust. I have not practised the Cathar creed in over two hundred years. My belief in any god has withered. Still, I do not think explaining I am a three-hundred-year-old atheist will get me off the hook. Not here.

Leo X once more arches an eyebrow. 'Serious charges that need answering, undoubtedly.'

I spring to my feet. '*Hospitium.* I claim the right to *hospitium.*'

'Is this a sleeping quarter? The only bed you'll find is the rack,' Cisneros sneers.

'That's our modern understanding of it, but the lad is right,' Isaac says, stroking his chin. 'While now we talk about beds added on to monasteries for pilgrims, the origin of the term is the right of the guest to be protected by his host. The Church invited us here, to make our case for the pardoning of the Cagots. To have this sprung upon us is… unseemly, Your Holiness.' He steps back and murmurs, 'Nicely played, lad,' as he passes me.

Leo X claps his hands in delight. 'A scholar and a sell-sword! Delightful!' His gaze lingers once more upon me.

'Nonsense!' the Grand Inquisitor cries, fire and brimstone burning in his righteous expression. 'Does not 2 John, 1:10 state: "If they come unto you and bring not this doctrine, receive him not into your house"? A heretic cannot claim the right of guests.'

This is turning into a disaster. Theological debates aside, the Cagots' case is unwinnable now. The whole court proceeding has turned from arguing their innocence, to me having to defend my own. And I know the look in the Inquisitor's eyes. He'll settle for nothing less than my blood. I suspect Leo X is too much the consummate politician to truly upset his leading firebrand supporter. My only hope now is to get Susane and Isaac out without revealing ourselves.

'A moment, please, Your Excellence, to speak to my compatriots?' I appeal directly to Leo X himself.

He waves his hand graciously. 'Granted.'

I huddle with Susane and Isaac. 'This will not end well. The appeal is a failure. You two need to leave.'

'What about you then, Paul?' Fear battles against her determination to see me safe as well.

'Don't worry about me, milady. I can take their ministrations however rude they be. Listen, follow my lead. Isaac, get her out of here safe and on the road back to Occitanie. The Cagots are going to need to go into hiding for a while, I suspect, until this righteous prick forgets his judgemental anger or at least until a different righteous prick with a different agenda takes his place. Get the message to Gwen-dolyne and get gone.'

'What about you?' she asks again plaintively.

'If they know some of my story and try to follow, I'll head up into Bavaria and onward from there. I'll be back in some few years, and on my return, I'll come searching you out and call in that favour.'

She seems almost breathless. 'Which would be what, Good Man?'

I smile my most hopefully charming smile even though Isaac told me it looks like I have ill humours trapped in my bowels when I practised it on him. 'Why, some time spent in your presence. A courting, true and official.'

I watch her struggle, but the smile wins out. 'My mother will be furious, but I think she'll agree.' Her seriousness comes back as quick as it went. 'Take care of yourself.'

'I shall.' I clap hands with Isaac and turn back.

'Who shall stand in accusation against me for heresy then?' I raise my voice, allowing it to carry to all assembled in the vast space. If theatre they want, it is what they shall have.

The strange knight, di Vico, steps forward. 'I shall.' I don't know if he is the origin of the idea or simply playing a pre-assigned role, but he looks eager to perform his part.

'I shall witness,' the youth adds, his voice tremulous with the change from child to man. I suspect I will not like him in either condition.

'And I shall prosecute!' the Grand Inquisitor crows, practically rubbing his hands with glee.

'Acknowledged,' Leo X says, a sadness in his voice that has more to do with my physical form than any spiritual concerns unless I've missed my guess.

Chapter Thirty-Six

FAERIE, 3 MAY, PRESENT DAY

Threatening the Lord of the Wild Hunt with an IED is a strong new entry on the list of 'Things I never imagined I'd have to do and hope I never have to do again'.

Oberon steps forward. There is something bizarre about his gait. It takes me a moment to realise his legs are back jointed like a goat's, something rarely seen in a biped. I wag the control at him. 'Ah, ah. Let me explain what this does first. Do you know what explosives are?'

He chuckles again but with less certainty this time. As I suspected, he is less confident about our world than he wants to let on. 'Of course. I've seen the cannons and the catapults, little thing. Your small iron will do me no damage.'

I match him laugh for laugh but mine carries both disbelief in his ignorance and surety in my position. 'You're out of date, Oberon. We've been somewhat obsessed over the last few decades about making everything smaller.

Smaller equals better. I know' —I gesture at his hulking form— 'that doesn't quite match with your world image, but that's how we've gone. Smaller, stronger, better. Oh, and deadlier. Definitely deadlier.'

I pull my jacket back again to let them see the small packages of plastic explosives. 'These little things? If I trigger them, everything in this room, *everyone* in this room gets ripped to shreds in the resultant explosion. The force will obliterate anything in its path for, ooh, about a fifty-metre radius.'

I feel him taste my words, my scent, undoubtedly searching for a mistruth, but I am being as fae-like as he is. Honesty is the best policy, especially when facing unfathomable powers. I sense him measuring the distance between us, working out how quickly he can back up. 'Wait, that's not even the best part of it.' I am grinning like a maniac now. Threatening a practical god is fun. Go big or go home. 'The iron you can detect? Steel ball bearings. I've got them in pouches covering the explosives. If I go boom, they're going to spray in every direction, a lot further than fifty metres. They're going to chew through wood, stone...' I give him a cheeky wink, nodding at his antlers. 'Bone.'

The room darkens. Where the roof parted to allow Oberon to stand, I saw blue sky through the gap. Now it is a swirling maelstrom, a storm of epic proportions. I don't doubt it can strike me down with a carefully targeted lightning bolt if the Lord of the Summer Court calls my bluff. Of course, I'm not bluffing. I am confident I'll come back even here. My reincarnation magic will probably latch onto one of their shredded bodies and rebuild it for me. It'll be a damn sight more comfortable than wearing Jack's marred face. I'm not going to kill them all just for that though, and I'm not keen to reveal the ace in my sleeve to Oberon. If we do all walk away from here alive, I will never be his favourite person. Hopefully, if he watches me die, he'll forget all about me again. Even more so if he kills me personally.

Of course, he wants to kill me right now. 'Just be aware, Oberon. If I let go of this trigger, we all go kablow. Kill me, you'll kill a good part of your court, and I don't think it'll leave you in an excellent state either.' I'm not foolish enough to believe I can kill the Lord of Summer that easily. 'Is it worth decimating your court and yourself just to stop me from going and hunting down a couple of fae renegades?'

'Disarm it.' His words carry down into my very bones and soak them in the demand. I know that for any of his court or for any normal Cagot convert, they'd have no choice but to obey. It is damn hard for me to resist, and there is only one reason I can.

'Sadly for you, this body doesn't belong to Summer. I'm as cold as ice.' I gesture sharply forward with the trigger, and the court falls back with a gasp that is immensely satisfying. Only Oberon holds his ground. 'Try me.'

We stay there like that for a minute, the king of the seelie, ruler of an entire people made of magic, versus myself, a washed-up has-been *talent*-wise still living it up off my one simple trick of not being very good at dying. The tension hangs between us, so taut you can peg washing on it to dry or get Dick Grayson to tightrope walk it. It builds, and that image of a storm is still omnipresent, this one amassing out at sea, envious eyes on dry land, squalling up a tsunami to drown out all who dare to stand against the air and water.

Then it breaks. Oberon smiles, terrible and bright, and it terrifies me far more than his brooding did even when I knew I was facing down a being who can snuff me out with a thought. He gives me the slightest nod and then waves to the doorway at the far end of the hall.

'Go, then, not-fae. You are free to hunt your two runaways. Me and mine will not halt or hinder you in any fashion.' It isn't couched as a promise, but it carries as much weight. Oberon said it. He'll not go back on it. Of course, though, he isn't finished. 'But be aware. Your little turtle-doves don't flutter their wings in my domain. They are not hiding anywhere where Summer holds dominion.'

Good God damn it. I hoped Oberon was sheltering them, and I would be able to intimidate him into bringing them to me. Susane would have seen the errors of her ways, confessing her crimes, and I would give my apparent son a spanking till I got the sceptre back. Not that I believe in corporal punishment for kids, but as he is a grownup and a thieving arsehole to boot, I'd have made an exception. But nope, that obviously would have been too easy. Instead, I have to go search...

'Sorry, where else could they be then?'

Oberon's smile isn't getting any more pleasant. If anything, it is becoming more unnerving. 'There's Winter's Court, of course. Though I don't think Maeve will be delighted to welcome you while wearing the face of her preferred envoy on Earth.' More of his teeth show, gleaming. 'You've managed to upset both Summer and Winter and are now in the Endless Lands. That is...very amusing.'

I fight down the panic threatening to overwhelm me. It is the prey instinct — not a common reaction in modern humans, but on some primordial level, down in my genome, some ancestral part recognises that we've always been quarry when the Fair Folk go hunting. Outwardly, I keep my cool even as sweat starts to drip down the back of my neck.

'Anywhere else they might be?' I am pushing it, but I've

come this far already. Might as well try to wring every drop of information out of this encounter before I get on my way.

'Well, between here and Winter is the Wilds. Land that belongs to neither one nor the other. Nothing in there owes fealty to either of us, and any that wander there do so at their own risk. Lands where all are fair game — for Maeve to seek amusement or for my hunts. They *could* be there, I suppose.'

The smile never leaves his face. It is uncanny, like he will never wear another expression or perhaps that he will fade away, leaving only his Cheshire smile hanging in mid-air. Instead, he stays motionless, his hand pointing towards the doorway, his eyes burning holes in my being.

I back up slowly until I touch the wall, feeling the rough bark press into my spine. I know dryads can be a potential threat, seeing as how the walls are living wood and they live in the trees, but I suspect they'll keep their distance at Oberon's insistence, if for no other reason. That being said, I don't put enough trust in his word to take my eyes off the fae king or his assembled court. I back up slowly, step by agonising step, expecting them to spring at me at any moment or for Oberon to decide the distance from him is sufficient enough to risk launching some of his minions at me.

The attack never comes. They all just sit and watch me with wide eerie eyes, and Oberon never stops smiling, never stops watching until I lose sight of him as I back fully out of the natural hall. The creepy bastard.

Once I make it outside without the hunting horn being sounded or a boggart trying to tear my face off, I relax but only slightly. Oberon gave me his word, near as damn it, but that doesn't mean he can't work a way around it. I bet he can come up with lots of ways of causing me intense misery without halting or hindering me. More likely, he'll wait until I pick up Susane and the other fae. The promise only extends as far as the hunt. There was no talk of my return with them after. I've gained a grace period, time to find them without Summer breathing down my neck. Afterwards, all bets are off.

Still, I'm safe for now. Or as safe as it's ever possible to be in Faerie when you've thwarted both its god-like rulers. I disarm the dead man's switch but keep it to hand. The risk of blowing myself up is too high to keep it constantly armed, but I'll not discard it entirely. I'm not that trusting of Oberon's word. Not that much of a fool.

I realise two things in quick succession. The first is that I should have asked for directions. The second is I don't need them. It's weird and sort of like how I imagine birds must feel, reading the magnetic lines of the Earth. I can feel the direction of Winter, an icy current pulling my feet in that direction, as though they know I have no right to be here in Summer and that path is home for this body. The way I see it, the Wilds wouldn't be anywhere but between the two kingdoms, acting as a buffer. So I let my feet lead the way, carrying me out of the eternal warmth and towards where the leaves turn blood-red on their way to die.

Chapter Thirty-Seven

FAERIE, DATE UNKNOWN, PRESENT DAY

Sadly, I suspect the Wilds aren't named after Oscar, who was full of social commentary and acidic, biting wit. More actual acid and biting.

I don't know how long I walk. Time feels elastic. There are cycles, sure. Days and nights come one after the other. But sometimes it feels like a year between my wary dozes under the limbs of a tree, my *talent* having spread wide into the ground to turn every grass blade into a warning system. Other times, it seems I only take a few steps before the sky darkens and I need to find a point of shelter somewhere I can defend. The day is dangerous in Faerie. The night is deadly. If I didn't have this compass tug of Winter growing stronger, I'd think Oberon tricked me, and I've not moved at all. I ration out the food in my etheric storage. There's no telling how long the stocks I put in there will need to last. I'm just grateful I can actually access it. The Good God knows what I'd have done otherwise. Starve, probably.

I feel the moment I leave his domain. I can see it too. A certain weight lifts off my frozen heart, and the blossoms and blooms grow faded. Things are dead here or dying or in the process of springing to life again. Tumbled branches that snapped from decay or damage obscure the path, and the air carries a chill that might not be the promise of Winter yet but which says it is not far away. Autumn and Spring chase one another's tails here, wrestling for dominance.

It is a dark time. I was already thrown from even a dream of a circadian rhythm by Summer's strange, constantly changing pattern. Now, I don't dare sleep properly. There is little life out here, but that just means I am even more of a tempting target for the weird few there are. Eyes gleam in the darkness and stalk along my path. I feel them more when they aren't seen. They hunt and harry me, only the presence of steel keeping them from open attack. But I've been treated as prey often enough to recognise it. I am an alien in a harsh and hungry landscape that will swallow me whole if I let it. After a few — days? It feels like days, but I can't be sure of how much time has passed. Anyhow, after an uncertain period without properly sleeping, I start feeling like Ogami Itto, the ronin samurai from *Lone Wolf and Cub*, who never sleeps but listens for the ninjas who never make a sound. I can't help thinking of the movie version, played by Tomisaburo Wakayama, who just progressively looks more and more insane from sleep deprivation as the films go on, walking the path of vengeance, pushing the baby cart of his son, killing everything he meets.

Of course, I'm not just wandering aimlessly nor was I during my days in Summer. I've been learning my new *talent*, testing it, working out what it can and can't do. Now as I walk, I attune myself to this barren land and listen to what it tells me. I walk towards Winter but don't allow myself to get too close, and slowly, the Wilds accept me. I am in a body that was born to belong to Summer, then remade by Winter's kiss, but I am of neither, just taking the shell for a ride. It is easier for me to sever my physical connections born of allegiances I never made to both Courts and connect myself to the Wilds.

It is a form of magic I understand, having walked my wards into the pathways of Toulouse over hundreds of years. I don't have that sort of time, but I can make a connection in footsteps, and I take advantage of that. Soon, I can sense much of what is out here — the monstrous shapes that lurk, obvious and hungry, and the hidden dangers that are unseen but just as ready to eat. It isn't long before I get a general feel for a direction to head in to find my wife and son. It isn't a radar exactly, pinging other fae out in the Wilds, but more a sense of invaders, foreigners, unknown bodies in the ecosystem that should have ended up swallowed whole but somehow haven't been.

By the time I see the cave, my confidence has grown. Now the things that go bump in the dark reaches never even think to bother me, giving me the equivalent of a nod of acknowledgement before seeking easier prey. My feet pick their own way through the pathless blasted forest without me needing to guide them, and I just listen to the way the Wilds tell me to go.

A fire crackles in the cave mouth, making shadows leap and dance, the orange glow so unfamiliar after the half-gloam the world seems stuck in that it is almost frightening. I wonder if it fulfils that primal role of keeping the darkness and the monsters it holds away or if it draws them in like it draws me, a dancing bright-petaled flower that my glacial body abhors by instinct but my mind misses and welcomes.

I sneak through the shadows silently, my feet always just missing crackly twigs, or else the land moves them out of my way. Now I am the silent, deadly hunting ninja. I can see a shape tending to the fire, feeding kindling in, though with them being behind the flames, I can't tell if it is Susane or the fae who claims to be my son or someone else entirely. Edging around the circle of light cast by the bonfire, I press myself against the hillside itself, far enough down to be obscured entirely in darkness, and wait.

It pays off. As I watch, the person comes to the mouth of the cave, and I can see it is Susane staring out into the distance. I have to bite my lip to stop myself from gasping and giving myself away. She looks terrible, gaunt and haunted, her eyes sunk back into that now-perfect fae face. That isn't the worst of it though. That honour goes to the bruises.

She has a black eye on the side facing me, a mix of purpled greens like poison beneath the skin. Though more like it is in the mind of the bastard who put it there. Mottled patches around her neck are too close in shape to be anything other than fingerprints, and she absent-mindedly worries at similar patterns covering her biceps and forearms. Looks like my instinctive judgement of that shitheel was entirely right.

She hugs herself tight, and I'll bet that is the only kind human contact she's had since leaving us. I haven't forgiven her for her betrayal, but Good God damn it, it looks like she's paid for it — *hard*.

After a few moments, she turns and heads back into the cave, and I creep after her. I wonder if I have better odds of talking her round now, or if she will still be as equally defensive of our son even after the way he's treated her. I hate him for that, for his contrived foppishness that he uses to hide this cruelty. The Wilds are more honest. They will tear you apart, but they won't hide behind quaint mannerisms. Their savagery is clear for all to see, while he keeps his beneath a veneer of charm and swagger. I don't much care if he is my son anymore. He is nothing but a bastard.

I round the corner and peer in. It isn't a large cave. The rear wall is probably only ten metres back, a flat slate-like surface covered in spiderweb cracks and pock marks. Most look like they've been there a long time, but it is hard to tell from this distance. A hefty rock seems to lean against it, like one of the menhirs I imagined for Gwen's faerie ring — a moment that seems like a lifetime ago.

There are also some basic supplies in the cave, including tins and a tin opener, some cooking utensils, and several oversized plastic bottles of water. Susane is now hunched up against the back wall, her head on her knees, her arms wrapped around them. She sobs quietly. What I don't hear or see, though, is my apparent son, who I dearly want a parental word with.

I slink forward, still pressed against the wall, slipping closer, and hiss, 'Suse!' to alert her to my presence. I haven't forgotten the power she hit me with in Melusine's chambers, and I don't want her to lash out in surprise if I get too close.

Her head comes up like a shot, and a flash of emotions flit across her face. Surprise, shame, hope, fear. Fear. I can hear her mother's voice in my ear. It breaks my heart.

'Paul, get out of here. Quickly! Now!' Her voice trembles, but I can hear the urgency in her urging. She isn't faking it. She is terrified for me now.

I advance cautiously, my eyes peeled for traps. 'Sure, Suse. I just need the sceptre, and we can go.'

She shakes her head disbelievingly. 'It's not here. He's got it, and you don't want to be here when he gets back.'

For a moment, I feel like Jack after climbing the beanstalk, talking to the giant's wife. I wonder if she'll get me to hide inside a wardrobe I can't see to keep him from grinding my bones to make his bread. Then I think that any creature, however large, however powerful, however *talented* who treats a woman the way he's been treating Susane is so small of spirit as to be insignificant. I'll not hide from the bastard.

I move farther forward. My priorities have changed. 'Come on then, Suse; let's be gone together. I can come back and find this scumbag and the sceptre later.' Right now, I just want to get her away from him regardless of what she did to me.

She shakes her head violently, desperately. 'He'll find us, Paul. He'll find us, and he'll bring us back. And…' She raises her eyes, seeking for understanding, for comprehension how such a strong-willed woman full of life could get crushed down to ruination, reduced to the fragment of herself that sits before me. 'And he's still our son, Paul. He's still our child. I can still save him.'

A mother's love is a powerful thing and can be turned to terrible desolation. 'Suse, you can't save anyone if you aren't safe yourself first. Let's get you out of here. We can worry about the rest of it later.'

I stretch a hand out to help her up. She looks up at me, torn, confused, lost in uncertainty. Then slowly, she raises a trembling hand towards mine.

Chapter Thirty-Eight

A prosecution by the Grand Inquisitor himself was certainly not a part of our original plan when we discussed what might transpire here in Rome. Still, I can handle what they throw at me. Protecting the others is my primary concern now.

'As a good and Christian man,' I say, stepping forward, ensuring all eyes turn towards me, 'I shall of course submit myself to the inquisiton of the courts right here in Rome. However, I ask you to extend mercy to my fellow travellers. This man' —I indicate Isaac carelessly as if I hardly know him— 'is nought but a paid scholar, hired for instructional purposes. And the lady' —I make a similarly lacklustre gesture, as though it matters little to me— 'came to seek the Church's blessing. Hardly the act of a witch.' I raise my hands before the raised objection. 'If there is heresy in the Cagots, then surely it must be rooted out. But under both *hospitium* and the laws themselves, allow her to return to her people, to report the accusations against them. Surely, the Spanish Inquisition will not struggle to find them afterwards?' I speak directly to Cisneros. 'Indeed, they are more easily located for you, being so much closer to home.'

I can see his thought process. He's already interrupted the Pope and turned the appeal into this charade. I doubt he's missed the Pope's displeasure about the whole affair, although that never turns one so full of zealotry from their actions. This, though, is a win for him. He can be both magnanimous to a group he considers easy to gather up again later while holding on to the officially accused heretic here and now. Doubtless, he hopes my testimony will provide the catalyst for further charges against the Cagots themselves.

'It is acceptable,' he states, a pompous air about him. 'If it so pleases, Your Holiness, I will take this foul bugger down to the Inquisition chambers, but his travelling companions might go free.'

'Agreed.' Leo nods magnanimously, and I have to stop myself from sighing audibly with relief. 'I will have this man brought down to you. Go prepare yourself. It will doubtless be an instructional opportunity for the boy as well. You' — he looks briefly at Susane and Isaac— 'are dismissed. Be on your way and swiftly so.'

The subtext is clear. The Pope is supreme ruler, but it is still a game of politics, and the Grand Inquisitor carries much sway here as elsewhere. Many have heard his public accusations and might feel tempted to act of their own accord in order to gain his graces. Better to be gone and quickly. I'm not worried. Nithael will take good care of them both from anyone who seeks to waylay them en route.

With a last worried glance from Susane and a supportive small smile from Isaac, they hurry from the room. That leaves me with the Pope and his guard.

'A word, my man, before you go to enjoy Cisneros' hospitality,' he says, beckoning me closer.

They searched me prior to entry, but still I see the readiness of all the swords and pikes as I approach the Holy Father, Pope Leo X. He gestures me nearer still, until I can hear his words at a quiet murmur.

'I cannot do much for you,' he says, 'not easily anyhow. There is, though, a way. My companions are my inspiration and known to be blessed. After all, who would dream of accusing a Pope's muse of heresy? If you would care to share, perhaps, some private time in my quarters, then I might deflect the Grand Inquisitor until his duties in the Kingdom of Spain call him back once more.'

So. An offer to warm his bed rather than the coals for the red-hot pokers. I keep my face neutral. There might be a bargain to be struck here. 'What of the appeal of the Cagots? Will you be able to think about that in a more positive light if I were to stick around some short while? Use your position effectively?'

My interests do not stretch towards those of my sex but nor does it concern me that his do — outside of the hypocrisy of those who suffer at the hands of his underlings. It is entirely natural despite what many others of the current age might think. If it will help the Cagot people, I can indulge this pope for a time without a question asked.

A pained smile answers my question immediately. 'I would were it possible, but Cisneros is much beloved by King Ferdinand. It was at his personal intervention that Cisneros became both Grand Inquisitor and a cardinal. He is good and loyal to both his king and his pope, but one must indulge his little passions where they arise. They are at least more easily assuaged than Torquemada's ever were, by all accounting.'

It is no surprise as far as answers go but nor is it the one I hoped for. I understand the politics, but they do not enamour me to the man. 'Then, Your Holiness, if it is solely to save my own skin, flattered as I am, I shall politely decline. I shall take first turn at the embrace of Cisneros' hospitalities and view what my friends might have to face in the name of appeasement, instead.'

His eyes widen slightly at that, and I think I detect a touch of hurt in his regard. Whether it is from the rarity of being rebuked or the truth therein, I do not know. 'A sad waste to stand so firmly on principles that you will swing when they get kicked out from under your feet. That said, I suspect it has been some time since anyone has been prepared to say their truth to me or to be guided by what they believe right.' He smiles sadly. 'It was a pleasure to meet a good man once more and a shame to send him on his way.'

He has no idea how right he is. For a politician, though, he is a reasonable sort. I've encountered much worse over the proceeding years. 'Well, this Good Man salutes you, Father. May the Good God bless and keep you.'

He looks faintly puzzled by my wording, but he makes a benediction. 'And you, my son. I fear your need may be greater than mine.'

The guardsmen who flank the Pope, Swiss mercenaries who are a recent addition to the Vatican by Isaac's accounting, lead me away from the Pope's chambers, towards what I suspect will be an entirely less accommodating form of chambers, deep underneath the floor of the Papal state. I run the calculations in my mind as they walk me down the steps that, while still carved elegant marble, become colder and damper the farther we progress down. It will take Isaac and Susane an hour at least to get back to our lodgings and gather our provisions, plus another two in order to cross the city boundaries. Once they are clear of Rome, it will be easy to lose any spies the Inquisitor might have set after them without revealing their supernatural capabilities. From there, no one will find or trouble them. Nithael will see to that. So I need only to stay alive for three hours, then I can be on my way.

Crossing my hands, I carefully rub open the loose stitching on my right sleeve and palm the two lozenges that drop into it. While I didn't expect what occurred, we knew we were walking into the lion's den. My reincarnation makes me the natural sacrifice when one is required. The two pastilles I hold are sufficiently different in size and shape that I can identify them by touch. One is instant death, drifting off into sweet dreams to awaken elsewhere. I keep that one curled inside my fingertips, and under the pretence of a yawn, I drop the other into my mouth, where I suck it until it dissolves entirely. The lozenge I just ate leads to a slower death. The time span is less certain, but it's around five hours.

If I am lucky, they will take me to a holding cell to await the Inquisitor's sweet ministrations, which will take the same amount of time as the lozenge does to kill me.

Instead, the guards lead me into a room covered in all the trademarks of the Inquisitor's trade. Two servants, their poles already inserted in the requisite holes of the rollers, man the stretching rack, ropes hanging loose but ready. Thumbscrews are easily identifiable on the tabletop even among all the sharpened implements scattered across it. The brazier burns, chock-full of red-hot coals, with a heavy-weight poker sitting inside it, already glowing with received heat. I have no idea if they keep it all ready in case of a heretic wandering past or if the Inquisitor sent word ahead.

Perhaps he notified the attendants to prepare prior to coming to confront us. The pair of iron boots that sit next to it, ready for their turn to be heated to flesh-scorching temperatures, do not fill my heart with joy.

Cardinal Ximenes Cisneros stands next to the bed-frame bench that is complete with head and limb restraints, carefully arranging the implements on the table next to it. The royal child lurks farther back in the shadows, far enough away that I cannot attempt to take him as a hostage but close enough he can enjoy every sizzle, every scream. His strange bodyguard, the supposed indirect descendent of that bastard De Montfort, looks at me with a gleaming anticipation in his eyes even as he pays careful attention to his charge, watching all who approach, his hand never straying from his sword.

'Well now,' the Cardinal says, only looking up briefly from his organising before returning to his meticulous arrangement. 'As you were so eager to come and confess your sins, I thought it would be rude to keep you waiting.'

Damnation. It looks like that dashes my hope of a delay. I let the other lozenge drop to the floor surreptitiously, kicking it into a shadowed corner. I've no wish for the Inquisition to get their hands on the apothecary recipes I know. Although, as they bring swift death, I doubt they'd be interested much. As my hands are to be fastened, the chances of me managing to imbibe it sneakily later on are nil. I'll just have to ride out the next few hours until the slow working poison takes effect.

That waiting period hardly fills me with anticipation as they strap me down. This isn't my first time being tortured; it's happened more often than I've wished, even if they always fail to make dying from it stick. But inside, under all the trepidation and steeling myself for the agonies to come,

I am practically bouncing up and down with excitement and glee. Susane agreed to allow me to court her! In a few mere years at most, I can seek her hand properly, and her mother cannot stand against it. I can take a few hours of torture to make that future a truth.

Still, it is not something I am relishing. You cannot acclimatise to inordinate amounts of pain. And the Inquisition are experts at inflicting the maximum a human frame can take without it giving up the ghost.

'Now,' the Grand Inquisitor says kindly as he plucks the now illuminant metal bar out of the coals. 'Tell me how you discovered and learned to practise the Cathar blasphemy. Who introduced you to it?'

The glowing metal comes slowly closer as he walks across to me. I remind myself that it is all in the name of a good cause, of the best cause I've had since I lost my faith, and I prepare myself to scream until my vocal cords snap or the poison kicks in, whichever comes first.

Chapter Thirty-Nine

A hand stretches out across a gaping chasm, created by
mistakes made over hundreds of years.

A loud *crack* is followed by a burning sensation on the right
side of my waist. For a moment, I think Oberon reneged on
his promise, and it is the feeling of being struck by lightning.
Then the burning spreads, increasing until it becomes a
hungry throat swallowing down my strength, like No Face
with the trays of food in the Spirited Away bathhouse. My
knees buckle, and I sink forward. The expression of horror
on Susane's face changes, now highlighted with sprayed
drops of paint flecks. Red paint flecks. I pull my hand away
from my side where I clutch it, and it comes away covered. I
am bleeding. A lot.

A voice sounds from behind me, close by. 'Not very
sporting of me, that, old chap, but here we are, needs must
when the devil does demand, and all that, what. There's
never been a better leveller with the fae than an iron musket

ball straight to the guts. Makes a bloody mess but calms us right down, doesn't it?'

His feet pass by my head, his heavyset boots ridging the dust. His hand seizes Susane by the hair and drags her up to her feet.

'I did tell you not to follow us, eh, old boy? Made it blasted clear — words and actions and a damned poor show to have done so after leaving you alive, eh, what? Still, it is what is; no point crying over spilt whatsit. Upsadaisy.'

His hand grips the back of my jacket and lifts me effortlessly to my feet before gently leaning me against the wall. Propped up, I can see him; he still looks like a swashbuckler, still talks like a twenties toff, still one of the nastiest pieces of work I've ever set eyes on. My son.

He's really committed to the pirate look since last we met. His loose-fitted poet shirt, frills decorating his bishop sleeves, is startlingly clean white. Rings adorn his ears, and he still has his Jolly Roger signet on his right-hand index finger. He only needs an eye patch and a parrot shitting on his shoulder, and he could get a job at Disneyland Paris for the *Pirates of the Caribbean* show. I think he thinks it makes him look like a force to be reckoned with. I reckon it makes him look like a twat.

He casually drapes his arm around Susane's shoulders and just as casually places a bowie knife to her throat. He regards me with that same intrigued bemusement, as if he can't quite believe I am here and doesn't quite know what to do next.

'Well, Papa.' He smiles jovially. 'Another joyous family reunion, pass the gravy, drinks all round, what. Still…' His expression looks playfully stern, like a schoolteacher trying to act cross but secretly delighted by the naughty pupil's shenanigans. 'I did make it clear not to come. Rather glad you did though, truth be told, eh? You, me, dear old Mama. Marvellous.'

He waves his hand, and fae *talent* spreads out around the cave, filling it like wildfire. It is potent and powerful and in sync with the surroundings. He smiles. 'You're not the only one to have tuned in, so to speak, to the frequencies of the Wild, what.' The monolith at the back of the cave lifts itself up, moving a metre to the side and revealing a deep dark hole underneath, a gaping wound in the rock floor.

'Mama is just desperate to know what's under there, afire with curiosity she's been, champing at the bit, what.' He gestures slightly with the knife, keeping it close enough to her throat to use it at will. 'Still, rather think that honour should be yours, old boy. Over you go, quick sharpish, tick-tock.'

I don't have much choice. The iron saps at me as much as it hurts, weakening me so that I am no match for him magically and am too spent physically to have a shot at disarming him. I have no idea if he is serious in his threat to kill his own mother, but seeing all the damage he's already done to her, it seems entirely plausible. I push myself up off the wall, staggering slowly towards the hole.

'Down we go then, old chap. Look smart, don't dilly dally on the way, and all that, what.' I can see the gleam of the blade out of the corner of my eye, too far for me to reach. I slide my feet over the edge and lower myself down.

'Ah, just a second, Papa. I'll be having that nifty little jerkin setup you're currently strapped up like a candy cane in. Quick sharpish, eh?' Damn it. I don't know what he has planned, but the iron ball-bearing explosive jacket was my last Hail Mary throw of the dice. Apparently, his eyes are keen enough to have worked out what I'm wearing. I consider for a moment arming it, trying to bluff him back.

But I can still see the blade at her throat, and the fact I've already surrendered shows I'm not prepared to hurt Susane. Threatening to kill us all is never going to convince him. The pain as I pull it off, as it rubs across the bullet hole is blinding. Carefully, I lay my rigged explosives at the edge of the steps. He moves forward and pulls them backwards with his foot, his eyes never leaving mine, the knife never leaving her throat.

There are some stairs carved into the rock, and I stand two or three steps down. The stone is cold, and a slight smell of musty damp reaches up from lower down towards me — not unpleasant, just the normal smell a closed-up cave gives. I turn back round to look at him. He stands at the lip of the hole with Susane still in his grip and points an old flintlock pistol at my face with the other hand.

'Right, let her go now then, son.' I hardly feel paternalistic towards the sod, but anything is worth trying to save her life.

He clucks his tongue. 'Oh yes, right you are, daddy dearest. In fact, you know what? She's been so desperate to bring you on board, to be by your side, why don't we let her join you?'

He kicks her in the back of her knees so she crumples forward as he pulls his hand up and back at the same time. The shock on her face, the disbelief, the hurt, and the pain of love betrayed, all dance in her eyes as her lifeblood splashes across me, half-blinding me in the moment. He lets her go, so she spins, pirouetting like a ballerina on the edge of the hole. Then she falls into my arms, the light already dimming.

'Forgive… me…cherie,' she breathes, bubbles of red forming at the corners of her mouth.

'Of course. Forgiven. Now hold on, belle.' No. It can't

happen. She can't die. 'Don't go again, please. Don't leave me again, Suse. I can't. Please, I can't.' I babble almost incoherently, holding her in my arms as she bleeds out, unable to control myself, unable to save her as the light goes out entirely. I press kisses to her still lips, utter promises of new chances, new lives together away from the hurt and pain. Of forgiveness, pure and true, for her in her mistakes. For me in all my endless ones, where time and again, others pay for my failures.

But it's no use. To love me, sooner or later, is a death curse. And the only woman I ever loved has paid twice for daring to return it.

I hold her limp frame, pain-blind, my vision ruined by the blood and the bitter agony of a loss I never realised could come again, let alone that it would. I look up at the murdering bastard who stands over us, wiping at my bleary eyes, trying to see him truly.

'Who are you? Were you even her son, our son? Who the fuck are you?' I yell, grief rebounding my voice off the roof of the cave to echo back, mocking my ignorance, my failure.

The fae shakes himself, stretching. It is like he just shed a skin, though physically there are no changes. His pretentious mannerisms are simply gone.

'Ah, that's better.' He smiles. 'I was so tired of that particular role. All that bastard "what" and "old chap" poncing about. Still, thought it was a character you might relate to, what with the whole devil-may-care attitude and flippant carefree charm, unworried by anything and everything. You can take a bow too if you want. After all, I based it on you.'

He brushes down his shirt's lapel, absent-mindedly worrying at a blood spot on the crisp white linen, though I notice the pistol never wavers from its trajectory. 'Still, to answer your question, the answer is no, I was never *your* son. Thank fuck for that. I was, of sorts, her son. Actually, more than that, I'm my own son, which sounds bloody confusing, and it really is. As for the latter part, well. Good to see you again, Good Man, though I've kept my eye on you for the longest time.'

He raises his free hand lazily to his face like a parent playing peekaboo with a baby, changing his expression as the hand passes, but instead it is the face itself that changes. In the place of the fae is that of a man — dark-haired, rugged faced, with the stout countenance of an innkeeper ready for a cosy chat over a well-pulled pint. Except it is the face of a man who would pull your guts out quicker than they would pull you a drink. A face I've not seen since the Albigensian Crusade.

'Simon De Montfort,' I breathe, my brain unable to process it.

He gives me a sweeping bow, his eyes never leaving me. 'At your service, you imperfect, interfering arsehole.'

Looks like I'm not his favourite person either.

Chapter Forty

No witticisms here. No clever little wordplay. Just absolute
certainty that one day I will get my hands on this bastard's
neck and watch the light fade from his eyes as I wring it with
all my strength.

I had posited Simon being alive as a possibility to Isaac, of
course, but my attention was more on if Arnaud Almeric
still lived. Almeric seemed more likely a candidate. He'd
been the one who'd slit my throat as the Grail had broken,
meaning he hadn't been much farther back than I. I was
ready for the possibility he might still be kicking around
somewhere, plotting some dark and twisted revenge.

I wasn't expecting De Montfort. He was unTalented as
far as I could tell and far back enough that I thought he
escaped the radius of energy escaping the Holy Grail.
Apparently not.

'How?' A dark thought crosses my mind. 'Did you kill
my son? Take his place?' I can feel the rage building at the

very idea. If I wasn't practically immobilised by the gut shot, I'd spring at De Montfort and take the risk. I'd probably die, but I'd give it a go. Slowed down as I am, that isn't even a possibility.

He laughs, that bawdy guffaw that reverberates round the cave, a warm sound that speaks of a shared joke by the firelight just before he slips a blade between your ribs. 'Oh no, didn't you listen, Cathar? This body was never your son. Hers, yes, but not yours.'

The first suspicious thoughts form, of what dark and evil shit he might have done to make it true. I'm not sure I want to hear the truth. I am certain he isn't going to give me the choice.

'Let me tell you how it went for me after you took my master away from me.' The humour is gone, and a savage snarl is on his face, giving the lie to any pretence of bonhomie. 'To shit. It went to shit, Cathar. My ascending star faltered. I was the equal of the Frankish King! Damn it, I held more land than he did by the time the Crusade was completing. But without Nicetas' *talent* to keep guard over me? Snuffed out like a witless, wickless candle by a rock hurled by some commoner bitch from the walls of Toulouse.'

Oh, I was delighted when I heard about that. I didn't even need to hunt him down like I'd done Almeric. Simon had died in the Siege of Toulouse, cut down by a direct hit from a mangonel. The walls had been manned by commoner women as eager to defend their city as the armoured knights. Eight hundred years later, he's still furious, outraged that he was cut down by a peasant and a female one at that. Good. Fuck him. 'It was only what you deserved, you stupid bastard.'

His eyes narrow, his nostrils flaring, and for a moment, I

think I see the brute of war come back. I have the impression he'll jump down into the hole with me and batter me bloody and blue with his bare fists. Then he exhales, pulling himself back mentally. It looks like he's learned self-control over the centuries, at least. That is bad news for me.

'Oh, I paid more than I should have had to, you heathen wanker. We all got it a bit differently, didn't we, this "keep coming back" curse? You got the best of it because of course you did, you lucky cunt. Poor old Ben wasn't so chancy, was he?'

Now it is my turn to bare my teeth. He just laughs like a man tormenting a tied-up hound, poking it with a stick to chuckle at its misfortune. 'Oh, yes, I know about him. Kept nearly as good an eye on him as I did on you. Who d'you think gave that skull to that *talentless* arse who caught you with your pants down? Who d'you think pointed him towards the veil? I'd have been satisfied with having you dead and gone, to have finally eradicated all of you Cathar shitheads off the planet once and for all. Still, it was a one-shot deal and just one of many plans in action to take you off the board, you poncy git.'

I breathe hard, still clutching Susane's empty shell to my chest, still too shell-shocked and numb to really understand anything. 'So what's the plan now then, De Montfort?'

He tuts, wagging his finger at me. 'Oh no, no, no. I'm not as daft as that bloody idiot Benedict. He wanted you to understand him, to forgive him. I want you to know why I'll never forgive you. How I've taken my revenge against you. You don't need to know anything else.'

He leans himself up against the huge rock he pulled out of the way with his *talent*, his pistol never wavering from aiming at my eyeball. 'I came back, Bonhomme. After that boulder caved in my head, I came back and not too far from where I was when I died. I didn't come back in a dead body, no, nor in a stranger's one.

'One moment, I was marching the lines, marshalling the men for action. I heard the sound, turned, and caught it straight in the head. Killed me instantly, they said. Still hurt like fucking murder in that moment, I can tell you.

'Next thing, I'm kneeling, staring at a half-laced boot. Except it's a smaller size than I wear, but it's on my foot. I recognise where I am; I'm in my private family tent, the war table just to the side. I stagger up, kicking my way through the scrolls and vestments to a burnished bronze mirror I kept and look at the only face I've ever loved.'

He leans forward, and I can see the edge of insanity in his eyes, how he is fighting to keep himself from tearing me apart with his teeth to gnaw on my bones. 'I'll give you a hint, Cathar. It wasn't the one I was born with.'

The answer comes to me, though I care little. I don't want to know the answer to his mystery. I only want two things. To defy the universe and breathe life back into the body I cradle in my arms. And to kill the bastard towering over me.

He sees the realisation though. 'Yes. It was my son. The apple of my eye. The one everything had been for. Why I followed Nicetas on his path to power.

'Nicetas swore to me he'd be ruler of the world once his master came through the Holy Grail. The two of them would rule the spiritual, owning all the hearts and souls. The physical would be ours, to do as we pleased with. They'd be gods. I'd be king. We'd have made the world anew, so much better without all this nonsense about freedom and choice. The strong lead. That's how it should always be.

'Instead' —the madness dances behind his pupils—

'your stupid, idiotic individualist creed ruined everything, and in my death, it made me take the life of my darling boy. Poor bloody Simon. All he ever wanted was to be like me. Instead, he became me and got lost for eternity in the process. A heavy fucking price to pay for your interfering, Paul Bonhomme.'

I am tired of this already. 'Okay, you hate me. You've got me. Now what? I don't care about any of this. None of it matters anymore.'

He smiles again, that malicious grin at the very edges of sanity; it would be terrifying if I had any emotions left inside my emptied-out heart. Of course he has something up his sleeve to deal with that. 'Oh no, I think you will care. Think it through now. Work it out. My reincarnation has a very specific flavour. I come back in the bodies of one of my children, taking them over while they still live, wiping my offspring off the planet each time I'm reborn. If I don't have a child, then the nearest relative instead. There's enough who are my descendants scattered around now. But I've also kept my seed well sown. What body am I wearing now? Who gave birth to it? Who was the mother?' He leans forward and hisses triumphantly. 'Who was the father?'

It clicks, and I snap. I leap from the hole or try to. My foot tangles in the sodden twirls of Susane's dress as I try to put her down and hurl myself at the monster at the same time. There is strength aplenty in my body according to my mind. My limbs have entirely different ideas. So instead of springing out at him, I slam into the edge of the hole, my arms over the top as I scramble to get out, snapping and raging at him like a rabid dog. It is a simple matter for him to step forward and kick me in the chin, snapping my head back, depositing me ungraciously in a heap on top of my now twice dead wife.

'You were always ready for magic, weren't you? Always prepared for attacks by other Talented.' He sneers, glorying in my reaction, my physical failure, my inability to do anything. 'Thing is, I never got any. Not till now. Not till this form. I just stole my boys' bodies from them time after time. I wanted it. I wanted that *talent* you all have and I never got. So I planned it out so carefully. Course, it was you who led me to the Cagot, Paul. You who brought them to my attention.'

He draws out a rolled-up cigarette and lights it, exhaling with that self-satisfied smacking of lips. 'I rarely smoke these days, but this is a special occasion.' He turns his attention back to me. 'It was a simple thing. When you were off travelling, I went to the Cagots as a magic-less trader, a back-packed tinker. An outcast among outcasts. No spells to weave. But I didn't need one, did I?' He leans forward. 'An apothecary's tincture in their drink, and they all slept like the dead. Meant I could go and pay your wife-to-be a visit that she'd never remember.'

His grin is a terrible thing. It speaks of glorying in misery and celebrating in bloodshed, and I'd say it is quite mad if I wasn't far from sure I'm still sane after what he said. He doesn't stop though. 'Fast forward nine months, and oh, the celebrations! A baby boy for the eternal blank-shooting boy-child. Ring the marriage bells!'

He chuckles, and it gives way to a genuine belly laugh. Tears spring to his eyes. 'Oh, I got you, Cathar. I got you good. Not only did you give me a way to get magic, but you gave me a way to tear your heart out. I got to fillet the love of your life and leave her as a wedding gift for you. I got to steal your son, a son who was never yours to begin with, and give you a taste of what I went through when I first came back thanks to your miserable meddling.'

He finishes his smoke and grinds it out underfoot. 'Now, that's all I wanted to share with you. I wanted you to know that I took your wife. I took your child. Everything that made you feel human again. I took them all from you, Paul Bonhomme. Me and me alone, without *talent*, without some team of do-gooding superpowers to back me up. I stole it all and brought you here to this place. And now I'm going to leave you here. Thanks to your delightful present.'

The pistol still has never wavered, and now he cocks back the hammer. 'Took me a while to make the prerequisite trips to get this cave all set up. I already laid this entire plan in place, but you made it so much easier by getting your magic eaten, you old horn-dog, you. I'm not sure how long you'll stay trapped here for exactly, but I know it's going to be a long, long time. And that you'll be quite mad by the time you get out.'

He flicks something at me. I fumble for it and miss, but as it sails past my hands, I see it is the brass Zippo lighter he used to spark his cigarette.

'You can have that as a gift, boy. It won't work on any of the flesh down there, same as violence against yourself won't work, but I want you to see where I've left you. I doubt our paths will ever cross again.'

'Wait!'

But there is a deafening roar, the terrible pain of bone shards hitting my brain as my one good eye socket splinters, and the iron ball he shot buries itself into my grey matter. Then darkness comes once more.

Chapter Forty-One

Just when you think you can't hate anyone more, Simon De
Montfort is there to prove you wrong.

I come to in the same darkness I left, alone and practically
talentless. It is pitch black, cold stone under my knees, under
my fingers. I'm prone, stretched out in the lightless chamber.
I stagger up, my eyes fixating on a tiny yellow window of
light that's wavering. It takes me a moment before I realise it
isn't actually wavering but rather shrinking, disappearing
rapidly. I hurtle towards it, but my foot catches on something, sending me sprawling. I skitter across the floor,
grazing my knee, the sharp pain only driving me forward,
but I am too slow. I've only found the first step by the time
the heavy stone slams into place and throws me into a sight-
less world.

I fumble around, trying to find what I tripped over. My
fingers trace the form of a body, a woman drenched in her
life force and cold to the touch. I know who she is and

where I am, though as I run my hand, wet with her blood and my tears, to touch her face, it disintegrates away, much as my own discarded forms do. I guess there is enough similarity between my resurrection magic and whatever Oberon worked on the Cagots, that when their second lives end, their bodies turn to dust. It is a small mercy. I don't think my mind can support wearing her dead form even if it might give me some *talent* back.

I grope around in the dark for what feels like hours before I finally find the lighter he threw down. A quick shake tells me there is little gas in it. I get myself up and spark the light.

It is a vast subterranean chamber, not immensely high, nothing compared to Lou's vaulted cavern under Hastingues, but it is deep, heading down into the earth. There is…nothing. Nothing here in the first visible part. The walls are smooth shaped granite, the floor the same. There are no stalagmites, no loose rocks. The absence of anything but walls, floor, and ceiling is the most striking feature.

It is only when I head deeper in that I find what De Montfort left me. Bodies. Rows and rows of bodies. Hundreds of them, maybe thousands. Men and women only, which is a small mercy, all naked, nothing unique about them, no connecting factor apart from them all being human. When I try to touch them, my hand slips off. They've been placed in some form of stasis, keeping them fresh like a cold-store freezer. I can't get a grip on them magically either. These bodies are normal humans, so I'm back to my post-Melusine level of *talent*, and my magic is far too weak to penetrate the weavings cast on the corpses. Not to mention, it's fae magic, making it all the harder.

I explore as far back as the cave goes. It's no short

distance; I walk for nearly an hour by my internal clock. Every step takes me past more bodies laid flat on the ground, utterly naked, perfectly preserved, and untouchable. I make my way deeper in but cautiously, mainly by touch. I am terrified my lighter will run out of fluid already, so I only flick it now and then to check I've not missed anything as I run my hands along the walls and floor, looking for a forgotten object, a puzzle to solve to escape, a flaw or weakness to take advantage of. Except, of course, De Montfort isn't interested in playing. He doesn't want to give me a way to win. He wants me to suffer.

First thing. Escape by death. I have no magic anymore, so no interest in protecting this particular body. The way out seems easy enough. My initial thought is to search for a sharp rock, something I can use to cut open a vein, but I still want to protect my lighter fluid just in case. So I decide to pull the same trick I did when Ben had me strapped up in his lair, spare bodies arrayed around me. Head back, tongue out, bite through, with the plan to catch the severed piece and use it to choke myself to death. Painful, but I can handle pain.

Except when I snap my jaw back open, there is no severed tongue piece. It's intact. I try again, but same result, and my heart sinks. Now I'm remembering when the Nain Rouge took me prisoner in his twisted version of an escape game. How my attempts to kill myself to escape were thwarted by a form of fae magic that healed me instantly each time I tried.

Looks like De Montfort has used something similar here. Fuck.

The time drags, alone in the cold, lost in the dark. At first, I remain stoic. I've been through hardships, locked up in dingy cells and left to rot. I escaped then; I'll escape now.

Except there is nothing. No convenient secret passageways, and no tools to make my own. And of course my etheric storage is blocked. He was obviously watching me for a long, long time, unTalented and full of hate, searching for an edge over me.

I head back to the start of the cave, the lighter fluid running on empty, only the sparks from the flint throwing strobes of illumination out, momentary flickers, then gone. I crawl cautiously back up the steps, my hands patting every single centimetre, hoping against hope that either he or I dropped something when he killed Susane and threw her down upon me. No such luck.

I get to the top, then heave and strain against the monolith many times my weight, impossible for me to even budge no matter how desperately I try. Half-crouched, half-crawling, I make my way up and down the rows, counting the dead bodies. Two-thousand and six. That really bothers me, the extra six. The illogical decision to add six more on to make it uneven, it upsets me. It becomes like a scratching noise at the back of my brain, constantly asking why, why would there be these six more? Did I make a mistake? I count again and again, scuttling along rows of dead, touching them, demanding there be six less, finding the count correct. It enrages me. I swear at the last six and try to strike them, but my hands just glide off like non-stick Teflon. I weep, salt streaks forming as they run down my face, trying to catch them on a tongue cracked with thirst, my lips breaking and blistering as I cry at the injustice of an extra six.

Sometimes, I think they mock me. I think I hear voices, invisible fingers pointed straight at me, calling me out for my faults. Telling me I am weak, a failure. Recounting all the times I paid the price for my foolishness and all the others who paid in my stead. The dead come calling to clarify that it is all my fault.

I can't really move by this point. Too weak to try even, too dehydrated and hungry. I fluctuate between being glad and furious that Susane's body disintegrated, and both are for the same reason. I try to gnaw on the limbs of the corpse nearest to me, dragging myself closer by bloodied yet perfectly intact fingernails, but my teeth slide off, clacking together, the terrible echoing sound ringing like the bells of a belfry, swelling until I want to clap my hands over my ears, if I only had the energy to move them.

Three days. Give or take. That's how long they say you can survive without water. Three days and then you die. Maybe you'll get five. Maybe a little more. But most of the time? Three days. I don't have a watch with me. Don't have anything, in fact. But that seems about right to me. I go through the stages of agony, feeling my muscles waste away, my eyes sink back into my skull, my skin hang loose where the water drains from the flesh. My mouth and nose are a mass of cracked sores, weeping blood that I try to lick up, to claim some small moisture back. My breathing becomes heavy, difficult, my throat feeling thickened, constantly trying to swallow but never managing it. Everything hurts. Though by the end, among the sensory deprivation and hallucinations, the pain and misery, I find a small window of peace. In the last few moments, as I feel it all sliding away, I'm at ease. Mainly by blocking out what I know in my heart of hearts is to come.

It does but not immediately.

First, I find myself back in the hut on the infinite sands, back where I arrived when I first died. I'm staring at the fire, and the voice behind me says, 'There isn't much time, but you'll be…'

I am back in the cave, in a new body, a naked female.

My magic tries to change my appearance, to match my expectations of what I look like, but I am too weak, too wasted, and I don't give a damn, frankly. Nothing changes with a switch of gender, not locked in here anyhow.

I weep and scream until my vocal cords crack and cave under the pressure. I spend the last two days prone, unable to move, instead of just the last one before I draw a final croaking gasp, feeling my major organs shut down one by one…

As I blink back tears in the firelight, the voice speaks in a kindly manner. '… back soon. Sit down, Paul. Let's talk.' I take a step forward…

My eyes snap open, but they see nothing. I'm back in the dark. Two thousand and four. I cut this one short after twenty-four hours. I might not be able to sever my tongue, but I force the broken, useless lighter down my throat until it blocks, and I claw and gag at my airways as the world goes away again…

I stagger in my step but steady myself on the chair arm, turn, and collapse into the seat. The radiant warmth feels incredible after so long in the frozen dark. I turn my head towards the door, where the voice has always come from…

A male form. Two thousand and three. I don't move for the whole of this life, just stay wrapped up in myself, unable to even find the want to search for the lighter to swallow again, just whimpering and begging for the end to come, begging it to leave me be, terrified of every possibility the future can bring. Not that any of it makes a difference…

I can see a shape — a woman, I think. She speaks again, and her voice is full of pity and love. 'It's awful that it takes you dying like this for us to speak, Paul,' and it hurts. Oh god, it hurts knowing I won't stay long…

A female. I scream and rant, run and hurl myself

against the wall, sob and scratch my way along the floor until I should have nothing but bloodied stumps where my fingers are. The magic doesn't let that happen though. There's been little evacuated waste, but the few drops of piss that demanded to be expelled each time means there's an acrid smell burning my nose and seemingly my brain itself. I can't. I just can't...

The comfort of the chair seems obscene. I've forgotten there is any sensation other than icy rock. The woman steps forward. She's middle-aged, at the top end, with a tender expression and a kindly smile. There's something else, something familiar about her. I can't place what it is...

A female. I can't remember. I can't. I can't remember how many there's been, how many left. I count the bodies again, over and over feverishly. Two thousand and one. It can't be. I must have been here longer than that. It shreds my consciousness, thinking about it, but I can't stop counting them, not until I can no longer drag myself down the line anymore...

Then I realise. She looks like my mother, like the face I forgot so long ago, and that I've wished I could remember. I'm haunted by so many hungry ghosts. I often wished she could still frequent one of my dreams. This woman isn't my mother, but her maternal aspect suddenly brings back that long-forgotten face to crystal clarity, the first thing I lost from my mind before I learned to build my mind palace, and I cry, sobbing, heaving tears for my long dead mother...

A male. I'm broken. Bestial. A hunched howling thing, the noise reverberating off every corner, half-screaming, half-baying at a moon I won't see for over a decade and a half. I can't bear it. I can't. I can't. I can't...

She sits in the chair opposite and lays her hand on mine. 'You've suffered so much, my brave Cathar, for doing that one correct, coura-geous thing. And still you're suffering...'

A male. Scrabbling, scrabbling at the stone, I search for purchase, driving my fingers into gaps that just aren't there, trying to force them in, to use them as levers. I'll snap them off, my arms too, anything if it'll give me purchase, if it'll move the stone.

There are no gaps. Just blood and pain, and slow, thirsty death…

Her expression is so sad, so weighed down with understanding and suffering on my behalf. 'It's not done yet, Paul. Not until we meet again. There's so much still ahead of you.' Her hand on mine turns gauzy, translucent, and I can see the bones underneath. 'Remember the key, Good Man…'

A male. There's something strange. Burning. Good God, it's so strange, and it burns. My eyes hurt at the bright, and I scream, terrified, scrambling backwards. As much as there is light in that other world, I feel like I am two different people. The calm homeliness of that place doesn't take me away from the madness and miserable despair I've fallen into here. So I scurry away from the unknown, the blinding light that pierces my eyes and makes no sense in the unending dark that is my universe here.

I hear the footsteps, cautious at first, then hurrying towards me quicker, then feel a strong, supple arm wrap around me, hoisting me gently but firmly, leading me towards the incomprehensible brightness, up the steps, and out. Out.

She holds me as I twitch and murmur and wail, as my eyes adjust again, and some small shard of sanity comes back to me. I cry and howl my madness at a moon I thought I'd not see until there was nothing left of the man I was, nothing but a gaping black hole born over and over into a different brain. It isn't the moon I was born under, but I recognise it for what it is, as a celestial body, and that is a victory. I am still here. I am still me. Damaged. Perhaps more so than I've ever been. But still me.

I want to ask how she is here, how she found me, why she even still cares, but I can't make the sounds, not yet. Words are beyond a man too broken to be coherent. It doesn't matter anyhow. If there was ever a debt between us, this squares it, not that I'll ever believe there was one. Not truly.

Aicha Kandicha has saved me.

Chapter Forty-Two

Is there nothing this woman can't achieve? She is definitely
Aicha Kandicha, not Kan'tdicha.

It takes several days before I can talk. Aicha makes me soup,
feeds me slowly, stays close, keeping physical contact to reas-
sure me she is here. Despite her freeing me, I'm not ready
yet to step outside the cave. I can see there is a world
outside. That is enough for me, for now. Knowing I can go
out is enormous freedom. Actually doing it is more than I
can manage.

One of the first things I asked her to do was destroy the
room below. 'Magic... fire-resisting...' I managed through
juddering breaths that hitched at the thought of what lay
beneath us. She went down there, and I tried not to mewl in
abject terror at being alone again. After what seemed
infinitely long to spend without her, she returned tight-
lipped and furious. The expression only softened when I
cowered back from her. She patted my arm, keeping her

hand there until she felt my heartbeat calm to normal levels. Then she walked me to the edge, reassuring me all the way, letting me stop each time I needed to, for me to regain my courage to go anywhere near there again. She poured her magic into it, *talented* fire roaring down like a dragon's breath into the cave, filling it and scorching it until the very rock itself melted under the extreme heat.

'They're all gone, Paul,' she said afterwards, and I wept, gulping down sweet, clean fresh air in between sobs at the thought I would never go back there, no matter what happened. I would die again, come back again, but not there.

I wonder if I'll regain my casual attitude towards dying, if time will erase the trauma. The very thought fills me with such existential dread. I watch constantly where I walk, terrified I'll trip and break an ankle or that some poisonous beast is lurking, ready to sink their teeth into my tasty flesh. Is this what it is like for normal humans all the time? It's been such a long time since I was one, I can't remember anymore.

There is only one thing I took from my time in the blind dark, outside of the mental damage, and it almost makes it all worthwhile. A woman's face, lined with worry and care and love, proud of her son, full of hope for where his future will take him. Sometimes, when the nightmares come and the dark calls me back, when I whimper and whine in my sleep, that face comes back to me, and it is like the fire at the mouth of the cave, keeping all the monsters at bay. Then I get some small amount of proper sleep, and slowly, I heal.

Epilogue

There's a way through loss and pain. There always is. I just
have to find it.

After two weeks, I start to handle existing again, though I
won't say I am getting better. I'm not sure I'll ever fully
recover from what I went through. If Aicha took any longer
in reaching me, I doubt I would even be sane.

I get her story from her — or as much as she is prepared
to tell. Of course, being Aicha, she was a mile ahead of me
the whole way. Knowing that both Susane and De Montfort
were fae and that there was nowhere on Earth they'd be
able to hide from a betrayed Mother of the Sistren of
Bordeaux, it was obvious to her that I'd head to Faerie. It
was equally obvious to her that I'd probably get myself
killed. Or to put it as she did, 'You're a fucking useless dickhead, Paul Bonhomme, and I wanted words with the fuckers.' She only used that word to describe them both once.

Susane doesn't get included in the same category as that human shitstain De Montfort. He played her like a fiddle.

She was investigating her own ways to get to Faerie with little success when the magic she used to find me in Ben's laboratory — the little speck of her own essence she lets hitchhike on my body-hopping soul let her know we'd headed for Lyon. Assuming we'd found a portal through carving out the Tarrasque's heart (I don't think she really assumed this, more likely just hoped it was true), she headed after us just in time to see the Tarrasque do his Dumbo impression. We sped off, and she tracked us back to the Pyrenees.

Once we left, she approached Gwen, only to realise that portal was shut to her. Since her other research was a wash-out, she went searching for the White Lady once more. She didn't want to admit it; I had to work hard to wangle it out of her, and it fills me with dread. Not because of the White Lady being evil or anything. I'm sure she isn't. But what she is, is other and a major Power. You don't make deals with the likes of her lightly. Certainly not twice.

Of course, that time she didn't have the Nain Rouge's finger to get him to hunt out the Lady for her, so it took her a bit longer. And the White Lady, guardian of the portal, allowed her into the Wilds.

There are few better than Aicha at hunting, but time obscured my trail, cold for over two weeks. It took her another week to find traces of my passing, to catch the scent of De Montfort, and to track it back to the cave. Once there, having a gander underneath the monolith, the only object in the whole smooth, worn grotto, was a no brainer.

I fill her in about Susane, about De Montfort, and how he came back. It takes me a while, but once I feel able to, I tell her about my visits to the cabin in the other world and about the woman. It is hard to talk about, to think about. As safe as I felt for the moments there, the torment of my captivity permeates everything, and my mind keeps skittering away from it, slipping off it like my hands did from the magically preserved corpses. Aicha can see the pain it causes me to talk about it, and we leave it for now, returning to more pressing matters.

Going after De Montfort is obvious. I have no idea what he is up to, but he knew about Ben, and he was watching me for a long time. He wanted me to suffer, to be broken, but he also wanted me out of the way. I need to find out why almost as much as I need to pay him back for what he did to me. And Susane.

Good God, that hurts. More than the madness maybe, more than that core of fear and doubt that's instilled in my mind, causing my eyes to twitch to every movement, every sound. More than her betrayal, throwing *talent* at me rather than trusting me enough to tell me what was going on. More than the knowledge of what he did to her, sneaking into her bedchamber. More even than knowing how I failed her, how I never knew that she'd been violated, that she'd lived after death, that she'd suffered — first in Faerie, then under his thumb.

All of that could have been repaired. He took away any fresh chances, any sunlit days after the dark and stormy nights that we might one day have reached.

He took away hope. He took away her. He took my heart even more effectively than he nearly took my mind. Would have done if it wasn't for the warrior, the woman, the true friend sitting opposite.

Perhaps I've a little of my heart left after all. Perhaps she kept it safe for me, tucked away where he couldn't find it. My sister-soul wrapping it up for safekeeping.

Of course we still have to get out of Faerie, and Oberon isn't going to let us get back out the way I came in, even if Aicha could pass through the portal there, which I doubt. That only leaves us with one option.

I look at Aicha, and a smile cracks across my face. By the Good God, it doesn't still the pain, but it still feels good. I wasn't sure I'd ever smile again. 'So how do you feel about storming the Winter Court?'

She stops chewing, motionless, then flashes me one of her momentary wicked grins. 'Beat up evil Elsa? Sounds like a whole lot Olafs.'

She watches the confusion settle into my expression, then sighs, frustrated. 'Olafs? O'laughs? He's the animated snowman. It sounds like the abbreviated form for "of laughs"? Jesus Christ, Paul, it ruins the whole joke if I have to explain it. Keep up, will you? Fucking eedjit.'

She can have that one. I can't keep the smile off my face anyhow. Even though I have a dead wife to avenge twice, to bring peace to an almost entirely broken heart, and another eternally living dead man to see sent to the damnation he so richly deserves. Even though I have no magic again, stuck in a practically unTalented human form, and we are about to take on the actual embodiment of Winter, a being possibly as ancient as the world, certainly as long-lived as our species' nightmares about her cold cruelty. With me entirely powerless, we are going to waltz into her territory, as terrible and as merciless as she herself is, and try to find our way home, an impossibility even if I was still packing the metaphorical big guns magic-wise.

And still I smile. Because, luckily, I have the one thing I value most in the world.

I have Aicha Kandicha. And that makes the impossible...well...

It might not make the impossible possible, but it means we'll have a whole lot of fun and cause a whole lot of mayhem finding out along the way.

Afterword

Ah, Paul. He tries so hard. One could even say he's distinctly trying. But try as he might, he can't do it on his own. Luckily Aicha's back. Both for his sake, and for mine, as several members of my Facebook reader's group — the newly renamed C.N. Rowan's imPerfect imPs as Meta got very upset by me using the word Gang — have been threatening stealth ninja excursions to steal hair in order to make a voodoo doll of me.

Of course, they may yet decide to get one done. The path ahead isn't about to get any easier for our poor imPerfect Cathar…

In terms of the historical aspects of the book, the Cagot petition to Pope Leo X, claiming Cathar ancestry for the Limpieza de Sangre, despite them having existed long before the Good People so-called heresy, actually happened. We don't know many of the details, but considering the Cagot's isolation continued for centuries, we have to assume it failed. Leo X's reputation — as both a patron of the arts, and an intimate patron of the male artists — is renowned, and he was known as one of the better of that period's popes. Albeit that didn't mean the tolerance towards homosexuality extended beyond the Vatican's walls, nor that he stepped in to stop the Spanish Inquisition, headed by Ximenes, from wreaking murderous slaughter in their terrible search for heretics. Charles Hapsburg was indeed under Cisneros's watch, and did grow to become the Holy Roman Emperor — bad news for Muslims, Jews and anyone else he considered even vaguely different. The Di Vico were an actual Italian noble family who, after falling on hard time, fell into mercenary work. They also had direct descent from De Montfort after his great-grandson married into them, as the De Montfort star began to wane.

The traboules of Lyon absolutely exist, as do all the places therein mentioned in the book. You can walk them and follow Paul's path taken — or run frantically like an out of shape headless chicken, if you're really going for accuracy — and the stories of their usage during the Silk Worker Rebellions and the Second World War are totally true. There are maps available from the Tourist advice centres. Of course, only the locals know where all the traboules are.

We're halfway through the first story arc, and at last Paul has some idea what's going on, some slight indication as to who he's up against.

Of course, before he can do anything about that, he still has to get the hell out of Fae. No problem. Right?

vinci-books.com/imPerfectbones

Steal from the Winter Queen? What could go wrong.

We need out of Faerie—but first, we have to break into Maeve's realm, rescue stolen kids, and escape unnoticed. Or start a war with the Unseelie Court. No pressure.

Turn the page for a free preview…

imPerfect Bones: Chapter One

FAERIE, 3 JUNE, PRESENT DAY

Sometimes escaping from the dark doesn't mean you leave it
behind. Sometimes, you just carry it with you.

I don't know why all my ancient ghosts keep getting dressed
up in suits stitched from skin.

There was a time when phantoms knew their place.
One simple job — hang around in musty old mansions,
bewailing their miserable existence, in desperate need of a
psychotherapist to help them learn to just let it all go.
Worst-case scenario was one chucking a tin of beans at you
if they felt particularly pissed off.

Now they all seem to be eager to try their long-
discarded flesh on for size again, like a wedding dress pulled
out from the back of the cupboard by a widow at a nursing
home. It seems like everyone I've ever cared for and had to
watch die has come back for a visit. After sipping several
pints of evil juice first.

My best friend and student from my life as a Cathar

Perfect tried to punch a hole in reality in order to jump off the reincarnation Ferris wheel and take me with him at the same time. Then Susane, my dead wife, turned up just in time to stab me in the back. Why? Apparently for our son, who had been ripped from her belly, supposedly killed, when she'd been murdered the first time.

Except the ghost pretending to be my son, wasn't him at all. Couldn't be, in fact, because I became infertile the first time *I* died. And our believed miracle baby was never mine — something I didn't find out until Simon De Montfort — yet another ghost— revealed he, too, had jumped onto this flesh-again fad. But where I can reincarnate into the nearest dead body regardless of its relation to me, Simon's spirit can only reincarnate in the bodies of blood relatives.

I avoid thinking too much about how he made that happen without Susane's knowledge, else I'm likely to go mad and start killing everyone in sight until I wrap my hands round his wretched neck and watch the light dim in his eyes one last, final time. Well, *more* likely. And more mad.

Plus, I don't yet feel like I've been reunited with the whole wretched gang of ghosts. When Ben first pulled his "fuck the world; I wanna get off" manoeuvre, I intended to look into whether Arnaud Almeric, the psychotic priest known as the Butcher of Beziers, might also still be kicking around in another body. My reincarnation and Ben's and, it turns out, Simon De Montfort's, were all caused by being splashed with the essence of stolen Cathar souls when I broke the Holy Grail during a magical tug of war with the treacherous Bogomil Cathar Papa Nicetas back in the twelfth century. Nicetas got blown up along with the Grail, but Almeric caught a bit of the ectoplasmic backsplash along with the three of us, so it seems highly likely he might still be around.

I lie huddled up inside my blanket, thinking about all this inside the lean-to shelter Aicha and I hammered together in the Wilds of Faerie. It's less warm and dry and honestly, probably less safe than the cave we left, but there's no way I'd ever have managed to get a good night's sleep in there. Even with water now dripping through the roof of woven wide-leaved indigenous ferns directly onto my nose, I sleep better. Too many of my own ghosts, fragments of myself I left lingering, hang around that cave full of vacuum-packed corpses, where Simon left me to go insane, starving and dying of thirst over and over again.

I'm still inside my blanket when Aicha comes back. For most people, Aicha Kandicha's a closed book. Not just closed but bound in five-inch-thick chains, then locked with an industrial-sized padlock. Then put in an uncrackable safe that would make George Clooney think twice. Then covered in concrete and buried at sea. Unreadable is the point I'm making. I, though, can gather more than most; her micro-expressions, tiny movements, and creases in her otherwise immobile face tell me box sets of stories missed by everyone else.

For example, at this moment, having come in and dumped down the miscellaneous weird vegetation she's identified as edible, she seems completely emotionless. Her short dark hair clings to her forehead, slicked by the soaking she chose to take rather than burn her *talent* to keep the rain off her. Features that are sharp enough to cut yourself on —or for her to do so with a swiftly delivered headbutt— are hard to see in the half-light, but the siyala tattoo on her chin stands out still, the curling fronds around the black dots a story of personal growth worn for all to see. Her coal-black eyes would be unreadable to most, buried behind the shadows of a nose Cleopatra would have killed for. But I can read the concern, the worry she carries for me — the relief that we've patched things up marred by whether I'll ever be quite the person I was before my imprisonment. I can see her heartache where no one else can.

She turns and sees me looking, obviously reading her thoughts. 'Are you over that whole bullshit yet, or are you still being a massive pussy, dickhead?'

See? Totally torn up inside by angst over my wellbeing.

'What are you staring at?' She waves her hand up and down. 'Woohoo, Earth to Major Knob?'

I snap out of my reverie. 'Sorry, *laguna*, miles away for a minute there.'

She grunts an acknowledgement and turns back to preparing a salad gathered from her foraging. Again. Bless her, she must be utterly fed up with the whole thing. Aicha isn't vegetarian, but she's been keeping our diet strictly herbal for two reasons. First, because I am vegetarian unless necessity really leaves me no choice. Second, just because something is four legged and furred or feathered doesn't mean it isn't sentient in Faerie. Hell, you have to double-check half the mushrooms aren't going to burst into song. And then try to eat your ankles.

I scoot over. While it might not be entirely watertight, we've made a reasonable and camouflaged space about ten metres squared. The failed waterproofing isn't surprising. The weather in all its forms in the Wilds (the unclaimed part of Faerie between Summer and Winter we're currently in) lives up to the area's name. The heat is baking; the cold is biting; the wind is tempestuous. And the rain? The rain is incessant.

It comes down in sheets. It drizzles like a fine mist. It hits with droplets that feel as large as my thumb. No matter what we do, it always finds a way in, and we've learned to live with constant damp as a companion. Aicha's affinity with the elements means it's bearable; she operates as a portable radiator, cranking heat out of her pores to dry the place and keep us warm. It stops us having to use a fire that might give away our position. Of course, it means she glows in the magical spectrum instead. Still, we're on a plane made of magic. Practically everything is luminescent with *talent* here. Apart from me, of course.

I got my magic back for a while. Well, not mine, as such. Reincarnating inside a fae body gave me access to their wild form of natural power, and it was a giddy feeling to be *talented* once again. Of course, Simon De Montfort made sure all the bodies he stored in the cave were normal, unTalented human ones. He didn't want me using fae magic to get out of his trap.

Now I'm fucking useless again. That's the official diagnosis. An acute case of *fuckingus uselessosis*. The worst I've ever seen. If I were a dog, they'd put me down. Sadly, because of my reincarnation magic, I'd just pop up again like a bad penny in another body. A fucking useless bad penny. Not even a bad penny. A mediocre penny.

Aicha can see I'm tormenting myself again. It's like a knife in her gut to see me so reduced, so full of self-doubt. She rubs at the corners of her eyes.

'Oh, boo hoo,' she says. 'I'm Paul Bonhomme, and I'm so very, very sad. I can't do much magic, and I had a rubbish couple of weeks, so I'm just going to sit here and whine and cry rather than doing anything about it. Weaaaaaahhhh.'

Okay, that one was just mean. Still, she saved me from that hellhole trap of De Montfort's making. 'You've made your point. I've not been coming up with much in the way of a plan. Have you?'

'Yep.' She carries on tearing the vegetation up, shredding it with one of the innumerable blades she keeps concealed around various points on her body.

I wait for a minute. A very annoying minute. 'Do go on?' I eventually prompt.

'Go to Winter. Find Simon. Kill the queen if she doesn't give up Simon. Go home.' She chops up something that doesn't look a million miles away from pak choi...if someone dipped some in neon paint and then injected it with gadolinium.

'Hold on, what?' I can't believe my ears. 'That's not an "Aicha" plan. That's a "Paul" plan. That's a "the plan I present and then you tell me it doesn't even count as a plan and that I need to sit in the naughty corner and think about what I've done until I come up with something that is actually a plan" plan. You can't put *that* forward as a plan! That's my job.'

Aicha is entirely unfazed by my outburst. 'Tell you what, dickhead. If you don't like that plan, come up with a better one.'

'All right, I will!' I feel righteously indignant. I'm the act-now-regret-it-later actor in this partnership. She holds the plan-rigorously-and-save-Paul's-bacon-with-it role. Not content with making me stop sitting around and moping, she's going to make me think as well. It's outrageous. Outrageous!

I sit furiously (which is quite a skill — taking a simple action and imbuing it with a ten-megaton emotional charge). Aicha pays me precisely zero attention and just gets on with preparing our food.

After a while, the intensity of my anger reduces, and the thinking starts properly. 'The problem is,' I say as she plonks down what looks like a bunch of leaves shredded into smaller leaves and served on one huge leaf, 'that we don't really know what we're up against.'

Aicha widens her mouth into a shocked O shape. 'You don't say?' she deadpans. 'Please, Mister Obvious, please tell me more of these reality-shaking revelations.'

'Queen Maeve rules Winter,' I continue, choosing not to dignify her sarcasm with an answer. 'We can only assume that if we go into her territory, she's going to know about it. Instantly. So we're going to be targets the moment we arrive, with no idea where Simon is or where the portal to get out of Faerie and back to Earth is. If we don't come up with a proper plan, we're fucked.'

'Paul,' she says, rolling her dark eyes, 'that's not a plan; that's a precis.'

'Yes, I'm aware of that. I'm hoping if I lay it out clearly, maybe it'll jumpstart my brain into actually coming up with a solution.'

'Is it working?'

I shake my head. 'Nah.'

'I can slap you really, really hard. Maybe that'll get your grey matter going again?' She bats her eyelashes at me hopefully.

'It'll get my grey matter going, Aich. It'll get it going straight out of my nose and splatter it across the nearest wall.'

'Right, which might —and hear me out— actually make you smarter.' I look at her in disbelief. 'Well, it can't make you any stupider, can it?'

'Okay, tell you what, let's take that idea, okay, and put it over here, on the conveyor belt into the incinerator.' I mime the required action and then watch it until it passes out of sight. 'Now, let's never talk about that ever again.'

'Still haven't got us any closer to an actual solution though, have you, *saabi*?'

'It'll come! Just give me some time.'

She finishes up her hardcore leaf-on-leaf food action, then sighs. 'You've had time, Paul. Plenty of it. We need to do something.'

I understand her frustration. For all the jokes, we are both creatures of action. Part of being extremely *talented* and virtually indestructible is it makes you more ready to get up in the mix, more quick to throw down when the moment demands it. Problem is, we're a long way from Kansas. We're on the Winter Queen's home turf, and I just can't see any way this is going to end well.

We sit in a companionable silence, and I bash my head against the problem from every angle. It seems impossible to crack. Luckily, my head is exceptionally hard. An idea suddenly comes to me.

'How did you get here again?' I ask Aicha, the first hint of excitement creeping into my voice.

She shakes her head at me. 'A deal with the White Lady. I already told you I can't tell you the details, and it was a one-way trip. She can't help us here.'

'Okay, no, I get that, but hear me out. How did you find the White Lady the first time?'

'I can't tell you that either. That was when I was off hunting down the Nazi bastards.'

Interesting. She mentioned having met the White Lady before, but I didn't realise it was so relatively recent. It's beside the point though.

'Okay, the second time — or the second-to-last time — or, fuck, I don't know how many times you've actually met the White Lady. Right, the time you got through Melusine's barrier with her help, how did you find her?'

Aicha rubs her chin slowly. 'I called in the favour the Red Nain owed us, settling his debts.' A sudden grin splits her face. 'I guess you could call it Red Nain Redemption.'

I groan. 'Dreadful, Aich. Still, it didn't settle *our* debts. It settled yours.'

I reach into my etheric storage, which is still accessible with some difficulty despite my depleted power level thanks to years of practise. Rummaging around, I pull out a shiny red finger, the knuckle-bone protruding at the bottom.

I grin. 'I can think of a winter fae who still owes me a favour.'

imPerfect Bones: Chapter Two

I guess it's time to knuckle down and really put a finger on the problem.

Aicha looks carefully left and right, then raises a hand. I point the dismembered Nain finger at her. 'Yes, you, the annoying one at the back with the Takeshi 6x9 tribute facial tattoo?'

Aicha blinks disbelievingly. 'Okay, well, first, I'm going to skin you alive and then make you tattoo, "I must not mock ancient and wiser cultures like an ignorant fool" on your flayed hide five hundred times using your sharpened little finger as the needle for that comment. But after that, last time I looked, we aren't in the Pyrenees.'

'Look, I get it. You're right…'

She interrupts. 'Say it again.'

I pause. 'Err, you're right?' I'm not sure which bit she means.

333

'And again.'

I sigh. 'You're right.'

'And one more time'

'You're right.'

I can see she's deep in thought. 'Nope,' she says at last. 'I'll never tire of hearing it. Sorry, go on.'

'Right, thanks, The Incredible Id-Woman. Look, this is my thought process. What the Nain Rouge gave us is summoning magic, okay?'

She nods. 'Yep, totally.'

'So why did he say that we had to be in the Pyrenees to use it?'

She shrugs. 'Because he lives there.'

'What, in the whole of the Pyrenees? That's a massive bit of land to claim as property. I'd think some other monsters and magical beings might dispute that slightly.' I'm a lot tougher than him — or was before my magic got eaten by Melusine, and I only own the city of Toulouse, France. Not that I'm in a measuring contest with him, but he isn't exactly a "capable of keeping strong Talented out of an entire mountain range" kind of guy. He's a "use sly magic to trap a more powerful Talented inside a dumbass escape room and then shriek like a little bitch when said Talented gets out" kind of guy. 'Plus, we know he lives in a collection of shipping containers in a pocket dimension. So why the Pyrenees?'

I can see her chewing it over. She's not looking to take the piss out of me anymore. Playtime's finished. She's got her serious thinking hat on. 'Because he feels an affinity or a connection with the mountains?'

It's my turn to nod now. 'Right. That's his focal point on Earth. Now, again, pocket dimension. Do you think he's powerful enough to have just carved that out of the ether?'

I can see her joining the dots together as I say it. 'No, not at all; else, he'd have made a better show at resisting when I kicked his arse and burned his house down.'

'Right! He's a trickster — sneaky, clever even but not a magical powerhouse. So where is his pocket dimension likely to actually be?'

'Inside of Faerie!' She grins suddenly, just for a moment. 'Bloody hell, *saabi*, every now and then you're not a complete idiot.'

'Thanks?' I'm not entirely sure how to take that.

'So what's the plan? Burn his finger?' That's how we can summon him. A flame flickers up on her fingertip.

I shake my head. 'Not straight away and not here. We already said he's got an affinity with the mountains. I say, let's look for any serious hilly area in the Wilds and do it there. What do you reckon?'

'That is actually very sensible and extremely well-reasoned out.' She puts her hand on my forehead. 'Are you sure you're not running a fever?'

I push her away and get to my feet. 'That's just the radiant heat of my genius. Come on. I've spent enough time waiting for you to get your shit together. Let's rock on.'

I manage to half-duck the cuff she aims at the back of my head as I waltz past, so it only makes half my brain bounce off the front of my cranium like a crash-test dummy. I try not to let her see me wince as I carry on towards the exit of the shelter that has been a safe haven for the past few weeks and into the unknown weirdness of the fae Wilds.

It's harder than I expect, walking out from that shelter. And I'd known it'd be difficult. I've witnessed the effects of trauma firsthand a hundred times over, probably more. Still, it's something else to feel it. That sensation like a physical barrier; an unpassable air-wall that squeezes you tight as you try, all the way inside to your very heart. My lungs must be compressed. I can't get my breath.

Aicha doesn't help. Not physically. She doesn't grab my arm and yank me out, however much a part of me might wish she would. She stands. And waits. And that in itself — having her just calmly standing, as if she has all the time in the world — is enough to get me moving. With a last shaking push I force myself through that self-imposed limit to my world and sail off the edge of my traumatic map.

Those first few steps are infant-like, a trembling toddle out into the unknown. Every step is an opportunity for terror; my heart is palpitating, leaping each time a leaf crinkles. The wind whispers threats that fill my bones with lead. I was once attuned to the Wilds. Not now. Not when my head is full of prey-thought.

Luckily there's an apex predator by my side to keep me safe. And more than that, her presence lends me the strength to still move forwards.

We walk for about half an hour, tromping through feathered bracken that crackles like brushfire under our feet, stamping past curled, thorned vines that seem to snatch at our ankles, winding themselves into the perfect position to obstruct our way before Aicha asks me the most important and pertinent question possible.

'So where exactly are we going?'

I stop suddenly. 'Ummm.' I was so taken with the whole "get off my arse, stop moping, and actually do something", that I didn't give any thought to *where* I should go once I did it.

Aicha sighs, a long-suffering sigh. 'And Bonhomme is back with a vengeance. I suppose it was too much to ask that thinking things through became a habit rather than just a once-in-a-blue-moon occurrence. So I take it that means you've no idea where the high terrain is then?'

'Err, not precisely,' I say, trying to work out how to save the situation. 'I mean, I know I'm keeping equidistant from Summer and Winter, so I thought...'

'You thought you'd just keep walking until you stumbled over a mountain range? Because obviously it would *have* to be in the middle between the two courts? Because the fae are so well organised and logical and love everything to be neat and tidy?'

'Hobs do!'

'Hobs are just brownies with OCD; doesn't count.'

'Do you have a better plan?'

'Absolutely.'

There's silence for a moment. Fucksake. 'Can I hear said plan?'

'Yep.' She nods. 'It's very simple. You ask me if I know where there any mountains.'

'Aicha Kandicha, Druze Queen, good friend, and massive pedant, do you know where there are any mountains?'

'Of course I do! I thought you'd never ask. Follow me, dickhead.'

She brushes past me. I guess that one was payback for my comment as we left the lean-to. I can't really argue with her. Plus, after my time trapped underground and then huddled up under dripping fronds, trying to hide from my sense of failure, getting out and just going for a walk is doing me the world of good. I suspect that's why she left it so long before mentioning it to me. She's just glad to see me doing something, *anything*, again.

Once Aicha corrects our trajectory (or 'turns around and goes the actual right way instead of just wandering about like a dickhead,' as she puts it), I lapse into silence, my earlier high from a sense of positive action dissipating. Instead, I find it harder and harder to catch my breath, my lungs feeling too small for anything but tiny, shallow ones. I can hear my heartbeat in my eardrums, which is weird as I'm fairly sure it's supposed to be in my chest, and my palms become slick with sweat despite it being tenaciously cool in the forest. Then we break through the foliage, and the mountain Aicha has been leading us to comes into view.

This enormous wave of relief hits me, and the weird symptoms reduce down to manageable levels even if they don't disappear entirely. I realise suddenly that I was terrified Aicha was taking us back to the hill I'd been imprisoned under, that maybe that place was the high terrain she was thinking of. It's only now that I see it isn't, that I realise how terrified I was of going back there.

Aicha seems not to notice, but considering she can spot a leaf falling unexpectedly half a mile away in sheeting rain, I think that's pretty unlikely. I appreciate the effort of her pretence.

The forest breaks against the slope of the mountain like a green wave, sparse hardy trees clinging to rocky outcrops. It looks almost vertical, and I feel dizzy just considering trying to clamber up it.

'How far up do you think we need to go to get it to work?' I ask doubtfully. I'm having second thoughts about the entire plan.

Aicha already did me the favour of ignoring one moment of weakness from me. She's not about to make a habit of it. 'How far do you think?'

I point at where the first of the tenacious few boughs poke out at what looks like almost ninety degrees. 'There?' The tremor to my voice is just to underline the question...

Though the trunks do look threateningly high. At least two, maybe three metres off the ground.

Aicha points at them, then lets her finger trace the path of the ascent all the way to the top. It's only when she swivels her hand around to point at me after that I realise it's her middle finger.

'The top, you twat,' she says, kissing the tip of her digit, then pretending to blow smoke off it. 'All the way to the tippy-top.'

Of course. Looks like I need to get my climb on. Fuck my life.

I might be from the lowlands of the Haute-Garonne, but I've spent literal lifetimes in and around the Pyrenees. I would normally be moving up this path like a sprightly mountain goat. Instead, someone seems to have surreptitiously operated on my kneecaps and swapped them out for jellyfish when I wasn't looking, which is a bitch move, in my opinion. I heave myself up one wobbling step after the other, from trunk to trunk, trying not to lose my trembling footing or face-plant when my sweaty mitts fumble as I crawl up a particularly steep bit. It's, well. It's frankly humiliating.

Even Aicha can't ignore it or just continue to take the piss out of me. 'Are you all right, *saabi*?' she asks eventually, after she comes to a grinding halt to allow me to catch up for what feels like the zillionth time.

I sink down against the tree I used to heave myself level, keeping my back to the slope, using the gritty irregularities of the wood to anchor myself into it, to feel safe. I don't mind if it scratches my skin. It makes me feel more connected to the mountain, less likely to slide back down all the way I climbed up.

'No, I'm really not, Aich.' I can't deny it. 'It fucking

sucks. I lost my *talent* — or as near to all of it as matters, and now the slightest difficulty has me shaking like a leaf. In my head, I feel fine, but nobody seems to have passed that information to the body I'm borrowing because it's on the verge of having a heart attack every time I see my own shadow. And I'm sick of it, Aich. I want to get out there and kick De Montfort square in the nuts, and at the same time, I want to go hide in the nearest dark hole.' I shudder. That's not true. 'Actually, not a dark hole. The opposite of a dark hole. Yes, to the hiding. No, to the dark hole. '

I never expected this. I don't know what I had expected, but it wasn't this. I was so blasé for so many years about the idea of being trapped. Sure, someone might torture me, I might suffer and die, but then I'd just dust myself off in a new body and get on with my life. The cave was the first time I really felt imprisoned, totally ensnared. The situation seemed helpless, the trap inescapable, and I really thought I was going to spend the next sixteen years, roughly three days for each corpse De Montfort had left down there for me, living it over and over. The first sixteen days alone reduced me to a shadow of who I once was.

I'm furious with myself for being so affected by it, but it doesn't change the truth. I'm terrified of dying now. Terrified I'll end up back there. That somehow Aicha didn't destroy all the bodies with her fire and didn't leave the hole open. That I'll wake up back in that cave again and never make it out. Each time my foot slides on the loose gravel, my heart feels like it's ten sizes too big for my chest, like someone hooked it up to one of those air compressors used to blow up a bouncy castle and threw the switch to maximum pressure. Just moving at all is taking every inch of my willpower, and I'm sick of it.

'It doesn't get better, you know,' Aicha says quietly.

I blink. 'What?' If this is her idea of a pep talk, she needs to do some serious work on her people skills.

'It doesn't get better. That sort of trauma. It just gets... usual.'

'Usual?' Apparently, although it's starting to look like my career as a wise-cracking, ass-kicking magician might draw to a close, at least I'll have the job of "annoying parrot" to fall back onto.

Aicha scratches the nape of her neck, knocking away whatever little flying beastie is trying to feed on her. Because we are in Faerie, I think I hear it vaguely cursing her out in a Scottish burr as it flies away. The drunken weave to its movement certainly looks Hebridean.

'You don't get over these things, Paul; you know that. Did you ever forget watching Ben bleed to death at your feet when you couldn't move? Can you honestly say that if you closed your eyes right now, you can't see Susane lying in a pool of blood on your wedding bed?'

I don't trust myself to speak, so I just shake my head. There's no way I can say that.

'So why weren't you still weeping into your pint for Ben's loss when we first met? How come you aren't still elbow deep in an opium den, blotting out your existence right now over Susane?'

I think about it for a minute. Even though I did fall back into the pint after I lost my magic, and Isaac, my father-figure and mentor, had to pull me out, he only managed to pull me out because *I* was ready. 'Because it won't help.'

That gets me the gun fingers. 'Bingo. It won't. When shit goes catastrophically tits up, we all catch a grace period where everything is allowed to fall to pieces. Might not be straight away. Might have too many other pressures. Too many responsibilities. Others who need us to hold it together. But the collapse, when it comes, is understandable. Maybe it's a week, maybe it's a year. Maybe it's just ten minutes of screaming and punching the wall. Not my place to tell anyone else how to handle things. Eventually, though, you've got a choice. Do you stay there? Or do you live again? If you choose the latter, it doesn't mean suddenly it all just goes away, does it? Just pack it all up neatly. Then carry it with you forever. Get so used to carrying it, sometimes you forget you even are, but when you think about it, it's always there. Over time, it just becomes usual.'

I ponder this. 'Have you ever thought, *laguna*, that we might be in desperate need of some serious therapy?'

She rolls her eyes. 'Well, duh. Let me know when you find a therapist who won't yeet themselves out of the nearest window if we start telling them our story.'

It's a valid point. Looks like there's a market opening for a Talented therapist. Maybe that could be my fall-back career if I never get my powers back. I'd be rubbish at the whole "caring, listening ear" thing, but at least when I add to their trauma instead of helping them heal it, they can Cathartically murder me at the end of the session. It could be the equivalent of one of those rage rooms where you pay to smash the place up. Don't like my advice? Stab me in the face. I'll make a killing. Well, they'll make a killing, but you get what I mean.

The changing light shakes me from my reverie. The shadows are elongating, dancing across the carpet of fallen leaves to intermingle, grouping together to solidify darkness' hold on the land itself. Night doesn't so much fall as hurtle downwards at terminal velocity in Faerie, and if we want to make it to the top before it becomes pitch-black, we need to get going. I'd rather defend the high ground if any of the

Wilds' hungrier denizens come sniffing about in the nighttime.

I push myself off the supportive bough, feeling like I have a second wind. I guess I just need to get used to my new normal. Funnily enough, I do feel better. It doesn't make sense; I've just been told I'll be carrying this forever. But maybe it's because I've now accepted that as the case instead of fighting myself every step of the way. Okay, I'll be more afraid, more nervous and cautious. To be honest, my overconfidence and reckless behaviour didn't really stand me in good stead. I can do with being a bit more careful in my everyday actions.

When I think back to my first life, I was terrified plenty of times. Hell, I was a named heretic with the considerable combined weight of the Catholic Church and feudal society chasing after me with a tinderbox and a bunch of kindling. Maybe I need to get back to my roots. Not in the religious sense — that's never going to happen, but in terms of finding a bit of courage even when I'm scared stiff. There's no bravery in genuine fearlessness. Just idiocy.

I use the gnawing worry about falling as a tool to choose my next branch to grip more carefully, to think out my path more precisely. I look farther ahead, working out where I'm going. If I don't want to plunge off the side of the mountain —and I don't want to plunge off the side of the mountain — then I better do something about it.

I feel Aicha prowling behind me, far more graceful and confident in her movements than I am. I mean, she's far more graceful and confident in everything than me, but it's the moving part that stands out right now.

'Appreciate it, *laguna*,' I say softly. 'Appreciate you.'

'Yeah, yeah, soppy bollocks. Less talking, more climbing.' Her words might be disparaging, but I notice she stays behind me, positioning herself in just such a way between this tree *here* or next to that boulder *there*, that if I slip, she can catch and brace me. She's back again in her role as my safety net. Only literally this time.

It's good to have friends who love you. Even if they'd rather swallow their own tongue than tell you that.

imPerfect Bones: Chapter Three

There's about half a second as Aicha hisses for quiet when I walk in, where I consider playing with her. Perhaps slamming the door or bellowing questions at her about what she wants for breakfast and why do I need to be quiet, fixing my decibels at just-below-eardrum-popping levels. Then I see her face and realise precisely what effect that will have on my life expectancy for this body and probably several other bodies as well.

Aicha isn't the most outwardly expressive person, excluding her artistic use of violence that she can use to express anything from slight annoyance to utter contempt. If there is a message to be given, it won't come couched in a grimace or a frown. It'll be visible in her eyes. Right now, they burn like coals dropped in the snow, the smoke rising off them almost visible. She is, as the kids these days would say (and even thinking that makes me feel every single one of my eight hundred years at once), "buggin' out".

A moment or so after deciding not to commit seppuku

via Aicha, I clock what has her attention — the wireless radio chattering away in the background.

'...*since the evening. Both the gendarmes and the military police are blocking all access points from the Ile d'Yeu but believe that the thieves may already have absconded off the island with the coffin prior to the forces' mobilisation. Authorities are appealing for any witnesses in the case of this egregious crime to contact them immediately. The telephone number to do so is...*'

Aicha leans forward and switches off the radio, tension radiating from the swift precision of her movement, as though it took all her concentration to stop at turning the knob to off rather than tearing it from its Bakelite frame. I suspect, had she done so, it wouldn't be the first time she tore a knob off.

'What's going on?' Part of me, the selfish part that values my own well-being, wants to just back out of the room slowly. This is my friend though, and if she needs to vent her spleen, I'm here for her. Even if venting her spleen means stabbing me in mine.

Aicha turns to me, swivelling on her heels before brushing past as she marches out the door. 'Tell you on the way to the Ile d'Yeu,' she shouts, stomping upstairs.

I sigh. Apparently, we're going on a road trip.

It's a long drive up to the island situated just off the west coast near Nantes. Work has started on a major motorway between Toulouse and Bordeaux that will knock a fair chunk of time off the route, but for now, we're stuck bumbling down single-lane roads, limited more often by haulage traffic or the occasional tractor than we are by the speed limit of a hundred kilometres per hour. It's frustrating. I've only just picked up my Citroen DS23, its burgundy spaceship curves as fabulously aerodynamic as they are impossibly futuristic, and I'm desperate to open it up and see what it can do. The other road users make that an annoying impossibility.

I let Aicha stew in her fury for an hour or so. Once she simmers down, letting a little of that righteous anger evaporate into a condensed but more controllable amount, I risk trying to extract some information out of her.

'Know what I love?' I inject a breezy tone into my voice to match the whipping air currents sliding in through the cracked window. Despite the winter month, the sun's strong enough to heat the cabin up sufficiently as to want some fresh air. Also, the pressure of Aicha's fury is stifling.

'Being a twat?' Good. She's still got her sense of humour. Because of course she's joking. Of course.

'Besides that. I love going for nine-hour drives to the other end of the country without knowing the reason why.'

'Not the other end of the country. Toulouse: southwest. Ile d'Yeu: northwest. West even, arguably. Hardly fucking Calais.'

I wonder if it might be advisable to look into a future career in dentistry because this is like pulling fucking teeth. 'Yeah, I think you might have focused on the wrong part of that sentence. It wasn't so much the geographical precision I was concerned by.'

I catch the faintest flash in her eyes. We've been friends for closing in on thirty years now, but she went off hunting Nazis for a good portion of that and was an almost entirely closed book prior. Even after her return, she's hardly thrown it open, pages out on display like some form of hussy literature, parading its verbs and adjectives for all the world to see. No, just occasionally, she'll crack open the tiniest sliver.

So now, twenty-eight years since I got her out of that hell-hole at La Rochelle, I'm still only just learning to read her. Most people wouldn't have noticed that micro-expression. The few who did would probably have interpreted it to be tamped down rage considering the rest of her body language and demeanour. I'm pretty confident it is amusement. We're developing a way of talking to each other, a back-and-forth banter that I hope will help her relax and open up further. Generally, I say something, and she insults me. It seems to work well. So I'm confident what I saw was amusement. Either that or tamped down rage, and I'm about to get murderised. One or the other.

She huffs slightly, the tiniest expulsion loaded with all the wearying weight of having to be in my company on a daily basis. See — told you I'm getting through to her. 'Not hear the news?'

'Not really.' I shrug. Normally it would be a wasted gesture, what with her eyes being fixed on the road, but I know perfectly well that Aicha sees more with her peripheral vision than most people see when they're looking straight at something. 'I was too busy hunting for the particularly gigantic snake hissing at me like it was about to strike when I came to offer you breakfast.'

She ignores me. 'Actually been listening, might have realised why. Took Petain's coffin.'

I sit upright. Ah. 'Who?'

I see her shake her head, doubtless in disbelief at my stupidity. 'Who? Fucking Nazis.'

I slink back in my chair, abashed. Right. Who else? Petain was a French hero in the First World War, a respected general at the start of the Second…and then a reviled traitor by the end. He set up the Vichy regime, the collaborative government that surrendered to the Nazis and was responsible for loading up Jews, travelling folk, homosexuals, and basically anyone Hitler didn't like onto train carriages, heading off towards Auschwitz and the like, never to be seen again. After the war, he landed a death sentence, but that got commuted to life imprisonment.

Post war, Germany grappled hard with what they did; there was soul searching aplenty. They acknowledged how much they'd fucked up — the evils done either by them or in their name.

But France never really went through that same self-analysis. Everyone miraculously became a former member of the Resistance, statistical evidence be damned, and there's a significant element of the hard- and far-right wingers that try exceedingly hard to gloss over the truths of the Vichy Regime. They want to present collaboration as having been a good thing — saving lives rather than the cowardly craven surrender it actually was.

Part of that whole "reframe our evil deeds" drive has been to present Petain as some sort of military hero who bravely defended France by licking Hitler's boot. I've not paid too much attention to it. I try to avoid listening to fascists' demands as it makes me want to kill large swathes of humanity, ironically. I know they want Petain buried in one of the main national cemeteries with full presidential honours. I have no idea which. Doubtless Aicha knows. Stick him in a plague pit or a pauper's grave, far as I'm concerned. None of his previous actions repudiate what he did when the Nazis came knocking.

A thought occurs to me, and I narrow my eyes. 'Did you kill Petain?' I can't remember the details.

Aicha scoffs. 'Yep. Made him be ninety-five years old. Super-secret Druze magic called "time".' She sobers. 'No.

Thought about it. But he was found guilty. Imprisoned. Enough. Just.'

Of course, that makes sense. Aicha had only "gone hunting", as the note she left me said, after news of some Nazis having slipped away, often getting quietly scooped up and pardoned by countries like the USA, came to light. Most of us who are Talented aren't big on killing ordinary mortals, though for particularly execrable scumbags like Nazis, we might make exceptions. That's obviously the line in the sand Aicha has drawn for herself. If they are caught and tried and found guilty by the authorities, she'll leave them be. If they escape the law, well. Then they're fair game.

I consider the information I've got now. 'Do you think it could be magic? Is that why we're getting involved?'

I see her start to shake her head, but instead, she cocks it, obviously intently listening to her own internal dialogue, considering my question. 'Possible. Not considered it. More likely not. Still, it'll become a rallying point for the Nazis. Breathe life back into their ideology here. Not having that.'

Again, it makes sense. Considering her own suffering at the hands of the far-right regime, she'll not want to see it coming back into prominence ever again. End of the day, this is fascists doing fucked-up fascist things. Enough of a reason for her to get involved. And if becoming their worst nightmare helps to keep her own nightmares under control, I'm happy to come along for the ride.

We pass most of the rest of the journey in silence. I occasionally re-tune the radio as we pass out of range of one antenna, chasing a new station that started up a couple of years back called FIP. Their music selection's eclectic, covering a plethora of modern wonders from around the world, particularly some of the more obscure funk and Motown you aren't likely to catch on the other French stations. Even better, they don't allow adverts, and most of the interruptions between songs are semi-snarky traffic advisories, as useful as they are amusing. I pore over the Michelin road map, guiding us away from any hot spots. I don't want Aicha to end up taking a traffic jam personally. In her current mood, she's likely to explode the other cars to clear them out of our way. After getting the occupants out, of course. Probably.

By the time we arrive on the island, night hasn't just fallen, it's tripped over its own feet and then face-planted spectacularly, so that seeing anything outside of the halogen glows of the streetlamps is difficult. The carpark on this side of the ferry dock is much like the other side was — a mixture of official vehicles, TV and radio branded mini-vans, and the rest undoubtedly ghoulish sightseers. Aicha pays them no mind but heads the short distance to the Pont Joinville Cemetery. It's a quick drive, less than five minutes, and all we have to do is follow the general traffic and buzz. Parking is more of an issue, but we find a spot on a side road where traffic can pass without side-swiping my gorgeous motorcar, then get out.

The front of the cemetery is a mass of bodies pressed up against the official cordon, where several police officers wearing harangued expressions more crumpled than their uniforms push people back. Occasionally they force an opening to allow senior ranking detectives, their jobs as clearly displayed on their faces as the stripes on the beat bobbies' shoulders, access in and out. It's a media circus, full of noise, a hubbub of hullabaloo. I need to check my copy of *Dante's Inferno*, but I'm fairly confident this is one of the circles of hell he described with such great accuracy. There are certainly enough politicians around for it to be the Underworld.

I turn towards Aicha to suggest coming back at a quieter time, like in about three years, only to find she's already marching with great purpose and determination towards the throng.

Looks like we're going to be fighting our way through the lion's den of press and police after all, exactly the sort of mundane humans I desperately try to avoid whenever possible. This is just what I want to be doing on a Monday night.

imPerfect Bones: Chapter Four

When Diana Ross wrote, 'Ain't No Mountain High Enough', she clearly wasn't on a walking holiday in Faerie.

We make it to the top of the mountain before it plunges into absolute darkness. That's a win. Faerie is full of wild, insanely dangerous creatures, the Wilds even more so. Luckily, I'm human — the most dangerous animal of all. Except for honey badgers. Those little bastards are vicious as fuck. Also — Aicha. I have Aicha. She's even more vicious than a badger. High praise indeed.

It's mainly a level surface at the top, the scrubby grass broken by rocks that push up and out like undead trolls digging themselves out of their graves. If that doesn't sound like a particularly cheery mental image, this is not a particularly cheery place. It's freezing cold, the wind whipping up the slopes behind us and accelerating over the top before launching into free fall down the other side, trying to carry us with it. The rain is holding off for once, though, so I'm thankful for small mercies.

Aicha does her award-winning impression of a portable radiator, and the whole place becomes more bearable. I'd love to start a fire as well, but that would be akin to shooting fireworks off that explode into a beautiful arrow pointing straight at us with the words 'COME GET YOUR WALKING BUFFET' picked out in twinkly curly script. I've enough *talent* left I can augment my night vision a small amount, meaning I can keep watch on a part of the perimeter, at least. I huddle over my sword, the cold returning as Aicha walks the rest of the boundary of the open space, securing our six. Attacks can and probably will come from any direction. Knowing how and where they are likely to come from is essential.

I beckon her over when she makes her way back. Simply improving my night vision fractionally has taken it out of me, so I hand the severed Nain Rouge finger over to Aicha.

'Burn that for me, will you?' She plucks it from my outstretched hand. Without her even blinking, it ignites, a momentary miniature beacon that I know she effortlessly wraps a protection around to keep it from keen predatory eyes. In a matter of seconds, the finger turns to ash, disintegrating into dust as the wind whips it away.

'Now we wait.' I crouch down next to Aicha, resisting the urge to warm my hands against her like a fire as that would be a good way to get them snapped off at the wrist.

'Yep. Thanks for stating the obvious, Hermione.'

I notice that although she's turned her back, she's angled herself to be closer to me. The temperature warms accordingly, and it's a massive relief. My teeth stop chattering, and I bask in not feeling like my bone marrow has been hollowed out and replaced with Mr Freeze ice popsicles (which would be as painful as it would make your skeleton delicious).

We don't have to wait long. There is a puff of red smoke because the Nain's a showy bastard, and the little red-devil-wannabe steps forward, out of the last few plumes before they disappear.

He's an ugly bugger. That's only by my, admittedly human, standards. Maybe for other vertically-challenged fae, he's a prime specimen, but shiny bright red leathery skin has never been my cup of tea. The stubby little bumps on his forehead, too tiny to even really be considered horns, don't help. As for his personality…he's the sort who thinks sticking your leg out and tripping someone over is peak hilarity. If they face-plant onto a bed of spikes, all the better. The Nain Rouge is a vindictive little trickster and an all-round shithead.

He capers forward, probably thinking he looks mysterious and otherworldly instead of how he actually appears, which is like a proper twat. 'Hello, hello Cathar…' he starts, then blinks. He looks around, whipping his head back and forth, his brow furrowing like a field ready for sowing. 'Where are… Where are we?' He backs up a couple of steps, his head still swinging around wildly. 'You're in Faerie — we're in *Faerie*!' The first trickle of sweat forms on his temple. 'What are you doing in *Faerie*? *In the Wilds*? Are you fucking suicidal, Good Man? Why, why would you call me *here*?'

His screeching gets higher and higher in pitch. He starts to make sudden tense movements. Each step carries a juddering readiness that speaks of the fight-or-flight mechanism, and if I'm any judge, he's about to make a run for it.

'Wait!' I hold up my hand. 'You owe me a favour.'

'A favour? A *favour*?' I can see his little hoofed feet

scraping at the floor, gouging a hole in the soil. 'I'm here now with you, aren't I? I'd say that's the favour done. Good day, Cathar. I need to get somewhere less deadifying.'

He tries to bolt, but Aicha was waiting and seizes him by the scruff of his neck so that his momentum just makes him do a pretty good impression of a fairground Pirate Ship ride, his skin folds operating as the pivot point. Once he swings back from the horizontal, he dangles from her grasp above the ground.

'Not how this works, Nain. You know that.' There's a tone to Aicha's voice that promises a detailed explanation of why can easily be forthcoming. It can involve diagrams and everything. Carved directly into the retina with a red-hot knife blade. 'You owe us a favour, and it has to be agreed to by both parties.'

The Nain continues to flail his stubby legs as if he thinks he might suddenly get purchase with the ground half a metre below them and disappear in a cloud of dust. 'This isn't fair! Isn't fair!' he wails. 'I stated to call me in the Pyrenees, and I'd come. I said nothing about Faerie.'

'Well, true,' I say. 'But that's because you never expected us to be in Faerie. And the fact you've turned up suggests the magic you made doesn't see the difference. As long as it's somewhere you're attuned to. And last I looked, you're still fae.'

'Very wriggly fae, actually,' Aicha pipes up, watching in intense fascination the Nain's entirely unsuccessful attempts to work himself free and head off.

'Still not the agreement, not the agreement, was it?' The creature looks like he's about to burst into fits of tears any moment. 'Do you even know where you are right now?'

I roll my eyes. 'Well, duh. You just said it at least once. We're in the Wilds of Faerie.'

'No, no, you dunderhead. Do you know where in the Wilds you are?'

I resist the urge to poke holes in him with my sword for the insult. Just. 'No, my geographical knowledge of "Lands where humans never willingly go" is somewhat limited. Lack of serious cartographers and all that.'

'This is Coin Mountain. Coin Mountain!'

I scratch my head. '*Con* Mountain? Like, there's a lot of *connards*, dickheads, that congregate up here?'

'No, no!' the creature shrieks at me, trembling in Aicha's grip. 'Coin. As in the plural of Cu sidhe. This is the mountain of the Coin sidhe.'

As if on cue, I hear a mournful howl echoing up from down below, on the slopes we just climbed up. It carries easily, mainly due to it being approximately the same volume as an entire pack of normal wolves turned up to eleven. When it's joined by another howl, then another, then a third, it becomes so loud, the very earth trembles. At the far reaches of my field of enhanced vision, I see the first gleam of massive glowing eyes. What's much worse is that they also see me.

Grab your copy…
vinci-books.com/imPerfectbones